the girl with the
golden bouffant

Also by Mabel Maney

KISS THE GIRLS AND MAKE THEM SPY

THE CASE OF THE NOT-SO-NICE NURSE

THE CASE OF THE GOOD-FOR-NOTHING GIRLFRIEND

A GHOST IN THE CLOSET

THE GIRL WITH THE GOLDEN BOUFFANT. Copyright © 2004 by Mabel Maney. All rights reserved. Printed in the United States of America. No part of this book may be used or reproduced in any manner whatsoever without written permission except in the case of brief quotations embodied in critical articles and reviews. For information address HarperCollins Publishers Inc., 10 East 53rd Street, New York, NY 10022.

HarperCollins books may be purchased for educational, business, or sales promotional use. For information please write: Special Markets Department, HarperCollins Publishers Inc., 10 East 53rd Street, New York, NY 10022.

FIRST EDITION

Designed by Adrian Leichter

Library of Congress Cataloging-in-Publication Data

Maney, Mabel, 1958–
    The girl with the golden bouffant : an original Jane Bond parody / by Mabel Maney. — 1st ed.
        p. cm.
    ISBN 0-380-80311-9
    1. Women spies—Fiction. 2. Lesbians—Fiction. I. Title.
    PS3563.A466G57 2004
    813'.54—dc22   2003056747

04 05 06 07 08 WBC/RRD 10 9 8 7 6 5 4 3 2 1

the girl with the golden bouffant

AN
ORIGINAL
JANE BOND
PARODY

Mabel Maney

HarperEntertainment
An Imprint of HarperCollinsPublishers

the girl with the
golden bouffant

prologue

AMALGAMATED WIDGET, INC.
AKA HER MAJESTY'S SECRET SERVICE
HEADQUARTERS, SECRET LONDON LOCATION
12 SEPTEMBER 1966

On her seven years with the British Secret Service, Miss Tuppenny had become accustomed to many things: long hours, low pay, insufferable secret agents. None of the powers that be at the British Secret Service remembered her first name; the silver-plate stapler she received at her five-year anniversary luncheon had been engraved MT—Miss Tuppenny. Composed and efficient, she was the principal secretary to N., the head of the double-0 division, and was the only female employee allowed inside his inner sanctum, a windowless office with lead-lined walls and fireproof filing cabinets full of top-secret information.

Each day, after Miss Tuppenny turned off the company cryptogram machine, ate the queen's daily directive (company policy as ordered by Her Royal Highness—at such a young age, QE2 had proved to be quite shrewd, so Miss Tuppenny was happy to comply), and vacuumed N.'s low-pile gold carpet, she went home to feed her cat, Mary Queen of Sniffles, before heading to a warehouse on the East End of London to start work at her secret side job as the head of Girls in Europe Organized to Right Grievances and Insure Equality, G.E.O.R.G.I.E. for short. After years of filing state secrets, fetching coffee, and fending off agents' advances, Miss Tuppenny had finally lost her temper, recruited some like-minded women, and founded G.E.O.R.G.I.E., an all-girl spy agency, dedicated to circumventing government policies deemed antiwoman. Miss Tuppenny had witnessed the winds of change blowing through free countries and had taken advantage of the fact that women were no longer content with their subservient roles. In the last three years, twenty-seven agents had come aboard. Their cover as door-to-door cosmetics salesgirls—pretty girls on pink scooters—allowed them to roam London, gathering information and blackmail material that would persuade politicians to see their side of things. Behind the scenes a retired university chemistry teacher with whom Miss Tuppenny had studied for A-levels brewed up small batches of exquisite lotions and creams, the sales of which subsidized the small spy group. It was these funds, and the constant stream of information that Miss Tuppenny obtained surreptitiously from the British Secret Service during her regular nine-to-five job, that made G.E.O.R.G.I.E. one of the most successful underground women's spy agencies in the world.

"What would I do without you, Miss Tuppenny?" N. said each morning when he arrived at work and discovered that she had sorted the field reports from secret agents into neat stacks on his desk, bitten the end off his morning cigar, and dusted his collection of African death masks. She would smile and nod, then go back to her desk to switch on the miniature Dictaphone machine hidden in her tape dispenser, recording N.'s meetings through a transmitter concealed in the plastic rubber tree plant in his office.

Despite the plentiful opportunities for snooping, Miss Tuppenny's job was far from pleasant. Although she had been named Best Secret Service Principal Secretary five years in a row, could type 195 words per minute, and had had an island in the Galápagos named after her, she was fair game for every agent who passed her desk on his way to N.'s office, men like 0010, a new recruit who was obviously too stupid to be a secret agent. Today 0010 was punishing her for laughing when he asked if she would consider becoming *Mrs.* 0010, and had handed her his expense records written on Vapor Paper instead of the requisite company form; ten seconds under the harsh light of her desk lamp and the paper would vanish in a puff of smoke. Struggling to interpret evaporating figures was causing her head to ache, so she swept the papers into the dustbin. On the main report next to "0010," she typed, "No Expenses Incurred."

The remainder of the afternoon was hers to do with as she pleased; she had finished her duties, N. was lunching with the PM, and the secret agents had left for their Friday-afternoon pub-and-bird crawl. Women's voices echoed through the hall as secretaries queued at the lift on their way to the clerical staff's cafeteria for afternoon tea. It was the loveliest part of the week, one Miss Tuppenny looked forward to, a chance to catch up on company gossip—often as accurate as the files she secretly

photographed with her steno-pad camera—and visit with her fellow suf-
ferers. Today, though, she had a bit of unpleasant business to attend to
first. She plugged in her electric kettle and locked the door. After insert-
ing an invisible ink ribbon in her gunmetal gray Smith Corona, she began to type:

12 September 1966
MEMO: To all G.E.O.R.G.I.E. Agents
FROM: Agent Louise Tuppenny, Chief of Operations
TOPIC: Status report regarding Agent Mimi Dolittle, reassigned to
    our Iceland office, 11 September 1966
CLEARANCE: Top-Hush

Agent Mimi Dolittle is a bright girl with great potential but is under-
mined by her refusal to follow orders. While her espionage skills are
top-notch—she graduated third in her class, excelling in disguise
and deception—her reports are frequently late and often unintelligi-
ble. Great pains have been taken to redirect Agent Dolittle's talents,
with limited success. The following is a chronicle of reasons for her
reassignment.

   • On 12 July of this year, she was given the assignment of infil-
trating a foxhunt club's annual ball; instead she attended a Dusty
Springfield concert with a forged ticket.

   • Last week (2 September) a shopping list on the queen's personal stationery surfaced. Only after it was determined that Her
Royal Majesty has no use for Twiggy Mod-A-Go-Go Fashion Tights
or a Beatles Wig for Female Fans of the Fab Four did Agent Dolittle
confess to printing the letter paper and matching envelopes on the
company mimeograph.

   • More troubling is her fixation on British Secret Service Agent
007-and-a-half, Jane Bond. Approximately one year ago, during the
investigation into Jane Bond's life to determine if she would be
amenable to G.E.O.R.G.I.E. philosophies, Agent Dolittle was
instructed to keep an eye on her. Instead Agent Dolittle drugged
Bond, took her home in the boot of her car, and tied her to her bed.
She later claimed it was a romantic encounter. One year later, and

despite Agent Bond's denials, Agent Dolittle still claims that their encounter was of a romantic nature and that their affair continues. Her insistence on sticking to this fiction puts into question her mental well-being, and her nonstop gossiping about the alleged love affair has created an atmosphere akin to a soap drama, distracting agents from their vital work.

• On 10 September I delivered a warning to Agent Dolittle about ringing the queen with unwanted fashion tips. Shortly thereafter, on the same day, Agent Dolittle engaged in a scuffle with 007-and-a-half after 007-and-a-half asked Agent Dolittle to stop stealing her potted-meat sandwiches from her desk. According to witnesses, Agent Dolittle threatened to "put a quick end to Agent Bond's lying," and then threw at her head an open jar of Vanishing Cream #739-A, a highly experimental product in the early stages of development, which she had stolen from the laboratory. Except for a small bald patch behind one ear, Agent 007-and-a-half was unhurt. However, after a thorough investigation of this latest incident, I decided to place Agent Dolittle on probation for one year and reassigned her to our Iceland office to study the potential of puffins as carrier pigeons. Her work and behavior will be monitored. (The expense of repairing the hole in the wall, caused when Agent 007-and-a-half ducked, will be deducted from Agent Dolittle's salary.)

In addition to her obsessive personality and dangerous behavior, Mimi Dolittle was probably the laziest agent in the history of spydom, Miss Tuppenny mused as she pulled the carbon paper from between the duplicate pages and burned them in the wastebasket. She then poured water over the tea leaves and set the pot aside to steep. The results of Dolittle's intelligence gathering—incomprehensible reports, transcripts of seemingly innocent conversations, and details about surveillance subjects' personalities (that is, revealing that Lord Sillitoe suffered from dyspepsia, had bleeding gums, and was fond of cats), were turned in looking like the work of a child with sloppy penmanship and unwashed hands, and smelling of nail-varnish remover and curry. It was obvious that she wrote up her reports while painting her nails; drops of Nude You and Paisley Pow! were dripped on her confidential documents.

Miss Tuppenny understood that the best agents were often ruthless and cunning, hard to chain to a desk. She had become accustomed to Dolittle's sloppy work and had even developed a solvent that would remove curry sauce while leaving the ink underneath intact. But the young agent had stepped over the line when she endangered the life of fellow agent Jane Bond. And she was concerned about Mimi's inability to let go of romantic notions involving Jane Bond, despite Agent Bond's open involvement with another G.E.O.R.G.I.E. girl, Agent Lady Bridget St. Claire, cousin to the queen forty-seven times removed and G.E.O.R.G.I.E.'s only operative with access to Buckingham Palace. The only reason Dolittle hadn't been sacked outright was that Miss Tuppenny was convinced she could be rehabilitated. A year in Iceland cooling her heels should do it.

Dropping two lumps of sugar into her tea and stirring, Miss Tuppenny debated whether to include details of her last meeting with Dolittle in the memo, during which the girl wept piteously as she handed in her last can of bulletproof hairspray, her transmitter compact, and her decoder ring in exchange for a snowsuit, fur-lined boots, and a copy of *Puffins from A to Z.* "You'll have to earn your way back into our good graces," Miss Tuppenny told her firmly, too angry to be swayed by tears. The girl's hot temper could have cost them for the second time the only agent who could provide access to institutions and events the small spy organization had thus far been unable to infiltrate.

It was a stroke of luck that Miss Tuppenny had been at her desk that Saturday one year ago when Agent Cedric Pumpernickel had brought a tall girl with sultry dark looks and a familiar face to N.'s office. The subtle appraisal the girl had given her on the way in had made Miss Tuppenny blush and, the minute the door to N.'s office was closed, she grabbed her compact so she could check her lipstick. After a reassuring peek in the mirror, Miss Tuppenny put on her Dictaphone headphones and turned on the machine, tuning in the hidden microphone in N.'s potted plant, eager to know more about this girl.

The first part of the conversation—a chat about 007's health—did not surprise her. Jane was, it turned out, James Bond's twin sister, and while many agents chose to keep their work a secret from their families, it was not uncommon in cases of severe injury or death for N. to deliver the news himself. Nothing in the spare, dark rooms indicated that the business inside involved anything other than the affairs of Amalgamated Widget, Inc., as it said on the sign out front.

Miss Tuppenny wondered what Jane's relationship with her brother was like—were they close, or was he threatened, as some brothers were, considering a lesbian sister competition? The answer, when it came, was clear. When N. informed Jane that her brother lay in a drug-induced stupor strapped to a cot (in the Secret Agent Psycho Ward at the Secret Spy Sanatorium in Switzerland, Miss Tuppenny filled in, mentally) in complete mental collapse (after a career of too much boozing, bullets, and broads, was the rumor), Jane had laughed. Not just the usual short yip of surprise followed by noisy tears but a hearty belly laugh punctuated by an exclamation of, "It's bloody well time someone committed that blighter!" Miss Tuppenny could hear Agent Pumpernickel trying to silence her with a, "There now, Miss Bond, this is a serious matter!" and N.'s heavy footfall as he paced the dark-paneled room, stomping out his frustration.

When Jane stopped laughing, blowing her nose noisily into one of Pumpernickel's starched handkerchiefs (Miss Tuppenny heard him clear his throat uncomfortably and imagined he would carry paper hankies from then on), N. offered her a cup of tea, a sign that their "little conversation" was far from over.

"Just tell me why I'm here," Jane said.

"Very well. There's no sense stringing this out, is there?" N. sounded nervous. This was getting good. Kicking her door to the hall closed so she would not be interrupted, Miss Tuppenny switched the Dictaphone to "record," so she could play this later for the G.E.O.R.G.I.E. girls.

"Miss Bond," N. started, "I'm going to tell you something very few people know. But first you must promise that this conversation will go no further than these four walls." There was a muffled sound; Jane must have nodded. Miss Tuppenny heard the groan of N.'s chair as he sank into it, heard his humidor open and close, and the click of his lighter.

"You have been led to believe that your brother, James, is employed at Amalgamated Widget, Inc. In truth his work is of a highly specialized and secretive nature that directly affects the well-being of the most beloved person in England." His words tapered off to a reverent hush, and Miss Tuppenny pictured him smiling smugly as he leaned back in his chair and puffed self-importantly on his Cuban cigar.

"Benny Hill?" said Jane, sounding completely sincere, and Miss Tuppenny put a hand over her mouth to stifle a laugh. This is serious, Louise, she told herself. In all her years of snooping, this was the first time she had heard N. purposefully blow an agent's cover. She swore she could hear N.'s teeth grinding as he stiffly replied, "Her Majesty, Queen Elizabeth."

"Good guess, though, Miss Bond," nosed in Pumpernickel. Always the peacekeeper, Miss Tuppenny thought. "Benny Hill is well liked by all of England, but the queen is beloved. It's important you understand the difference between a man who dresses in women's clothing for entertainment and a *real* queen." The man annoyed N. no end, but after Agent Pumpernickel had saved the queen from kidnappers intent on stealing the throne for the exiled Duke of Windsor, he was impossible to get rid of. Her Majesty would not be happy to discover that her savior had been relegated to the scrap heap.

"What does he do?" Jane chuckled. "Mix her martinis?" N. must have been midpuff when Jane said this; Miss Tuppenny heard him sputter and gasp, then someone thumping him soundly on the back. No doubt Pumpernickel's first-aid effort.

"He's telling the truth!" Pumpernickel cried, with a passion in his voice she'd heard only once before, when 007 broke into Pumpernickel's desk and replaced the erasers on his pencils with smoke bombs, driving Pumpernickel out of his office for the better part of a week.

"Your brother's absence has put the queen in a precarious position," N. said with all seriousness.

Jane was quiet, and Miss Tuppenny imagined that the truth about her brother had sunk in. "You see," continued N., "within certain foreign circles, there exist people with a lunatic hatred of England."

"It's probably that nasty habit we have of taking over their countries," Jane suggested dryly.

Pumpernickel's "Oh, dear" was silenced by N.'s curt "Zip it." He continued, "In one week the queen will present your brother and one hundred thirty-three other loyal subjects with the coveted Jolly Good Show

Medal. Death is the only excuse for not attending; your brother's absence is . . . well, we might as well print his obituary in the *Times*. Your presence at the event would be much appreciated."

"How will my being there affect anything?" asked Jane.

"You won't be there as yourself, Miss Bond. With a little help from our experts in Disguise and Deception, you're going to play James."

"And I'm going with you!" cried Pumpernickel.

After some haggling over the terms of her employment—Miss Tuppenny was a little jealous that Jane's starting salary was double hers but impressed that she held out for a month's paid holiday—Jane Bond agreed to let the Secret Service transform her into her brother's surrogate for public events. It was then Miss Tuppenny hit upon a brilliant idea. If the secret service could have a James Bond look-alike, why couldn't G.E.O.R.G.I.E.?

That was one year ago. In the time since, Jane, escorted by Agent Pumpernickel, had donned man-drag eleven times and made public appearances as James Bond for the British Secret Service. Except for her refusal to use the men's loo, that first mission and several others had gone off without a hitch. Her affair with G.E.O.R.G.I.E. Agent Bridget St. Claire had turned into a real romance, and six months into her tenure as 007-and-a-half, she had decided to stop playing at being a spy and become the real thing. Six weeks of G.E.O.R.G.I.E. spy school later, she had graduated from student to apprentice agent, and was eager to show off her skills as a double agent, the first British Secret Service agent to throw her allegiance to G.E.O.R.G.I.E. Miss Tuppenny smiled at the thought and initialed the memo, then zipped it into the secret compartment in the lining of her Burberry slicker.

Her tea was strong and sweet, and this, combined with the biscuits she kept in a tin in her top drawer, would be her supper tonight, which she would eat while finalizing some new G.E.O.R.G.I.E. plans. Last week N. had had her type an interoffice memo requesting a lightweight James Bond suit with featherweight padded shoulders, good for a desert climate; two tickets on British Airways to America; and a copy of the book *How to Be a Hotshot Gambler or Just Look Like One*. The rumor that surfaced at last week's Friday-afternoon tea explained N.'s purchases: an American agent was alleged to have invented a truly remarkable device, the best thing since invisible ink, to be unveiled at the annual men-only Spy Convention in Las Vegas, Nevada, and sold to the highest bidder. Even if females *were* allowed into the exclusive group, Miss Tuppenny thought, her small operation could never afford to compete in a bidding war with larger, government-funded agencies. What G.E.O.R.G.I.E. needed was an agent who could infiltrate the gathering, locate the gadget, and steal it.

It was time to call in Agent 007-and-a-half.

one

The request had come, as usual, in the form of a telegram slipped under her door. AUNT HARRIET AILING. REQUIRE YOUR IMMEDIATE ASSISTANCE. TAKE THREE O'CLOCK TRAIN TOMORROW. UNCLE FRANK. "Aunt Harriet" was her brother, James Bond. "Uncle Frank" was N., head of the notorious double-0 department of Her Majesty's Secret Service. "Immediate assistance" meant that Jane Bond would soon be packing her spy kit for another appearance as her brother, 007. Whether she was at the opening of a new branch office or the retirement luncheon of a beloved Secret Service secretary, she had only simple tasks that required little more than donning a special suit and spending a few hours smiling, smirking, and sneering. She had wrenched her neck once attempting all three at the same time, while trying to inject some humor into the typically dull assignments. Still, it was better than being on the dole. Since her work for the Secret Service was strictly top-hush, kept from agents and bureaucrats alike, N. paid her in cash and put her on his expense account under the heading of "Necessary Evil."

In the past year, since agreeing to the charade, Jane had averaged one assignment a month and was still making three times what she had earned at her last job as a bookshop clerk. Thirty-two years old and she was back in her brother's shadow, working for a man she detested, for an organization whose policies she abhorred, all for that envelope of crisp pound notes shoved under her door every Monday morning that allowed her to live as she pleased. Her James Bond kit contained a suit, a martini glass, stick-on scars, and *The Bachelor's Guide to 101 Pickup Lines*, but no Walther PPK, Bondmobile, or state-of-the-art spy gadgets. She knew that her appearances were meant to undercut rumors of her brother's decline; she was window dressing, her brother's stand-in when he drank himself into a coma or broke both legs while mixing martinis on skis. She had been content with her lightweight role, and then G.E.O.R.G.I.E. Agent Bridget St. Claire came along and offered, among other things, to make her a real secret agent. And the double-agent aspect appealed to Jane's twin nature. After six weeks of G.E.O.R.G.I.E. spy school, spent learning to mix incendiary devices from biscuit powder and invisible ink from commonly available citrus fruits, becoming a top-notch shot and a fair cryptographer, she was eager for her first real assignment. She had waited long enough.

But not for this. When N. announced she would be attending the Spy Convention in Las Vegas as her brother, in hospital recovering from a nasty burn, her first reaction was to decline the job. It was too risky; her true identity would surely be revealed the minute she walked into a room filled with her brother's colleagues. "I'll be with you all the way," said Agent Pumpernickel from underneath N.'s desk, where he was searching for a boiled sweet he had dropped. Cedric was technically retired after twenty-five years' service, and when he wasn't parading Jane around town, he was in front of the telly in his dressing gown and slippers, eating Violet Crumbles and wondering why love had passed him by. "And I could stand a holiday," he said, holding up a sourball covered in gold carpet fuzz. Jane had left N.'s office unconvinced.

The next day Miss Tuppenny contacted Jane and made it clear that her days as a simple stand-in were over; she was as skilled, if not as practiced, as any G.E.O.R.G.I.E. agent, and it was time to get her out into the field. No beginner was sent on a mission alone, however, and especially not that far from headquarters; Jane's backup, Agents Bridget St. Claire and Bibi Gallini, would fly to Las Vegas with her (but not *with* her) and maintain undercover status while remaining available should the mission prove more difficult than expected. Jane was to behave as if she were on her own, calling on Bridget and Bibi only in a pinch. Miss Tuppenny had also ordered that if Agent Pumpernickel, who had almost no field experience, having spent the majority of his career behind a desk ordering office supplies, should happen upon the invention first—an unlikely scenario—Jane should let him have it. There was no sense putting her job with the Secret Service in jeopardy when Miss Tuppenny could arrange for the invention to "disappear" from the weapons closet. This way nothing could possibly go wrong. It was, Miss Tuppenny was convinced, a perfect way for Jane to stretch her double-agent wings.

When Jane heard this, her reservations about the mission were replaced with a determination to prove herself by securing the invention for G.E.O.R.G.I.E. without involving Bridget and Bibi. She would not ring them on her spy phone—a plain, black men's wallet that became a telephone with the addition of a ballpoint-pen antenna and receiver hidden in a Kennedy half-dollar—until she had the invention in her hands.

So, on the fifteenth day of September, Agents Jane Bond (as James) and Cedric Pumpernickel boarded a British Airways 707. Their cover: two British gentlemen, members in good standing of the International Association of Accident-Prone People, heading for their organization's convention in Las Vegas. Their mission: to approach the unidentified creator of a top-secret invention and secure exclusive rights for Britain. After they'd settled themselves in their seats, Jane turned and looked seven rows back at her lover, G.E.O.R.G.I.E. Agent Bridget St. Claire, disguised as a bored Italian contessa, and winked. Bridget smiled and then quickly ducked behind her Italian *Vogue* when Cedric turned around to ask the child behind him to please refrain from kicking his seat.

At Bridget's side was her partner, Agent Bibi Gallini, disguised as the bored Italian contessa's pouty French maid. Bibi was a compulsive womanizer and a practiced thief—she had once lifted the queen's purse and then returned it, all without being noticed, when she found that it contained dog biscuits, bunion pads, and a collapsible rain bonnet but not rubies, emeralds, or diamonds—and part of Bridget's job was to restrain Bibi's wilder impulses, to keep her from stealing the store when all they needed was a pack of chewing gum. Unaccustomed to taking a backseat, Bibi had the job of reining Bridget in should she interfere before she was needed. Miss Tuppenny had warned Bridget against crowding Jane on her first mission as a double agent; she and Bibi were ordered to wait for Jane to contact them.

The thumping on the back of his seat abated, and Agent Pumpernickel strapped on his seat belt. While he was looking forward to his first visit to America, and his only chance to see Liberace live in concert *and* visit Hoover Dam, he felt some apprehension about Miss Bond's sudden personality shift. She had begun acting more professional and less like a child at a costume party. Her interest in the logistics of this trip, always his department, made him wonder if she thought she had outgrown him. He hoped that this mission, her first introduction to spy society, would not go to her head. Another arrogant Bond was the last thing Cedric needed; before he retired from daily office life, part of his job descrip-

tion, or so it seemed, was to provide a target for 007's sophomoric high
jinks. (James had glued Cedric to his chair, and switched Cedric's cheese
sandwich for one made of paste, and put mackerel in his electric heater.)
By the end of Cedric's tenure, rubber spiders regularly jumped out of
his desk drawer, and due to his arachnophobia, he had to open his drawers with a ruler, taking cover behind his desk chair. James would stand
in the doorway giggling, saying, "Come on, mate, you need a bit more
exercise anyway." And so the zeal with which Jane had thrown herself
into this mission worried him. She had agreed, for the first time, to wear
knuckle-hair patches, and it seemed that overnight she'd acquired a definite 007 swagger that hadn't been part of her routine before now. She
even *welcomed* the addition of uncomfortable latex forehead and chin
prosthesis that made her disguise all the more realistic. For Pumpernickel the line between the two Bonds was blurring, and, despite the
friendship he had developed with Jane and her lover, Bridget, a sweet
cosmetics salesgirl by day and the daughter of a duchess by night, he
was once again beginning to check his pockets for moldy jam.

16 SEPTEMBER 1966
LAS VEGAS, NEVADA

Say cheese!" said Agent Cedric Pumpernickel. "This one's for the company newsletter." Jane smiled and pointed to a faded picture of flapjacks
featured in the Teepee Village Motor Court Coffee Shop's menu, then
waited, feeling like an idiot while Cedric searched his camera bag for a
fresh flashbulb. Every moment of their trip so far had been documented
by the budding photographer, who had shown up at her flat with an Instamatic glued to his eye. He had insisted on snaps of her sleeping in the
taxi on the way to Heathrow Airport, ignoring the preflight safety
demonstration, repelling a stewardess's advances, receiving her tin
flight wings, and, now, perusing the plastic-covered menu. "I want to remember our very first meal in America," he explained, finally snapping
the portrait of Jane and then turning his eye to the still life created by
the table setting—two yellowing Melmac plates bordered with turquoise
teepees, two earthenware mugs with chipped rims, and two sweaty red

plastic water glasses. Arranging the salt shaker so its shadow dramatically intersected the butter, he wiped his camera lens with his handkerchief before capturing the scene on film.

"You might want to get a chair," Jane said to their waitress, who responded with a shrug and a weary sigh. The red script embroidered
above the left breast of her imitation buckskin uniform read WANDA.
Wanda looked like she slept under a sun lamp. The rich nut color of her
skin was several shades darker than her fringed, cap-sleeved dress, the
apron of which was smeared with egg and ketchup. On her forehead a
bubble of peeling skin peeked out from under fluffy bangs the color of
cirrus clouds. The rest of her hair was glued in a gravity-defying upward spiral, like a serving of spun sugar atop a paper cone, and covered
with a nearly invisible hair net. I've got no place to go, Wanda's posture
said. Leaning back on the heels of her worn moccasins, shoulders sagging, she began examining her nails, painted frosty white and beginning
to chip.

Jane's heart went out to Wanda, and she hoped those moccasins were
orthopedic. Since their trip began—no, since their *association* began almost one year ago—Jane had spent more time waiting for Cedric—to tie
his shoe, drink his tea, or finish complaining about the collapse of the
empire—than she had posing as James Bond.

It was hard to believe the man across the table had been the first
double-operative. In 1931 a young Pumpernickel had been dropped onto
a remote South Pacific island with orders to assassinate a mad biologist
breeding wolf spiders as big as Volkswagens, intending to turn them
loose at one of the queen's teas. To get to the madman's laboratory,
Cedric had had to fight his way through dense cobwebs and had been
bitten several times, blowing up like a blimp. The mission had been a
miserable failure. Not only had the evil scientist used Cedric's bloated
body to float to Brazil (rumors of a spider man living in the dense jungle
still surfaced every few years), Cedric was left with an extreme aversion
to spiders. Shattered by failure, he had asked to be reassigned to a job
suitable for a man with jangly nerves, one that would not bring him
into close contact with anything hairy, squishy, or with multiple legs.
Luckily, the head of the department of desk accessories had just hanged
himself out of boredom, using a rubber-band rope that had taken him

fifteen years to weave, and so the keys to the storage closet became Cedric's.

Twenty-five years behind a desk had made him as slow as a slug, and if Jane tried to hurry him along, he sulked. Little wonder he had hadn't had a boyfriend since 1947. He was no oil painting to begin with, not homely so much as bland as a bowl of cottage cheese, resembling a thousand other middle-aged white-collar men with pasty skin and rounded shoulders from decades hunched over a desk. Years of drearily shuffling papers and sharpening pencils had dulled his features into a perpetual saggy frown. Jane had seen photographs of a young Cedric, before his father had *forced* him into a job with the Secret Service. It was not age that had taken the shine off him, but boredom. It was only when N. complimented him on a job well done, or Jane admired the newest addition to his snuffbox collection, that he showed any sign of passion in what was an otherwise carefully ordered, hermetically sealed existence. His fusty mannerisms, inherited from Mother Pumpernickel, a relic of the Victorian era, aged him far beyond his fifty-two years, making him both a sympathetic figure and an irritating travel companion.

"Foreign customs are so confusing." He shook his head and held the menu close to his face, having left his reading glasses in the Heathrow gents' loo. "I can get eggs and sausage and flapjacks and toast and juice— tomato, orange, or prune—or eggs and sausage and potatoes and toast and juice—orange or tomato. Why can't I get potatoes *and* prune juice?"

"You can," said Wanda, using her pencil to flick a piece of dried egg yolk off his menu. "See right here—prune juice."

"We're out of prune," said the man behind the counter, a tubby fellow in a dirty T-shirt and limp feathered headdress, leaning against the griddle and reading a racing form.

"We're out of prune," she repeated.

"That does put a wrench in the works," sighed Cedric.

"Look, they have buttered eggs. You like buttered eggs," said Jane. They had nearly missed their connection in New York because he couldn't decide between a Hershey bar and a roll of fruit Life Savers.

"Why come this far for something you can have at home?" Cedric snapped.

"Christ on the cross," said Jane, turning over a grape jelly packet to check the ingredients: sugar, corn syrup, Blue Dye #3. "It's not your last meal." Too nervous about her first flight—and first actual G.E.O.R.G.I.E. assignment—to eat a proper breakfast, Jane had eaten only one meal the day before, the snack served on the last leg of their trip, over the American Midwest. "I flew this far on a glass of Tang and a Hostess Ding Dong," she said, eyeing Wanda, who was gnawing off the white lipstick that made her mouth look like a skinny slice of frosted cake. "You had both our in-flight meals, chocolate bars at every stopover, and half of the cabdriver's ham sandwich. Pick a dish before I cover the menu in jelly and eat it." Wanda brightened, licking the end of her pencil and holding it ready above her order pad.

"I hardly think this kind lady is interested in what I eat," Cedric huffed, holding up his hand. He would not be rushed. Food was a sensitive subject for him; he had put on a little weight since his retirement, and even his socks were tight. His new Bermuda shorts were two sizes bigger than his last pair, purchased years ago for a holiday in Greece, and he had carefully scissored off the tag inside the waistband that gave away his love of mash and bangers.

Jane rolled her eyes and thought back to their first meeting, an overcast September morning at the London Zoo. Dressed in a dark trench coat buttoned to the neck, looking like a perverted vicar, Cedric had approached Jane as she fed peanuts to the gnus. "I'm Mr. Pumpernickel from Amalgamated Widget, Inc., your brother's place of employment. His boss would like to have a little chat with you." Thinking her brother had gotten some poor stenog preggers, Jane started to walk away. She had stopped cleaning up James's messes long ago, when she grew tired of playing agony aunt to his ex-lovers. It was only when Cedric began talking about insurance papers and hospital forms and her responsibility as James's next of kin that Jane agreed to the meeting, an act she regretted in her lowest moments. Like this one.

"Just pick something, Cedric," Jane said, ripping open the jelly packet and poking at the gelatinous cube inside. It didn't look like any jelly she had ever seen.

"What about the Bucking Bronco Biscuits with brown gravy?" said Wanda. Her shoulders were slumped from exhaustion—she had been up since 4:00 A.M.—and her Eighteen-Hour Bra had gone on strike at

6:00, but her voice was as chirpy and bright as the song of the mourning doves that nested under the eaves of the teepees and helped her greet the day.

"Is that a genuine cowboy dish?" Cedric asked. Jane checked her watch and groaned, remembering his hourlong conversation last night with the owner of the motor court about the authenticity of the concrete teepees.

"Yup, it sure is," Wanda said patiently. "It's Lorne Greene's favorite dish." She pointed at a signed photograph of the actor hanging above the cash register, but it didn't seem to sway him. Cedric wrinkled his brow and went back to examining the menu, trying to concentrate over Jane's sighs. This was far more complicated than the choice of dinner on the plane, which had been limited to Swiss steak and tomato salad or fish sticks and Tater Tots. Unsure of what a "tot" was, not wanting to appear unsophisticated, he had ordered the steak, which, when it arrived, bore no resemblance to Swiss cuisine.

"What's in brown gravy?" he asked Wanda, and the toe of Jane's Cuban-heeled Beatle boot made contact with the hairy white flesh of his shin, airing in public for the first time in over a decade. The stewardess on the flight over, a young trainee from Wales, had cried waiting for him to make up his mind. Bridget had kindly taken the young girl to the lav for a mop-up, swearing at Cedric in Italian as she passed by.

Wanda laughed and spit her gum into a paper napkin, wondering if she could unhook her bra through her uniform without their noticing. "Don't ask, hon. What about the Git Along Littl' Doggies Gastronomical Delight? It has one of everything. That way you don't have to decide." She patted his shoulder and smiled, as one would comfort the afflicted, and gave Jane a conspiratorial wink. Jane rolled her eyes and mimed shooting herself in the head, making Wanda laugh. His head stuck in his menu, Cedric didn't notice their little game, didn't notice when Wanda pretended to hang herself with her beaded belt. From London to Las Vegas, his neurotic behavior had driven Jane, the airline pilots, the customs inspectors, a bevy of stewardesses, and the taxi driver crazy. Wanda seemed built of sturdier stuff and, like Jane, accustomed to annoyance.

"Too rich for my sensitive stomach." Cedric burped delicately.

"You ate both our dinners on the plane!" Jane reminded him. "You were halfway through your plastic plate when the stewardess informed you it wasn't part of the meal."

He slapped his menu on the table, almost upending his water glass. "How was I to know it wasn't one of those awful crisp American salads?"

Wanda began chewing on her pencil. With the casinos practically giving away food, following the principle of fattening sheep before the slaughter, establishments on the edge of town, like the Teepee Village Motor Court, barely made enough to pay the electric bill for the coffee shop swamp cooler that helped make the stifling desert air bearable. Except for an earlier rush of harried truckers wanting fried eggs and brown gargle, these two men were her only customers, and the first real company she'd had all day. "You in town for a convention?" she asked, picking a yellow splinter off her tongue. Her husband, the owner, manager, and cook, was after her to give up the filthy habit. Perhaps if she smoked more, she wouldn't crave the pencil.

"Yes, we are," said Cedric, wondering why Wanda was staring cross-eyed at a gnawed No. 2 pencil. "We're a group working to meet the needs of the habitually unlucky." He took his wallet from the back pocket of his mustard-colored Bermuda shorts and showed her his official International Association of Accident-Prone People membership card. This year, despite his retirement, Cedric had had the honor of choosing the theme.

"You're not Mormons, then," she said, tapping the eraser end of her pencil on the arm of Jane's black jacket. "You, hon, look like a first-class converter in that preacher's suit."

The invitation had said to "dress casual," so Cedric had parted with a tidy sum for a casual-wear wardrobe from the Dorcas Collection. For the opening day of the convention, he had slipped on Bermuda shorts, a stretchy short-sleeved golf shirt, and leather monk sandals over black socks—Jane had convinced him to throw caution to the wind and go without garters. But Jane had to suffer in the black Bond suit she wore on all her missions. There had been insufficient time to acquire an entire holiday wardrobe to disguise her feminine form, so the padding that thickened her waist, disguised her hips, and broadened her shoulders had been tacked inside a new, hastily stitched rayon suit that was still too heavy for hundred-degree weather and contained the occasional stray pin trapped in the turned seams.

"We're Church of England all the way," Cedric assured Wanda. "But not men of the cloth." Before he could launch into an explanation of the marital troubles of Henry VIII, Jane shoved her menu under his nose, pointing to the picture of the Trapper's Delight, a six-egg omelet stuffed with seven kinds of meat. Cow, sheep, pig—how many more could there be? She decided not to pursue the thought. "How about this?" she asked. She glanced at her watch, a gift from Miss Tuppenny upon her graduation from spy school. The face of the watch was a camera lens, the rim was a powerful cutting tool, and the "diamond" chips circling the face were tiny knockout darts activated when she pushed the stem. They had another hour to kill until it was time for the drive to the Las Vegas Strip and, beyond that, the convention center, and she feared Cedric would go on like this until doomsday.

"It does look good enough to eat," he said grudgingly, fiddling with the Royal Navy ring on the pinkie of his left hand. It had been his father's, and, as time passed, his. As his girth expanded, he had moved the ring from his middle finger to his ring finger and, the last stop, his pinkie.

"But it's awfully hot, don't you think, for a griddle dish? And fattening," he said, patting the strained waistband of his shorts. "As soon as our feet touch British soil again, I'm beginning a slimming diet," he announced, looking down at his thighs spread over the booth's cracked red leatherette covering. Pinned to his gold Dacron golf shirt was his Order of the British Empire medal, given to him for his part in the rescue of Her Royal Majesty from a band of disgruntled aristocrats determined to snatch the throne from under her royal rear. He hoped the opulent ornament would distract attention from his flabby arms.

"Well, it's awfully hot to be wearing this bloody monkey suit," snapped Jane. "Come on, we have somewhere to be." Eleven hours in this straitjacket, and when they arrived in Las Vegas, Cedric, who had kicked off his shoes midflight because they were pinching, scolded her in the taxi for undoing the top button of her shirt. "You never know who's watching," he had said, throwing his lightweight golf jacket over her head.

"How about the Chubby Cowboy Breakfast Plate?" said Wanda. "Ripe tomato slices, cottage cheese, and dry toast. Nothing hot about that."

"I've put on a half stone or so since retiring, but I'm hardly chubby." He sucked in his stomach, aware that the clingy fabric of his shirt did nothing for his chunky physique. The man in the headdress, the owner of the establishment, cleared his throat and started to scrape the griddle, a sign he was ready to call it quits. Jane grabbed Cedric's menu, soft and sticky where his fingers had been clutching it, and shoved it into the tomahawk-shaped menu holder on the scratched red-and-gold Formica tabletop.

"We'll have the Pecos Pete Pancakes. And I'll have coffee."

"Two stacks splatter dabs, chief!" yelled Wanda. The man fired up the griddle, sending a wave of heat across the room. Jane leaned over to open the flyspecked window at the end of their booth. "It's nailed shut," Wanda said. "Keeps the flies out. The sand, too. In '62 a dust storm swept through this place, took us days to sweep it out. We had to throw away the condiment bottles on every table." She ticked off the different types on her fingers. "Ketchup. Mustard. Salt. Pepper. Relish. There was sand in my teeth for days." When she finished, Cedric snapped her picture. Wanda's hands went immediately to her hair, which Jane imagined would stay put in a tornado.

"You've got to give a girl some warning," Wanda told him, patting the stiff white column. Throwing her shoulders back and smiling, she exposed evenly spaced white teeth and a strip of pink gums. Cedric obliged by snapping another one.

"Make sure I get a copy," she said over her shoulder as she went to get Jane's coffee.

"I hope the food here is better than the tea," said Cedric. "This looks like dishwater." He bobbed a Lipton tea bag furiously in the small tin teapot, his lips pursed in disapproval. "How can anything steep properly in lukewarm water?"

"Ask her to boil some more."

"It's best not to draw attention to ourselves," he sighed, braving a sip. "She could be working for the KGB. Imagine what kind of target a roomful of top spies would make. Despite our brilliantly inventive cover, anything could happen." He lowered his voice and leaned across the table, blasting Jane with a cloud of Old Spice aftershave. "In 1951, at the inaugural spy convention, a secret agent fell to his death whilst on a tour of the Eiffel Tower."

"I hadn't heard that one," Jane said, leaning to catch his words while keeping an eye out for their waitress. "What happened?" Cedric loved to gossip, and in Jane he had found the perfect listener, for she was an unrepentant nosey-parker. She even liked hearing gossip about herself, especially if it was salacious or untrue. It wasn't until Agent Mimi Dolittle threw that jar of vanishing cream at her head that Jane realized the trouble that unrestrained chitchat could cause. Most gossipers did not graduate to attempted murder, but as a precaution G.E.O.R.G.I.E. had asked its agents to abstain from all forms of gossip, including speculation, tittle-tattle, and rumor. All Jane had now were Cedric's stories, culled from old government case files, his mother's diaries of her life on the stage, the society pages, and things he had overheard on the bus. This was one of the best parts of their partnership.

"Absolute cat lap," he shuddered, emptying three sugar packets into the tan liquid and sipping it slowly, enjoying Jane's interest. "According to witnesses," he began, putting down the offensive brew and picking up his water glass, "the man, an Icelander, tripped over a schoolgirl's book bag. A red one."

"That's it?" said Jane, turning up her nose at this so-called piece of scuttle. Good gossip did not typically involve an unfortunate death from a very high place or a child's red school bag.

"Those in the know suspect it was *murder!*" he whispered dramatically.

"Bo-o-r-ring," said Jane, leaning back against the leatherette banquet and pressing her sweaty water glass to her forehead.

He sniffed, deciding to keep other prime tidbits to himself for the time being. "In our world there are no accidents. Remember that, Jane." He reached for his teacup, an automatic gesture, then pushed it aside with a grimace. "If this is an indication of the sophistication of the American palate, I'll fade to nothing by the time we return to London. Did you get a look at the back of the menu? They have apple pie, rhubarb pie, peach pie, but no kidney pie. Honestly, when we let the colonies declare their independence, we should have given them a cookbook as a parting gift."

Jane dipped a paper napkin into her water and wiped the back of her neck. She was sweating under her forehead prosthesis, which, in this heat, felt like a big hot hand clamped to her brow. "The decline of many civilizations can be traced to bad food. Quit complaining, or I won't go see Liberace with you," she said, knowing it was the surest way to get him to put a lid on it.

He stopped wiping his fork on his shirt and stared at her. Was it her imagination, or were those tears in his eyes? "I'm not complaining," he insisted. "I'm merely narrating. Since you didn't take the trouble to educate yourself about American customs, it's my duty to help you through uncharted territory."

Jane rolled her eyes and launched into an impression of her "guide."

"*Your duty?* 'A child is kicking my seat. I can't see the safety demonstration through that nun's wimple. How come my packet contained only eight peanuts and yours nine? Must they land so rapidly that my ears pop? I'm certain the customs official in New York stole my socks. Why is it so sunny here? A dollar-fifty for a taxi ride? It's highway robbery! My teepee is stuffy. I think I saw a spider. Motor-court soap gives me a rash.' Christ, Cedric, today I have to walk into a room filled with my brother's friends and colleagues and make them believe I'm 007. If I'm not spot-on, by day's end the entire spy world will know that 007 is out of action, and that N. has sent his sister in his place. If I were you, I'd worry more about *that* than a pair of missing socks."

"Three pair," he said sulkily. Jane had shocked him into silence, and, glad for the quiet and a little ashamed by her outburst, she looked down at her hands, at the hair that had been painstakingly glued to her knuckles, which now itched. The night before the flight, she had spent hours with the Secret Service's top disguise artist, and as a result she sported hair on her toes and on the rims of her ears. She felt like a werewolf.

"Don't scratch," said Cedric, slapping away her hand when he saw her rubbing the thatch of wrist hair peeking out from under her sleeve.

"Sod off," she said.

He raised his eyebrows at her insubordination, and Jane wished she could take back her words. They were quarreling like an old married couple, and it had to stop.

"I must be allergic to the glue," she said weakly. As soon as this mission was over, she was going to shave her entire body.

"Nonsense, the adhesive compound is of the highest quality. It's your nerves, but you have nothing to fear. The chaps in makeup did a splendid job on you. Why, if I didn't know it was you . . ."

". . . you'd be checking your drawers for spiders," Jane finished his thought. "But I'm not my brother. See?" She turned out her pockets. "No creepy crawlies here."

Cedric smiled and relaxed, and the tension between them dissipated. "You needn't worry, Jane. If the fakery is discovered, I'll simply pull the chaps aside and explain that your brother had another commitment that precluded him from making this year's meeting."

"And how will you explain the woman in the Bond suit?"

"You needn't worry about a thing," he repeated. "I've been trained to handle just such a situation. You've already enough to think about." If Jane was unmasked, his instructions were to drop a tranquilizer in her martini and put her on the first flight home, explaining to the other agents that she was an escaped mental patient with a Bond complex. Their friendship would be over once she awoke, but he was confident it wouldn't come to that. Her transformation over the past year had been remarkable; even when she was just plain Jane, she retained elements of her brother—his sardonic smile, dramatically cocked eyebrow, the queen's diction, and of course the Bond passion for beautifully tailored menswear. Except for the skirt and sweater she wore to somber occasions like weddings and funerals and St. Claire family dinners, her wardrobe would be at home in her brother's closet. A passable Bond impersonation had become a great one, with the addition of caps (the front tooth cracked to mimic one 007 had broken while wrestling a shark), manly body hair, a more pronounced forehead, a square jawline, shoe lifts, and a little practice. Jane was perfect, Cedric thought, until she opened her mouth and a girlish voice tumbled out. N. had suggested a simple operation to bring down her voice—"a little snip"—but withdrew his offer when Jane suggested he undergo a little snip of his own.

Wanda set down stacks of pancakes nearly as tall as her hairdo, and Jane dug in, cutting a wedge eight pancakes high, dripping with syrup, and shoving it into her mouth, washing it down with a big gulp of coffee, black and strong.

"My, my, my," Cedric said, polishing his fork on his shirt. Taking little bites around the perimeter of the stack until it began to resemble a lace doily, he made a show of enjoying his meal until Wanda crossed the room, unlocked the jukebox, and started waxing the records.

"Isn't this better than the Marmite and melba toast you were going to have in your teepee?" said Jane, popping a piece of crispy bacon into her mouth.

"I'd heard American food was terrible. I had no idea it was this dreadful," he said, syrup dripping down his chin. "Watch you don't drink too much of that," he added when Jane took a sip of water. "Full of fluoride, you know, bad for the teeth." Taking a bite of the melon wedge on the edge of his plate, he scrunched up his face and spit it out. It was crisp and cool, nothing like the stewed fruit he enjoyed at home. Looking over his shoulder to make sure Wanda wasn't standing there listening, he said, "I hope I don't contract George Washington's revenge. Perhaps dining in a restaurant catering to truck drivers wasn't the wisest choice."

"You're the accommodation man." Having sat through Cedric's long-winded rant on the sorry state of the British economy, Jane had expected to stay at a modest motel. Not one of the Goliaths on the Strip, with neon lights and Olympic-size pools and glittery showgirls, but something older, less ostentatious, with fluffy towels, morning coffee service, and perhaps even a small swimming pool. So when their taxi had pulled into the gravel drive of the Teepee Village Motor Court late last night, Jane knew that Cedric's lecture was meant to prepare her for this: eight concrete teepees arranged in a horseshoe around a run-down two-story adobe structure, the bottom floor a diner and the top floor the owner's home. The exteriors of the concrete teepees were hot to the touch and the view a dusty carpet of barren desert. No maid service, no morning coffee, and no swimming pool, unless one counted the drainage ditch by the side of the road that gave off a fetid odor. Last night Jane had slept in a funnel-shaped room with concrete walls, on a twin bed made of rough-hewn logs, under a scratchy Indian blanket.

two

W hile Jane was sitting in a hot diner, feeling her fake forehead sink down her face and eating what Wanda colorfully called "splatter dabs," her lover, G.E.O.R.G.I.E. Agent Bridget St. Claire, was relaxing in a cool blue pool at the Sands hotel, stretched out on an inflatable raft, peeking through oversize dark glasses at the celebrity lineup around the kidney-shaped pool. Singer Sammi Martini was trying to woo a blonde in a gold bikini, Rock Hudson was admiring his reflection in the water, and Lorne Greene was stretched out on a chaise longue working on his tan. Bridget gave a little start when her raft bumped against the side of the pool, made of brilliant Moroccan-blue glass tiles that sparkled in the sun. She used her feet to push off, admiring her toenails polished in Revlon Jack O' Diamonds Red, which was part of the hotel's welcome package for female guests. The ripples she created made the tile mermaid at the bottom of the pool appear to undulate, her half-closed eyelids giving her a languorously seductive look. Gilt-edged green gills ended in a pair of enormous, cartoonish breasts partially covered by long golden locks. The Twiggy aesthetic hadn't reached Las Vegas, and Bridget didn't mind one bit.

Themes from popular American television shows, interpreted by a perky guitar quartet in the cocktail lounge, jangled out of the casino each time a waitress opened the sliding glass door to the patio, carrying a tray of drinks capped with tiny paper umbrellas and skewers of pineapple, mango, and kiwi. To get to the pool—to get anywhere in the Sands—hotel guests had to walk through the casino, past roulette wheels and blackjack tables crowded with high rollers. Visitors to Las Vegas were assaulted by noisy slot machines as soon as they crossed the Nevada border. As their plane slipped over the state line, stewardesses had wheeled out battery-operated slot machines, and passengers played feverishly until the PLEASE FASTEN YOUR SEAT BELT sign flashed. Gas stations and grocery stores, highway rest stops and roadside cafés competed for the millions of pennies, nickels, and dimes fed each year into the one-armed bandits.

Standards were different in Monte Carlo, where she, Lady Bridget

Genevieve Norbert-Nilbert St. Claire, had spent every summer of her youth trailing behind her mother, the oft-married Emerald St. Claire, Duchess of Malmesbury and England's best-known hostess, clad in a junior-miss version of her mother's couture costume. Parading through a casino in a terry-cloth shortie robe, cork-heeled sandals, and bare legs was simply not done there, unless one was purposefully courting ridicule, but here no one had blinked at her getup. Attention was paid only to the piles of chips atop the gaming tables' green-felt surfaces. There was no one here who would recognize her and ply her with bloated compliments in an attempt to acquire an invitation to one of Emerald's celebrated soirees, and Bridget relaxed into her newfound peaceful anonymity, her dark glasses curtaining off the world.

So far the mission had been the most relaxing of her career as an underground girl spy. She had spent most of the flight over flipping through fashion magazines, part of her role as European royalty (no great hardship) and watching Cedric drive the stewardesses crazy. (Her girlfriend had a similar affect on them, she knew, but all she could do was put on her dark glasses and try not to look.) Being married to a facsimile of one of England's most notorious mashers could work a girl's nerves.

With a glass of chilled mango juice in hand, Bridget kicked to the shallow end of the pool, where Angie Dickinson, in a curve-hugging gold lamé bathing suit, was stretched out on a chaise longue. The movie star was talking into a black telephone patiently held at her ear by a bellhop, his glance torn between the glamorous movie star and the long cord snaking back to the casino, a trip wire for those who had taken their breakfast, tall, cool, and on the rocks. He waved Bridget away. Feeling a blush begin at the V of her white one-piece Catalina swimsuit, she put her drink on the side of the pool, stuffed her newly tinted black hair into her daisy swim cap, and slipped gracefully into the water, surfacing by the floating craps table at the deep end, where she played one of the complimentary chips she received with her eggs Florentine breakfast, and won fifty dollars.

Angie Dickinson was even prettier in person than she was in the movies, and Bridget would have told her so had that irritating little man not interfered. Aware of how oppressive public attention could be—the crowds who gathered outside Buckingham Palace knew Bridget and her little pink Vespa by sight, thanks to an unauthorized newspaper article about unmarried royals—she would have been pleasantly low-key.

Climbing out of the pool, she toweled off, dropped onto a chaise, and applied tanning lotion. She could still smell the dye in her hair, a temporary stain that was not going to wash out of her natural strawberry-blond hair without a fight. New hair color, heavy makeup, and an Italian accent had changed her identity so successfully that when Cedric, who had known her a year now, stood next to her at the airport shop flipping through *Queen* magazine, he hadn't given her a second look.

When they landed at the Las Vegas airport, both she and Bibi had "become" American. They had traded their Italian accents for one straight out of Indiana and changed into outfits more suited to two entertainers. Bridget had swapped her Chanel suit for black capris, ballerina flats, and a peasant blouse, and Bibi, though reluctant to shed her sexy French maid's outfit, donned a similar outfit only after Bridget promised her she could wear the short black dress, frilly white apron, and cap in their hotel room.

After all, they were dancers now, making their Las Vegas debut in *Frost Side Story*, an original interpretation of the hit Broadway play and film *West Side Story*, written specifically for the Dorothy Duncan Defrost-Off competition, being held at the Las Vegas Convention Center, in the hall next to the gathering of spies. They had secured the job through a somewhat confusing connection between a series of hairdressers—beginning with Emerald St. Claire's beloved Mr. Francis, a big fan of Bridget's sudden "burning desire" to try her luck on the American stage, and ending with the man who designed the costumes and hairstyles for the show. Dancing in *Frost Side Story* was their way of being available should Jane need them, and much more fun, Bibi had argued, than entering a cooking competition. The words "dishpan hands" had ended the discussion over which cover would be more desirable before it even began.

After ordering another fruit juice, Bridget perused the thick color entertainment guide to Las Vegas that arrived with her drink. There seemed to be dozens of amusements to choose from on any given day on the Strip: magicians, animal acts, and girls, girls, girls. Since *Frost Side Story* was based on a dark study of racial tension in America (albeit with snappy musical numbers), Bridget hoped their roles would not require costumes as embarrassing as that of the poor showgirl wrapped up in the elephant's trunk at magic act at the Rancho Rivera. Bridget knew that even Bibi would rather be a dedicated defroster than a sequined peanut.

When a woman in a mink bikini walking a leopard on a silver chain strolled by, Bridget suppressed the urge to snap her picture with the miniature camera hidden in a paperback copy of Betty Friedan's groundbreaking book *The Feminine Mystique.* Bridget had traveled the world, as both a spy and a student, visiting every country that would grant her a visa, and even a few that wouldn't, but since the beginning this place had surprised her. From the sky the night desert looked like a flat black sea, but as they descended, she could see a pink haze seeping over the mountains, and suddenly Las Vegas burst into view, sparkling like a Windsor-cut diamond. She had edged closer to the window to get a better look, knowing that Jane, who had flown only once before, twenty-eight years ago in a wooden airplane at Brighton Beach, would have her eyes squeezed shut. "Darling, it's safer than my scooter," Bridget had assured her, succeeding only in giving Jane something more to worry about. In a city where the temperature was a hundred degrees and climbing, there was no better place to be than at the edge of a cool blue kidney-shaped pool, her delicate skin shaded by an umbrella. Bridget marveled at her partner's logic—Bibi had picked the Sands out of a guidebook simply because the name sounded so right for a desert town. Mimi had forged a coupon giving them three nights' stay for nineteen dollars plus tax—her last decent act before losing her mind.

"Paging Mamie Eisenhower. Mamie Eisenhower. Is there a Mamie Eisenhower in the pool area?"

For this mission Bridget and Bibi had needed two identities each, European and American. Generally, when constructing new identities, great pains were taken to match the name to the girl, something easy to remember but not too close to the original. Miss Tuppenny had originally handed the job to Bibi, who had passed it on to Mimi and then, without contemplating the consequences, broken up with her the following day. By the time they saw their passports, it was too late, and their American names made the ones on their European passports—

Contessa Fagiolo Ravioli and Mademoiselle Pierette le Pew—seem playful by comparison. The conspicuousness of the names negated the good that Mimi had done with the forged discount coupon. Reason enough for her transfer to Iceland, Bridget thought.

Cringing, Bridget raised her hand. Two women with creased, leathery skin, wearing deep-cleavage swimsuits and enough jewelry to sink a battleship, giggled at her behind thick fashion magazines. Bridget realized she had been wrong; this place *was* just like Monto Carlo. The bellhop rushed to her side, staring at the dark-haired woman in the short terry-cloth robe and large dark glasses, more Audrey Hepburn than first lady. He handed her the telephone, waving off her tip, and crept away. People stared, as they had in the airport when it was announced that Mamie Eisenhower had left her prescription depilatory cream at the luggage counter, another going-away gift from Mimi. Bridget grasped the phone eagerly. Although she and Bibi had been ordered to stay in the background, Bridget thought Jane could at least have rung her to let her know where she was staying.

"Darling, how good to hear from you!" A day apart and she felt the same kind of thrill she had when they first met.

"So you're not annoyed at me anymore for pinching the tablecloth at breakfast. Good, because tomorrow I'm getting the dishes that go on top of it."

"Oh, Eleanor, it's you."

"Of course it's me. I'd told you I'll ring when I was through gambling away our travel allowance. Where did you think I was?"

"In jail," Bridget said flatly. She wouldn't be at all surprised if a slot machine turned up in Bibi's luggage. The girl was that good.

"No, but I'll give it my full attention after we pinch the invention. You thought I was Jane, didn't you? I knew Tupps shouldn't have sent you two on a mission together; you just can't stay away from her."

"I know we've been forbidden to contact her, but I had hoped she'd at least check in." Bridget lowered her voice. "Bibi, I'm afraid she's been taken by the KGB," she whispered.

"You always think that. Remember what Tupps said—Jane will ring *if* she needs us."

Bridget knew she was being unreasonable, but she did worry about

Jane, and sometimes thought that one spy in the family was enough. "Still, I'd like to know where she is."

"At the convention, silly. And we will be, too, in a little while."

"Yes, but we can't go near her." What if Cedric recognized Bridget despite the disguise? Jane would have to admit that Bridget knew of the arrangement with the British Secret Service, and Cedric, who always played by the book, would launch an unwelcome investigation into the life of Lady St. Claire, learning several things she'd rather he didn't know, like the name of the girl she'd been with before Jane, or that the relationships had overlapped by a few weeks; that she had a beauty mark on her bum and could play the piccolo. And that she was a secret agent for a spy-girl organization headed by the venerated Miss Tuppenny. "What if something goes wrong when her convention is not in session and we have to get to *her?* I'm just trying to be sensible," she added, afraid that she sounded like a possessive girlfriend.

"I'm sure she wanted to ring you but misplaced her wallet. You know how absentminded she can be. Honestly, the next time I find her gun on top of the office candy machine, I'm keeping it."

"She could ring me on a landline."

"Don't hold your breath," said Bibi, knowing that there was no right answer. Loving someone seemed to involve an enormous amount of fussing and fretting, which is why she avoided it. Trying to keep up with fashion trends on a secret agent's salary was drama enough. "You know what it's like to be a new agent. Miss Tuppenny's word is God. And when would she get the chance to ring? You know that Cedric sticks to her like the queen to her pocketbook."

Bridget relaxed, aware that Bibi had a good instinct about things like this. "I'm just worried because it's her first time out."

"And Mother's not there to tie her shoes and load her gun?"

"Okay." Bridget shuddered, never, *ever* wanting Jane to see her as a mother figure. "I'm cured. And speaking of psychological problems, have you lost all our money yet, Mrs. Roosevelt?" Refusing to appear in public in a swim cap, Bibi had opted to stay indoors and try her luck at the slots. Bridget hoped Bibi hadn't added gambling to her long list of compulsive behaviors.

"I'm up twenty dollars."

"Splendid!"

"And down twenty-nine," she added ruefully. "But I am having fun."

"I've spent as much on fancy fruit drinks," Bridget admitted. "And I have my eye on a platinum bracelet in the gift shop."

"I'd love to hear more about your enormous wealth and expensive accessories," interrupted Bibi, "but I actually called for a reason. Have you forgotten? The shuttle bus will be here in a half hour to take us to the convention center for rehearsal. It's time for two former first ladies to put on their tap shoes."

"You're a funny girl," said Bridget, and put down the receiver. She swung her legs over the side of the longue, belted her robe, and put the entertainment book in her pocket. It contained a one-line description of their show, and she knew Bibi would want it for her scrapbook. The leopard and its mink-clad mistress took Bridget's place on the chaise, and Bridget made her escape as a nervous waitress bent to take their order.

• • • • • • • • • • • • • • • • • • • •

three

a battered blue country car, the Teepee Village Motor Court rental, was waiting for them in the parking lot—a "station wagon," Wanda called it—with the keys under the mat, a melting St. Christopher statuette on the dash, and a dog-eared copy of Arthur Hailey's *Hotel* in the glove box. "It's not the kind of thing my brother would drive," remarked Jane as Cedric piloted the long, clumsy car, its imitation-wood side panels flapping, onto U.S. State Road 1.

"We're undercover," he said, tossing her a pair of Ray-Bans, standard issue to all agents working in sunny climes. "Something along the lines of your brother's car would be too flashy for our mission." The limits of Cedric's driving ability were instantly apparent. He had been a city driver all his life, and an incompetent one at that. Uncomfortable driving on the right side of the road, he compromised by staying in the middle, straddling the yellow line, jerking to the right for the occasional oncoming car. "I can't imagine why N. lets your brother choose his own vehicles," he mused, ignoring the enormous aqua Cadillac riding their tail. "Anyone with half a mind could guess his occupation from what he drives."

"The rear-mounted machine guns and British Secret Service parking pass are a dead giveaway," Jane agreed, watching the Cadillac's progress in the side mirror. "Let that car pass, will you?" she begged as an entire lemon meringue pie hit the back window of the wagon.

Sighing, he pulled over. "Your brother drives like that," he said when the women behind the wheel gave them a one-finger salute and disappeared in a cloud of dust. "But when he guns his motor, a flame appears out of his tailpipe. And when he arrives at the office, he draws more even attention to himself by parking on the footpath and using the ejector seat. I imagine the secretaries find it amusing. A few years ago, he picked up the American custom of plastering pithy sayings on one's vehicle. 'God Save the Queen.' 'Spies Do It Undercover.' N. made him remove that one, on my recommendation." Cedric sucked air through his teeth, then jerked hard to the left to avoid a tumbleweed. "He doesn't like me, your brother. He thinks I'm a tattletale."

"My brother. What a clot. When I was getting fitted for my suit, I overheard the rumor that he had planted a bug in the ladies' lav, in the soap dispenser, so he and his mates could find out what the secretaries were saying about them. He was the same way as a boy. He'd listen to your problems like a regular agony aunt and then use the information to get what he wanted."

"A portrait of a secret agent as a lad. You must have hundreds of stories like that. It's a shame you can't write a book."

"It would be called *Why I Hate My Brother*," Jane said. "Forget everything you've heard about twins and their special bond. You don't think he invented the rubber-spider-in-the-drawer trick just for you, do you?"

"Do I detect a tinge of jealousy?"

"'Jane, you're just a girl. No need for you to go to university. You don't want to scare off the chaps, do you?' That, by the way, was an imitation of my father."

"And a good one," said Cedric. "You forget I knew him casually, when he worked as a courier for us during the war. A nice chap."

Jane stuck her head out the window, seeking relief from the stifling car interior and wanting to end the direction of this conversation. Cedric both feared and admired her brother; Jane loathed him and was, she admitted only to herself, a little jealous of the ease with which he moved through the world. "That waitress was right," she said, catching a glimpse of her short hair and dark suit in the side mirror, held on with gaffer's tape. "I look like a missionary hell-bent on chasing sin from Las Vegas."

"We're not authorized to do that," warned Cedric, fumbling with the airflow knob until hot air blew into the car. "Our directive is simple: find this remarkable new device and secure it for Her Majesty's Secret Service. I hear," he added confidentially, "that she has been informed of its existence and eagerly awaits news of our success."

Great, thought Jane. When she pinched the invention for G.E.O.R.G.I.E., she would be disappointing N., Cedric, *and* the queen. The new information made her double her desire to make the theft a clean one, without tarnishing Cedric's reputation. This mission weighed heavily on Jane's mind; since all her brother's assignments were solo jaunts, no one *really* knew how he behaved when left to his own devices. All she had to go by were his reports, misspelled tales of sexual conquests, bizarre bad guys, and multiple martinis. She prayed they were exaggerated accounts, for she was definitely *not* arriving at *this* spy convention in a one-man rocket accompanied by a busty blonde who would later flower sexually under her touch. There was no room in the Secret Service budget for a rocket to replace the one her brother had crashed into the side of Mount Kilimanjaro, and it was decided that a busty blonde would only get in her way. (Bridget had seconded this decision.)

"Did you hear me, Jane? Even the queen is crossing her fingers for our success." The image pleased Cedric, and he burbled happily for a few minutes about his conversation with the queen at a tea party at the palace, a pleasant chat that ended when she'd thanked him for saving the House of Windsor from collapse and he had bowed so low he threw out his back and had to be carried to his car by the Keeper of the Silver Stick. "Imagine the reception we'll receive when we walk into Buckingham Palace with it." This time he'd wear a back brace.

"Unless it's an invisible space rocket, in which case we'll fly in," she said dryly. When Cedric read the report of this new invention, he had latched onto the only description available; "better than invisible ink."

For this reason he had come to believe that this new gadget was invisible. Jane believed that they were looking for something typically American: big and shiny, expensive and flashy, perhaps involving espionage in outer space, given the American government's obsession with controlling the universe. Either that or it was strawberry-scented invisible ink, for today's swinging secret agent.

"Airspace over the palace is strictly regulated," Cedric warned. "We'd be tangling with the RAF."

"I said *invisible*."

"They have special equipment to detect the presence of such a craft. I read all about it in *Spy Digest*, in the April first edition."

"All right, what do *you* think it is?"

"So many fine things have been invented in the last decade—the waterproof carrier-pigeon anorak, the toupee life raft, the edible gun—I can't imagine what's left. I do hope it's not something along the lines of the Twister Gun," he said with distaste. That "remarkable invention" from 1964 had turned out to be no more than an expensive party gimmick. "Sure, for a few months it made people twist until they dropped, and then broke as soon as the warranty expired. We were left with twelve dozen of the faulty weapons, which ended up in *my* office, since the basement was filled with your brother's old furniture."

"My Great-Aunt Honoria's antiques," Jane corrected. "Left to me and hijacked by James for the sheer sport of it." Miss Tuppenny had arranged for its return to the rightful owner, and, piece by piece, Jane was walking four rooms of furniture out the back door of British Secret Service headquarters.

"I did happen upon an idea whilst being fitted for my new warm-weather clothes. I've been hearing about a new material called Teflon that can repel any substance known to man; imagine how something like that can be used in our line of work."

"Things just bounce off of it?" said Jane, thinking she had heard of it. "Like bullets off Superman?"

"According to what I've been reading, yes. They say, if used correctly, it has the power to transform life. I remember where I was when the idea first came to me. I was being fitted for shorts at Harrods, and when the tailor mentioned a new fabric spray that repelled dirt, the gears in my mind started to spin!" He stopped to swallow the lump in his throat. At the mention of his tailor, he automatically sucked in his stomach, wishing he hadn't finished all eight pancakes and glad he had gone for the shorts with the elastic waistband. Belly flab was a source of shame for a man who had tried to keep himself fit all these years, walking to the office instead of taking the Tube, the stairs in place of the lift, and sitting at the farthest table from the door in the secret-agent cafeteria. Feeling Jane's stare, he fiddled with the side mirror, noticing the beginning of a double chin.

"I imagine plaid isn't easy to work with," kidded Jane, seeing him tug on his shorts in an attempt to hide his chubby knees. "Burberry, are they?"

"They're from the Dorcas Collection, an American line of clothing carried at Harrods. I'm only sorry you couldn't use your share of the wardrobe allowance. Your arms and legs are too slender to pull off your brother in short sleeves and Bermuda shorts. The clerk said they were just the ticket for this desert weather."

"The medal goes nicely with your shirt," she said, being swept with a sudden desire to cheer him up; if this mission turned out to be a pleasant holiday as well, perhaps the happy memories would offset his feelings of personal failure when G.E.O.R.G.I.E. ended up with the invention.

"I noticed that, too." He smiled, visibly relaxing. "I don't know why I'm so nervous." He burped. The Pecos Pete Pancakes rested heavily in his stomach. Tomorrow it would be Marmite on melba toast in his teepee; he'd save thirty cents and avoid another bout of dyspepsia.

"It's because this mission is a tricky one," she pointed out. "We don't know what we're looking for. We're competing against the best spies of the Western world, and we have no real secret-agent skills." He looked terrified, and she felt like a bloody idiot. While she didn't want to wholly damage his fragile ego, she still needed to keep him off balance, insecure about his ability to perform at this level—her reasoning was that he would be only too glad to step back and let her take the starring role.

"'Tis as murky as the London fog," he agreed. "N. was no help. 'Don't muck this up' are hardly comforting words. And going up against the Americans is a heady proposition. With their enormous wealth, unlimited espionage budget, and history of underhanded behavior, we've got to be especially clever. I suspect their man has a much larger check pinned to his sock than do I." A check bearing N.'s signature—and nothing more—was fastened to his left sock, and, should he lose it, anyone could fill in his or her own name and the amount. N. had brushed away Jane's offer to carry the check next to her skin, under the tight bandage wrapped around her chest—"All women are alike; you and Agent Pumpernickel will quarrel, and you'll go off and spend the money on feminine fripperies"—leaving Jane to wonder if N. had ever actually *looked* at her.

"But we've got something they don't," Cedric assured her.

This was news to her. "Indigestion?"

"We've got Agent James Bond *and* Agent *Sir* Cedric Pumpernickel, the man who saved the monarchy from collapse last year when he uncovered a nefarious plot to kidnap Her Royal Majesty. Outside of Batman and Robin, I can't think of a more impressive duo." He gave her a sideways glance, checking her response to his deviation from the script. N. had made him 007's manservant for this trip, something that chafed more than sweaty thighs in starchy shorts.

"But who's going to hold my martini?" Jane said jokingly.

"Why would the queen knight a valet? It rings false. Only *one* agent needs to recognize me and our credibility will *collapse* like one of those stale Violet Crumbles you are constantly leaving in my Morris. Why would someone as famous as *I* pretend to be a valet, unless he was up to no good? I did *not* come all the way to America, to my first spy convention, simply to hold your coat." Punctuating his words with corresponding tugs on the wheel, he almost landed them in a drainage ditch.

"You can be queen for all I care!" Jane cried as she grabbed the wheel. "Just don't kill us before we get there!"

There were hitchhikers along the road, men, mostly, in dusty jeans and T-shirts, with cardboard signs announcing their destination held above their heads, tilted to provide shade. A woman sat on a suitcase with a child, about eight, on the ground next to her. SCOTTSDALE, AZ was scrawled on their sign, in shaky red lettering.

"We should at least take them to the Strip. Buy the kid a Coke," Jane said.

Cedric looked at her with his eyebrows raised, locked his door, then commanded her to lock her own

"Come on, they look like they're baking. Mind you, it's not much cooler in here, but at least we've got a roof." Earlier, after she'd pleaded her case, Cedric had finally allowed her to unbutton her shirt a modest three buttons, exposing the top of the tight bandage squashing her poor breasts. "I'll button my shirt."

"Danger can come in any form, Miss Bond. That suitcase could contain an explosive device. The child? A midget agent. Not that I'm immune to human suffering. I did, after all, work in a small, windowless office for twenty-five years," he said, hitting the gas. "But my first obligation is to the queen. Then N., then the memory of my mother, and then you. But you've got to do your part. It's not enough to look like 007. You've got to *think* like him. Danger lurks everywhere."

"Except down women's blouses. And on ski slopes. And in one-man submarines."

"Your brother is equipped to handle himself in all situations. He has the mind of a true agent."

She bristled at his implication. "And I don't?"

He chortled.

"Tell me—what was my brother thinking when he lit his hair on fire in Monte Carlo?"

"That a gallant gesture had turned to tragedy."

Jane laughed. The accident that had resulted in her being sent here was vintage James: While bending over to light a woman's cigarette—and, according to witnesses, get a good look down her dress—his Brylcreem went up in flames. A cocktail waitress had tried to extinguish his hair with a pitcher of martinis, which only made the fire worse. The famed James Bond ended up with his head in the loo.

"I'd like to have seen him being carried out of that casino with his head packed in a tub of used shrimp-cocktail ice."

"There is nothing amusing about a grease fire, Miss Bond, or losing your trademark mane of luxurious hair. N. is furious. He even had Miss Tuppenny type a memo adding Brylcreem to the list of don'ts. And how do you know the details of your brother's mishap anyway? Only three people know: myself, Miss Tuppenny, and N."

Being a double agent did have its drawbacks, Jane thought. "You told me over a pint after we picked up our flight tickets."

He sighed. "I drink too much when I'm around you. It's too easy to let details slip when you're relaxed. Alcohol can muddle the brain, and familiarity can lead to a false sense of security . . ." He cleared his throat and tapped nervously on the steering wheel. There was something he had been meaning to take up with Jane for some time, and he decided that now was as good a time as any. so he continued. ". . . Especially with loved ones. Does Bridget ever wonder about your work at Amalgamated Widget, Inc.? Does she want to see where you spend your days? Come down to the office for lunch?" Cedric couldn't understand how the brave little duchess's daughter never complained about Jane's "job." Then again, he reckoned, she did work as a cosmetics salesgirl, trudging around filthy London on a flimsy scooter, in a pink vinyl minidress much too revealing for a girl of her pedigree. He wished N. would give Jane a raise in pay, so she could get Bridget off the streets.

"I forgot to tell you—I told her I changed jobs. Now I sell knickers door-to-door."

Cedric was not happy to hear this. Jane was supposed to clear all official lies with him, but it was too late to do anything about it. "When you're together and feeling close, you've never been tempted to tell her the truth? Pillow talk, I believe they call it."

Jane smirked. "Bridget and I don't chat about work in bed. We hardly talk at all, in fact. The walls in our flat are so thin we're forced to use hand gestures to communicate. Sometimes we use puppets. Bridget's gran gave her a set of the queen's coronation figures; we take turns playing Prince Philip."

"Miss Bond, that will be enough!" He slapped the dashboard to communicate his outrage and cried out when his hand hit the blistering plastic of the St. Christopher statue.

"Be careful," said Jane, laughing. In the last year, he had managed to fall into a punch bowl at a farewell luncheon for a retiring agent, impale himself on a pencil at the celebration of a secretary's promotion to principal secretary, and almost choke to death on a piece of watercress at one of the queen's teas. The incidents left him wondering how Jane, like her brother, managed to complete every mission without a scratch, as if

they had been born under a lucky secret-agent star. "Little wonder your
mother didn't let you cross the street by yourself until you were thirty,"
Jane scolded.

"Bugger," said Cedric, holding his wounded paw to his mouth.

· ·

four

ℐn order to make himself feel better, Cedric switched on the radio
and quickly found a twenty-four-hour Liberace station. Jane winced.
Within five minutes she couldn't remember the International Association of Accident-Prone People's secret handshake or the words to the official jingle, since this information, and most of her childhood memories,
had been expunged from her brain by the "all Liberace, all the time"
station.

She had fallen asleep twice, the slow drive through the hot desert
and Liberace's life story combining to make a potent sleeping potion. It
was a better sleeping aid than the tablet hidden in her signet pinkie
ring.

The plain, balding man at the wheel, whose conversation typically
centered on subjects like the queen mum's hat collection, remembrances
of his mother, and the aphids on his rosebushes, was positively smitten
with the popular pianist, and now he went into his familiar speech about
how he had been reared on the music of this piano-playing wonder. (To
be fair, Jane *had* queued for over an hour once to get Diana Rigg's autograph.) His mother had owned all of Liberace's early recordings, which
were now his own, and together they had once sat through three consec-
utive showings of Liberace's 1950 cinematic masterpiece *South Sea Sinner*, also starring Shelley Winters. Jane could picture Cedric and his
mother sitting side by side in the cinema sharing a bag of popcorn,
Mother Pumpernickel eating the kernels one at a time, ladylike, the way
she had done everything, as her son, unable to take his eyes off the
screen, told himself that he was sharing his mother's adulation for the
handsome piano man as a tribute to her good taste.

Cedric refused to let up until Jane agreed to go see Liberace. There were only two entertainments he was interested in: a Liberace concert and a tour of J. Edgar Hoover Dam. "Even *spies* are given the evening off now and then," he pointed out. "And we don't want to spend every night in our teepees washing out our socks. What luck that we're in town at the same time!"

"It's not luck, it's providence." Sending Cedric wandering down the Liberace path might distract him from their mission. "What are the chances that Liberace and one of his biggest fans would be in Las Vegas at the same time?"

"*Biggest* fan?" He tightened the muscles in his legs so his thighs would look slimmer.

"Most *passionate* fan. I propose we find out where Liberace is staying and get a room in the same hotel," she said, dreaming of a swimming pool—even if she couldn't go in, she could at least lounge around it—room service, and fluffy towels. "You can accidentally-on-purpose run into him. He pals around with the queen; you told me yourself they have the same dish pattern. Once he finds out you're *that* Sir Cedric Pumpernickel, you'll be in like Flynn. You'll be so busy meeting celebrities that you'll have to *send* out your socks to be cleaned."

He imagined going to parties where the elite of Las Vegas met to sing show tunes and sip champagne. "The idea is intriguing," he reluctantly admitted, not wanting to let fantasy overcome good sense. "But I'd settle for a balcony seat at one of his concerts. I'd be too nervous to actually meet him." He recalled his first meeting with the queen. At the precisely wrong moment, just as she leaned in to shake his hand, he had dropped a butterscotch Life Saver down the front of her dress.

"We have a shocking number of things in common, even though he was born in a place called Wisconsin, where they make cheese, and I was born in London, the cradle of civilization."

"Like what?" she asked, wondering how Cedric could explain this. She used this opportunity to turn down the radio. How many versions of "Chopsticks" *were* there? Dart watches are not to be used lightly, she thought, recalling Miss Tuppenny's words.

"We both had strict fathers who disapproved of our chosen professions," he continued. "And while Liberace was able to overcome this stern opposition, I, sadly, never made it to the stage as an adult."

Jane stared at him, unable to imagine her fellow agent in a theater as anything but an adoring fan. Money from a publisher—for he had been contracted to pen his memoirs—had certainly helped his appearance; he no longer cut his own hair or made his own shampoo, and the scar on his cheek, a crude S he had picked up during his one mission as a double-0 man, had all but disappeared under the surgeon's knife.

Jane checked her new watch, a gift from Miss Tuppenny. With it, she could climb tall buildings, cut through steel, and use the luminous face to read in the dark. And the strap was made of a vitamin-rich edible vegetable frond, should she need emergency rations. But it couldn't keep proper time. "Are we there yet?"

"There's no need to rush. I imagine today will be spent catching up with one another, with the lectures, demonstrations, and panel discussions beginning tomorrow. Tonight might be ours to do as we please. It would be pleasant to sample American culture, don't you think? Perhaps a Liberace concert?"

"It would be more pleasant to check into a hotel on the Strip," she replied. Jane would dearly love to be staying in an air-conditioned room with a toilet that didn't run all night, in a room where things didn't skitter away when she swung her legs out of bed. And then there was Bridget. They were accustomed to sleeping apart when one of them was on a mission, but this business of being in the same city yet forbidden to communicate until an emergency arose tugged at her. If they bumped into each other at the convention center, Bridget in her slinky showgirl costume and Jane surrounded by her secret-agent friends, they would meet like strangers. The secret agents would whistle at Bridget, and maybe worse, and, protecting her brother's reputation as a piece of slime, Jane would have to lead the pack. N. *had* tossed around the idea of assigning Jane a Las Vegas lover to complete the charade, and Miss Tuppenny, hearing of this, considered introducing Bridget to N. as their new temporary office worker, knowing he would find the pretty girl perfect for the role. N. changed his mind after calculating the cost of three airline tickets, twenty-seven meals, and the eight-hundred-pound fee he paid women to find 007 absolutely irresistible.

"Certainly not. I gave the woman two nights' lodging in advance; that would be sixteen dollars down the drain. When she gave me the keys and the can of Bug-Off, she told me there were no refunds. Yes, Jane, the Teepee Village Motor Court is perfectly fine for our needs. Entire Indian families lived in them long ago. Mind you, I'm not speaking of *our* particular teepees."

"Are we still in Nevada?" She yawned and stretched her legs, feeling as if she had spent more time in this station wagon than she had on the plane. He spread the map over the dash and tried to wipe away the blob of grape jelly where the convention center was supposed to be.

"You're suffering from jet lag," he informed her. "I tried to convince you to join me in my morning RAF calisthenics, but you insisted on sleeping in; it was the worst thing you could have done. And you can't sleep now. Besides, we're almost there. Look at that sign: 'Las Vegas five miles.'"

They had gone only seven miles in twenty minutes. Jane figured she had plenty of time for a nap, but she needed to keep her eyes open and keep him off the wrong side of the road.

"First of all, how could I—or anyone for that matter—sleep with the racket you made, jumping around in your teepee? And your exercise routine doesn't seem to have improved your driving skills; perhaps tomorrow you should try eye exercises. Honestly, if we ever decide to become bank robbers, you are *not* driving the getaway car. I refuse to wake at the break of dawn to move my arse and then stuff it into James's starched suit."

"Sunrise is a *perfectly* reasonable time to begin one's day."

"Not if our convention doesn't start until noon," she pointed out. "I don't want you to even *knock* on my door until ten A.M.—understood?" If she arose in the middle of the night, she'd have time to drive to town and snoop on her own. How hard could it be to break into an empty convention center? And if he kept with his habit of turning in after dinner, to relax into a detective novel over a glass of warm milk (spiked with G.E.O.R.G.I.E.-brand sleeping powder), she'd have the whole night to herself, assuming she could get away from her brother's colleagues, who, according all accounts, shadowed her brother like schoolgirls in love.

"Cedric? Are we in agreement?"

He shook his head out of frustration. "Your brother can go without sleep for a week."

"Yes, but he does manage to find his way to bed several times a day." She had read the same reports, arriving at a different interprotation.

"You do have a point." When Cedric had gotten to the more lascivious portion of the reports, he had shielded his eyes. "The next time we fly this far, just promise to get plenty of rest the night before we leave. When I saw you in the airport lounge, I thought you'd be checking those bags under your eyes."

"That's what every girl wants to hear," said Jane, taking off her glasses and glancing at her face in the side mirror. She was tired and looked it. "In fact, I did go to bed early. I went to bed before supper, in fact. Just ask Bridget when we get back to London. She was there." With that she played with the radio tuner knob until she found a pop station, sure the Liberace torture was past her. That put a cork in him, one that popped when a gold Cadillac convertible stuffed with women clad in skimpy bikinis and sipping champagne zoomed past.

"I wonder if the accommodation committee realized the bacchantic nature of Las Vegas when they made their decision," he said in disgust, rolling up his window as if he could shield himself from the debauchery. Their midnight taxi ride along the Las Vegas Strip, on their way to the Teepee Village Motor Court, had been a real shocker for them both. Never before had Jane witnessed such brilliant excess—a cluster of casinos, hotels, marriage chapels, and pawnshops—and she laughed thinking of how she would describe this place to her friend Edith, who had one lamp in her bed-sit, on a long cord so she could carry it around with her. Cedric had mentioned that the city had a "gay nightlife," but it hadn't prepared her for the giant neon cowboys, martini glasses, and pink flamingos rising out of the Mojave, outshining the stars, washing the dark desert in fluorescent colors. Afraid the bright lights would damage his retinas, Cedric had placed a handkerchief over his eyes. He always used the lowest-wattage bulb available in his lamps, he informed

Jane, and turned them off whenever he left a room. Jane, whose financial circumstance forced a similar economy, was enthralled by the dazzling electric landscape. The Supersonic Carwash, the Pair-a-Dice Motel, the Orbit Inn, the Desert Moon—every building they passed was lit up like a drunken Christmas tree. Even the crematorium sign on the Palm Mortuary glowed tangerine and magenta. "All night long these things are turned on," said their cabdriver. "A fellow can't get a wink of sleep." Cedric had sighed in sympathy for himself.

He was sighing again now, still troubled by Jane's lack of enthusiasm toward Liberace. His only chance to see his idol, and she was being characteristically stubborn. It had been like this from the beginning of their partnership, when N. had asked him to come out of retirement for "one special assignment." A year later, with almost a dozen "special assignments" under his belt, they were friends, but the type that bickered about the same trivial things over and over. Jane had many fine qualities: She went out of her way to fix him up with nice gents, was never mingy when the bar bill came due, and once she'd even taken him to the dentist, on the back of Bridget's scooter, for a frightfully painful procedure, then made him mushy peas afterward. But she could be willfully disobedient, being of the generation who thought they knew it all. And now he was forced to endure the sounds of the Beatles on the radio. As they hit the Strip and passed bright-colored hotels and shimmery signs, he tried to broach the topic of the piano man once again, hoping the festive atmosphere would sway her.

"They say you'll never see a show like his. He drives onstage in a mirrored Rolls-Royce, wearing ermine suits and mink capes and dozens of rings, and even a hi-fi diamond watch that plays tiny records. His, of course." Jane though it ironic that all this was coming from a man who was scandalized to learn that Princess Margaret used lavender ink to pen her personal correspondence. She was also a little jealous, wishing her watch played records.

"A bit of a Flash Harry, wouldn't you say?" she remarked.

"How else can a mature chap compete with those mopheads? Half the time you can't make out what they're saying."

"*'She loves you, yah, yah, yah.'* How hard is that?"

"It's not Shakespeare, is it?" According to people whose job it was to know these things, mass burnings of various items of Beatles memorabilia were taking place in a part of America called the Bible Belt, by people who blamed the British pop group for ruining family life by encouraging boys to wear bangs and girls to scream at deafening decibels. As a result of the success of the Beatles and other such bands—so many that it seemed to Cedric there must be a factory in Liverpool churning them out—sales of recordings by classy American singers like Pat Boone and Doris Day were down. Every penny he and Jane spent in Las Vegas would help heal the rift between the empire and her stubbornly independent offspring. Going to see Liberace would be a goodwill gesture. To avoid what would surely be a painful attempt by Jane to compare the popular singing group to the great Bard himself, Cedric turned the dial on the radio. "Let's get to know Las Vegas and its culture." Jane rolled her eyes yet again.

"KMOB time, eleven forty-one in the A.M. In the news today: Actress Vivian Vance appeared in court in Hollywood, California, to give testimony in her divorce action against her bullfighter husband. The opening day of the annual Dorothy Duncan Defrost-Off got off to a chilly start when contestants arrived to find that the air-conditioning units had been set to frosty. The Red Cross rushed in with grilled cheese sandwiches, coffee, and emergency cardigans until technicians were able to correct the problem. And now for the weather. It's hot-hot-hot today, and it's gonna get hotter! Expect temperatures to reach a hundred and seven by noon and stay there until sundown, when it's gonna be a cool ninety-one. Tomorrow's forecast: hot as hell. And for everyone who called in about the black plume to the west, that's not a nuclear bomb, folks, that's Vivian Vance, throwing off a little steam there in Hollywood, California! And don't forget—Wayne Newton begins a sixteen-year run at the Riviera tonight; tickets are half price if you mention KMOB radio."

"Half price! Now, that's a—"

"*'I want to hold your hand, hand, hand,'*" Jane cut him off.

"You wouldn't see Larry reciting those lines," sniffed Cedric, snapping off the radio, peered at her refusal to drop the subject. "And by Larry I mean Sir Laurence, of course. My mother shared the stage with

him in '27. She played a serving wench to his Hamlet. You must know—
it's in my manuscript. Page eight hundred fifty-seven, line thirty-nine."
To date, he had churned out over a thousand pages of his autobiography,
which he had carried to America in a briefcase tied to his wrist with a
clothesline. A carbon copy was hidden in his neighbor, Mrs. Figgis's,
sewing basket, and Jane was in possession of the other.

"Doesn't ring a bell," said Jane. "But then I've only read up to the
scene where your father teaches Lawrence of Arabia to ride a camel."
She didn't reveal that a majority of it was holding up a three-legged chair.

"If you can imagine, it gets better. The India years are full of strife
and struggle. Wait until you get to the part where my father must face
down a Bengal tiger whilst mother attempts to marry kidney pudding
and curry. Happy days, those. The happiest ever for my little family."
But Jane wasn't really paying attention. She had begun to blow down the
front of her shirt, which was getting wetter with every slow-passing mile.
She wished Cedric trusted her—or women in general—enough to drive.

"What are you doing, Jane?"

"Air," she said. "I'm dying in this. How on earth do women endure girdles?" Although she liked stepping into her brother's shoes for the free-
doms it afforded her, she would never get used to the bandage she had to
wear to bind her breasts, which was now fused to her skin. And the other
necessities that tormented her in the desert heat: the cheek inserts
clamped to her back teeth, the forehead and jaw prosthetics, all of which
made her face broader and more masculine; the facial scars that had
itched since New York; the heavy application of Brylcreem that made
her head slide off the back of the seat. But the worst of it was the patch
of hair glued to the space between her eyes, wedding her natural
shapely black brows into a hideous, hairy unibrow. Bridget had glued it
on for her, and been kind enough not to laugh. She had also closed her
eyes tight when she kissed Jane good-bye. Drops of sweat were gathering on top of the synthetic brow, like rain in a gutter, and she shook her
head, spraying the dash with her sweat. There were many things about
being her brother that appealed to Jane, who lived in a world that liked
short hair on a girl *only* if she was *also* wearing an even shorter skirt.
Forbidden to wear her disguise off-duty, she had begun to look forward
to her missions, to the walk through London unmolested, to the pretty

girls who slowed when she approached and tried to catch her eye, and, most important, to the pants with deep pockets. "Oh, get a purse, Jane," her father used to say when, as an adolescent, she lost another Tube token or her flat key. No one would ever tell James Bond to get a purse.

"It's so bloody hot here," she complained again.

"You can remove your jacket and roll up your sleeves for now," he said like a benevolent parent. He seemed afraid to let her remove even one piece of her Bond suit, as if it were imbued with magical powers. He tugged at his waistband, which was cutting off his circulation. He was hot, too, and the salesclerk had been less than truthful when explaining that wearing synthetic fabrics was like wearing nothing at all. In solidarity with Jane's long trousers and warm plastic facial patches, he had left his socks on. This sacrifice seemed lost on her.

Jane tore off her jacket and opened her shirt, using it to flap air up to her face.

"I can see the shape of your bosoms!" Cedric cried, putting up a hand to shield him from the shocking sight of James Bond with breasts.

"My *bosoms* are no bigger than yours," sniffed Jane, looking down at her breasts, wrapped so tight for these missions that she was sometimes afraid they wouldn't spring back. "In fact," she said, glancing at Cedric and his clingy shirt, "I think your bosoms are bigger than mine, with or without this straitjacket."

"Never mind that," he snapped, trying to suck in both his stomach and his chest. "What if someone sees the binding and tells the others that 007 has a chest injury? We'd be better off telling the truth: that he's under sedation at a secret plastic-surgery clinic, awaiting his donor eyebrows."

Jane buttoned her shirt, coming back to reality, and Cedric once more relaxed behind the wheel, a Sunday driver in a sea of race cars. "Have you noticed we're the only station wagon in sight?" she said. The road was thick with shiny, candy-colored cars, big as boats. "It hasn't turned out to be a very inconspicuous vehicle, has it?"

"Please, Jane, I'm trying to concentrate. We're supposed to turn left somewhere around here, I think." He slowed at the sight of a giant sultan standing atop the entrance to the Dunes hotel, the bright sun glinting off his enormous gold sword. The driver of a white Lincoln coupe, a brunette with a heavy foot who had been riding them since they hit the

Strip, laid on the horn and shot past them, gunning like a race-car driver trying to pull ahead of the pack. I SAW XAVIER CUGAT AT THE STARDUST! said the sticker on her bumper.

"Pull over and I'll get directions," said Jane, spotting the Sands, Bridget's hotel. Accidentally running into her in an *air-conditioned* lobby wasn't the same as ringing for help. But Cedric was too busy staring at a man in a hamburger suit standing at the entrance to a drive-in restaurant, waving at cars with his pickle, to pay attention to Jane.

Jane bounced on her seat and pointed. "There! Pull in!" He ignored her, and checked the map again, pushing aside the jelly blob to read a street name. She began to wish she had sprinkled sleeping powder on his pancakes and left him locked in his teepee to sleep it off, and slumped back in her seat as they rolled past the hotel.

"I promised Bridget I'd call her when I arrived," Jane said. "And I think my forehead is melting. We'd better go indoors."

"Nonsense—your face is made of the highest-quality rubber. And have you considered the cost of a transatlantic call? A postcard would be more economical and something she could keep forever. I've several from the motor-court gift shop; you may take your pick." He checked his watch. "It's five P.M. in London. She won't be home from work. You did remember to reset your watch?"

"Of course," she said, pulling her right sleeve over her wrist. She was afraid to fiddle with the stem, for fear of setting off a dart. "But I think Bridget deserves something a little nicer than a postcard of Wanda holding a stuffed rattlesnake. And I *promised* I'd call. She'll be worried about me."

"But what if the operator breaks in and Bridget realizes you're calling from America? She thinks you're in France, selling ladies' unmentionables. Poor Lady Bridget. I only hope your behavior on the plane isn't an indication of how you conduct yourself at home. Allowing an air hostess to sit in your lap while she's on duty! You put us all at risk." He was a funny one to talk, Jane thought, gripping the door handle as he played dodge-'em with bigger cars. "Right lane! Right lane!" she yelled, and when it became apparent they were not going to die at that very moment, she defended herself. "It wasn't *my* idea to masquerade as my depraved brother. And I didn't start it. I merely asked her to show me how the seat cushion turned into a flotation device."

"How many passengers get private seat-belt-buckling lessons? Making that poor nun wait for a second packet of peanuts because the air hostess was otherwise engaged—with you!"

"I held my tongue as long as I could. There is nothing in your directive about collecting phone numbers from strange women." Over Kansas a paper ball had landed in Jane's lap, a message from Bridget. Before she could read it, Cedric snatched it from her hand and ate it. "This is going too far," he said, bits of glossy paper sticking to his front tooth. Jane scribbled "Message intercepted" on the inside of a British Airways matchbook cover, but before she could deliver it, he ate that, too. "Cigarettes must be extinguished in preparation for landing," he huffed.

"How do you know it was a number?"

"Experience, Jane, there's no replacing it. I was able to distinguish the ink pattern with my tongue. It's the kind of thing you pick up after twenty-five years in office supply." Jane was not surprised by this remark; she could see him sitting at his desk eating paper scraps, tasting ink right from the pot, nibbling on nibs, and tinkering with the formula for envelope-flap glue.

"I assure you I have no intention of behaving in a manner that would harm my relationship with Bridget."

"That's good to hear. When you don that suit, your personality changes in subtle ways. Something comes over you—the ghost of your brother, perhaps? I worry about how far you're willing to take this masquerade."

"You mean the woman you caught me talking to the other day at the Indian take-away."

"I haven't wanted to bring that up."

"My brother loved her and left her. I wanted to make her feel better, so when she suggested we get together, I mentioned my recent medical problem."

"A cold?"

"The clap."

Afraid there would be no place to park at the convention center, Cedric had refused to stop for directions until he spotted the Riviera marquee that read, ONE WEEK ONLY! LIBERACE! WITH THE GEORGE LIBERACE OR-

CHESTRA! SEPTEMBER 10–16. SHECKY GREENE AND THE DOROTHY DURBEN DANCERS IN THE LIDO LOUNGE.

"Americans have the strangest names," Jane pointed out.

Cedric ignored her, screaming "It's the last day to see Liberace!" He cut off an armored car and hurled across the lot, almost running over a movie star, better known for his infidelities than his acting ability, who was wobbling through the parking lot held up by two young women.

Jane braced herself as Cedric hit the brakes, his targets too intoxicated to move out of his path. The girls, though barely of legal age, already had a deflated quality, their cheeks hollow and shoulders sagging. Their brilliant yellow bouffants, fluorescent in the sunlight, were beginning to cave in back, their skintight orange capris sagged at the knees, and their sleeveless muslin blouses, wet under the arms, were so sheer Jane could see their nipples, pointed skyward like missiles. Marvels of the modern age, their unnaturally large breasts were so firm that when one of the girls tripped and fell forward, she almost knocked an eye out. The dark circles under their eyes looked like a mix of exhaustion and old mascara; they were probably, finally, going home to bed.

"You act as if you've never seen a woman before," said Cedric, weaving around them and squeezing into a spot between two armored cars as they were pulling out. Leave it to him to scold her as *he* performed a death-defying stunt.

"Not one made of plastic," Jane said, clutching her stomach, dizzy from that last move.

"Let's go, then," he said, suddenly the perky scoutmaster. "We've seven minutes until the convention begins, plenty of time to run in for tickets." He pulled Jane up the steps to the entrance, gave her a nickel for the slots, and beetled off to find the ticket office. Jane stood by the door enjoying the cool air, until she was jostled inside by a group of women in tidy housedresses and starched aprons with DEFROST-OFF name tags on their chests, looking for the lav. The noise inside the casino rolled over Jane in waves, falsetto voices piped in over loudspeakers set into the ceiling sang about California girls, and slot machines—dozens of them—rang and chirped and spit coins. The wheel of fortune never stopped, the little ball clattering as players babbled excitedly about what they would buy with their jackpot. A new car, a color television, a boat. A fiftyish woman standing at the craps table in her Sunday best, holding a Bible and rosary beads, screamed *"Win! Win! Win!"* each time she threw the dice, less a prayer than a direct order.

At the bank of telephones near the front of the casino, the man standing next to Jane was trying to talk his wife into signing over the deed to their house. "Oh, come on, sweetums," His words were slurred, and by the looks of it, he hadn't been to bed for a few days. "I'm just about to hit the jackpot. I know it! Fella next to me won twenty-five thousand last night. Twenty-five grand! Think of all that money. Think of the kind of house we'd be able to buy! A fucking mansion!" He began sobbing into the telephone.

Jane dropped a nickel in the pay phone's slot. There was no harm in leaving Bridget a message, just to say hello. "The Sands, please," she said. When an operator came on line, she put a hand over her ear and spoke into the receiver. "I'd like to leave a message for Mamie Eisenhower, please. Room five sixty-four."

"Hardy-har-har," said the operator, who was accustomed to dealing with drunks. "I suppose next you want Mrs. Kennedy?"

No, Jane thought, Eleanor Roosevelt. "I swear I'm not having you on," she said.

There was a pause, then, "There's no one here by that name." Jane could hear the scratch of an emery board on nails. "Are you sure you have the right hotel? Not the Dunes or the Sahara?"

"I'm certain. She checked in around midnight, with Eleanor Roose— with a friend. May I leave a message in case she checks at the front desk?"

This complication smacked of Mimi's hand, another attempt to keep Jane and Bridget apart. Her previous attempts—planting fake love letters in Jane's desk, hiring a girl to break into their flat and slip into bed—had been the laughable exercises of a bratty schoolgirl. This time she was interfering with a mission.

"Go ahead," the operator said. The nail file never stopped. "Your name?"

"Bond. B-o-n-d. James Bond."

There was silence, then an angry, "Where the hell have you been for the past year?" A blast of foul language followed.

"You've confused me with someone else."

"I know it's you, James. Don't bother disguising your voice."

"Really, Bond is a common name in England. Like your Smith or Jones."

"Are you saying I'm common? I know it's you. 'Baby, there's only one James Bond.' God, I got tired of hearing that." Jane nodded when a waitress in a genie costume offered her a free cocktail. At a loss for words, she downed the drink, a sweet mix of gin and fruit juice that made her gag.

"Sure—now the cat's got your tongue," the operator raged on. "Too bad it didn't happen a year ago. For months I've searched for you, and now you blow into town without calling, then pretend you don't know me. And after what you gave me—"

"Did it require large quantities of penicillin?" Jane asked with a sigh.

"I can't talk now. My shift ends at three. Don't meet me here; I don't want the girls to know I'm seeing you. Meet me at the cocktail lounge. And bring your checkbook."

"What cocktail lounge? Where?"

"The place where you proposed, you cretin," the operator snapped.

· ·

five

a full inch shorter than the average British woman, Bridget had never been made to feel self-conscious about her size before. It had never interfered with her job as a secret agent. No lover had ever complained. Jane, who had a good five inches on her, with a rangy, slim build, was always telling her how sexy she was, small and curvy, with breasts, waist, and hips as nature had intended. "Jesus," Jane said the first time she saw Twiggy in an advert. "Forget about Oxfam—let's send *this* girl some food." Only once had Bridget tried dieting down to Twiggy size, under Bibi's influence, naturally. For a week the two secret agents lived on a strawberry-flavored drink, losing a dress size and becoming exceedingly bad-tempered. Diet-Eze turned out to contain a large amount of caffeine, a string of unpronounceable chemicals, not one strawberry, and something called Red Dye #27. Days after quitting, their symptoms—jumpiness, sleeplessness, leg cramps—persisted. Despite testimonials in the press about its damaging side effects—"*I lost four stone and a kidney!*"—the diet remained so popular that when it was banned, women smuggled it in from France in their underpants.

"This is a bloody disaster," said Bridget, fumbling with her tights, which were snug in the hips and long in the leg. Only by rolling the waistband several times, leaving a thick tire around her middle, was she able to make them fit. "What if we run into Jane between performances? She's never seen me dressed like a giant vegetable before."

"It is a bit embarrassing," admitted Bibi, "and frankly, you've looked better." But in these getups, no one will recognize us." She pulled up her stockings, identical to Bridget's. The dirt brown color made her arms look sickly pale by contrast, but the glittery gold high heels were divine, even if they were a size nine and she had to stuff the toes with the ladies pages of the *Las Vegas Sun*. "These girls have big feet," she whispered.

"These girls have big everything," Bibi said. A few feet away, the lead vegetables were practicing their steps, their almost comical conical breasts sitting stiffly on their chests while they bobbled about on six-inch heels. There was not a bounce in the group.

"I guess it's the miracle of plastic."

"What?" Bibi twirled in front of the mirror, admiring the way her legs looked in the heels. "I think I'll keep these."

"All the costumes have to be returned to the wardrobe mistress after each performance," said Candy Apple, a giantess in a green leotard and matching tights. She had been kind to them earlier, helping them rat their hair so they'd appear taller. "They get cleaned and resequined between performances. We don't get paid until the final show. No costume, no paycheck."

Their trip to Las Vegas had taken a decided downturn the moment the *Frost Side Story* shuttle dropped them at the rear of the convention center, an ugly concrete building, and the door to the entertainer's entrance had flown open and a slim balding man with a sinister mustache pulled them inside and ordered them into a lineup of gorgeous gals. Despite the stale, chilly air, there were sweat stains under the arms of his loose, bell-sleeved shirt, and his black-spangled pants—another unfortunate use of the polyester that was proliferating the world—were droopy in the drawers. A hair shorter than Bibi, Bridget was dead last in line. An airplane could have flown in the space over their heads, but Bibi, busy snapping her gum and admiring the scantily clad girls, didn't seem to notice how they stuck out. Or, Bridget thought, throwing back her shoulders, how they didn't.

The choreographer perused the lineup, nodding at the six bosomy Amazons, then made an ugly face when he reached the end of the line. "Let's see how you move." Feeling like cows at market, they performed the simple dance steps they had seen the other girls execute. A deep sigh was the man's only response. Whispered conversation with the piano player followed, and when he raised his hand to his chest, palm down, and shook his head, looking doubtful, a shiver ran down the line. "Fuck," said an Amazon near the front, kicking off her shoes. "I really need this job."

When it was decided that "the short, flat girls" *could* be worked into the show as potatoes, the starchiest of vegetables, trimming the number of leading roles from eight to six, a slim hour of rehearsal followed. As the man pointed out, his shoulders sagging, this wasn't Broadway, and most of the audience, every one a Dorothy Duncan contestant, would be too strung out on sugar and baking powder to understand his clever lyrics. *Frost Side Story* told the tale of fresh vegetables and frozen vegetables living side-by-side in an uneasy peace, until the day a pea rolls out of the freezer and into a salad. The fresh vegetables, thinking themselves nutritionally superior, defend their territory through song and dance. The drama would climax in a shocking scene in which the celery stalk, slipping on condensation, impales a tender eggplant, and before the roughage can come to their senses, a carrot is brutally julienned in revenge.

After the last girl demonstrated that she could tap her toe while thrusting her chest skyward, costumes were assigned—flesh-colored body stockings with hundreds of colorful sequins strategically placed to cover what the choreographer kept calling "the naughty bits." Bridget and Bibi were to be covered head to thigh, with just their arms and legs showing, by sequined, potato-colored cardboard shells. "At least he didn't call you," Candy said. Her stature and flaming red hair had landed her a plum role as lead carrot. "If you're going to work in this town, you've got to have height or tits. I can give you the name of a good breast man."

"No thanks," said Bridget. "We're just in town for this show." What had seemed so perfect on paper, jobs as dancers in a musical revue for a cooking contest, now seemed like a raw deal.

"No kidding, kiddo, you can have these"—Candy grabbed a breast in each hand—"by this time tomorrow. A few injections and *pow!* Feel 'em—they're almost lifelike."

"You've convinced me," Bibi said, reaching out to sample the merchandise.

"Help me get dressed," snapped Bridget. They had already drawn enough attention to themselves. If Bibi wanted to feel up showgirls, she was going to have to do it on her own time. With Bibi's help, Bridget stepped gingerly into the cardboard shell, thrown together by the wardrobe mistress from discarded fruit boxes and covered in brown sequins. The more glamorous getups—the pea pod and zucchini, the ear of yellow corn and long stalk of celery, the cucumber and the carrot—had required days of painstaking handiwork. The two top-notch secret agents had been reduced to props. As Bridget stood at the floor-to-ceiling mirror, which ran the length of the room, she heard the other girls giggle. When Bibi stepped into her spud costume and took her place by Bridget's side, the giggles exploded into laughter.

"Hey, Bridget, what has many eyes but cannot see?" Bibi, clearly amused by the horrifying sight before them, picked up the giant vegetable peeler and poked her friend in the posterior.

"What?" Bridget hiccupped softly, imagining Jane's expression should she ring them for help and two girls in dumpy potato costumes appeared.

"Us!"

*   *   *

From the outside, the Las Vegas Convention Center and Visitors Bureau had none of the flash of the nearby hotels and casinos. The front façade was tinted glass, gray as an overcast day, the building a low concrete bunker with a bank of porthole-size windows set under a flat roof, which shielded the building from the broiling sun. It was the size of a football field, and it typically housed a dozen gatherings at a time. High-ranking staff members were transported through the building and around the eighteen-hundred-car parking lot in golf carts manned by midgets abandoned by a magician sentenced to life in prison for making his wife disappear for good. Enormous air-conditioning units set into the walls blew frigid air on conventioneers all day long, creating the largest controlled-temperature system in the United States.

After ten minutes of circling the almost empty lot for "the best spot," and although he had secured tickets to the last night of Liberace's Vegas tour, Cedric finally admitted to a bad case of nerves. "Once we go through that door, there's no turning back," he said as he eased his body out of the car, the thin fabric of his Bermuda shorts sticking to the hot vinyl seat. "When you're in there, it's James Bond all the way. No more using the ladies' lav—I thought the security guard at the Riviera was going to have you arrested."

"The men's was disgusting. The worst part about this job is surely the urinal cakes," she snapped.

She was pissed that she hadn't gotten through to Bridget. Either the operator was lying—not about her brother, but about whether they had checked in—or Jane had indeed memorized the wrong hotel name. The Sands, the Sahara, the Dunes; all were variations on the same theme. Had Cedric not grabbed the phone from her hand and hurried her out of the casino, she would have called those places, and every other hotel on the Strip, until she found her girlfriend. She hadn't wanted to ring Bridget on her first day out, not wanting Bibi, who thought lovers should never be sent on a mission together, to think she lacked confidence in her ability to pull this off.

"I'll be sure to include that in my official report," he said, trying to smooth his wrinkled shorts, imagining how the plaid valleys must look on his too-big backside.

Jane got out of the car and examined her face in the side mirror, where Objects Were Closer Than They Appeared, and tugged on the glued-on bits to make sure the hold was strong. Everything was where it should be and would stay that way. "Does this look okay?" she asked Cedric, pulling her left ear forward so he could check her bald spot, courtesy of Mimi Dolittle.

"I do not understand how you ended up washing your hair with a feminine depilatory cream," he said, checking the tuft of artificial hair, glued firmly in place. He, of course, had no knowledge of Mimi's existence. "It's an excellent color and texture match," he said. "The chaps in Disguise should be proud; if he could see you now, your brother would think he was seeing double."

"I imagine he sees double quite often," Jane said. She studied her reflection in the car window, wondering if the rubber forehead made her look like a Neanderthal. "They did do a brilliant job," she admitted, and the little knot of worry she had carried in her stomach since leaving London started to melt.

"What are you thinking?" asked Cedric, putting his chin on her shoulder and staring at his own fleshy face, comparing it to Jane's strong, angular one.

"I'm wondering what we're having for lunch," she said. She was really thinking about the awards and honors her brother brought home each year. He had been voted Most Likely to Save the World from an Evil Genius every year since the convention began. He was clearly the favorite son, a role he had played most of his life, and instead of trying to compete, she would bask in this reflected glory. She grinned, realizing that her brother, with his fans and proclivity for grand entrances, was the Liberace of the spy world.

"I hope it's not Swiss steak," Cedric said, tucking in his shirt where it had started to pull out of his shorts. "I had that on the plane."

"Let's go, 007," she said under her breath, staring at the mirror. Unbeknownst to Cedric, whose idea of a weapon was a stern look, she had a G.E.O.R.G.I.E.-issue Glock in her ankle holster. There was nothing else she needed. The only thing left to do was walk through that door.

"Let's go, 007-*and-a-half*," Cedric said. "Into the greatest gathering of spies the Western world has ever known."

She laughed at his worshipful tone, and the sound of her own voice shattered her confidence. "My voice! I left the spray that deepens my voice back at the teepee!" Her morning application had worn off.

"Oh, my." Cedric mopped the back of his neck with a handkerchief and remembered something his father used to say: For want of a good waterproof sealer, a battleship was sunk. "Get in the car and *scream*."

"That *oven?*"

"Don't stop until you're hoarse. I'll tell everyone you have a terrible cold, that a woman seated next to you on the plane sneezed on your food."

"That was you!" Jane cried in protest as he opened the door and shoved her inside.

"Yes, but I don't have a cold," he said through the window. Already feeling faint from the heat, Jane was trying to unroll the window, but he planted his hand on the glass and pushed *up*. "If anyone asks," he said, "she was wearing a tailored gray suit. And pearls, a present from her mother. A single strand, I think, modest but genuine. The kind that can be worn with a skirt and jumper or a black cocktail dress. She turned around to ask you to please stop kicking her seat, and that's when she sneezed. She was most apologetic."

"I don't think that a scream is going to cut it," Jane said.

"It's obviously too late to say you've been studying the art of mime," he said. "That would entail keeping your mouth shut—and when have you ever refrained from telling your opinion on anything?" That was when Jane started to scream.

Ten minutes later, having been released from her sweltering prison just as she was about to shoot her way out, she leaned against the car smoking one of the frightfully expensive Turkish cigarettes favored by her brother, shading her face with a map of Nevada. The smoke was harsh against her raw throat, but she agreed that burning through a pack before going in would adjust her voice to its required depths. Cedric's quick thinking about the voice problem had impressed Jane, but she still wanted to kill him for locking her in the hot car.

As Jane smoked, Cedric rehearsed one last time the fun facts, pithy remarks, and tried-and-true jokes he had culled from old copies of *Spy*

Digest, should he be asked to make a few off-the-cuff remarks—not unthinkable, as surely he would be the only agent in attendance who had saved a monarch in her underwear.

"I'm thoroughly cooked," said Jane, crushing the fag butt under her boot. She was dying for a Coca-Cola. "I guess it's time to go," she said reluctantly.

"Tell me if I get this right," said Cedric, handing her a sheet of typewritten paper entitled "Opening Remarks, 1966 Convention, Las Vegas, Nevada, U.S.A.," and he began to repeat the text word for word. As they walked the long expanse of steamy asphalt toward the front door, she looked back on their time together; they'd had cocktails with politicians eager to meet the notorious 007, eaten bubble and squeak with the queen, signed autographs at the Secret Service's annual jumble sale, the proceeds of which kept the Tampax machine in the lav stocked. Until today indigestion and boredom were all she had to worry about. The first woman to enter a secret spy convention, disguised as one of the espionage world's top men, and the only person she had to rely on was rehearsing a knock-knock joke about Polish spies.

She ran her tongue over the capsule embedded in her molar, knowing she would save the emergency Valium for another time. She could handle this. She had been imitating her brother for a year now. Her disguise was perfect. She had graduated with honors from G.E.O.R.G.I.E. spy school. She had a fully-equipped spy watch on her arm and a dagger in her thin black tie. Sewn to her suit were three smoke-bomb buttons, and the last cigarette in her pack, marked with a spot of red nail polish, was a tiny explosive rocket activated by the heat of a match. And her belt . . . well, that just held up her pants.

"We're late," Cedric said, beginning to run. He grabbed the paper from Jane's hands and stuffed it in his pocket.

"No one expects James Bond to follow any timetable," Jane sniffed, successfully inhabiting her character by slowing her gait and puffing out her chest. Cedric squirted her with an atomizer of Hai Karate he had up his sleeve, and she sneezed. At the front of the building, they paused to look at their reflection in the glass door, polished mirror bright. The hot air wrapped around their bodies, making it appear as if they were underwater.

* * *

As they reached the welcome desk, in order to calm his increasingly jittery nerves, Cedric rubbed the pocket that held his wallet, in which, tucked behind a wedding portrait of his parents with his father scissored out, was a letter from FBI director J. Edger Hoover, something he treasured almost as much as the scrapbook of his childhood illnesses his mother had put together. *Good work. Signed, J. Edgar Hoover.* It had arrived after an American magazine had picked up the story of the plot against the queen, and Cedric considered it his good-luck charm. Never one of the popular boys at school, he had hovered in social rank a tick above the children scorned for their stuttering, thick glasses, and corrective shoes, children who grew up to be either wildly successful movie actors or perverted murderers who scattered bodies on the moors. Things were different now: Cedric "Knobby Knees" Pumpernickel had been replaced by *Sir* Cedric "Knobby Knees" Pumpernickel, a man who had taken tea with the queen.

None of this mattered to the woman at the front desk of the convention center. "Accident-prone or frozen foods?" she asked. The woman in a yellow twinset and nubby gray skirt, the first sensibly dressed person Jane had seen in Las Vegas, stood guard behind a table blocking access to an imitation-wood door leading to the maze of convention halls. Smiling, she used the eraser end of her pencil to push up her blue cat glasses, poking herself in the eye.

"We're accident-prone," Cedric said, showing her their falsified identification cards. "Sir Medrick Slumberknuckle and Mr. Jim Bland." Secret agents took turns choosing their cover for the annual Las Vegas meeting; they had been gynecologists, swizzle stick salesmen, astronauts, and bra designers. They couldn't, after all, announce that the free world's top spies were in town. The idea for this year's cover had come to Cedric after he received a nasty paper cut from the electric bill on the same day he'd fallen off a stepstool while straightening his linen cabinet.

Plastic name badges pinned to their shirts, they each received a *Welcome to Las Vegas!* information packet containing, among other things, a mimeographed list of local bail bondsmen, a coupon for a free backscratcher from the Hoover Dam gift shop, and a coupon for a free meal at the Hungry Honcho. The phone number for Gamblers Anonymous was slipped into the Book of Mormon and passed under the table to Jane with a little wink. "Call them before you trade your car for cash," the woman whispered, revealing herself to be an evangelist in a city of sinners. "Your Heavenly Father cares."

Before Cedric could explain that they were Church of England, a woman with stiff brown hair set in spit-curl precision raced up to the table, panting, the contents of her straw purse, squashed under her arm, spilling onto the orange indoor-outdoor carpet. Jane and Cedric chased after her things—a lipstick, a meat mallet, and a gravy boat—as she leaned her hip against the table and caught her breath, hugging her casserole to her chest.

"Darlin', I'm here for the Dorothy Duncan Defrost-Off, and I've got to get my Meat Loaf à l'Orange to a freezer toot suite! Marge Milligan. M-i-l-l-i-g-a-n. Incredible Edibles."

"Go through that door and to the right," the registrar said, tucking a complimentary plastic rain bonnet into the *Welcome to Las Vegas!* information packet and wiping the condensation off the bottom of Mrs. Milligan's casserole dish using a handkerchief she kept tucked in her sweater sleeve. "You're both in the East Wing."

"How did you know I needed a new bonnet?" said Marge Milligan with delight, as if she had been handed a diamond tiara. "And how nice to have such nice neighbors!" She indulged them with a sunny smile, and Jane wished they were attending *her* convention. Marge Milligan reminded her of her mother, a sweet, gracious woman whose sunny disposition tempered her husband's dark moods.

Cedric held the door for Marge Milligan. "That smells delicious," he said as the lid shifted and the scent of Meat Loaf l'Orange wafted toward him. "You come by for a piece anytime," she said. "I'll be in Aisle Eleven, Booth One Thirty-six." She marched through the door, balancing her information packet on her casserole dish, looking as resolute as any general going into battle. They trailed her determined step down a long beige corridor decorated with historical photographs of early Las Vegas.

"Perhaps there will be taste tests for the public," said Cedric, too busy trying to identify the wonderful smells filling the narrow corridor to pay attention to his surroundings. He tripped over a wire stand holding an enormous floral horseshoe, a flowery monstrosity for which hundreds of red carnations had given their lives, draped with a white satin sash with bloodred letters: GOOD LUCK, UNFORTUNATES! FROM AMALGAMATED INSURANCE, INC. He had found their convention.

Marge Milligan was the first to offer her assistance, shoving her casserole into Jane's arms and holding out a dishpan hand to help him up. Cedric struggled to his feet, then leaned against the cinder-block wall so he could pull off his left sandal and sock to make sure the check was still secure. It was.

Jane stood there awkwardly, feeling as silly as if she were holding a purse.

"You're with the International Association of Accident-Prone People, aren't you?" Marge Milligan clucked sympathetically, inspecting him for signs of damage. "You've skinned your knees, but some Bactine should take care of that."

"Yes, we're an organization of like-minded people working to bring relief to the habitually unlucky," he said, putting his sock and sandal back on and examining the raw skin on his chubby knees. He simply wasn't meant to wear shorts. "The idea for the organization came to me after I suffered three separate accidental injuries in the same day."

Jane swayed on her feet, humming the theme to *The Avengers* and practicing her theory that she could block unwanted sound by thinking of something pleasant. Fantasies of sex with Bridget usually did the trick.

Mrs. Milligan listened patiently until she saw water dripping from the casserole dish in Jane's arms, then grabbed it and disappeared around the corner. They could hear the heels of her sensible shoes slapping against the low-pile carpet as she ran away from them.

"You're making all kinds of friends in Las Vegas," Jane said, the woman's glazed expression reminding her of how Wanda had looked while waiting for him to order. "We'd best go in," she said, taking the last fag from the pack in her pocket, then returning it when she saw the red dot indicating that it was her explosive cigarette.

six

As they entered the room, a large, anonymous-looking space with the same orange carpet as in the halls, the walls a light tan tinged green by the long tubes of fluorescent lights that hung from the ceiling, Cedric paused to savor his last bit of anonymity. His fingertips caressed the medal pinned to his shirt, polished to a sheen.

J. Edgar Hoover, who knew everything about everyone, had undoubtedly informed the FBI agents in attendance that Sir Cedric Pumpernickel of Her Majesty's Secret Service was among them and should be given a hero's welcome. So while Cedric waited to be noticed, Jane stood quietly at his side, making a mental survey of the room, checking for exits, examining the walls, wondering if she could scale them with the collapsible rope ladder in the false bottom of her suitcase. There was no telling how this would play out, and Miss Tuppenny's directive—to find and steal the invention without harming 007's reputation—meant that Jane had to be especially clever.

Cedric chewed his nails and rocked on his heels and waited, wondering how long they'd have to stand alone before someone looked up from his drink and realized that Sir Cedric Pumpernickel had finally arrived. "This is no doubt the opening get-together, where agents catch up on the news before getting down to work," he said, trying to keep the disappointment out of his voice. A knight of the crown and its most celebrated secret agent had just arrived, and still the circulating cheese tray was of greater interest.

"Perhaps no one recognizes me without a martini in my hand," said Jane. She slapped Cedric on the back—a suitably masculine gesture—making him swallow his breath mint. "If we stand here any longer, we'll look like idiots. We don't want it to seem as if we've never been to the convention before," she said. "The bar is open. I suggest we pick up a few props." She needed something to do with her hands besides play with the wallet transmitter in her pocket. More than anything she wanted to ring Bridget and tell her that, yes, she did lack confidence in her ability to pull this off. When she looked in the mirror that morning, after donning full James Bond drag, Jane thought she could see the line that separated the false forehead from her own. Because she insisted on removing her face before going to bed, Jane had to do her own makeup in the morning. What if the scars were in the wrong spot? Her big feet, and tendency toward sarcasm, were the only authentic things about the disguise.

Fighting her impulse to run to the ladies' room for a private chat with her true love, she took the lead, her hands shoved in her trouser pockets to hide the shaking, and led the way to the well-stocked bar at the far end of the room, walking as if she owned the joint. A sea of men parted to let her through, some nodding as she passed. No one spoke except Cedric, who was right behind her, praying under his breath. No one stepped forward to identify her as an impostor, but no one stepped forward to say hello either. They got their drinks—a martini for her and a Tab for him—and started to mingle. Recognizing an agent from a photograph in one of her brother's reports, she threw back her shoulders, twisted her mouth into an ironic smile, and slapped him on the back. "Pierre!" she cried, her gravelly voice choking on the *r*s. Agent Pierre Camembert popped a Triscuit-and-cheddar-cheese canapé in his mouth, chewed, swallowed, and turned his back. "The French," Jane said with bemusement, turning to a chap who had wordlessly watched the exchange and shrugging. The man quickly backed away. Jane, puzzled at the look of revulsion in his eyes, wondered if her face had shifted. She put a hand to her head and felt the familiar slab of plastic molded to her forehead, with subtle painted frown lines and a jagged little scar from when her brother had been bitten by a shark. It was securely in place. Everywhere she went, men turned their backs. Her sparkling conversation openers fell flat, and when a chap from M1-5 pretended he couldn't understand what she was saying because of her accent, she got the point. James Bond was *not* going to be named Most Popular Attendee for a sixth year.

Many of the men were clearly on their second or third or fourth round, and Jane thought it might explain their reaction when she tried to engage them in conversation. Surely, if she *had* been recognized as a fake, they would have pounced on her by now. It wasn't suspicion, she decided, that made them hold back—it was something her brother had done. But what? His list of sins was as varied as it was long.

"This is nothing like I imagined," Cedric whispered. He had stood behind Jane as she circulated through the crowd, and in all that time, no
one had recognized him. "I guess this is not a literary crowd." He had
been the subject of a *Reader's Digest* "Drama in Real Life" story, and
still received fan mail from across the pond congratulating him on his
courage, but these men undoubtedly had little time for reading.

Jane decided to wait to tell him any more bad news, and they lingered
at the Space Food booth, the first in a line of tables and stalls set against
one long wall, covered in bright bunting and loaded with goods. The perfect place, Jane thought, to stash an invention.

"This place looks like the Bombay open-market bazaar," he said,
sounding disapproving but already picking through the items for sale.
She thought it looked more like a church jumble sale, the goods strewn
in messy heaps on a ragtag assortment of different size tables. The presentation lacked a woman's touch. "I think I'll be needing a rise in allowance," she joked to Cedric, who kept their funds in his other sock.
They browsed through the stalls, Jane sizing up the sellers' reaction to
her (neutral verging on indifference; apparently, 007's *money* was still
welcome here) and Cedric pouring his disappointment into souvenir
shopping. He thought about buying N. a FOR THIS I WENT TO SPY
SCHOOL? barbecue apron, tried out the joke shoe transmitter with plastic
dog shit glued to the heel, and made himself a little dizzy with the X-ray-
vision glasses designed to *See through today's synthetic fabrics!* "You'd
look good with a *Man from U.N.C.L.E.* tattoo," joked Jane as they
watched an agent get Napoleon Solo's head permanently inked on his
rear.

"I'm going to take advantage of the conventioneers' special interest
rate and get a Diners Club card," Cedric said, and while he filled out the
application form, Jane signed up to win a Bobby Darin wig at the Have
to Have Hairpieces booth, putting her entry in a goldfish bowl jammed
with dozens of slips bearing the name Dougie Smathers. At Cedric's be-
hest she looked over his credit-card application and then wondered if the
secret agent manning the hairpiece booth would recognize her brother's
signature. Good-bye, Bobby Darin wig, she thought as she fished her
contest entry from the bowl and ate it. She had just swallowed the last
shred when an agent leaning against the bar looked in their direction,

did a double take, and pointed excitedly. He ran toward them, his martini sloshing on his mud brown Bermuda shorts, and others followed, jostling for the lead.

"Well, well," said Cedric, smoothing his thinning hair in anticipation of a camera's flash. He was repositioning his medal when they flew past without a glance in his direction and tumbled to a stop, falling all over each other to be the first to have his picture taken with a cardboard cutout of Emma Peel in a skintight cat suit. "Hard competition, that," Cedric told Jane, swallowing his disappointment. "Perhaps Americans are more reluctant to foist themselves on celebrities than we are in England," he added hopefully.

"Perhaps." Perhaps her brother's reports of his godlike standing in the espionage community were a tad exaggerated, Jane thought.

"Something's not right," said Cedric. "Last year 007 was so busy signing autographs and posing for photographs it took him a full hour to get from the door to the bar. That didn't happen to you."

A stocky man in a baby blue bowling shirt with FEDERAL BUREAU OF INVESTIGATION in white block letters on the back and his name, Agent Dougie Smathers, embroidered in script over his left breast pocket, pushed past them, shoving Cedric with his elbow.

"Sorry," he muttered, and then turned to look at Jane. "Bond," he grunted.

Cedric patted his metal, smoothed his thinning hair, and stuck out a hand. "Sir Pumpernickel," he said. "Bond's travel companion."

"Smathers," Jane grunted back, thankful for the help the bowling shirt had given her. Ignoring Cedric's hand, Smathers belched in their faces and continued on his way. Cedric let out a whoosh of air. They both recognized the name from last year's report.

"Do you know who that is?" he breathed. She nodded. The puffy-faced man with a beer can in his hand and chip dip on his chin was the FBI's most cunning agent, her brother's closest American colleague, and the one she had feared would give her away.

"He didn't flinch when he saw you," said Cedric. "That's a good sign."

"He's drunk," said Jane. "They all are. This should be one hell of a convention."

The contents of the tiny bottle of concentrated truth serum in her pocket, disguised as nasal spray, should be enough to get these chaps talking. If she could pollute the liquor supply, she'd then be able to take each agent aside and ask if he had invented any good gadgets lately. No, getting the drug into these agents would not be a problem; most were drinking martinis made in a washing machine behind the bar that had been converted into the world's largest martini shaker. She looked at Cedric, who was flipping through a stack of John le Carré novels, one free with every purchase of a glow-in-the-dark toilet seat. He would be the problem.

After talking Cedric out of getting a tattoo of J. Edgar Hoover, Jane decided they would plunge headfirst into the cocktail party. She got a second martini, and another Tab for Cedric, grabbed a handful of Ritz-cracker-and-Spam canapés, and they joined a group of men toasting their good fortune in having dodged work and wives for three days of fun, fun, fun in America's Sin City. When she raised her glass and said, "Look out ladies, here we come!" the men grew silent. "You promised, Bond!" an agent said as he punched her on the shoulder, hard, and the men drifted away to take up residence in the Bachelor Pad of Tomorrow and shoot her dirty looks. After that, every agent they approached turned his back on them, and the more she and Cedric tried, the more obvious it became that they were not welcome here. It appeared to be an orchestrated snub. Only one agent seemed happy to see them, slapping Jane on the back before stuffing lit Cuban cigars in her and Cedric's mouths. The cigars burst into flames, curling Cedric's nose hairs and sending the lads into peals of knee-slapping laughter.

"It's dance class all over again," Cedric said miserably as they backed into a nice dark corner to discuss their next move. "I do believe that your brother left some things out. This is not the picture of convivial camaraderie pictured in your brother's report. There was nothing in last year's report to indicate that relations with France, Canada, Australia, or Kansas had cooled. And nothing looks as it should; there should be a lectern where the bar is, and rows of library tables so we can take notes while listening to lectures by the brightest minds in our field. Perhaps these displays of goods disappear into the floor and the real convention furniture pops up."

"You're confusing real life with *The Avengers* again," said Jane. "This *is* the great spy convention my brother has been raving about for years. A motley group of men in hideous clothing, drunk on cheap gin, and standing in line to buy glow-in-the-dark toilet seats."

Cedric chuckled at her naïveté. "I think I've been in this business a little longer than you, Jane, and I *know* this is not the true face of espionage. Mark my words, the next time we see this room, we won't recognize it. After these men get the blood and guts and grime of their last mission out of their systems, it's down to work. Perhaps everyone's put off because they know you'll get the gadget no matter what. They've already given up, which explains the almost desperate need for alcohol."

Jane shrugged. She knew her brother and had the feeling that this convention was no different than the others. Whether it was a drunken free-for-all or a sober meeting of minds, she was going to get that invention for G.E.O.R.G.I.E.

The motor on the circular bed, on display in the center of the room as the jewel of the convention, touted by a glittery sign that read $399.99, BLACK SATIN SHEETS EXTRA started to purr, and Cedric seemed to lose the strength of his convictions. "The reports your brother turned in chronicled three days of serious Cold War conversations and weapons demonstrations, followed by social events designed to foster understanding between nations. Where is the shoemaker to fit us for bulletproof rubbers? The haberdasher with the camouflage socks? I'm beginning to suspect that those reports are fiction."

"What?" Jane was too busy imagining the fun she and Bridget could have on the circular bed to pay attention.

"Who wants to take this baby out for a test drive?" an agent barked, demonstrating the patented E-Z-Use Ejector System. "Pull this lever and—*blammo!*—you've just solved a sticky social situation—how to tell some dame it's time to go home."

"I wonder if it works on wives," Jane overheard Dougie Smathers say. His companion guffawed and slapped him on the back. Agents began to quarrel good-naturedly, throwing hokey-looking karate chops at one another, each wanting to be the first to be flung out of bed. Cedric clutched the Tab in his hand, his eyes glazed over as he watched the childish display. The death of a dream was hard to swallow, and he lifted his can to his lips and drained it, wishing it were something a little stronger. A tasty, old-fashioned root beer would have been nice.

As a man wearing white trousers and an unbuttoned paisley shirt slid under the satin sheets and gave the operator the thumbs-up sign, Jane put her hand on the prayer book in her pocket, and bowed her head. "Heavenly Father, thank you for making me a lesbian," she murmured as he flew by, belly flopping onto the shag-carpet landing pad, a gold male-symbol medallion the size of a dinner plate smacking him in the face and knocking him out. His martini had made a perfect landing; not one drop had spilled.

A cheer went up, and Cedric looked at her, rolled his eyes, and said, "This display makes me wish I were a lesbian, too."

As she scanned the room, wondering which of these Neanderthals could have invented a device that could change the world, she noticed something strange. "Hey, Cedric, that chap at the Bulletproof Beachwear booth is staring at us," she said. "And it's not with hate in his eyes."

The man watching them had the pallor of a dedicated desk jockey; his legs, like Cedric's, were making their debut in polite society and were as white as the sheet Agent Dougie Smathers had taped to the wall on which to project the pornographic eight millimeter films he had brought from home. His shorts, lime and turquoise plaid, were too long by half— they almost touched the tops of his black socks—making him appear young and vulnerable, a schoolboy in his big brother's clothes. His bad taste had suggested he pair the shorts with a lemon yellow Ban-Lon short-sleeved shirt, a color better suited to a kitchen wall than a pale blond, and his awkward movements suggested he, too, was there for the first time.

Hiding in the corner of the convention hall like teenagers at a dance furtively passing around a bottle, Jane and Cedric watched the mousy man scrutinize bulletproof swim trunks—and them—for twenty minutes before finally selecting a pair of turquoise-and-orange vertical-striped trunks—vertical because horizontal stripes, he confided to the salesman, made him look hippy. After he paid, he carefully counted his change, put it in his shoe, and asked for a receipt for his expense report. Each time he glanced their way, he first looked over his shoulder to see if anyone was watching. This confirmed Jane's newly formed suspicion that her brother was not Mr. Popularity. It didn't surprise her that he wasn't well liked; she was his sister, and she wasn't that keen on him herself.

"Why is that chap looking at us?" whispered Cedric, nervously playing with his empty Tab can, pushing the sides together to make a tiny metallic "pop." Jane wrested the can away before he shattered her last nerve. "There was a little left in there!" he cried.

"Go get another."

"I refuse to venture forth into these shark-infested waters alone," he said. "I'm waiting for the real convention to begin. If there *is* a real convention."

Jane nodded. After the rude greeting they'd received, she was content to stand in this spot and mull over her next move, smoking Cedric's cheap cigarettes undisturbed and wondering why women were held to impossibly high standards of beauty when men could walk the earth in Bermuda shorts and black shoes without threat of arrest or a life of solitude. "I don't recognize the chap looking at us from any of James's snaps," she said. "Could it be we have an ally here?"

"Do you think he could be our inventor?" asked Cedric hopefully. "He looks like an inventor. See, he's squinting. He must wear glasses. Everyone knows glasses are a sign of intelligence. All inventors have bad vision. Well, in the movies at least. He's our man, all right. I have the check right here," he said, bending down to take it from his sock, breathing a sigh of relief; this could be the most efficient mission in the history of the Secret Service.

"You have that signed blank check in your sock?" Jane said. Visions of a smart new G.E.O.R.G.I.E. laboratory danced in her head until she realized N. would have Cedric's *head* if he returned with no invention and no check. "Don't flash it around. We don't know who that chap is—yet." She waved at the man, who quickly turned his attention to a paisley-print cabana robe. It was clear he was interested in more than safe swimwear, but more than likely he was a curiosity seeker, wanting a closer look at the unpopular James Bond.

"Research indicates we're looking for someone who stands apart from the pack," Cedric said, recalling an article in *Spy Digest* about men of science "He's his own man, an iconoclast with a brilliant turn of mind. Perhaps he's wearing brown shoes when others are wearing black. Or he eats catsup instead of ketchup on his hamburger."

"That one's definitely apart from the pack," said Jane, watching an agent bounce a beach ball off the man's head. She realized she should encourage Cedric's belief that Mr. Swimtrunks was the one they were looking for; it would give him someone to play with besides her. "Now that I think of it," she said, "in the movies the brilliant scientist *is* always the mild-mannered, clumsy chap." She was watching the man trying to get a straw through the opening of a can of Orange Crush. And failing.

Cedric's chest puffed like a pigeon when he heard this. It wasn't fair that Jane got to be both the handsome *and* the smart one. "Although I've never been on a real mission before, I think this one could turn out to be a rousing success. Why, if this man is the one we're looking for, and we can convince him to sell the invention to us without putting it on the auction block, tonight we could go straight from Liberace to the airport, saving the department two days' food and lodging." They would be victorious *and* thrifty.

"I think you're right," said Jane. "From now on you're the brains and I'm the brawn. Go get him, tiger!" He dug in his heels as she pushed him toward the man.

"He doesn't know who I am," Cedric protested. "No one here does. He's been staring at you this entire time. *You* go!" He grabbed her arm and tried to trade places, and they scuffled for a minute before Jane gave in, afraid they were drawing too much attention to themselves.

"Sorry," she said, wondering if the shirtsleeve she had grabbed hold of would always hang to his elbow or would bounce back.

"This is my last foray into the world of synthetics," he sighed, examining his lopsided shirtsleeve. A matchbook from Bob's Big Boy Family

Restaurant landed at his feet, and he kicked it back, a reflexive action. Their admirer with the dodgy taste in swimwear picked it up and used it to light a cigarette, watching them over the match until it burned down to his fingers.

"No wonder you don't have a boyfriend, if this is how you read signals," Jane said. "If someone tosses you a matchbook, you're supposed to pick it up."

"Why? I don't smoke. It's one habit I've managed to evade. Now, if I could only give up boiled sweets . . ." He patted his stomach.

"He was *communicating* with you. Secretly. As in secret agent."

Cedric's hands flew to his face, and he felt the rush of blood to his cheeks. "I was right! He *is* our man!" He turned his back, his breath coming quick and shallow. "I'm having a heart attack. I know it."

"You've got bacon in your teeth," said Jane, refusing to support his dramatics. He was always "having a heart attack" when forced into new social situations. "Right in front. Lower level. And you're not having an attack of anything but nerves." She had known this would happen, and had packed accordingly. "Take this," she said, handing him a mild sedative.

"It's against company policy to take medication whilst on duty."

"N. suggested them." Or would have, had he imagined this scene.

Plucking the pill from her hand, he stared at it as if he had never seen a Valium before. "I'll need some water."

"Swallow it dry. You," Jane said, raising her voice to be heard over the moans and groans of *Sexy Stenographers*. "Come over here."

A "who, me?" look in his eyes, the man sidled up to them, wiping his sweaty palms on his shorts. "These guys—they're kooks!" He smiled, making a sweeping gesture with his hand toward Dougie Smathers and a small gang of agents engaged in pulling the wings off robotic spy flies. "But a lotta fun, doncha think? I'm Agent Felix Bivens, FBI. Kansas City office." He stuck out his hand. "I work with Agent Smathers."

Cedric sucked in his gut and grabbed the outstretched hand. "One of Hoover's G-men, of course. Sir Cedric Pumpernickel of Her Majesty's Secret Service."

"Nice to know you, Pumperknickers."

"Pumpernickel. *Sir* Pumper*nickel*. Like your coin."

"Like the bread," said Jane. Sir Pumperknickers was holding on to the chap's hand like a drowning man. "I'm—"

"Everyone knows who *you* are!" cried Agent Bivens, using both hands to grab Jane's, pumping her arm until she was afraid her fillings would fall out. "Golly, I've been dying to meet you! You're just about the most famous Brit in the world, at least to those of us in the spy trade." Jane could hear a stream of air leaving Cedric's mouth. His last bit of hope had been punctured. "Why, you're more famous than the Beatles, if you ask me. Will you sign my cocktail coaster? Here—sign the back." He handed her a pen and a stained cardboard coaster with a rude cartoon of a naked woman riding a rocket. "Please make it out to 'My good friend Felix.' This is going up on my bulletin board at work," he told them, hopping excitedly from foot to foot. He was giving Jane a headache. "Right next to my autographed picture of Wally Schirra. I'm hoping to get Liberace's autograph, too. I understand he had a fondness for dogs, so I brought my autograph hound. We drove all the way from Kansas together. I could have flown, but there's nothing like the great open road. The desert's awfully scenic, don't you think? Although for my money nothing's as pretty as autumn in Kansas. Mother Bivens loves it. She refuses to leave, even to come here and see Liberace. Of course, she doesn't know anything about my work; she thinks I'm an accountant at a wicker-chair store."

"So you know Dougie?" Jane said. "We seem to have had a falling-out." The trick was to get him talking without raising any suspicion. Shouldn't James Bond know what had happened to turn Dougie against him? But James Bond was in a private clinic, getting new eyebrows. "My memories of last year's convention are dim. Right after it ended, I had a run-in with Dr. Yes and his memory-erasing machine."

Felix started to shift uncomfortably. "The truth is, we work in different departments. He's a field agent, and I'm in supplies." He brightened. "Office supplies. I do the purchasing for the western states. Seven offices, all needing toilet paper, memo pads, file cabinets—not exciting stuff, but it makes the Bureau tick. We couldn't catch crooks without paper clips, after all!" He flung his arms wide, smacking Cedric in the chest with the Instamatic camera hanging from his wrist by the strap. "This is my first convention. The office staff never gets invited to these things, but an agent in the Reno office met with an unfortunate accident, and I won his spot in the office pool. One day I'm sitting at my desk, comparing one-ply to two- and the next I'm at Sears looking over the Dorcas Collection of warm-weather clothes."

"I'm wearing something from the Dorcas Collection as well!" Cedric said, sounding as excited as if they had mutually discovered the cotton gin.

"But you *do* know Agent Smathers?" Jane prodded.

"We-e-ll-ll." He looked down at his sandals. "Not really. But I had hoped to get to know him a little better during this trip. We were supposed to share a room—the Bureau got us a suite at the Desert Inn—but Dougie thought he might be entertaining quite a bit, and so I volunteered to sleep on the fold-out sofa. My opinion of him changed somewhat when I awoke this morning to find I had been folded inside. Luckily, the maid was changing the sheets and heard my cries for help."

"You weren't able to disassemble the fold-out mechanism and free yourself?" Cedric sounded disappointed, and Jane grabbed him by the elbow and pushed him behind the booth.

"Excuse us, Agent Bivens."

"I'm not so sure anymore," said Cedric. "If he's so clever, why didn't he disassemble the fold-out mechanism and free himself?"

Jane smacked a hand to her forehead and then felt to see if she had done any damage. She couldn't cope with Cedric's mood swings, and wanted to keep him busy while she did the real work for G.E.O.R.G.I.E. "He might well be the inventor. An unpopular squinter wearing too much aftershave who has no taste in clothing? He fits the three basic criteria mentioned in a recent article in *Spy Digest*." It was just what he wanted to hear, for she suspected he found Agent Bivens attractive. God knows they had a lot in common: Both were annoyingly obtuse, mad about plaid, and devoted to their mothers.

He nodded, relieved. "That issue must have come out the month I spent at the seashore. What do we do now? Should *we* mention the invention or let *him* do it? We don't want to scare him away." Despite the chilly air, Cedric was sweating.

"I don't think that's going to be a problem," Jane replied calmly. Felix was staring at them with a goofy smile on his face, and when he bent over to pull up his socks, she saw the KICK ME sign on his back. "I think he's adopted us. He seems very taken with you—one secret agent to another, of course," she added when she saw fear wash over his face. He *did* like Agent Bivens, and now Jane was going to play them like violins.

"He does seem out of his element," Cedric said, flapping his arms in an attempt to dry his underarms. Felix did the same. "Geniuses often don't fit in."

"Exactly my point," said Jane. "I may intimidate him, so it's up to *you* to make him feel comfortable. It seems you two have a lot in common."

"You think I'm a genius?" Cedric squealed. Jane could tell that the Valium was beginning to kick in.

"You both have autograph hounds. I'd open with that. Now, I need a drink. I'll leave it to you, *Agent* Pumpernickel," she said with a wink. Ignoring his silent plea for help, she emerged from the shadows, her expression set on scowl, to a barrage of olives thrown her way. Cripes, what a bunch of babies! It was hard to imagine any one of them as the elusive inventor. She pushed her way through a cluster of secret agents toasting the Cold War, ignoring their rude barnyard noises and pausing to capture each man on her wristwatch camera, certain their agencies would appreciate pictures of them "hard at work." She managed to anticipate the second olive bombardment, catching a few and dropping them into her drink. Someone chortled and was hushed by an angry Dougie Smathers. He was, apparently, the source of the snubs, and Jane again wondered what her brother had done to deserve this treatment. She took up her post against the wall, between the Bachelor Pad of Tomorrow and a booth selling twelve different types of inflatable women, and ate her gin-soaked olives. She imagined her report to Miss Tuppenny. Day One: I discover that the top spies of the free world are a bunch of drunken louts. *Careful, Jane,* she imagined Miss Tuppenny's response. *Drunk or sober, these men could prove to be formidable foes.*

She smiled like a proud parent as she watched Cedric fumble all over himself in an attempt to impress Felix, who seemed to hang on Cedric's every word. Everyone's got a twin, Jane thought wryly as she watched them take each other's picture, then switch Instamatics and do it again. She propped the stem of the glass against her chest, watching Cedric admire Felix's swim trunks, wondering what else he admired about the little man from Kansas City.

After a couple of demonstrations, the revolving bed finally spun off its tracks under the weight of a dozen men, who came to rest on a pile of inflatable Angie Dickinsons. As Jane watched them scramble to pick up their pocket change, she laughed along with them, trying to fit in. She was ignored in favor of an arcade attraction called The Love Tester. One by one the agents stepped up to a wooden box housing a rubber hand and squeezed, each time sending the "mercury" in an outsize thermometer to the top. Everyone here was, it seemed, a "Stud," and the machine spit out wallet-size cards to confirm it. They seemed pleased, as if they had just received their diplomas from Love University, and Jane was not surprised when the chap who had singed her eyebrow earlier now waved her over. Time for more public humiliation, Jane thought, wondering how much more she'd have to put up with before being allowed back in the club.

"Come on, Bond. What kind of lover are you?" he called out, and the men around him snickered. She knew that her brother wouldn't have turned down an offer to show off, so she put her martini on the coffee table of the future and stepped up to The Love Tester.

"007! 007! 007!" the agents chanted as she squeezed the rubber hand as hard as she could and hoped someone wasn't putting knockout drops in her unattended drink. The "mercury" in the giant thermometer rose, passing "Big Loser," "Lazy Lothario," "Sexy Son of a Gun," and "Ladies Man," all the way to "Stud" before the machine sputtered, the mercury suddenly plunged, and machine spit out a card declaring Jane a "Big Loser."

"You're not a Stud anymore!" Dougie Smathers cried, taking his foot off the cord running from the back of the machine to an electrical outlet. Jane retrieved her drink with new insight into the fun and games Cedric had suffered through in his years with the Secret Service. Certain now that they would *not* be invited to the afternoon clambake in the dining hall, she ventured over to the Space Food booth and grabbed a complimentary ice cream bar. She ripped the foil package open with her teeth, the powdery vanilla-flavored substance fizzing on her tongue while she watched Cedric stare as Felix tried his new swim trunks on over his shorts. It was nice that he had made a friend, but she could use someone to talk to. A race began down the middle of the room, between the idiotic French chap and Dougie Smathers. Wearing glow-in-the-dark toilet seats around their necks, they bounced on inflatable life rafts, keeping rhythm to a Sammi Martini song blaring from the bachelor pad's hi-fi. The agents cheered as Dougie Smathers won the race by a nose—a great big red one—and hoisted him over their heads. He was clearly their leader, and Jane knew what she had to do. She had to get Dougie Smathers to like 007 again.

How would one go about getting the attention of someone like Dougie Smathers? Put him in peril and then save him? Get him a discount on nose-hair clippers? Bibi, Jane knew, would just unbutton her blouse and, when he rushed over to investigate, shoot him. What the girl lacked in subtlety, she made up for in results. What did Jane have to offer that Dougie would want? Correction—what did 007 have?

Jane made a mental inventory of the various weapons hidden on her person and realized she didn't want to part with any of them. He could ruin his own toys, she decided, watching him put out his smelly cigar in the bottom of his rubber lifeboat. The only other thing he could want was the one thing she wouldn't get him—a woman. But she could do the next-best thing.

"Give me your biro," she said to Cedric after sending Felix off to for another round of drinks.

"Glksimgh?" said Cedric, his mouth filled with dehydrated space jellybeans. She had found them sitting on the Sofa of Tomorrow, Felix perched on the edge as if he were afraid it, too, would close on him. He seemed relieved to be on his feet again, and perfectly happy to do her bidding.

"I need your biro," said Jane. The pen in her pocket was filled with invisible ink, which would never do for what she had in mind.

Cedric's hand went immediately to his shirt pocket, where he kept his favorite pen, the one with which he was writing his memoirs. "I'm afraid I'm running out of ink," he demurred, thinking it bad luck to lend it to anyone, even Jane.

"I'm not going to *lose* it," Jane assured him, snatching the Montblanc from his pocket. Felix returned carrying a tray of soft drinks and a bowl of Chex Mix.

The Coffee Table of Tomorrow was made of bouncy rubber, and Jane had to write slowly to keep her handwriting even. After a handful of the salty snack, Jane opened the Book of Mormon and, in the space between prayers, listed all the girls she had ever known, liked, dated, loved, and lost, starting with her eighth-form gymnastics teacher. When she reached number 47—Swiss Sonya—she went back and made up Nevada phone numbers for each of them, variations of the Bob's Big Boy Restaurant number on Felix's matchbook.

"Why are you using my Montblanc to deface a prayer book?" Cedric held out his hand, and Jane surrendered the pen and waved the small black book in the air to dry the ink.

"I've got a plan," she said. "In a few minutes, Dougie Smathers will be in my back pocket, and we'll be the toast of the convention."

Felix pricked up his ears at the "we." "I'm ready for action, Agent Bond," he said, saluting her with the hand holding the bag containing the bulletproof swim trunks—the very *heavy* bulletproof swim trunks. He knocked himself out, hitting his head on the Ottoman of the Future as he went down.

"He's going to have a hell of a headache when he wakes up," said Jane as they picked him up off the floor, checked to see if he was breathing, and placed him on the sofa. Cedric unbuckled Felix's belt and undid the top button on his shorts. Jane slapped his hand away. "There's plenty of time for that later," she said. "Come on. We're going to get back into Dougie's good graces."

Dougie was sitting on the steps of the mock lunar space capsule with Agent Pierre Camembert, drinking a martini while perusing a *Playboy* magazine. "I'm going to sneak behind the lunar capsule and listen. You go get another drink for Dougie—and one for me." Cedric seemed stunned by her sudden assurance, and it wasn't until she clapped her hands like a stern schoolmistress that he trotted off to do his part.

Upon closer inspection, Jane saw that the NASA prop was a tin trailer on wheels covered in shiny aluminum foil, with a television antenna hanging off the back. Agents Smathers and Camembert were having a burping contest, and Jane plugged her ears. Could anything be more obnoxious? A minute later they proved the answer to that question, and she held her nose, waving the book in an attempt to clear the air.

"Martini," someone whispered in her ear, and she turned around and saw that Cedric had brought a martini for her, a Tab for himself, and a plate of deviled eggs. "They're loaded with protein and just eighty calories apiece," he whispered, stuffing one in his mouth. Jane ate the olive in her glass and sucked on the mermaid swizzle stick. Unlike her brother, she took her martinis stirred, not shaken.

"Okay, then," said Jane, needing to put all her soldiers in a row. "It seems that Dougie Smathers hates me. My brother. Why?"

"Because you're an obnoxious egomaniac? I mean, your brother," he added hastily when Jane raised an eyebrow.

"Yes, he is an obnoxious egomaniac, but he's always been one. What happened last year to make James alienate his little band of merry men? What's a typical James thing?"

"Drinking. Spending money on expensive clothes. Flying around in rocket ships, in cars that sail and boats that fly. Sleeping with every woman he meets. I'd say your brother's a womanaholic, if there was any such thing." He looked at her accusingly, as if she were one, too.

"That's it, Cedric. He slept with Dougie's *woman*. But what kind of woman would *be* with Dougie Smathers?"

"Mrs. Smathers?" Cedric guessed, and when Jane started to laugh, he clapped his hand over her mouth lest they be overheard.

"My guess is that Dougie and James went after the same girl at last year's convention. Guess who won?"

"So you're trying to convert him by defacing a sacred book? This is not making sense. And now, more than ever, I fear for your mortal soul."

"It's unfortunate, but it was the only little black book I had. This had nothing to do with religion and everything to do with what's *inside:* phone numbers for Genevieve and Colette and Astrid and Babette. Agent 007 is going to retire from the girl game and hand the crown to Dougie."

"And I? What is my role in this charade?" He popped the top of his

Tab, getting the metal ring stuck on his finger. "Shall I try to fight you for it?"

Jane suppressed a laugh. "You stay here," she said, putting the book back in her pocket. "If I need help, I'll say, 'Looks like rain.' Understand?" She picked up her drink, took a sip, and crept around the side of the lunar module, rehearsing her opening line.

"Right-o, Agent Bond," Cedric whispered. Although it involved the destruction of a holy book, he admired her quick, if misguided, thinking. Playing up to Dougie Smathers was completely unnecessary; turning their backs and walking, heads high, out of this room with the inventor in tow would show these men how a true secret agent behaved. Cedric was certain, after chatting up Felix, that he had found his man. He would have communicated that to Jane had she not been so eager to put herself in her brother's shoes. She was obviously enjoying her little foray into spydom, thinking herself quite the secret agent. One thing nagged at him as Jane disappeared around the front of the module. He had seen James Bond's *real* little black book, and it made the London telephone directory look Lilliputian by comparison.

"What do *you* want?" Dougie Smathers said when he saw Jane. He was still wearing the glow-in-the-dark toilet seat around his neck, and in the dim corner of the room, the seat glowed green, giving the whites of his eyes a yellowish cast.

"I want to talk, man to man." Agent Camembert eyed her warily through bloodshot eyes, picked an olive out of his martini, and took aim. Dougie shoved him off the stoop, an act Jane would expect from a schoolyard bully but not the FBI's top Kansas City man.

"Go away, Frenchie," said Smathers. He stuck his face in his martini glass, sucking up three olives with red, rubbery lips. He looked up. "You seem different, Bond. Have you been on a diet?" He punctuated his words with burps. "You're not the man you used to be, are you? The work getting to you?" The belly hanging over the snug waistband of his powder blue slacks jiggled when he laughed. Never had she met a man so in need of a good girdle.

"Let's call a truce, Smathers," she said. "Let bygones be bygones and all that." Pierre was leaning against the side of the module, his arms crossed, listening. Jane tried to sit down, but Dougie planted himself in the middle of the step, like a petulant child, so she leaned against the mock NASA barbecue pit.

"We used to be friends—" she began, and then stopped. If her brother's reports were all fabrications, what *was* their relationship?

"*Best* friends," he snorted, grinding his cigar under his shoe and lighting another. "But not anymore."

"If there's something I've done, you should tell me," said Jane. "After last year's convention, I had a run-in with Dr. Yes and—"

Dougie put up his hand, meaty and pink like a small ham. "I've heard that story, Bond. Remember? I *invented* Dr. Yes. You don't have memory problems, you have loyalty problems. Why, my dog, Dougie Smathers Jr., has more loyalty in one paw than you do in your entire body. We've been friends for . . . how long?"

"A long time," said Jane solemnly.

He nodded and looked into his empty glass with the same wistful expression with which Dougie Smathers Jr. would have looked at an empty water bowl. Jane leaned over and poured half of her drink into his glass, and he brightened. It was something. "Look, Bond, I've put up with a lot over the years. You've stolen every woman I've ever wanted, except my wife. You borrow money and never repay me. You use my clothes to polish your rocket. I never said anything because it was fun being your friend. But last year, when you stole every one of our dates *at the same time* . . ." He shook his head, his big ears, hairy as caterpillars, flapping. "One hundred and thirty-seven women! They *had* to know they weren't the only ones! Where on earth did you put them?" He hiccupped into his glass, lapping up the rest of the gin. "I promised the boys we're not taking the bus to Reno again to look for desperate divorcées." On top if it, the girls had refused to refund their money.

The combination of Space Ice Cream and this disgusting pig made Jane nauseous, and she took a sip of her martini, hoping it would settle her stomach. "How *is* Mrs. Smathers?" asked Jane.

"The missus? She's same as ever. I'm bringing her this toilet seat." He tapped it. "She's home papering the bathroom, and I thought this might be a good gift. No more complaints about late-night mishaps."

"That's thoughtful of you," Jane said. He was a cheap bastard. While he should be bringing her the standard I-cheated-on-you gift of jewelry, the toilet seat was probably all he would be bringing home—besides the clap.

His eyes narrowed. "But never mind my wife. Just lay off the broads."

"I've repented," she said, taking the book from her pocket and tossing it in his fat lap. "Las Vegas is all yours. I have no interest in shagging any woman who would even *think* of shagging you."

Dougie stared at the embossed gold cross on the book's black cover. "You? A Mormon?"

"Open it."

Dougie's mouth fell open when he saw the women's names penned between psalms, and realized what had been given him. "James Bond's little black book," he whispered reverently, wiping his hands on his trousers before flipping through it. "Hey, it's not encrypted. I always imagined it would be."

"It is. I decoded it to save you the trouble."

"Gee, thanks, Bond. I could never make sense of those codes."

"You tell them I sent you," Jane said. "And that you're the FBI's top man in Kansas City."

"'Ow 'bout yor l'ttl bruvah?" he asked, in a dreadful Cockney accent.

"Or sister, if you like."

"Luverly!" he cried, and they had a good chuckle over that, but when they stopped laughing, he looked at the book and scowled. "It's not funny." He tossed the book onto the Astroturf lawn surrounding the module. Someone's idea of life on the moon involved a neat lawn and roasted hot dogs. "I don't believe it. Why would you give up all these broads?"

Because there is a limit to what penicillin can cure, she wanted to say. "Because . . . I'm getting married."

"There's going to be a Mrs. 007? Really? Hey, fellas!" he cried, jumping off the stoop to retrieve the book. "Bond's getting married!" It may have been her imagination, but she thought she could hear Cedric's screams over the hoots and hollers. Suddenly she was the belle of the ball, and agents ran over to toast 007's—and their own—good luck. Champagne was poured all around. Talk of a suitable wedding gift—a

riding mower? a circular bed?—was cut short by Dougie's announcement that *he* would be best man. And, as best man, Bond's little black
book naturally went to him. This last announcement sent a hush over the
room, and Jane could feel the transfer of attention from her to the lucky
winner, which suited her just fine. She had gotten what she wanted. Anyone who wanted to speak to her, from the bed salesman to the inventor
of the top-secret gadget, could without fear of retaliation.

Smathers proposed a toast. "To wedded bliss. If I didn't have my
Daisy, I don't know what I'd do." Surprised and a little touched, Jane
started to raise her glass when he amended his statement. "Why, I'd
have to do my own laundry. *Ha-ha-ha!*"

At the last "ha," Cedric, who had crept around the circle of revelers,
tapped Jane on the shoulder. Startled, she jumped, the leather soles of
her new boots slipping on the slick new Astroturf. She lost her grip on
her glass, and it rolled over her hand; when she grabbed it with her
other hand, she accidentally put her thumb on the stem of her watch,
sending a knockout dart into Dougie's fleshy thigh.

"*Sacre bleu!*" Agent Camembert cried as Dougie fell to the ground, a
tiny trickle of blood running down his powder blue trousers. "There is
an assassin in our midst!"

· ·

seven

The humiliation of appearing in public in a potato suit was too much for
Bibi to bear, and while Bridget, who possessed a more developed sense
of confidence, walked proudly through the Sands casino, her head held
high (not that anyone could tell, as it was covered by a brown shell), Bibi
held back. After a dismal rehearsal, they had taken the bus back here,
bouncing on the seats in the potato-shaped costumes, their clothes having disappeared sometime during rehearsal (they suspected it was the
celery stalk, a tall, cool number with shifty eyes, who stole their cute
Mary Quant shifts).

Having endured more than enough spud jokes from badly dressed tourists amused to find potatoes hanging around the casino entrance, Bibi jumped to life when she saw a truck carrying individually wrapped perfumed hotel soap go around the side of the building. She followed it to a loading dock and, more important, the service lift. When the elevator doors flew open, she stepped inside and rode all the way to the penthouse level before realizing she had missed her floor, and was punching buttons when a man stuck his shoe between the closing doors, forcing them open. In walked two burly men holding up a familiar-looking singer in a paisley-print Nehru jacket. Sammi Martini, America's answer to Tom Jones, was drunk, had been crying, and had obviously allowed too much time between shampoos. His hair seemed to grow only on one side, and when his head flopped over, his bald pate was revealed. Seemingly unaware of his appearance, he leered at Bibi, tripping over his own feet as he lurched in her direction.

Bibi was shocked. This was, after all, *the* Sammi Martini—the warbler with twenty-four-karat pipes.

"You're a beautiful chick," Sammi Martini sobbed at her before collapsing on the dingy, gold shag carpet. Knowing she would always have a head of long, luxurious hair, Bibi decided to feel sorry for him, so when he threw up down the front of his Nehru jacket, she held her nose and handed him a tissue before stepping as far away from him as possible, given the size of the elevator. Sammi Martini's bodyguards stared at the acoustic tiles in the ceiling, rocking on their heels and pretending that Las Vegas's most admired song stylist was *not* on his knees trying to kiss a reluctant potato's hand.

They rode down in silence, two muscle men, a talented girl in a potato suit, and America's coolest cat curled in a fetal position on the floor, sucking his money clip. Covering the singer's head with a black satin pillowcase, one of the bodyguards dragged him through the loading dock to an idling car, a gleaming gold Cadillac with leopard bucket seats and gold piano-key bumpers. The other picked up Mr. Martini's alligator overnight bag and snarled, "You keep your lips zipped, girlie," while pulling a fat finger across his throat. "Or else!" He peeled a couple of C-notes from a thick bankroll and threw them in her face. Bibi let the bills fall to the floor. She didn't like being threatened, especially by a man holding luggage smarter than he was. Had she not been stuck in an awkward cardboard shell, Bibi would have made him pick up the money with his teeth. It was only after the doors closed and she bent down to retrieve the bills—no small task given the bulk of her suit—that she saw the gold martini-glass charm, with an emerald olive and ruby pimiento, nestled in the carpet.

She looked closer. It wasn't a charm, it was a key chain, with one key. She picked it up and examined it. Engraved on the back was SAMMI MARTINI'S PENTHOUSE SUITE, THE SANDS.

"I deserve something for all I've been through," she said. "No one should have to see an aging world-class entertainer in a Nehru jacket!" Emboldened by her prior generous act, she decided to do Sammi Martini one more favor and prune his wardrobe. Bibi thought of what Miss Tuppenny told her before she had left for the States: "Remember, Bibi, you're there to work, not cheat at cards or pick up showgirls." But the boss had said nothing about trading up to a penthouse view, especially one whose occupant had just left for a slumber party in the dypsomaniac ward. Her natural and healthy curiosity about the lives of famous entertainers overtook her, and Bibi folded her fingers around the key to the most luxurious penthouse in Las Vegas, which was also currently the emptiest.

The view from Las Vegas legend Sammi Martini's penthouse suite was a panorama of monotony, miles of flat land dotted with low, boxy buildings and bordered on the west by haze-covered mountains. Inside, the walls were blanketed with platinum records and martini-glass art rendered in every medium imaginable, from neon to string art to the Andy Warhol olive wallpaper in the guest bathroom, where the toilet was a giant hand-blown martini glass. PUSH DOWN ON SWIZZLE STICK TO FLUSH, read the framed needlepoint over the stainless-steel tank. Judging by the hundreds of framed photographs crowding the tabletops, their host had met every celebrity worth meeting: Jackie Kennedy, Frank Sinatra, Minnie Mouse, the entire cast of *Bonanza*—they all had scrawled their admiration to the man whose voice was as intoxicating as a dry martini with a scotch chaser.

"Look—he knows the pope," Bibi said to Bridget as they wandered through the suite trying to shake off the embarrassment of rehearsal. "And Ringo Starr! And here he's got his arms wrapped around Twiggy." She picked up the framed picture and examined it. "He looks drunk. And she's just standing there, letting him hang all over her. *And* he's wearing that same shameful Nehru jacket. What was she thinking? I'm never going to wear my Twiggy-A-Go-Go false eyelashes again!" Bridget grabbed the frame before Bibi could break the glass and tear up the picture.

"Bibi, that's the flagpole out front he's got his arms wrapped around," she said, putting it back on the black marble piano. "We're guests here, and we're going to leave this place in the condition we found it." She was always tidying up after Bibi, and, as much as she disliked playing mother, she couldn't imagine going out on a mission without her. The complete disregard Bibi exhibited for the rules of society made her a good secret agent, and her self-absorption made her a formidable foe, for she was determined to leave every situation the victor. She had a heart of pure larceny and the protective instincts of a guard dog.

Bibi stretched out on the black-and-white-checkered op-art sectional sofa that was as inflated as Sammi Martini's ego; it looked like the most comfortable place to land in a room full of cartoon chairs come to life. Was she the only one who recognized the relationship between blow-up furniture and humiliation? It was sticky in summer and brittle in winter. And forget about sitting on it naked: It clung to bare skin, was difficult to get out of gracefully, and released its grip with a sucking sound that made everyone look at you for the wrong reason. So what if it was easy to move? It was just as easy to go to the bar and flirt with a couple of big butches who would gladly move furniture to Mars in exchange for a date with a friendly girl.

"I wonder if this fabulous pad is how he gets all those movie starlets," Bibi said. The long shag of the white carpet had acted like a million fingers grabbing onto her heels until she fell on this conveniently placed bag of air. She needed a drink, and then another. The one-hour rehearsal had seemed endless, because each time Bridget cried, Bibi had to unscrew the lid of her potato so she could mop her mascara. Big brown lumps at either side of the stage, they had nothing to do for most of the show, just sit and bake until the "Farewell to Freezer Burn" finale. Each time they wobbled to their feet and took their places next to the more glamorous vegetables, Bridget would start to cry and the choreographer would insist they begin at the top.

"I suggest we keep details of our theatrical debut a secret from the girls back in the office," said Bridget, trying to get comfortable on a chrome-and-leather chair shaped like a martini glass, with clear plastic ice cube pillows. "If I see one mention of potatoes in your report to Miss Tuppenny, I swear I'll de-daisy every one of your Mary Quant outfits. What kind of nut has chairs you can't sit on?" she cried, banging her elbow on the chrome frame. "There's a swizzle stick up my bum!"

"Well, darling, you should talk. Your mother has the kind of chairs you can never sit on; either some old king sat there a billion years ago or the queen or her mother sit there when they come to tea. 'Oh, don't sit *there*, dear. See those dimples in the seat cushion? That's the queen mum's bum.' "

Bridget laughed. Bibi always had a wonderful insight into Bridget's unusual upbringing. In Emerald's quest to stay "youthful and now," she had recently furnished her country estate with migraine-inciting op-art inflatable furniture, her passion for plastic lasting an entire week before the furniture was deflated and sent to a missionary school in the Congo.

"If you're not going to make me a drink, peel me off this thing so that I can," Bibi said.

"We were told to go have *lunch*, Bibi." They had taken the box lunches provided them and decided to have their cheese sandwiches, apple, and cookie with a view. They had forty-five minutes before the shuttle bus would be back for them, plenty of time to relax and eat. Unlike most Las Vegas entertainment, *Frost Side Story* was for the Defrost-Off attendees alone, and therefore was strictly matinee material, with daily performances sandwiched between the one o'clock Dinah Shore show and the three o'clock coffee klatch. While performing for a dining audience wasn't uncommon for Las Vegas entertainers, it was when the menu was tuna sandwiches, celery sticks, and Jell-O cubes. Everyone hoped the crunching was kept to a minimum.

"Please," Bibi begged, making a slurping sound as she pulled her head off a Peter Max pillow; one she'd like for her very own. "I need something refreshing and reviving." Bridget unwrapped a sandwich, but Bibi turned up her nose at the Velveeta-and-white-bread confection. "I'm having a liquid lunch today; otherwise I won't be going on that stage," Bibi said.

"You wouldn't be so tired if you hadn't played spin the salad-dressing bottle with Candy Apple while the rest of us were memorizing the Food Pyramid," Bridget said. She headed to the chrome-and-black-leather bar, crowded with tiny airplane bottles of off-brand alcohol. While mixing Bibi a weak scotch and soda, adding three cherries per her request, Bridget noticed the bar's cash register. "Cheap bastard," she said, taking a Tab from the refrigerator for herself and putting a quarter in the drawer. The man had more platinum on his walls than Emerald had in her jewel vault. "He charges for drinks, using airline bottles of alcohol."

Bibi sipped her drink, wrinkling her nose when she tasted it and realized it was more soda than scotch. She raised her glass. "Speaking of cheap."

"Yes, let's," Bridget said, ignoring the implication. A few stiff drinks and Bibi would swing from the chandelier—and Sammi Martini's looked fragile. "Why does a wealthy man who steals airline liquor and sells it to his friends give his penthouse key to a stranger he meets in a lift? Free of charge. Bibi, tell me you didn't spend all our money renting this place."

"No money changed hands. I told you, we struck up a conversation about breaking into show business. He told me about his first singing job at a potato-chip factory's company picnic."

"Something about that does not sound right."

"I told him how mean our choreographer was, and he was so moved I had to give him a tissue."

"And *then* you threatened him."

She shook her head, a cherry stem hanging from her mouth. "The key was out of his hands without any prompting from me. Honest, Bridget, he's just helping two kids with stardust in their eyes."

"Well, this place does have a pool. I guess we could stay until the end of the day."

"Until the end of our visit, you mean. I gave up our room. The luggage is being sent up."

"Bibi, I wish you'd discuss these things with me before changing the plans! If she's lost her transmitter wallet, how will Jane be able to find us?"

"Relax. She knows where we're staying. And I left a message with the hotel operator. If James Bond telephones for Eleanor Roosevelt or Mamie Eisenhower, he's to be put through to Mr. Martini's suite. The kind lady swore she'd handle the message herself."

At 2:50 P.M., Bridget and Bibi walked through the front door of the convention center and showed their badges to the woman at the desk, who examined them carefully and then waved them past. It was a town built around money and the proposition that anyone could strike it big, and it attracted high rollers, many of whom used the excuse of a convention as an opportunity to try their luck. Gem dealers, gun buyers, the makers of Hostess snack cakes—all had visited the convention center at one time or another, and all had been promised a safe and secure place to meet. No one was allowed in without a pass, and anyone caught wandering the halls without one would be chased to the door by a golf-cart jockey.

They arrived in the dressing room with only minutes to spare, thanks to Bibi's refusal to leave the penthouse until she had peeked in every closet, and slipped into their tan tights and gold pumps. "Do *not* lose this," said Bridget, picking up the badge Bibi had left on the dressing table while she did her makeup. "We can't get into the building without it. And why are you putting on lipstick? No one's going to see your face."

"If you *feel* pretty, then you *are* pretty," Bibi quoted her mother. Or was it Audrey Hepburn? She slid the suit over her head, buckling it between her legs, and looked in the mirror. She'd rather be wearing a paisley Nehru jacket. Her last act before making her stage debut was to spray Bridget's very expensive perfume on her shell. "If you *smell* pretty, then you *are* pretty," she said as Bridget tried to wrest the perfume, a gift from Jane, out of Bibi's hand. There was a sharp rap at the dressing-room door. The show was about to begin, and they hurried to take their places at either side of the stage. They plopped themselves on the uncomfortable wooden floor and watched through peepholes as six beautiful, lanky showgirls walked onstage, shoulders thrown back, right hips thrust forward, perfectly balanced on stiletto heels despite the twenty-pound feather-and-steel headdresses. Chins high, the women glided into place in perfect synchronization, their frozen smiles unwavering. The excitement of the Defrost-Off audience seeped through the

closed curtain; they could hear chairs scraping against the floor, programs rustling, and a hundred pairs of sensible shoes planting themselves on the floor. "It's show time!" the choreographer whispered as the
curtain rose and the smell of tuna on white bread wafted toward them,
making Bibi hungry. The three-man orchestra struck up the overture,
and the floorboards began to tremble as the vegetables started to dance.

While they rumbled and sang, parried and stabbed, Bridget kept losing herself in a delightful daydream in which Jane secured the invention,
dropped it in her lap, and then made wild love to her. Becoming sleepy in
the stifling costume, she put her mouth to an airhole disguised as a potato eye and sucked in fresh air, then swiveled her costume so she could
look out into the audience. Rows of neatly dressed women in aprons and
easy-care hairdos sat quietly, clutching their programs, some swaying to
the music.

*"Tonight, tonight, won't be just any night, tonight we're having green
bean amandine!"* the vegetables sang. Bridget sang along softly to keep
herself from nodding off. She could tell that Bibi was having the same
problem. Her arms had fallen to her sides, and she was tilting ever so
slightly toward the audience, worn out, no doubt, from the treasure hunt
through Sammi Martini's closets and the heat of the lights on the cardboard costumes.

Audience members gasped as the ear of corn brandished a giant vegetable peeler. There was cheering when the carrot pulled out an enormous wooden spoon and the two began to spar. Set off by the jumping
and twisting, Bibi began to rock, slowly at first, picking up momentum
when the carrot fell to the floor, fatally sliced. Bridget realized Bibi was
in danger of tumbling off the stage, and she put her hand low to the
ground and pushed the stem of her Ringo Starr watch. A thin invisible
thread with a tiny grappling hook at the end shot across the stage,
catching on the bottom of Bibi's costume. She pulled, jerking Bibi
awake, but the pea pod tripped over the line, setting off a chain reaction
that literally brought down the house.

The corn fell on the rhubarb, who rolled into Bridget, who tumbled off
the stage onto the lap of a Mormon housewife attending the conference
hoping to pick up tips on freezing food for the afterlife. The woman
screamed, and Bibi immediately followed Bridget's elegant example by

rolling off the stage onto a carrot sheet cake baked by a member of the audience for the cast party. While trying to retract her hook from Bibi's potato, Bridget accidentally set off the smoke bomb on her charm bracelet.

"That potato's overcooking!" yelled an audience member, and an exodus ensued; women grabbed casserole dishes, forgetting first to put on oven mitts, and the zucchini raced off the stage sobbing, "My career is over!" The confused musicians launched into "I Feel Gritty," and the choreographer picked up the giant vegetable peeler and chased Bridget and Bibi around the auditorium.

"There's been a costume change!" he cried, swinging the enormous peeler over his head. "We're going to try the potatoes with the skins *off!*"

Cosmetics cases in hand, their clothes in a paper sack, no sadder potatoes could be found in all of Las Vegas. They had lost their jobs and, with them, their excuse for being at the convention center. Even worse, they were forced to take separate taxis back to the hotel because they were too bulky to fit in the same back seat. And when they walked through the casino, they had had to endure clever spud remarks from drunken gamblers. As they ascended to the penthouse in Sammi Martini's private lift, Bridget mixed a shaker of very dry martinis. She had made her stage debut by falling off it, and her pride, like her tailbone, was bruised. "You can walk around half naked in this town and no one notices," Bridget grumbled. She had icing in her shoes, in her hair, and down her back.

"It's absurd! Did you see the leopard walking a woman in a fur bikini?" asked Bibi, using an entire package of cocktail napkins to wipe the remains of a tuna sandwich from her costume. "And yet they make comments at us."

Bridget handed her a drink, and they hopped on barstools and decided to enjoy the ride. The ascent to Mr. Martini's suite was a slow one, no doubt designed that way, to give the singer enough time to ply his victims with alcohol and flattery. Staring at herself in the mirror-tiled wall, Bibi assured herself that even through cardboard she looked good. "I'm keeping the suit. It's not exactly slimming, but I've earned it. No paycheck, no costume."

"You do know it's illegal to smuggle produce from the United States into Britain," Bridget joked as the lift purred to a stop and she knocked back the rest of her drink. The gold doors slid open, and she searched for the key to the suite, taped to the inside of her costume.

"I'll wear it, then. British Airways has no dress code. Did you see that girl on our flight wearing a baggy black dress that did nothing for her figure, with a weird white hat that looked like a seagull?"

"That was a nun, Bibi. Anyway, we have to make other plans. How the hell are we going to tell Jane we're not just down the hall? What if something goes wrong?" As performers for the 1966 Dorothy Duncan Defrost-Off, they were invited to attend any of the panel discussions and demonstrations as long as they stayed in costume and agreed to be photographed with the contestants. It would have been so much simpler to have just *enrolled* in the cooking contest.

"Why *should* we tell her? She hasn't bothered to ring us to make sure *we're* okay."

Bridget frowned as she fumbled for the key. "Agents need full disclosure so they can decide how to operate. As embarrassing as it might be—and I can't believe this is happening on our very first mission together—Jane needs to know what's happened."

"Does she have to know everything? If she needs us, we can always grab a couple of golf-cart jockeys in the car lot, steal their uniforms, and drive right in the front door. Honestly, Bridget, you act like this is a dire situation. We *are* spies, you know."

"You know I hate to lie to Jane." The key in hand, Bridget paused in front of the Mediterranean-style dark wood door. Despite Bibi's objections, once inside, after removing her shell, she was going to ring Jane with the bad news.

"Does she *really* need to know?" Bibi pleaded, certain that Bridget was about to do "the right thing."

"I could say we had to bow out of the show for personal reasons: You slept with the carrot and rubbed her raw." Bibi gasped and Bridget giggled, and fitted the key in the lock, noticing the scratch on the brass fitting. She ran her thumb over it, wondering if it was their doing, and then realized it was a blond hair with a dark root caught on the elaborate scrollwork. No doubt one of Mr. Martini's fans, in need of a touch-up, had peeked through the keyhole and left behind a souvenir.

"I'm beat!" said Bibi when the door swung open. She ripped off her potato shell and stood in the foyer in her bra, tights, and gold high heels and looked around. In the short time they had been gone, the room had been scrubbed and fluffed. The Twister-mat scatter rugs had been polished to a high sheen, new dribble glasses in sanitary plastic wrap were lined up in a neat row on the bar, and the pool water sparkled. The suite smelled of chlorine and pine air freshener. And Jean Naté After-Bath Splash.

"Come on in, girls, and shut the door."

• •

eight

While Dougie Smathers snored inside the lunar space capsule, Jane was tried by a tribunal of drunks and judged guilty of assaulting a federal agent. She was banished for life from all spy get-togethers, and the victim's new best friend, Agent Pierre Camembert, was given the right to decide the punishment. Felix, who had been locked inside the closet of tomorrow by one of his hotel suitemates, had been freed only to find that, in absentia, he had been tried and found guilty on four counts: for consorting with the enemy, having girlish mannerisms, possessing too much enthusiasm, and wearing mismatched socks. Captured at the Soap-on-a-Rope booth trying to buy an Irish Spring gun, Cedric was thrown onto the revolving bed with his friends, their hands lashed to the headboard.

"This is highly embarrassing," Cedric said to Jane as the bed began to spin, picking up momentum until the faces of their tormenters were blurred. "You'd never catch you-know-who in this situation."

"Eyebrow implants!" Jane yelled back, trying to be heard over the cheering. Then she started to giggle, her reaction whenever someone strapped her to a bed and rotated her.

"*Good night ladies, good night ladies, good night ladies, we hate to see you go!*" the agents sang as they gathered behind the headboard and pushed it toward the door. One man ran ahead to measure the width of the double doors, while another calculated the trajectory of the bodies. The doors were pulled open, the cords binding their hands cut, and as they flew through the air into the corridor beyond, Jane vowed that Dougie Smathers would suffer for her humiliation.

When they landed in the corridor, a man in a golf cart cornered them like stray cattle, and a pinch-faced woman wearing a name tag—MRS. VERDA TAYLOR, *1965 HONORABLE MENTION, E-Z BREEZY MARSHMALLOW DOTS*—aired her complaints. She had called security when she heard the ruckus. "What if a soufflé had fallen?" the woman cried, and the man in the golf cart agreed. After a consultation with the building manager via walkie-talkie, it was decided that the convention experience would be nicer for everyone if these three miscreants were removed.

"Thank you, Mrs. Verda Taylor," sneered Jane, reading the woman's badge as theirs were ripped from their shirts. They were herded toward the lobby, the driver of the golf cart poking them with his nine-iron.

"You're welcome, young man," the woman called out, no trace of irony in her voice. Jane looked over her shoulder and saw her smirk.

Bruised and battered, she managed to limp to the station wagon and crawl behind the wheel before Cedric could beat her to it. It was nothing to brag about, really, since he was busy propping up Felix, who had taken a rather nasty hit to the knee. As Cedric eased Felix into the backseat, Jane fished around the glove box for the crumpled grocery list she had seen in there earlier. Thoroughly cheesed, she did a quick sketch of the woman's face—just in case she was a spy sent to keep James Bond from attaining the invention—and wrote the woman's name underneath. Mrs. Verda Taylor. E-Z Breezy Marshmallow Dots. Jane shoved the pad back into the glove box when Cedric slid into the passenger seat and handed the keys to her without a word.

"I believe it's my turn to scream," he said miserably as Felix moaned in the backseat.

"Hold off," said Jane, looking in the rearview mirror and seeing three golf carts headed their way. "They'll think I'm kidnapping you." The engine gave Jane a little trouble, but once she got it started, it purred under her touch. "Hang on, chaps," she said, revving the motor and squealing out of the parking lot.

"Right side! Right side!" Felix shrieked, forgetting his aching knee.

Jane corrected herself, and the ride was smooth after that initial moment of terror. No one said much as they turned onto the main highway and headed for the Strip. Felix passed around Bazooka Joe chewing gum. Cedric wondered if there was too much air blowing from his window. They took inventory of their assorted bruises and bumps and decided they would all live.

Jane punched in the lighter and reached into her jacket pocket for a cigarette. The pack wasn't there. "Have one of mine," said Felix, who leaned over the seat with a pack of Kools in his hand when he saw her frantically check her pockets. She took the cigarette, wanting to appear calm and . . . well, "kool," but felt herself starting to sweat under her jacket. If her cigarettes were gone, the tiny rocket had gone with them. Her wallet wasn't in its usual place, her breast pocket, and it was only when she had checked every possible spot—the space under her seat, the glove box, her shoe—that she admitted to herself that it was gone as well. Someone would find a plain-looking black men's wallet containing a picture of Bridget St. Claire astride a Vespa, a faded picture of Jane's childhood dog, Minnie, a key to a flat in London, and a strange piece of metal hidden behind a leather flap that beeped on occasion. At least she hadn't left it on top of the candy machine at work. "Lost in the line of duty" sounded so much better.

"You shot Dougie Smathers in the thigh with a sleeping dart." Felix Bivens was jumping around in the backseat like a kid, and Jane was beginning to suspect he was *not* the brilliant inventor of a radical new spy gizmo. "Gee whiz. You shot Dougie Smathers in the thigh with a sleeping dart." He sang this refrain over and over, tapping the back of the seat with a swizzle stick, the only souvenir that had survived their launch into space. Poor Felix. His bulletproof swim trunks had been forgotten in the fray.

"It was an accident," Jane said. If the French chap hadn't made such a fuss, she knew she could have smoothed things with Dougie Smathers by offering to set him up with Twiggy. When Agent Camembert had raced to Dougie's side, his arms pinwheeling in an attempt to block another assault, he had knocked Dougie Smathers ass over heels off the stoop. Dougie had, in turn, split the seat of his trousers, revealing a pair of official FBI underwear bearing J. Edgar Hoover's face.

"Do you know *who* Dougie Smathers is?" Felix's backseat bouncing made the car shudder, and the Space Ice Cream in Jane's stomach threatened to make an encore appearance.

"Please . . . sit . . . down," she said, the threat of punishment behind her words. "You're making my eye hurt worse than it already docs." Frenchie had socked her when Dougie went down.

"He's just about the best FBI guy in the entire Midwest. You're name's gonna be mud from Oklahoma to Ohio." He tapped the swizzle stick on the back of her seat for emphasis, and Jane snatched it from him, broke it in two, and tossed it out the window.

"That's littering," said Felix. "In Kansas that'll cost you three dollars."

"We're not in Kansas."

"Kansas." Pumpernickel sighed. "It must be lovely this time of year, especially since people aren't allowed to litter."

"You shot Dougie Smathers!" Felix began all over again.

"I will commit an even greater crime than shooting someone in the thigh if Dougie Smathers is mentioned again," promised Jane.

"James!" Pumpernickel cried.

Felix pinched his forefinger and thumb together and zipped his lip. A companionable short silence followed, while Felix chomped on gum and Jane was able to relax into her own thoughts. How was she going to tell Miss Tuppenny that she had been banned for life from the spy convention?

After a few minutes of blessed peace, Felix leaned forward again and rested his chin on the seat back. "In the thigh," he said. "With a sleeping dart." Then a quick, "Sorry.

Jane grabbed Cedric's soap gun and clocked Felix on the head. Felix grapped with the door handle in an attempt to escape, and Cedric wrestled the gun from Jane's hand.

"I have a compulsion," Felix confessed. "I always have to—"

"Shut your cake hole," Jane snapped. Pumpernickel was still high, but her martini had worn off, and the eye that had made contact with the French chap's fist was killing her. "An eye for an eye," he had said before punching her in the face.

"—finish sentences."

"It's bad manners to leave people hanging," Pumpernickel agreed.

Felix wilted quickly under the heat, and soon he was stretched out on the back seat, snoring lightly. Jane looked over at Cedric and tried to read his mood. She knew he was dying to know where she had gotten a dart gun. "I almost had him," she said quietly, not wanting to wake Felix. "When I gave him the book, all was forgiven." Dougie's thigh would heal and his trousers could be mended, but his ego would not be so easily repaired. It was considered unfashionable to wear official underwear.

Lighting a Kools, his new choice of smokes, Cedric fiddled with the radio knob, searching for the Liberace station, finally tuning into a country-western station. Jane kept quiet. She had lost her brother's place in the spy community, and with it her job. They'd be going home with nothing to show for their stay but some bumps and bruises, a postcard of Wanda holding a dead rattlesnake, and a few thin bars of perfumed motor-court soap. And it was her fault.

"We'll send Agent Smathers a nice fruit basket," Cedric said, surprising Jane. She had expected chilly silence. "Tomorrow all will be forgiven and forgotten, eh? And if it isn't, then the lot of them can just sod off." He pressed back into the seat, one arm out the window, kicked off his sandals, and wiggled his toes, the picture of relaxation. Either he had lost his mind or he was extremely susceptible to the effects of Valium. "When Dougie's boss reads next month's *Spy Digest* and finds out that his top agent threw the great inventor out of the convention, he'll suffer a punishment far greater than the wee prick of a dart. By the way, we'll talk later about how one came to be in your possession. Mark my words, next year we'll be in charge of this meeting. The first thing I'll do is ban alcohol."

"What if you're wrong?" Her voice was a near whisper. "What if Agent Bivens isn't who you think he is? We're looking for someone smart enough to invent something every spy agency wants, and clever enough to pit agents against one another. He hardly seems cunning enough for the job."

"Oh, that's just an act. Under that silky blond hair is the brain of a scientist, under his gold shirt is the heart of a spy, and under his Bermuda shorts—Watch out!" he cried as she ran over a tumbleweed.

"You were saying?"

"Agent Bivens—Felix—had me hold his jacket while he tried on something sporty from the Sammi Martini collection. I peeked in the pocket. Guess what I saw?"

Jane raised an eyebrow. "The invention?"

"Glasses. Thick ones. In a plaid case from a place called Sears. And you know what that means."

"That he has bad vision. We've covered this. I still don't buy it." Jane popped a piece of gum in her mouth and, mindful of Felix's littering ban, tossed Bazooka Joe and his pals into the ashtray.

"I'll wager a penny for a pound that if we got into his suitcase, we'd find a white coat."

"A dinner jacket?" Jane blew a pink bubble, enjoying the *snap* when it popped.

"His laboratory coat!"

Rolling his souvenir dice between his palms, Cedric glanced around the Hungry Honcho, a rustic restaurant that looked like something out of *Bonanza*, with its log walls and antler hat stands, wondering where the cowboys in chaps were. Men in spurs were said to sing Roy Rogers tunes nightly, beginning at five o'clock, and it was already 5:03. Feeling peckish after an afternoon of strenuous sightseeing, he turned his attention to the menu, an Old West wanted poster, the words WANTED: HUNGRY HONCHOS beneath a sketch of a skeleton partially buried by sand.

"I'm a hungry honcho. How about you, Jane?" It was Jane whenever Felix was out of earshot, and Cedric had slipped up only once, turning it into a weak joke about 007's multiple personalities. He blamed it on the relaxant Jane had forced on him earlier, and he swore to stay off the dope from then on. It had served its purpose. He had felt comfortable around Felix, as if they had always been friends. The drug had its uses, but it was not an experience he wanted to repeat on a daily basis. Not even weekly. Perhaps on special occasions, he decided, smiling at Jane, who had been miserable all afternoon and showed no sign of cheering up.

After they fled the convention center, they had gone straight to the Desert Inn so Felix could retrieve his suitcase before Dougie and his friends returned and threw his clothes off the balcony, as they had done the night before, and checked him into a room at the Lady Luck, in downtown Las Vegas, far from the Desert Inn. The first day of their convention was over, and Jane couldn't face spending the day in her hot teepee, so she agreed that some sightseeing was in order, as long as the attraction was air-conditioned. Leaving Cedric and Felix in the car to pore over an entertainment book was a mistake; Jane returned from a quick visit to a service-station lav to find that their next stop was a dice factory in a small town an hour outside Vegas. And now, three hours later, she was in a cowboy restaurant watching a courtship unfold, stuck in the middle of the desert, with a love-struck Cedric and a paper-clip-ordering bloke from Kansas, who was across the restaurant debating a purchase of a porcelain cowgirl statuette for Mother Bivens.

While watching the dotting machine churn out dice, Jane, doubtful that Dougie Smathers's mood tomorrow would be much improved, worked out a plan. If the inventor hadn't already sold to the FBI, out of sympathy for Dougie's tragic tumble off the stoop, the invention could still be in the convention center, hidden amid the merchandise. And, given that Jane was a skilled spy, there were a number of ways she could proceed. Taking a page from the G.E.O.R.G.I.E. playbook of recommended strategies, she could scale the convention center's wall tonight and drop through a window. Not knowing what it was she was looking for would only make the search that much more interesting; that's how she'd play it in her report at any rate. And if the gadget *wasn't* hidden in one of the piles of merchandise there, it was on to Plan B, a search of the Desert Inn—"The conventioneers' friend!"—where the Americans were staying. It would mean donning a maid's uniform, which would mean shaving her legs.

The things she did for England.

"I say, Jane, are you a hungry honcho?"

"No." She put her menu facedown on the wagon-wheel tabletop. Now that she had a minute to sit and think, she wasn't sure if either of her plans was all that good.

"You're worried about Agent Smathers, aren't you? You seemed awfully quiet in the car ride back. Well, you needn't worry about a thing." Cedric seemed unusually relaxed, which Jane put down to a mix of Valium and the pigheaded idea that Felix was *the* one.

"I think *someone* should be worrying," said Jane. "We looked like idiots today, and if we don't go back and claim our ground, the inventor is going to think we're weak." Perhaps Princess Margaret's private number would buy her way back into the club. "I'd be happy to do it alone," she said, making an unsuccessful grab for the keys he had tossed on the table. He got to them first. For a large, slow man, he was incredibly quick.

"That is completely unnecessary," he said, putting the keys into his coin purse and tucking that into his bag of souvenirs. "The 'inventor' thinks of you as his hero. He told me so in the factory gift shop while he selected fuzzy-dice key chains for his bowling team." He sounded a little unhappy about it. Jane could tell *he* wanted to be Felix's hero. She wanted to hit her head on the table until she was unconscious. Must he fall in love during her first real mission?

"If Felix has invented something and wants us to have it, why doesn't he just say so?" she asked irritably. As long as Cedric had the keys, she was dependent on his moods, and today his gauge seemed stuck on daft.

"In a way he has. Before the trial, when we were simply unpopular and not yet hated. Felix and I were in the Bachelor Pad of Tomorrow, testing the lawn furniture of the future, and we had a frank conversation about our experiences in office supply, about the desire to make our mark—*ha-ha-ha*, it's an indelible-ink joke!—on the greater spy world. To be remembered for more than our ability to put a poison-tip pencil in every secret agent's pocket. He revealed that there's something he's hiding from the other chaps in the office. Some *thing*, Jane. I pretended I didn't know what he was talking about, but *I do.*"

"So do I," Jane said, figuring Felix was hiding something more personal than an invention.

This pleased Cedric. He outranked Jane, but she, like his mother, was a person with strong opinions and little patience for his more analytical turn of mind. Finally they were on the same page. Tapping out "God

Save the Queen" on his front teeth with his new plastic-dice key chain, he wondered if it would be unmanly to have a manicure while he was in town; after all, Liberace had them. "Before Felix comes back, there are some things we need to discuss."

"I won't use the women's lav again, I promise."

"Good, because at the factory I had to tell Felix you were in there chatting up the ladies."

Jane shuddered, imagining her brother lounging against the Tampax machine, offering his phone number with every purchase. "He must think I'm a first-class wanker."

"And rude," Cedric added. "I'm afraid that, along with his parking spot and Savile Row discount card, you've inherited the less savory aspects of your brother's reputation."

She reached for the basket of roasted peanuts and popped one in her mouth. "But *you* must insist Felix stop calling you *Sir* Pumpernickel; it's intimidating. I'm James Bond, and you hold a patent for a new type of paper clip; isn't that intimidating enough?"

"*And* I saved the queen," he added, "but let's not quibble. Your point is well taken. I will hide my light under a bushel basket if you will. And you are to apologize for threatening to stuff him into the dotting machine. Thanks to their childish pranks, the Americans have ruined their chances at securing the invention. If you harm Felix, you harm England's chance at spy superiority. Do you want the French to get the invention?"

"Of course not!" she replied adamantly. She popped a peanut out of its shell and flipped it into her mouth. "Fine, no more threats. But *you've* got to stop bending over to pull up your socks. Number-one rule for plaid-Bermuda-shorts enthusiasts: Bend at the knee."

"That's sound advice," he agreed.

"I have some more advice—ask Felix if he's the inventor! What are you waiting for? Mind you, I'm not questioning your judgment; there is certainly something to be said for taking it slow, but, given our circumstance—if he isn't our man, we've got a lot of apologizing to do— wouldn't it be nice to know now, so the question doesn't nag at you all night?"

"Miss Bond"—it was always "Miss Bond" when he was exasperated with her—"in the race between the tortoise and the hare, who wins? Patience, Jane. It's something your generation lacks. Let's have a relaxing meal, open a corridor of communication through convivial conversation, and convince him that the British Secret Service is the best home for his remarkable invention. I'll make him an offer when I'm ready. And you are not to interfere!" He wagged a red-ink-stained finger at her, the one he had caught in the dice-dying machine.

"I have no doubt you will," said Jane, playing with her ring, wondering what would happen if Cedric and Felix were suddenly struck down by narcolepsy in the middle of their meal. She quickly abandoned the idea as reeking of desperation, which she certainly was *not.*

As they had settled the manner, Cedric began perusing the menu, and Jane had a flashback to their breakfast at the Teepee Village, wondering if the guns that were part of the waitresses' red cowgirl outfits here were real, and if they would hesitate to shoot. Cedric read the extensive menu in silence, and when he began to make check marks next to the dishes he would consider ordering, Jane threw down her menu in disgust.

"It's not to your liking?" He raised an eyebrow.

"I'm not eating buffalo," she declared, "if that's what you're thinking. Or a Meat Mountain smothered in A.1. sauce."

"Please eat something. You look pale and tired, and we've got a long and exciting night ahead of us." He responded to Jane's puzzled look with, "We have tickets to Liberace. You didn't forget?"

"You *still* want me to go to the Liberace show?" Fishing an ice cube from her water glass, she held it to her black eye.

"*Shows,*" he corrected her, taking six tickets from his sock and placing them on the table. "Eight o'clock, ten o'clock, and midnight."

"Aren't you going to spend the rest of the night in your teepee worrying about what N. will say?"

He looked at her as if it was the craziest thing he had ever heard, and that's when she knew for sure that he was in love.

"I'd like a scotch," Jane to a passing waitress holding a platter of pork-kabobs, and she imagined her evening with a few hundred other Liberace lovers, when she could be out looking for the invention—and for Bridget.

"Change that to two Clamatos, please. Tonight you'll want all your wits about you."

Jane reviewed her options. She could say it was "that time of the month," but she'd used that excuse last week to get out of a farewell luncheon for an agent who had disappeared in 1952 and had *finally* been retired. She had to get Cedric to ask Felix. It was a match made in Liberace heaven, but Cedric was too clueless—or stubborn—too see it.

"What if Dougie Smathers finds Felix and threatens to kidnap him until he turns over the invention? Or worse, what if he shoves Felix into the sofa and *steals* the invention?" She was getting to him; he was shredding his napkin and wearing his Cedric-to-the-rescue expression.

"I never thought about it like that! Why, Smathers can be an animal!" he cried. "I can't go if Felix will be in danger!"

She groaned and looked around for her scotch. "The correct answer is, you both go. The only way to protect Felix is to never leave his side, and you can't expect him to spend the evening in your teepee. It's like an oven in there; you saw how the heat did him in today."

"But if he takes your tickets, you'll have to stay in."

"But I'm not a brilliant inventor," she pointed out. "No one wants to kidnap me. I have plenty of ways to entertain myself. For one, I'm reading your manuscript. And I want to write a postcard to Bridget. I haven't touched that informative booklet about the Hoover Dam you gave me. And I need to soak my knickers." The mention of knickers was always a good way to kill a conversation.

Cedric looked anxious at the idea of being alone with Felix, so Jane decided to play to his ego. "Cedric, you've been doing this longer than I have, and if anyone can crack a nut like Felix, it's *you*. This is your chance to prove he's *your* man." He nodded knowingly, and Jane knew she had successfully convinced Cedric to ask Felix on a date in the name of the queen. She lit a cigarette, crushed the match in the cowbell ashtray, and looked around for the third member of their party. "Do you think he's jumped ship?"

"I told you, he's calling Mrs. Bivens."

"For the last twenty minutes?"

"Mother and I could talk for hours," Cedric responded matter-of-factly as Jane's scotch arrived, so cold it made her teeth hurt.

"I say, where's my Clamato? It seems to me, Jane, you get served in half the time. On the plane I thought I was going to expire from hunger waiting for my peanuts. Then I got one package to your three. And there were only four nuts in mine. You had an average of six. Why is it you elicit such eager attention from waitresses?"

"It's the old Bond charm," Jane said, propping her elbows on the table and holding out her hands. The waitress put a drink in each. The Clamatos were nowhere in sight, and Cedric coughed loudly, hoping his expression of thirsty consternation would prompt their waitress into re-membering he was there. "Drink this," Jane said, pushing a scotch and soda across the table.

"How do I know if I'm pushing too hard too fast?" Cedric said as he took a sip, angling his head toward Felix, standing at a call box having an animated conversation. Before Jane could answer, the Clamato arrived, with two lemon wedges floating on top and a red plastic lobster stirrer upright in the thick juice. "At last!" Cedric exclaimed, and for a moment he forgot the subject at hand. He took a long sip, letting the goodness of clam and tomato wash away the taste of scotch. "Delicious!"

Averting her gaze, a little queasy at the thought of marrying clam to tomato, Jane said, "You've only just met him; it's too early to say. Some people hang back and take their lead from the other person, and some jump right in. Who do you want to be—Fred Astaire or Ginger Rogers?"

"I'm not much of a dancer," he said. "And I'm not certain secret agents should dance while on duty."

"You're a Ginger," Jane laughed, knocking back her drink. There was nothing she could do right now, stuck out here on a dusty road between Las Vegas and Boulder City, so she might as well enjoy it.

Jane saw Felix heading back to the table, looking pleased and holding a Hungry Honcho bag, and Cedric, nervous about extending the invita-tion to see Liberace, started to fold his napkin into an Appaloosa, as demonstrated on the back of the menu, running out of napkin before running out of horse. He stuffed the lopsided creature into his pocket, and Jane knew that, in the privacy of his teepee, he would fold it until he got it right. Though naïve as a schoolgirl and stuffy as one of the queen's Christmas radio addresses, he had qualities, too, that she admired: his attention to detail, for one; fierce loyalty, whether to queen, country, or a boiled-sweets brand; and a memory so precise it made Jane, who sometimes couldn't remember what she had eaten for breakfast, feel ancient.

"I'm back," Felix said. "And I brought presents, but first you have to answer a riddle. What's fossilized, lumpy in places, and has spent too much time outdoors?"

Cedric blanched, which made his sunburned ears appear even redder, and Jane examined Felix for hint of malice.

"A petrified wood paperweight!" he laughed, opening the bag and dropping three fist-size gray rocks on the table. "Petrified-wood paperweights for everyone!" The composure returned to Cedric's face.

"Sorry I made you wait so long," he said, pulling up a chair next to Cedric. "My mother tried to talk me into coming home. Her lawn needs mowing."

"I did most of the yard work, too, when Mother was alive. Well, I hired a local lad to do it, but I stood nearby to make certain he did a bang-up job."

"She acts helpless, hoping I'll move home," said Felix. "I should have known better than to call her from Las Vegas. She's certain I'm going to let some showgirl talk me into marrying her. I said, 'Mother, there's not enough liquor in the state of Nevada to make that happen.'"

"You don't live with her?" said Cedric, sounding stiff and disapproving.

"Not everyone is lucky enough to have the perfect mother," Jane said, patting his arm. Was she going to have to keep him drugged for the next three days?

"Sir Pumpernickel, my mother is a hysteric. She'd love it if I lived with her, but the next stop for me would be the nuthouse. Say, I think I'll use my wood as a paperweight in my home office."

Suffused with a rush of tender feelings for the man who might as well be motherless, Cedric replied, "Please call me Cedric. And thank you for the authentically western gift. I'm putting mine in the glass case where I keep my snuffbox collection."

"I'm going to use mine to kill Dougie Smathers," said Jane, hoping to lead the conversation around to revenge. (What good was a humiliating situation if you couldn't talk about it later?) But the subject was paperweights.

"Howdy, pardners!" Maxine, their waitress, must have been pushing seventy. The authenticity of her costume, a red cowgirl suit with horseshoe appliqués and pointy white western boots, was diminished somewhat by the addition of support hose and a glittery poodle pin.

"What's your pleasure, cowboys?"

"The chaps in chaps!" Cedric said.

"There's no floor show tonight, folks. It's just me and the mister. What can I get you?"

"Another scotch," Jane said.

Cedric sighed and looked at the menu. Felix was conducting an experiment to see how many napkins his new paperweight could hold in place. Jane was beginning to believe he *could* be the inventor. He kept inventing new ways to drive her crazy.

"How about steak, baked potato with sour cream, and salad all around?" chirped Maxine.

"As long as my sour cream is made of scotch," said Jane.

Seated near the large picture window, they watched the sun sink below the horizon and the neon signs in the distance flicker to life, eating their steaks while Cedric and Felix launched into a political debate that threatened to become interesting. Who was prettier, Lady Bird Johnson or Queen Elizabeth? Which breed of dog was superior, the beagle or the corgi? And what was it like to always be driving on the wrong side of the road? This last, said in unison, caused a fit of giggles that drew queer looks from the lanky cowboys leaning against the bar. Swinging her feet in the silver stirrups attached to her chair, Jane began to relax, her embarrassing exit from the convention drifting away. Someday it would make a good story. And it might have been worse—when they were marched toward the front door, Jane could hear music from the auditorium, and she had been seized by an impulse to break free and run to Bridget. She was glad now that she hadn't panicked and acted like a novice spy. All that mattered was that she obtain the invention, not how she did it.

Mr. Frontier, Maxine's better half, judging by his age and costume, took a seat on the cowhide-covered bench in front of an electric organ, cracked his knuckles, and dove into a loud, off-key rendition of "Tumblin' Tumbleweeds." Holding their forks about their heads like conductors' batons, they sang along, reading off a cheat sheet on the back of the menu. When Maxine trotted out a length of thick rope for the knot-tying demonstration and called for an assistant from the audience, Cedric jumped to his feet. "Pay attention," hiccupped Jane to Felix as he was lassoed and hog-tied in under a minute.

"Huh?" said Felix.

Flushed with excitement, Cedric returned to his seat holding a souvenir rope belt he had made with help from Maxino. Picking up the check with the élan of a man who parted easily with his money, he left a whopping tip, and Maxine and her husband serenaded them all the way to the door.

"Espionage becomes you," Jane whispered in Cedric's ear when Felix crouched down to adjust his sock.

"Tish-tosh," he said, reddening.

Lying across the backseat, her feet propped on the windowsill, Jane drifted off to the sound of the wood-look panels slapping gently against the car, the noise insinuating itself into her sleep, making her dream that someone was being given a paddling. She awoke with a start, feeling disoriented that she wasn't at home in her own bed. Neon lights winked through the window, and she shielded her eyes and looked around. They were parked in front of the Lady Luck hotel, and Cedric and Felix stood in the parking lot saying their good nights. Jane slipped into the front seat and rolled down the window. Mumbling so quietly she could barely hear, Cedric leaned against the car hood and said, "I was curious—would you like to sit together at the closing night banquet?" She recognized Cedric's strategy; the question was intended to suss out Felix's interest in spending more time with him before the real proposal: A night with Liberace.

"I think the seating arrangement's been decided. If I'm correct, we're supposed to sit with our home state. But I'm not pleased at the idea of sharing a tray of crudités with the same men who sent me into orbit."

Jane stuck her head out the window and, seizing the opportunity, said, "Felix, do you want to go see Liberace tonight?"

"Jim, I'm flattered, but—"

Christ, Jane winced. "Not with me. With Cedric."

"Oh! I'd love to go." Felix's voice went up a whole two octaves. "Do you think you could come back and pick me up? That will give me time to shower and change."

Jane had never seen Cedric move so quickly. Felix had barely finished answering when Cedric was back in the car, topping the speed limit by a good two or three miles per hour, the car shaking from the effort.

"The first show is in two hours," he said anxiously, more to himself than to Jane. "I'll need to bathe, shave, comb my hair, and get dressed. Crikey! I don't have a thing to wear! If only mother were still with us, I'd be prepared."

"If your mother were with us, you wouldn't be going out with Felix. You can wear my tux if you promise not to spill Clamato juice on it." Jane was now officially in a better mood, knowing she was free of them, at least for the night. Her first stop, after a long cold shower, would be the convention center.

. . . .

nine

Seated stiffly on Sammi Martini's purple paisley-print inflatable sectional sofa was a plump, fortyish woman with frowsy, dirty-blond hair and dark circles under her eyes, in baggy tomato-colored capri slacks, a stained sky blue blouse, and scuffed white Keds. It was the kind of outfit one might throw on during the night, fleeing from a fire. There was no other way, Bibi thought, to explain the hideous color combination.

Seemingly unsurprised by *their* outfits, the woman spoke in a calm, raspy twang. "Eleanor Roosevelt and Mamie Eisenhower?" There was no trace of irony in her voice when she said their Vegas names, as if the last twenty years of American history had disappeared down her throat from the gin glass clutched in her hand. They nodded, sweating despite the air-conditioning, wondering who this stranger was and how she had entered the suite.

"Who are you?" Bridget finally asked.

"I'm Arleen." The woman picked up the Peter Max pillow and hugged it to her chest, looking as lost as a showgirl without a strut. "But you can call me"—she tried to sit up and make her back a ramrod of indignation but shrugged, as if the effort were too much, and sank back into the sofa—"*Mrs. . . . Sammi . . . Martini!* Now, where is he? Where is my cheating husband?" Her words were meant to be threatening, but she had rushed them out and they tripped over one another. She burst into tears, her jagged nails, bitten and chipped, digging into the groovy pillow. While Bridget fumbled in her purse for a tissue, Bibi ran into the bedroom and dressed quickly—she pulled a hot pink A-line over her head, paired it with white daisy stockings, and finished off her outfit with Mary Quant patent-leather slides—then bounced onto an inflatable purple paisley-print love seat, a match to the sectional sofa occupied by Mrs. Martini in the next room. It would have been nice to come home with a complete set of living-room furniture for once, she thought as she pushed out the last bit of air and stuffed it in her suitcase, behind a black-velvet painting of Las Vegas at night from their original room.

Bibi emerged from the bedroom carrying her locked suitcase, dropped it, and rushed to Mrs. Sammi Martini's side. Despite Bridget's ministrations, the woman seemed no more relaxed than when Bibi had left to pack, clutching the Peter Max pillow so hard Bibi feared it would explode. "There, there," said Bibi, putting her soft hands over Arleen's dishpan ones, and squeezed until she let go of the pillow. Bibi gave her Bridget's pink vinyl cosmetics case to clutch instead. Peter Max pillows were almost impossible to get in London these days, Princess Margaret having snatched up an entire boatload for a swinging pool party.

"It's not what you think," said Bridget soothingly, handing her a cup of instant coffee.

"We barely know your husband," said Bibi. "He was kind enough to let two kids with stars in their eyes and no money for a room of their own stay in his suite." Mrs. Martini calmed down enough to listen to Bibi's explanation, that her husband had given her the key to his penthouse in the midst of an emotional collapse, after she had tended to him as devotedly as any nurse. "Imagine Florence Nightingale, only more attractive." But this seemed to further upset Arleen, unleashing another torrent of tears, sending Bridget to the guest lav for more tissues. She emerged with a glass of water and a Valium, found in the medicine cabinet in a bottle marked "iron pills."

"Arleen, take this. It will calm you down." The Valium was rejected in favor of another gin and tonic. Obviously accustomed to being waited on, Arleen shoved her glass at Bridget, accidentally knocking her onto the Twister mat that united the grouping of mod furniture into a cohesive conversation pit. Righting herself by placing her left foot on blue and her right hand on yellow, Bridget pushed to her feet, aware of how ridiculous she looked, then ashamed that concerns over her appearance took precedence in a situation where they were clearly in danger of being exposed. After preparing another drink for the distraught wife, Bridget followed Bibi's lead and excused herself to go into the bedroom. She slid out of her potato, peeled off the brown tights and matching leotard that were stuck to her skin, ran a comb through her hair and put it in a simple ponytail, all the while assessing their situation. One unhappy wife was no match for two quick-witted girls spies, she told herself as she changed into a lacy white minidress and trendy plastic black-and-white mules. She shut and locked her suitcase and went back into the living room, hoping Bibi hadn't tried to steal the sofa from under the weeping woman. A few comforting words and they'd be gone, back to their old room with no harm done.

The sofa was still there, but Mrs. Martini was not on it. Bibi hardly seemed concerned about the angry woman in the suite; she was measuring the ottoman, wondering if it would fit in her purse, as Mrs. Martini wandered around the room in a daze. While running her finger over the black marble piano bench, Arleen studied the grouping of photographs on the piano top. "There's no picture of me here!" she said sadly, taking in the signed photographs from some of Hollywood's most important stars. "Shirley Booth, Vivian Vance, Debbie Reynolds—how can I compete with *them?*"

"Let's go," Bibi mouthed when Mrs. Martini peeked into the bedroom, shrieking again when she got a look at the light-up mirror over the kidney-shaped bed.

"I'm going to be sick!" Mrs. Martini cried, fleeing the bedroom and dropping onto the chrome-and-leather martini chair. She kicked off her Keds and pulled off her sockettes, white with yellow bobbles at the heels. Curling her toes around the orange yak rug, she looked at them with moist brown eyes. "In just one day, my entire life has been turned upside down," she sighed dramatically. Bridget looked at Bibi, who nodded, and both took a seat on the sagging sofa. They wanted to get out of there, but who could resist juicy celebrity gossip? Sex and sin *were* part of the Las Vegas experience.

Mrs. Martini waved her arms around as if conducting the music of her messy marriage, her gin slopping in her glass. "I was at the dentist getting a crown replaced," she began, "when I was shown an article on Las Vegas's classiest pads in an interior-decorating magazine. Sammi doesn't let me read them—he says they're full of lies that will only upset me. The hygienist saw it and brought it to my attention. You can only imagine my embarrassment. I had just rinsed and spit when I found out my husband has a secret penthouse with fake zebra sheets. Fake zebra sheets! And his kids are sleeping on poly-blend!"

"It's always the children who suffer most," Bridget said wryly. Bibi could only stare at the woman's toes. While her fingernails were chipped and her mascara was flaky, Arleen's feet were beautifully cared for; the skin looked soft and smooth, and the polish, a deep pink with a frost of white, was the same color Bibi was wearing. Bibi didn't know whether to be proud or worried about her own color selection.

"The question is," Bridget continued, "are you going to let him get away with this?"

"You should steal all his stuff," suggested Bibi. "That'll teach him. And because we are *shocked* that a man would lie to his wife, we'll help you. I'll just go powder my nose, and then we can think of something that will get his goose," she said, stepping into the guest bath off the foyer, cosmetic case in hand. There was a nice set of cashmere towels in the bathroom's closet she wouldn't mind having.

"But he's still my husband. *And* the father of my children."

"Hardly reason to let someone cheat on you," Bridget said. Women could be so very silly.

Mrs. Martini's eyes narrowed. "How much does purple shag wallpaper cost, do you think?" she asked.

"What?" Was she redecorating or plotting revenge? Or both?

"I could never figure it out. His records sell in the millions, he gets a nickel every time someone drinks a martini, and his line of men's wear is sold at better department stores everywhere. And yet we're months behind on our bills. Now I know why my household budget hasn't increased since 1959—it's so he can live like a *playboy!*"

"You should leave him," Bridget said automatically, as if she were speaking to her mother about any one of her seven husbands.

"It's my fault." Wiping her nose on the sleeve of her blouse, she implored Bridget, "Be honest. Is it my *hair?*" With a closer look under the lava lamps, Bridget spotted the gray strands in Arleen's faded, shoulder-length, dull blonde flip, which had lost its height in the Las Vegas heat. Like many celebrity housewives married to men who were seldom home, Arleen Martini had made the obvious mistake of using the medicine cabinet in her bathroom solely to store her pep pills. Had she bothered to look into the mirror on the front of the cabinet, she would have seen a lackluster mane and a faintly perceptible mustache.

Bridget's green eyes shone with determination as she flipped open her cosmetics case and took out the bottle of peroxide she used to bleach Bibi's roots. There was little she could do about a bad marriage to a selfish spouse, but she could make Arleen Martini feel a bit better about herself. "Is there a plastic shower curtain in there?" she yelled to Bibi, still shopping in the guest bath. "And there have got to be rubber gloves somewhere around *this* place."

Bibi flushed to cover the sound of a diamond-encrusted towel hook's being yanked off the wall. They were going to either kill Arleen Martini or do her hair, she thought, and the cheerful quality in Bridget's voice helped Bibi guess correctly that it was the latter. She knew that tone. Another poor little kitten had lost its mittens. The self-absorption of the distressed was always exhausting; still, a new look did tend to revive one's spirits. Perhaps Mrs. Martini would stop crying long enough to realize she was not the *only* one with problems. She may have a cheating husband with bad taste, but at least she had never been tossed out of the convention center as women in aprons threw carrot sticks at her.

Bibi ripped down the shower curtain and emerged from the bathroom with the makeshift apron to find Mrs. Martini with her hands flattened over her hair while Bridget mixed a white paste that would brighten her natural blond color and hide the gray. "Is it going to make me look cheap?" whimpered Mrs. Martini. "What if people can tell?"

"Only your hairdresser will know for sure," Bridget assured her as she cut a hole in the shower curtain and pulled it over Arleen Martini's head. This was like the old days, when she and Bibi went door-to-door giving free beauty makeovers to the wives of high-ranking government officials. Bibi would give them a facial, covering their eyes with cucumber slices, then go off to snoop through their husbands' study while Bridget colored their hair. It was a strategy they used until last month, when they were promoted to full-time spy status.

While Bridget and Bibi touched up her dark roots, Mrs. Martini told them about her home in Indiana, a happy home with a sturdy picket fence, an automatic lawn-sprinkler system, and a double-car garage, but no husband.

"Sounds lovely," Bridget said, thinking the woman should thank her lucky stars and just go home and change the locks.

"I had the perfect life until I found out *from my dental hygienist* what kind of man my husband really is. When she showed me the magazine, I told her that it must be another Sammi Martini they're talking about, but the photograph of him sitting in that ridiculous olive chair did it. She swore she'd keep it to herself, but by now it's all over town. If it weren't for the kids, I'd climb to the top of the giant neon martini and jump." Bibi blanched and shot Bridget a look of alarm. Why were they doing this woman's hair if she was just going to mess it up?

Bridget put a thin rubber swim cap over Mrs. Martini's head and set her under the hood of Bibi's dryer for twenty minutes with an Italian *Vogue* and another cup of Nescafé. Mrs. Martini exclaimed over Italian fashion and hairstyles one minute and lamented her own cruel, drab existence the next, talking loudly enough to be heard over the hum of the dryer. *"When I married that man, his own mother told me that I'd regret it. His own mother! When a man's mother knows he's no good, he's no good!"*

Trying to ignore her, Bridget and Bibi lounged on the Twister mat, playing crazy eights with a deck of nude-showgirl cards from the bar.

"Let's go," said Bibi, knowing that Arleen couldn't hear them with hot air blowing at her head. "Let's grab our suitcases and run."

"We can't leave her with wet, unset hair," sighed Bridget. "It would be cruel. I guess it's no worse than listening to *your* romantic problems."

"Do you promise that the next time you have the impulse to do good, you'll ignore it?" Before Bridget could consider the question, the egg timer chirped—it was time for Mrs. Martini's wash and set.

The next twenty minutes tried Bridget's patience almost to the breaking point.

"I sacrificed everything for that man," complained Mrs. Martini as they washed the bleach from her hair. "I gave him a home, two children, and the biggest closet in the master bedroom. What more could he want?" she moaned as they set her hair on empty orange-juice cans.

"And now the best years of my life are over, and his are just beginning!" she wailed when Bridget put her back under the dryer.

"He used to say that we were like a pair of old shoes together," she sobbed as they unrolled her hair. "A perfect fit!"

"I like it!" she cried when they brought her a mirror and she saw her glamorous new blond bouffant. "Now there's only one thing I need," she said, and reached into her battered straw purse to remove a pearl-handled pistol.

"Bullets?" gulped Bibi.

"No, I've got those." Mrs. Martini smirked. "Your money. Give me all of it, or it's *finito* for you two." If was as if she were just realizing *now* that she was supposed to dislike the two young beauties she had found in her husband's secret penthouse. She took aim at Bridget.

When Bridget gasped—armed robbery hadn't been the crime that had come to mind the first time she stepped over the threshold into this monument to infidelity and bad taste—Mrs. Martini looked puzzled, then realized it was the ladylike pistol in her hand that was upsetting her. "I'm not going to shoot *you*," she said. "I was aiming at the swag lamp in the corner." Obligingly, Bridget ducked, and Mrs. Martini laid waste to the lamp and a smiley-face candle in one shot. "I used *finito* to mean the end of your visit to Las Vegas. I'm not going to hurt you, but if you don't cooperate . . . well, my husband has friends. Big friends. And I'm friends with their wives."

Mrs. Martini made them empty the contents of their purses on the coffee table, and Bibi hoped she wouldn't notice the Peter Max pillow in her pocket. "*Finito* sounded so final," Bibi said, hoping to distract Arleen with a chat about foreign languages. "Really, who uses it in everyday conversation these days?"

"My husband," Mrs. Martini said. "After relations."

"I wish she hadn't finished the gin," Bridget said under her breath as she emptied her change purse onto the coffee table and slid the contents across the glass top. When her thumb brushed a smoke-bomb nickel, she hesitated, considering their options. Their cosmetics cases, containing their weapons, were parked in the foyer, too far away to get to without a fight, and despite the woman's assurance that she was merely "redecorating" her husband's home-away-from-home and could never shoot a human being, Bridget didn't trust her. She pushed the coins across the table, palming the smoke bomb.

While Mrs. Martini robbed them of every penny, including the cheap poker-chip earrings Bibi had lifted from the gift shop, she did a spot-on imitation of a broken record stuck on a song called "My Man, He Done Me Wrong." "I've got people waiting to be paid—the grocer, the dog groomer, the pool man. And what does my husband do? Have a flip-out without giving me my allowance first when he knows perfectly well the bug man is about to sue us." She took aim at the piano and with three shots laid waste to three starlets' photographs.

"That's some sharp shooting for a nutcase," said Bibi, deliberately wanting to unhinge her. When Mrs. Martini whirled around to confront her, Bridget jumped her from behind, and the three tussled on the shag carpet until Bridget was able to relieve Mrs. Martini of her weapon. While Bridget held her at gunpoint, Bibi frisked her, getting their money and her earrings back, then tore the Twister mat into strips and tied Mrs. Martini to the heated towel rack in the guest bath, leaving enough slack so she could use the facilities or lounge on the polar-bear bath mat. Before they left her, Bridget made sure their prisoner had a glass of water, a snack, a portable radio, and a fashion magazine to read, in accordance with the Geneva Conventions.

"We'll call the front desk in an hour and tell them you're up here," promised Bridget. That would leave them enough time to decide on new identities, create a disguise, and check in somewhere else. Mrs. Martini struggled to say something, but Bridget refused to untie the dotted strip around her mouth for even a moment. "If you take a nap, do it sitting up. Otherwise you'll ruin your hair," she said helpfully.

"It really does look nice," said Bibi as they tried to wipe every surface clean. Rather than wash the entire plastic sofa, which was especially dangerous as it retained fingerprints beautifully, they deflated it and shoved it into Bibi's suitcase. Bibi had gotten her wish—she now owned her first set of matching living-room furniture. Before they left, Bibi pulled a twenty from the wad of bills she had recovered and stuffed it down the front of Mrs. Martini's blouse. "Buy yourself something nice, Arleen. Baggy capris and a shapeless blouse don't do your figure justice."

"We left our potato suits!" Bibi cried as Sammi Martini's private elevator delivered them, in air-conditioned comfort, to the lobby.

"Never revisit the scene of a crime," said Bridget, behind the bar making a couple of quick margaritas. Honestly, she had become quite a lush on this trip. "I don't know why you would want those ugly things anyway." She handed Bibi a frothy pink drink.

"I wanted the gold shoes," Bibi confessed. "They made me feel tall." British fashion favored low heels or flats, and the gaudy high heels appealed to her. "I wouldn't have worn them very often. Just on *special* occasions."

"I'll buy you a pair that fit," said Bridget, raising her glass, refusing to admit she'd had the very same thought. The ride was over far too quickly, and they took their drinks with them, mindful of fingerprints.

"It's the least I deserve, considering what I've been through today," said Bibi as the elevator came to a smooth stop and the doors opened onto the lobby, across from the front desk, in clear sight of a row of bellhops. "There are ladies in need of assistance," Bridget muttered, dragging their luggage out of the elevator as the men pretended they weren't there.

"There are ladies in need of assistance!" Bibi yelled.

"We're not allowed to help any of the *ladies* coming from Mr. Martini's penthouse," one explained, leering at them. "On orders from Mrs. Martini."

"She lied to us!" Bibi hissed as they struggled with their luggage, much heavier after her shopping spree. "She knew all along about this place!"

"Well, she fooled me. We might have to lose some weight," Bridget said, helping Bibi push her suitcase while holding onto her own bag, cosmetics case, a hatbox filled with shoes, and her margarita glass. If James Bond could drink while skiing, surely she could move a little luggage through a hotel lobby while imbibing. "What did you steal when I wasn't looking?"

"Just a few things for the flat."

"Good." She took a sip. "I noticed while I was wiping down the lava lamps that the yak rug was missing."

"Actually, while you were busy rinsing Mrs. Yakety-yak's hair, I tossed that fabulous rug over the balcony so we could get it later. I think it might have fallen into the pool." She looked at Bridget with puppy-dog eyes, but her friend shook her head and gave Bibi's luggage a kick forward. "'She couldn't resist stopping for the yak rug—and ran right into the arms of the law.' Is that how you want to be remembered?"

Bibi looked horrified. "I want to be remembered as a top agent and a great kisser."

"Then push!" Between the front desk and the front door was a long aisle that ran through the casino, flanked by slot machines. A short time ago, they had passed these very same people, their heads bowed from the weight of their costumes and shame. They were going to exit with dignity.

People seemed amused by the sight of two pretty girls loaded with luggage slowly making their way toward the door, but none of them offered to help, afraid to break a winning streak or lose their place at a slot machine that was surely on the verge of paying off. They made it to the last row of slot machines, and Bridget went outside to hail a cab. Perched on her suitcase, Bibi opened her cosmetics case and fished out her compact. Her face was shiny from the exertion, and she ran a powder puff over it, then redid her lips. Reflected in her compact mirror was the pool area of the hotel, and Bibi squinted, certain she could make out a furry orange blob on a chaise longue.

"I'll give you a dollar to watch our luggage," Bibi said to an elderly woman in a pink-and-white sleeveless gingham shorts set, pointing to her suitcases. The old woman's face, wrinkled as unpressed linen, lit up at the offer. She looked into her bucket—the white paper bottom was visible beneath a thin layer of coins—then looked at Bibi. "Five dollars."

"Mother, don't be greedy. A dollar will do." The woman's daughter, a perfectly attractive middle-aged woman, seemed to be trapped in a peculiar kind of hell reserved for daughters with overbearing, unfashionable mothers: Her outfit was identical to the old lady's, down to the white patent-leather purses hanging from their arms. "We'll guard your things with our lives."

Bibi smiled her thanks, then skipped back through the casino and out the side door to the pool, and came back cradling the rug. The daughter helped her squeeze it her suitcase, sitting on top so Bibi could snap it shut. The sides bulged, and Bibi knew it wouldn't be long until Bridget guessed what was inside.

"There's a cab waiting," said Bridget, returning for the luggage. Bibi picked up her suitcase to drag it behind her back. It became clear to her that her greed had finally overcome her good judgment, when she could hardly stand up straight from the heavy bag. She vowed to rein in her less savory habits and count to ten before nicking something again. (And to invent an expanding suitcase in case she broke her vow.)

Just as she was about to embrace reform, a loud *pop!* made her turn her head in time to see her bag explode dresses and nighties and knickers. The yak rug, the source of the problem, knocked over a tall, cylindrical ashtray, and cold ashes and sand flew into her face, making her sneeze. When she sneezed, she dropped her cosmetics case, which, like her suitcase, popped open. The gun she had taken from Mrs. Martini flew into the air, hit a slot machine on its way down, and went off. The bullet narrowly missed giving a card dealer a new part in his hair, embedding itself in a portrait of Sammi Martini hanging above the blackjack table. The eyes-in-the-sky surveillance cameras, set into the ceiling and operated by men crouched in a crawl space, started to swivel.

"Let's go!" Bridget said, grabbing Bibi's arm.

"Please don't kill us! Darlene, give them your money!" The old woman who had watched their luggage stepped back, her hands in the air, the palms black from the nickels she'd been greedily stuffing into the slot machine.

"We don't want your money," said Bridget.

"It *would* come in handy," said Bibi.

Darlene held out her bucket.

"We're not going to take your nickels," Bridget said. "This is *not* a stickup."

The old woman leaned closer, cupping her ear. "What'd she say, Darlene?"

"She said this was a stick-up, Mother."

"*No!*" Bridget shook her head. She glanced out the door. The cab was still there. "I said this is *not* a stickup."

"Huh?"

"I'm being taken hostage, Mother. Don't wait dinner." Darlene took her mother's coin bucket and smiled demurely, like a girl earnest to be asked to dance, and patted her straight brown hair, held off her face with a red plastic kitten barrette. "I like your outfit," she said to Bibi as she left her mother's side to help them with their luggage.

"Thanks," Bibi said. "It's Mary Quant."

Casino guards, alerted to a robbery in progress on the floor, closed in on them. Tossing the smoke bomb on the stained red carpet, Bridget grabbed Bibi and with Darlene's help, made it to the door with both luggage and nerves intact. Once outside, Bridget and Bibi ran as fast as two girls wearing leather-soled slides and carrying heavy luggage could, throwing their bags, and then themselves, into the cab.

"Thanks, Darlene," Bibi said, shoving the overly helpful woman out the door. They already had enough baggage. "Don't forget," she waving, the bucket of nickels out the window. "*Mary Quant!*"

They changed taxis three times along the Strip, then hitched a ride with a woman headed west in an old aqua Cadillac, who dropped them at the Teepee Village Motor Court outside the city limits, which offered the cheapest rates around and was a comfortable distance from the Strip, where it was widely known that Mamie Eisenhower and Eleanor Roosevelt were wanted for armed robbery. According to KMOB radio, they were the leaders of a gang of female casino burglars, preying on trusting tourists: *"Last seen carrying a bucket of nickels and a stolen yak rug, they are to be considered armed and extremely wily. Be on the lookout for two girls, short but still attractive, with New Jersey accents."*

As spies, Bridget and Bibi were accustomed to being misunderstood. It rankled a bit that the Indiana accents they had worked so hard at weren't as spot-on as they had imagined, but it was the "short but still attractive" part of the description that bothered them most.

"'Short but still attractive.' What is this—the land of *giants?*" Bibi snorted as they entered their teepee and dumped their luggage on the bed. "Look at this room, for example. The ceiling must be ten feet tall in the middle. No one seems to care that the *men* are runts. I'll bet Sammi Martini's trousers would look like clam diggers on me."

"There's nothing we can do about our height," said Bridget. "But, clever spies that we are, we *can* change our identities." The woman who dropped them here had been nice enough to take them to a grocery store and wait while the girls ran in for Lady Clairol Ash Brown #31 and two cans of Aqua Net. Bibi had been too busy perusing the candy selection to realize that ash brown looked exactly how it sounded.

"I'm too dusty to think about a new identity right now," said Bibi, going into the bathroom and turning on the cold tap, waiting for the rusty water to clear. The concrete teepee was a far cry from the luxurious penthouse they had occupied a scant hour before. The room was stifling, with only a tiny window for ventilation, its panes coated with dust and dead flies. The bed, a hard twin mattress set atop carved logs and covered with a scratchy-looking Indian blanket, did not vibrate, rotate, or levitate. Even with the door wide open, the air was thick and oppressive. The closest thing to a pool was the plastic ice bucket.

Bridget stripped the blanket off the bed and fell onto the cool sheet. "The proprietress didn't even ask my name. She just took the four dollars and gave me the key to this palace."

"We can't stay here," Bibi said, emerging from the bathroom with a scrubbed face. "This soap has left a nasty film on my skin."

Bridget fanned herself with the *Nevada Racing News* she found in the top drawer of the bedside table, stuck in a Gideon Bible. Kicking aside her ruined sandals, Bibi gingerly lowered herself into the twig chair facing the bed, immediately feeling a splinter in her left buttock.

"We've really botched this mission," Bridget sighed in defeat. "Why did this have to happen on Jane's first time out as a double agent?"

"Isn't there *any* comfortable place to sit in this town?" Bibi said, pulling the splinter from her bum. She picked at the pink polish on her nails, gummy from the heat. "If you really think this through, Mimi's the one to blame. She worked our nerves for months, so naturally we're all off our game."

"How did she work *your* nerves? She wasn't harassing *your* girl-friend."

Shrugging, Bibi finished one hand and started on the other, leaving pink specks on the orange yak rug she had placed under her feet. "This may come as a shock, but I was shagging her. I'm sorry I didn't tell you sooner."

"I live with you—I knew all along. I recognized her evil cackle through the bedroom wall."

"I didn't set out for it to happen. We were in the darkroom developing microfilm, and she said the safe lights really brought out the blue in my eyes."

"They're brown."

"Last month I found out she was sleeping with another agent," Bibi said, chewing on a nail. "It's almost too painful to discuss."

"Who?"

"Sylvia Birdsworth, the cute brunette from the cosmetics factory. The one who was developing the vanishing cream. Mimi must have stolen it."

"There's a thief in our midst? Shocking. Anyway, weren't you sleeping with Agent Birdsworth, too?"

"I found them in bed together. That's when things got really sticky."

Groaning, Bridget put the thin, lumpy pillow over her head. "I don't want to hear how this story ends."

"You will eventually," Bibi shrugged. "You're not going to tell Jane I slept with her archenemy, are you? I really don't see why you should."

"I haven't yet and won't, if you promise to get your head examined." Bridget tucked the pillow under her head and closed her eyes. "I'm too hot to care. Sleep with anyone you like. Except Jane."

"She won't even flirt with me, and I'm the prettiest girl I know," complained Bibi, flipping open her cosmetics case and examining G.E.O.R.G.I.E.'s new line of nail colors. "I think I'll try Orange Flip." The description of the robbers had mentioned pink nail polish. Someone in that casino had been watching her closely. It had to have been poor, desperate Darlene, so eager to be kidnapped and made over.

"If Mrs. Martini hadn't caught us, we'd be swimming in a cool pool, in an air-conditioned room," Bridget sighed. She was weighing their options; none involved running to Jane for help.

"We'd be sitting in a better class of uncomfortable chairs." Bibi propped her feet on the edge of the bed and unscrewed a bottle of nail-polish remover. She could think more clearly with prettier toes. "Who do you think told her we were up there?"

"I suspect she has an arrangement with the bellhop who brought up our luggage. You didn't tip him, did you?"

Bibi scowled. "Men have enough of our money. But it could have been anyone. The choreographer, say, or any one of the vegetables. I might have mentioned our new accommodation to the carrot."

"Oh, Bibi, We've made so *many* new friends here."

. . . .

ten

*J*ane's tuxedo fit Cedric well enough, with the padding that camouflaged her curves removed and the cuffs and sleeves taken up a few inches by Wanda, who told them her story while measuring Cedric's inseam. Wanda turned out to be the wife of the owner, manager, and sullen short-order cook known as the Chief, who had owned the motor court for almost twenty years, buying it after the war from the original owner who was happy to retire to Arizona and leave his beloved teepees in the hands of a former Marine. Shortly after purchasing his first headdress, he met Wanda at a strip joint on the seedy side of town and proposed to her that very same night. She was happy to say yes, to exchange her high heels for a pair of comfy moccasins. It was getting harder each year to make her tassles twirl, and the idea of owning a small business, even concrete teepees in the middle of no-man's-land, made her snatch up the proposal the way a gambler pounces on a stray chip.

"It's not a woman's town," she told them, kneeling on the buffalo-hide rug and pinning Cedric's cuffs. "In this place there are only two ways a girl can support herself without landing in jail: You're either dancing for men or cleaning up after them. Now I do both," she laughed. "And I've got a life sentence. I told him the day we got hitched—if he screws around, I'll kill him." Holding his arms stiffly at his sides, like a soldier at inspection, Cedric let a small, dry laugh escape his lips.

"No kidding, Sir Slumberknuckle. I keep a gun in my hair-dryer hood in case he ever comes home smelling of someone else's cheap perfume," she said cheerfully. He stood very still as she threaded a needle and made a series of quick, neat stitches. "Turn around," she ordered. The suit judged a perfect fit, she removed the pins from his cuffs and sleeves, stuck them in her beehive, and sat back on her heels to survey her work.

"There you go, you're all set. The monkey suit's real nice. Very sharp. But I'd ditch the horsehair if I were you. I made the Chief get rid of his right after we became man and wife. I buried it in the cactus garden." She said this to Jane, who knew tonight she would find a shovel by her door. "Really, Sir Slumberknuckle, whoever this gal is, I guarantee she's going to like you just the way you are," Wanda insisted. "With your classy accent, all you'll have to do is spread some dough around, and the dames will be dropping like flies."

"How disconcerting," he murmured, patting his new toupee.

Rolling her eyes at Jane, Wanda pointed out the window, then pantomimed digging a hole. "Well, fellas, I gotta get dinner started before *The Dating Game* comes on." She tidied as she talked, straightening the cowhide lampshade on the wagon-wheel lamp, wringing out the soppy bath mat Cedric had left on the floor, and checking under the tub for scorpions. "Centipedes—ugh," she said, peeling three of Jane's scars off the sink basin and flushing them down the toilet.

"Do you really think she'd kill him?" asked Cedric after Wanda had gone, as he combed his new hair in front of the lav mirror. Wanda's words hadn't dampened his enthusiasm for the mat of lustrous blue-black hair perched atop his head.

"And miss all that stimulating conversation?" Jane pocketed the roll of wig tape from his open suitcase. Standing in the doorway, she looked over his shoulder into the mirror; under the bare bulb, even her brother's face looked unattractive.

"With your pale complexion, I think a light brown would look more natural." Picking the cellophane wig bag out of the trash, she pointed out the color guide printed on the package. "It says here, 'If your complexion is pasty, stick with the medium blonds or subtle warm browns, in the lighter shades.' Is that my comb?"

"Is it?"

"It has my name on it. See—007-and-a-half. It's from the shaving kit N. gave me for Christmas. Where's yours?"

Cedric stopped admiring his dashing new do. All he had gotten was a card—a pencil drawing of the Secret Service's secret London office building, dripping with fake sparkly snow, and a rubber-stamped *'From all of us to all of you'* on the inside.

"Don't you think it makes me look like a matinee idol?"

Jane shook her head. "Bridget says harsh color ages pale skin."

"She *is* a cosmetics sales representative," he sighed. "And she did pick out that blue sweater everyone compliments me on." Jane leaned over and peeled the fake stab wound off his cheek and sent it down the toilet after the centipedes. She had dozens more, on a handy stick-'em roll. "I don't understand why you're adding new scars to your face when you paid through the nose to have your real one removed."

"But that was ugly. Yours are dashing."

"They're itchy."

"What about these? I got them today at the Have To Have Hairpieces booth." He held two narrow, furry strips of synthetic hair to either side of his face and gave her a toothy smile.

"You look a Labrador retriever. Felix already knows you're a little thin on top. So is he. If you show up wearing that thing on your head, he'll feel bad he didn't pack one, too. He likes you. Fake scars and hairy flaps aren't going to change that."

He peeled off the toupee, made in India of 100 percent human hair, gave it a final pet, and handed it to her. "It's so soft," he said.

"It's just like having a little dog," Jane said, stuffing it back in the bag.

A half hour to show time, and he was finally ready. Standing stiffly by the station wagon, blinking from the flash of the Instamatic, his smile was tight. Even she was nervous.

"Have a good time," she said. "Good luck opening that corridor of communication." Felix was not the inventor, Jane thought, but he was a lifesaver. "Stay out as late as you want. Don't worry about me. I'm turning in early. Do you have enough money?" she asked, brushing dandruff from his shoulders.

"I've a ten in my wallet and another in my sock."

"Tickets?"

"In the other sock."

"The blank check?"

"It's where no one would think to look for it," he assured her.

"Don't put your hands in the pockets," said Jane. "It ruins the line of the suit."

"You're certain my medal from the queen isn't too ostentatious? I wouldn't want to outshine Liberace."

"Not bloody likely," she said, opening the car door. "Better get going."

"Mother always said medals make a man more attractive than he actually is," he explained, sliding into the car after first wiping the seat with his handkerchief.

"Do you have another handkerchief—a clean one?" Cedric was a man who was always leaking—runny nose, watery eyes, clammy forehead. "If you need to blow or mop, do it in the gents'. Secret-agent liaisons should have a little mystery to them. Hurry. You don't want to miss Liberace flying onstage in his ermine cape." Feeling like a proud parent, she sent him on his way, waving until the rusty station wagon turned onto the highway and disappeared into the inky night.

Cool from a nice long shower, the bandage that bound her breasts in an untidy pile on the bathroom floor, her fake forehead cooling in the ice bucket, Jane stretched out on the thin patched sheet in an undershirt and boxers, smoking and finishing the now lukewarm Fresca that Wanda had left behind. Cedric had left her his manuscript should she become bored while all alone at the edge of civilization. Half expecting a pop quiz in the morning, she propped the 1,257-page manuscript, including a dedication to his mother that ran on for twelve of those pages, in her lap and adjusted the cowhide shade on the lamp next to the bed. Fanning herself with the *Nevada Racing News* she'd found in the Gideon Bible in her nightstand drawer, she flipped through the manuscript until she finally came to Cedric's account of his birth, 613 pages in.

Chapter Seventeen

I Am Born.

As you may have already guessed, it is I, dear Reader, who cut short my mother's theatrical career. A gifted thespian, she had shared the stage with Sir Laurence Olivier and appeared for well nigh onto a decade as the Virgin Mary in hundreds of religious tableaux enacted in theatrical venues throughout England. On 3 October, 1917, this great lady stepped down from the stage to give birth to her only child, not the son of Christ but rather the progeny of Captain Ethelbert Thaddeus Pumpernickel of Her Majesty's Royal Navy, a ten-pound bouncing baby boy imbued with his mother's flair for dramatics and, as the years would reveal, his father's somewhat unfortunate hairline. Whilst in bed recovering, this shining example of maternal love was visited not by three wise men bearing precious gifts but by three stagehands with knitted booties done up by their wives, in the colors of green and yellow and blue.

Jane hoped that when he left his mother's womb, the pace would pick up. She flipped ahead; a few hundred pages later, he was still in nappies. Definite doorstop material. There should be one in every home, that's what she'd tell him, wishing she knew how to help without damaging his fragile ego. This book meant the world to him, and he had worked on it night and day for seven months. The publisher was expecting a boffo bestseller, full of juicy royal tidbits and heart-stopping action. Jane knew someone had better tell Cedric he was prancing down the wrong path—and soon, so he could fix this sodden lump.

"Another job for Bridget," Jane said, tossing the manuscript on the bed. Not only was her girlfriend a better spy—Jane should have *never* relied on her brother's reports—she always knew what to say and how to say it. She'd tell Cedric the truth and make him feel grateful that someone with her taste and refinement had taken an interest in his success. Bridget's sweet nature tempered Jane's impatience with Cedric's stubbornness. The subject of Cedric's love life came up one night when Jane and Bridget were lying in bed, Jane exhausted from work but unable to sleep after a day filling out expense reports for her last mission and listening to Cedric complain about the lonely life of a bachelor. Joining the Lonely Gents' Pen Pal Club had only brought him smutty pictures and requests for cash from prisoners at Wormwood Scrubs, and the Flaming Gardenias had turned out to be a gardening club for female retirees. Jane announced that she was going to get him toasted and drop him off at a sailor bar. "And he won't be allowed to go home until he's made three new friends," she had said. Jane always favored the direct approach.

"He's a romantic at heart," Bridget had insisted. "Just like the Duke of Windsor, my third uncle twenty times removed on my mother's side. He needs a soul mate, someone as sensitive as he is."

Jane ran her fingers through her damp hair and decided she was ready for her first solo spy act. She would find the invention on her own and be home before Liberace could take his final bow of the midnight show.

She stood at the bathroom mirror making up her face and hating her brother. Under the harsh light of the bare bulb, the prosthetic brow looked almost primordial; all she needed were bolts sticking out from either side of her neck and she'd be Frankenstein's better-looking brother. She had a carpet burn on her cheek, a black eye, a bump on her head, and the skin on her chest was raw from sweating all day under the tight bandage. She put on a fresh suit, leaving off the tie and undoing the top two buttons of her white shirt. She looked like an office worker on holiday, she thought as she rummaged through her suitcase for her five o'clock shadow kit. At the bottom was a package wrapped in Tuesday's *London Times* obituary pages, with a note attached: "*And you thought I was going to make you suffer! Cedric.*" Tearing off the paper, she found size-nine-double-E brown leather monk sandals, just like Dad's, and adhesive toe-hair patches. If her behavior at this convention weren't enough to ruin her brother's reputation, these shoes were.

*   *   *

"Wanda?" she called through the ripped screen door to the kitchen, then knocked and waited, not wanting to barge in on anything unbecoming. The Chief, in the same dirty T-shirt he had worn that morning, only filthier and wetter under the arms, waved her inside.

"*Dragnet,*" he said, rolling his metal office chair across the small room to fiddle with the improvised rabbit ears, two wire hangers attached to a black-and-white television with gaffer's tape. Wanda, hunched over a yellow mixing bowl, said, "Hey, Jim, I'm making meat loaf! We're going to eat it during the show. You're welcome to join us." A piece of onion clung to her cheek, and she flicked it away. "Hon, there's a new box of foil under the sink if you want to fix those ears." The Chief fiddled with the coat hangers until a man holding a gun shifted into focus.

"Dum-dah-dum-dum," he sang while Wanda squished raw hamburger between her fingers and smiled affectionately at him. Love was a funny kind of sickness, Jane decided. The Chief rotated his clothes weekly, bathed only when Wanda threatened to turn the hose on him, and spent more time with Batman than he did with her, and still she was happy. What did they talk about? If the castaways would ever get off that island? Maybe they didn't talk, Jane thought, after the Chief asked Wanda to please squish her meat a little quieter.

"Wanda, I hate to bother you," Jane whispered.

"No bother, hon." Wanda wiped her hands on her apron and pushed the bowl across the table to her husband, who was leaning back in his chair, his feet on a sack of potatoes. Without taking his eyes off the Chef Boyardee commercial, he divided the bowl's contents into three loaf pans. "You're going out for a night on the town, and that black eye is going to put a crimp in your plans."

"I don't want to scare my girlfriend," said Jane.

"You got a girl already?" Wanda asked her with raised eyebrows. "You Brits sure do move fast." The Chief grunted; Joe Friday was being called out on a case. Jane followed Wanda upstairs to a surprisingly feminine bathroom, with cabbage-rose wallpaper, pink tile, and a blond-wood vanity with a frilly pink skirt. The *101 Bathroom Jokes* paperback on the back of the toilet somewhat ruined the effect.

"At least he reads something besides those damned racing forms." Wanda shrugged and smiled, tapping Jane's shoulder and indicating she should take a seat on the edge of the tub. "Where'd you get the shiner anyway?" she asked, mixing foundation to match the olive undertones in Jane's skin. A layer of this, then a concealer stick, then powder; she repeated this until the bruise was covered. "Was it a fight over this girl?"

Jane nodded.

"Better watch yourself. They frown on that here. Gives the city a bad name. There was a guy a couple of years ago in town for a bra-sales convention that got tangled up with twin showgirls. They hog-tied him and threw him on a bus to Tijuana." She handed Jane a mirror. "Looks good. You might want to shave, though. Gee, you've got a heavy beard. If you ever want that eyebrow plucked, come see me." She looked at Jane queerly. "Didn't you have a scar on your cheek this morning?" Jane's hand flew to her face, feeling for the ridge that wasn't there. "I remember thinking it made you look like Errol Flynn. I thought maybe you fell down some steps or ran with scissors. Oh, maybe it's my eyes," she decided. "I need reading glasses. No fighting tonight, okay?"

Jane nodded. "Wanda, you're a doll."

"I know," she said, washing her hands with Dove and drying them on the HIS towel.

Jane waited with her thumb in the air by the side of the road, the teepees steaming from the day's heat behind her. A dozen gleaming white limousines had passed her by when a dented aqua Cadillac, the trunk tied down with a rope, slowed to a halt. Jane knew that this trip to Las Vegas would be her only one. Her friend Edith Liversidge, a pensioner who lived in her building, had been terribly excited about Jane's *fabulous* trip to *fabulous* Las Vegas, begging her to get Sammi Martini's autograph should their paths cross. Edith would be expecting a full report about Sin City, and Jane wouldn't disappoint. She would recast Wanda as an ingenue who saved her tips in a jar under her bed, until the nickels and dimes added up to a bus ticket to Hollywood. There'd be no mention of the brutal sun and bone-dry land, or the fact that Jane had to hitchhike to the Strip.

The woman behind the wheel gave her the once-over. "I've got a pistol in my purse," she said.

"Me, too," said Jane, and the driver laughed and used a pliers to unlock the passenger door.

She could have been Wanda's mother, created from the same vat of peroxide and Aqua Net. Her face, dark and shiny as a burnished walnut, had obviously been pulled taut by the surgeon's scalpel. Like a paint-by-number portrait, her face had been subdivided into distinct color fields: The slices above her eyes were as blue as a robin's egg and as bright as neon, and were outlined by liner, black and thick, jetting up and out like ravens' wings. The circles of rouge on her cheeks made her look feverish, and her white lipstick had been drawn outside her mouth in an attempt to turn thin lips into a Louise Brooks pouty cupid's bow. Her upper lip had a two-tone look, like a brown spectator pump with a white toe, her dark skin peeking through the lipstick. Rhinestone-studded black cat glasses hung on a gold chain around her neck while she squinted at the road ahead.

"I'm going as far as the Stardust," the woman said after explaining that the door had to be slammed to get it to close properly. "With a little detour to pick up a friend."

"Me, too." Anywhere she could get a taxi would do. When Jane reached into her pocket for gas money, the woman shook her head.

"You'll be parting with that soon enough, mister. Besides, I'm going that way anyhow." Jane slipped a dollar between the seats, knowing that the woman would find it the next time she cleaned her car, which was old but immaculate inside and out. The vinyl seats smelled of vinegar and lemon, the cracked dash was waxed, and bath mats with the Sands logo—a desert scene with topless showgirls astride a camel—covered the floor. Even these were pristinely white. Jane, afraid to dirty them, put her feet on either side so it looked like she was straddling an imaginary horse. Noting Jane's discomfort, the woman shook her head, her dice earrings smacking her cheeks. "Go ahead. I've got dozens more in the trunk."

"I'm James," Jane said, offering her hand.

"Sandy." Her palm was callused, the skin dry and cracked. Before her "premeditated assault" on Dougie Smathers, Jane had overheard some chaps talking about redeeming their "buy one, get one free" massage-parlor coupon; young or old, women did all the dirty work in this town. If this old car was any indication of how Sandy lived, her reward wouldn't come in this lifetime. Sandy was probably in her sixties but looked older, despite the face-lift. Maybe it was the sun-damaged skin or the cigarettes she chain-smoked—three Lucky Strikes since Jane got in the car a few miles back—or the tired and tough quality to her rawboned features.

With one hand simultaneously on the wheel and holding a cigarette and the other hanging out the window catching the breeze, Sandy explained that she was headed to the Stardust to play the penny slots with her friend Betty, and to take advantage of the free midnight buffet. "No kidding, mister. Once you're in the door and drop some hard cash, it's all yours for the taking." She gestured at the open bowling-ball bag at Jane's feet. It contained a roll of antacids, a moist washrag in a plastic bag, and several empty Tupperware containers. In one smooth movement, Sandy took her right hand off the wheel and, using her knees to keep the car on course, extracted a cigarette from the cracked plaid plastic case on the dash.

"Me and Betty eat all we can. They have roast beef and chicken and shrimp and canned ham and all kinds of side dishes, potatoes and vegetables and more kinds of salads than you've ever seen, even those real pretty Jell-O salads with grapes and cottage cheese. I don't like to waste, and so what we don't finish we take home for later. When I host poker night, I like to serve something nice, like shrimp and Jell-O salad. I can get a whole pie in there, but you gotta be careful. I learned the hard way you can't put beans in your bowling bag. Betty came up with the idea of the bag; we used to make sandwiches and stuff 'em in our purses, but this way we can bring home a healthy four-course meal. She's a smart girl. She got her boyfriend, Chickie Skeets, to buy her a little ranch house before he got eighty-sixed. That means dead. Wanna hear how it happened?" She looked sideways at Jane, clearly hoping the answer was yes.

"*Naturally,*" said Jane.

"Oh, I just love your accent. New Jersey?"

"England."

"That's a nice place, too. Never been there. Anyway, he was sitting in the barber chair, getting his ear hair trimmed, and this mug Chickie owed money to comes in, pretty as you please, and gives him a new part with a .38 slug. Chickie wasn't completely dead—he had a plate put in his head during the war. He was tough as a rattlesnake. So they took him on a scenic tour of the desert, and that was the end of Chickie Skeets. Poor Betty had her heart set on being Mrs. Skeets. We all called him Ears, because they were so big. Stuck straight out from his head. We used to tease Betty in the old days, when the army tested their bombs out here: Better hold on to Chickie so he don't fly away. It would get real windy on those days. Now they say we should have stayed indoors. Who knew?" She shrugged.

"Wanna cold beer?" Her knees still steering the car, she twisted her body so she could reach the cooler in the backseat. Sandy's black stretch capris hugged a slender figure, but her lime green peasant-style blouse, worn low on one freckled shoulder, drew attention to a neck creased from age and untouched by the surgeon's scalpel, as if she had run out of money when he reached her chin.

The cold beer went down well, and this time Jane insisted on paying for it. Cedric had left her a dollar for a sandwich and a cold drink at the coffee shop, so before she set out, she picked the lock to his teepee and searched for his money roll, finding two hundred dollars precisely where she, and every burglar in the world, imagined it would be—in a sock in the back of his shipshape underwear drawer, under a *Muscle Man* magazine. She took her half.

"Buy yourself something pretty," said Jane, placing a five under the cigarette case, patched with clear tape, now yellowed and crumbling.

"What are you—a millionaire?"

"That's right. I only walk for my health."

"This is America, Jimmy. Nobody walks." An Old Milwaukee tucked between her thighs, she turned off the highway into a development of ranch homes, modest and neat, each with a large picture window overlooking a plot of manicured grass. Televisions glowed through each window, and as they snaked past children playing in the street, Jane turned her head to look into these rooms, struck by a powerful longing to return home. Occasionally one of the dark shapes on the sofa would get up to stand at the window, at the children playing freely in the safety of the suburbs. The shrubs in front of each house created a pool of shadow that swallowed them as they ran across manicured lawns lit by brilliant streetlights. Jane had expected neon.

"This used to be a mob dumping ground before it became Shady Acres. Downtown is strictly cowboys and winos, but the casino workers with kids live out here. There are bodies still buried here. During construction they kept diggin' em up—finally they gave up and poured concrete over 'em. It's all this sand—it makes it easy to dig, and the night wind covers up any tracks. Let's take a cab ride, they'd say. Everyone knew what *that* meant. Here's Betty." A woman in a modest cap-sleeved sundress with a gauzy yellow scarf tied to her bowling bag sailed toward the car as Jane got into the backseat. "This is Jimmy," Sandy explained. "We're giving him a lift."

"You're not gonna strangle us, are you?" Betty poked her head in the car and checked Jane out.

"I might," Jane said, and Betty cracked a smile.

"*I* could strangle Sandy sometimes," Betty confessed as she slid into the passenger seat and took a cigarette from the pack on the dash. "Yakety-yak-yak—it can get to you sometimes. That quack who lifted her face should have sewed her mouth shut." Whoever had lifted Betty's face had been more skilled, the results subtler and softer. High cheekbones and large dark eyes were framed by a soft auburn bouffant with a slight fringe, and her makeup—powder and a light touch of coral lipstick—added to the overall appearance of a woman unafraid of aging. Sandy's junior by ten years or so, whatever her age, Betty was a looker.

After backing carefully out of the driveway, no easy task considering the size of the old Caddy, Sandy dinged a tricycle left unattended at the side of the street and roared off, her exhaust pipe scraping the concrete. "I'll be hearing about that in the morning," said Betty. She didn't seem upset. "As long as she doesn't hit my new garbage can or a kid. Most people here work nights," she told Jane, sitting sideways so she could talk to them both. "And the kids run wild."

"Tips are better at night," explained Sandy. "So it's desirable."

"After midnight, people are too drunk or too tired to notice what they give you. They just hand you whatever they've got in their pocket. Right, Sandy?" Betty winked broadly. "Sandy used to make out fine when she was young. Her headlights are real, if you get my drift."

"Betty, you're shameless." Sandy slapped the dashboard and chortled. Jane could hear a smoker's rattle deep in her throat.

"You two should be onstage," Jane said, laughing.

"We used to be!" they said in unison, and they all laughed.

"What's your profession? What are you besides tall, dark, and handsome?" quizzed Sandy. "In some circles that is a profession," she added knowingly.

"I'm in insurance," said Jane. "James Bland—London, England." She passed up one of the phony business cards Cedric had had printed for her. Her specialty, naturally, was accident insurance.

Betty turned around so she could scrutinize their passenger. "I thought perhaps, with your looks, that you were an actor."

"Or a gigolo," said Sandy, examining Jane's face in the rear-view mirror.

"Someone did the cha-cha on your face recently, and whoever tried to cover it used cheap concealer. Maybelline, it looks like," continued Betty.

"In her spare time, Betty's an Avon representative," explained Sandy. "She knows quality.

"Or did some girl give you something to remember her by—an old puncheroo in the face?"

"I fell down," said Jane. "I'm in Las Vegas to attend the International Association of Accident-Prone People. We're having our annual convention. I'm here to learn how to live a full and rewarding life despite my chronic clumsiness." Cedric had made her memorize the spiel, and he'd been right—it had come in handy.

"We're going to a convention, too," said Sandy. She slowed for a four-way stop, stuck her hand out the window, and made a left turn.

"The Dorothy Duncan Defrost-Off. We're going the last day, when Dorothy Duncan *herself* arrives to tape her weekly show. We're going to get on that show! But I can't tell you how. It's top-secret. But I can tell you that when we walk out of that convention, everyone's going to be sorry they treated us so shabbily all these years. We've gone fifteen times, and we've never won a thing!"

"You never win because every year you make the same dish—beer and mustard soup," said Betty. Sandy hooted and tossed a matchbook at Betty. This was obviously an old act, making Jane think this Dorothy Duncan competition was just something they did for kicks—a respite between stealing hotel towels and racks of lamb.

"And *you* never win because every year you make Cottage Cheese Cutie. Jimmy, it's a very popular dish here in America. A scoop of cottage cheese on a bed of lettuce, with a raisin and maraschino cherry face and parsley curls. The problem is, every other contestant makes one. This year, cottage cheese scoops and beer-based soups were banned from competition, so we decided not to bother."

"*I* wanted to go for the opening day festivities, but I was afraid we'd run into our archenemy, Verda Taylor," said Betty. "She hates us because we're happy, even though we're not housewives."

"Each year, she volunteers to be the registrar only so she can give everyone a hard time."

"Are you going to see the dancing, singing vegetables?" Jane asked. Where had she heard the name Verda Taylor before?

"I just don't see how a celery stalk or an ear of corn can take the place of Natalie Woods." Betty wrinkled her nose. "They come up with the dumbest ideas. Last year they had a cookbook come to life and a giant tap-dancing oven mitt introducing the recipes. Verda Taylor was in that one; she stepped in after the nutmeg broke a toe."

"Speaking of show business, I wanna show you something," Sandy said, reaching into the glove box for a worn red wallet. "Since you're an insurance agent, you'll appreciate it." The Caddy stalled, then died, and Betty took charge of the wallet while Sandy pumped the gas pedal and got them moving again.

Betty handed Jane a picture of two women in modest bathing suits holding a rattlesnake. The platinum hair on the older one was the giveaway. "That was in the old days, when shows didn't have insurance. If a girl was bitten, it was her tough luck."

"That was about the time Bugsy moved in and gave this place some class," Sandy said. "After that, people started coming here by the boat-load. Everyone was hiring, buildings were going up 'round the clock. A lot of women came here to keep house while their husbands built the dam, then got divorces. There were so many jobs they didn't need to put up with some jerk. We'd walk down the street and casino owners would run out and make us an offer. Of course eventually we got a little too old to be showgirls—"

"Our warranties had expired," Betty added.

"—but there were still lots of jobs, and interesting ones, too. I was sawed in half for years by Marvelous Marvin the Magical Magician, over at the Flamingo."

"I sewed tutus for a dancing-dog act," said Betty. "*Nothing* takes pee out of netting. This girl here"—she pointed at Sandy—"was the assistant head sequiner at the Stardust for nine years."

"I make all my own clothes," said Sandy proudly. She fingered the ruffle on her peasant blouse, proud of the workmanship. "I've got kitchen curtains of the same material."

"Yeah, when she stands in front of the window, she disappears," snorted Betty. "Hand me a beer, Jim."

"Betty was Mrs. Atomic Blast 1951," Sandy said. "She was never married, not really, but unmarried gals over thirty were all put in the same category."

Glowing, Betty swiveled her head so she could see Jane's expression. "The blasts were a big tourist attraction back then. The hotels set out deck chairs on the hillside and packed big hampers of picnic lunches, cold chicken sandwiches, macaroni salad, fruit cups, and there'd be a bar on a cute rolling cart. When the cloud appeared, we'd mix up some zombies and watch it float away. I got to see one closeup after I was crowned. Not many girls can brag about that."

"It's why she looks so good," said Sandy, pulling into the Stardust parking lot. "She's been preserved. All out for the Stardust!"

Losing them proved impossible. Jane walked into the casino with them, kissed them both on the cheek, handed Sandy a ten-spot—"the price of a ticket for the best show in town"—then ducked into the men's room and waited for them to disappear into the casino. A real spy would not let two dizzy dames keep her from her work, no matter how charming the company and cold the beer. Five minutes passed, and, the coast clear, Jane went outside and hailed a cab. She had just given the driver her destination when Sandy and Betty descended on her.

"Why didn't you tell us you were headed for the convention center?" asked Sandy as they pulled out of the Stardust lot and back onto State Road 1. "Old broads like us have all night to do as we please. The free buffets don't open until midnight, and we're in no hurry to part with that ten. We coulda just dropped you there to begin with."

"What are you doing out there this time of night? That place shuts down at five. That way, the conventioneers *have* to go to town to have some fun."

"I'm meeting someone," Jane said.

"I knew there was a girl involved," said Sandy. "When I saw you sneak out of the casino, I told Betty you were headed to a romantic rendezvous."

"Sandy, that's his business," Betty scolded, remembering how many people had hounded Chickie about things that were none of their business. So what if he was involved in shady deals, in trouble with the IRS, and had a mistress? "Live and let live, that's my motto."

Sandy snorted, knowing that, the minute they dropped Jim off, Betty, a romance-novel addict, would start speculating about his love life.

"Just be careful, Jim," Betty added as the convention center came into sight. In his own way, Chickie had been an insurance man, too, and look what had happened to him! "People can get into a lot of trouble in this town. If anyone offers you a pep pill, *just say no*. People take 'em so they can play the same machine until it pays out. Those are the ones who wind up in the wacko ward at Vegas General, thinking they're Sammi Martini or Shecky Greene."

"They sure don't put *that* in any of the travel brochures," said Sandy. "Once I saw newlyweds being carted off, and it gave me the idea to design straitjackets for women, in colors we gals like."

"Sandy's always coming up with some get-rich-slow scheme. Always thinking, that one."

"My first idea was a salon hair dryer that cuts your bangs, but that didn't work out because my prototype cut off more than the volunteer's hair. And then I came up with the idea of an alarm-clock coffeepot, so you can wake up to the smell of fresh-brewed Nescafé."

"I keep telling her it's a swell idea," said Betty. "Especially for busy people on the go. She gave me and Chickie one to celebrate our anniversary, only the Creamora clogged up the works."

"I've had other great ideas! When I worked at the Flamingo, I made pretty paper swimsuits for guests who had left theirs at home, only they fell apart when they hit the water."

"I cut mine up into place mats," Betty reported.

"Waste not, want not," Sandy said approvingly.

Jane sat back and enjoyed the banter. Soon enough she would be breaking in to the convention center, praying that her first serious criminal act would go unnoticed. The night ahead could be treacherous, making this time with them all the more enjoyable.

The Caddy was stalled behind a group of limos. Dozens of tourists with Instamatics at the ready stood in front of Caesars Palace, the newest and brightest jewel on the Strip, craning their necks to try and spot Elvis and Priscilla Presley climbing out of a powder blue limousine with gold hubcaps. Betty and Sandy shrieked when they saw who they were stuck behind.

"Hit them, Sandy, and we'll sell the paint scrapings!" said Betty excitedly. A woman threw her hotel key, and it lodged somewhere in Mrs. Presley's jet-black, foot-high beehive. "I read in *Ladies' Home Journal* it takes her hairdresser two hours to do Priscilla's hair," said Sandy, still craning her neck. "As soon as things start looking up, I'm going back to Mr. Donald. You just can't get the same lift at home. I tried, but my automatic beehive machine was a bust."

A white limo pulled up, and a tall, handsome man in a plain blue suit unfolded himself from the backseat, holding on to the bony arm of a stick-thin, petite woman with a stiff helmet of hair, wearing a sparkling blue gown with a modest neckline. A plain cloth coat hung from her shoulders. A murmur of disappointment swept the crowd, but the couple didn't seem to notice, or care. They smiled and waved, the woman holding up her hand, palm facing inward, making stiff little circles in the air.

"Only the queen's allowed to wave like that," said Jane in a rare flash of nationalism.

"That's the fellow who's running for governor of California," said Betty. "Used to be an actor. Roger Reagan."

"No, Ronald Raydon," Sandy corrected. "I hope he's a better governor than he is an actor; Chickie once took me to see him in a movie with some chimps. It stunk. If he hadn't been an animal lover, Chickie woulda shot up the place, it was *that* bad." Used flashcubes littered the red carpet as an actress better known for her infidelities than her roles went through the door, and people began to wander away.

"See you later, alligator!" Sandy cried out the window as she and Betty sped off, leaving Jane in the convention center's empty parking lot with a can of Old Milwaukee and another warning about accepting drugs from strangers. She popped the top of her beer, thinking it would make her seem more like a conventioneer, and splashed a little on her clothes, thinking it would make her *smell* more like a conventioneer. She crept to the front doors and peeked inside. As Betty had said, the place was deserted. A long burp was the next thing out of her, and she took deep gulps of cool evening air, to clear her brain. If she kept drinking like this, she'd end up in the Secret Service Swiss Spy Sanitarium Dipsomaniac Ward. Trying to keep up with Sandy and Betty had been a dumb idea, and Jane took one last sip from the can and poured the rest on the cactus beds flanking the doors.

She stole around the side of the building, keeping low to the ground, and hid behind a large humming metal box, the main air-conditioning unit, she guessed, to examine the rear of the building, a blank cinderblock wall with a fire door that doubled as the entertainers' entrance, and a scrubby-looking patch of parched soil to one side where people tossed their cigarette butts. After looking around to make sure she was alone, she went to the door to try the handle—just in case someone had been sloppy. The handle refused to budge, and the steel door was bolted in several places. She could take it off its hinges, had she brought a blowtorch and someone with more skill and experience. She let go of the handle and stepped back, imagining Bridget going through that door each day and slipping into some sexy, sequined, barely-there costume and feathered headdress. The headdress didn't do much for Jane, but the idea of Bridget in a nude body stocking and strategically placed sequins made the back of her neck burn. She understood now why Miss Tuppenny insisted they stay out of each other's sight *unless absolutely necessary*. Jane was going to get to absolutely necessary any minute unless she stopped thinking about Bridget and started thinking about that invention.

Still thinking of Bridget, only in a professional, secret agent way, Jane pressed the starfish-shaped gold cuff links on her sleeves and watched, always impressed with the sight, as they sprouted sharp grappling hooks capable of holding three hundred pounds. She looked over her shoulder for the telltale red lights of a police car, aware that, should she be caught, she'd face almost certain deportation. Explaining her behavior to Cedric, on top of the dart gun, would be the killer. Then, feeling a little foolish, she crouched low to the ground and began hopping, getting a few feet higher with every jump. Before leaving her teepee, she had changed from her beloved leather-soled, Cuban-heeled Beatle boots to Flubber-soled, Cuban-heeled Beatle boots. Flubber® was a miracle polymer compound discovered after the war but forgotten in the mad rush of scientific research that followed. As it absorbed energy, the grayish material grew in strength. The trouble with Flubber was that its powers wore out easily; this was especially true in hot weather. Jane had been warned to limit the use of the shoes to five minutes at a time, to give them a chance to cool down, and when the timer on her watch beeped, she realized she had wasted a few of those precious minutes marveling at the sight of the nighttime Strip from a bird's-eye view. With one more strong push that made her knees groan in protest, she flung herself upward at a slight angle, activating her cuff-link grapping hooks and reaching out for a steel-framed window, missing it by only a few inches.

"'It's not unusual for it to take a novice agent several tries to get her grappling hooks in place,'" she told herself, quoting from *The Textbook of Spy Tricks.* Her second try was worse, and she swore angrily when she grabbed for the hook and cut her palm.

She heard Cedric in her head: "Between the hare and the tortoise, who wins, Jane?" He was always preaching patience to her. When they first met, she had thought he was a religious nut trying to sign her up. Turned out he was a spy. And here she stood a year later, trying to break into the Las Vegas Convention Center with Flubber and cuff links. Before she'd joined G.E.O.R.G.I.E., the tallest thing she had ever scaled was her ex-girlfriend Astrid, an Amazon beauty with the heart of a devil. Compared to Astrid, this concrete block should be easy to penetrate.

One more time Jane built up her speed, aware that the clock was ticking. Flubber softened under friction, and soon her shoes would lose most of their bounce-ability and need a cool-down period. Once inside, she could search for the invention sans her Flubber-soled shoes, but first she had to *get* in. One more hard jump brought her face level with the bank of windows, and she flung her arms forward and hooked the steel edge of one of the frames, smiling when she heard the sound of metal scraping metal. She had made it. Hanging from her wrists, with her face pressed to the cool concrete, Jane remembered Bibi's remark when the new product was unveiled: "It sounds too much like blubber."

Drawing herself up until she could rest her elbows on the window frame, Jane peeked inside. From her vantage point, the room looked like a pub after a soccer win. Beer cans littered the floor, someone had fired up the barbecue grill and left glowing embers behind, and it looked as if the martini-shaking machine had been used to do a load of laundry. Suds soaked the floor, and wet clothing was heaped on the circular bed, ruining the silk sheets. When one of the lumps of clothing rolled over, Jane was startled, lost her grip and started to fall, held only by the thin wire attached to the right grappling hook. She swung there for a minute, reviewing her choices, until a patrol car turned into the front lot, red lights flashing. Feeling she might indeed look a little suspicious hanging off the side of the building, Jane retracted her cuff links and dropped to the ground, using her last bit of Flubber power to jump over the patrol car and disappear into the night. What she had to do next would probably be her greatest sacrifice for G.E.O.R.G.I.E.

eleven

When Jane opened the door of the suite Dougie Smathers shared with four other agents, a cloud of noxious gas smacked her in the face. "Jesus Christ!" she cried, trying to breathe through her mouth as she waded through a sea of twisted clothing, Chinese carry-out containers, empty beer cans, and girlie magazines. "Yeech." She shuddered, stepping on something squishy. This was clearly the worst room of the lot she had searched. Twenty bucks had bought her a Desert Inn maid's uniform, purchased from a woman just leaving her shift who mentioned that this was the third time that month some guy had gotten into her dress. Then she winked, and Jane handed her the twenty, shoved the uniform under her jacket, and ran. The black stockings made her skin itch, and the dress length was unflattering, but she felt like a real spy as she picked the lock (it took five minutes, but she got it) and walked right in.

The rooms, four in all, opened out onto this space, a sitting room with thinly padded angular wooden sofas, the fabric brown to hide stains, plain wooden side tables bolted to the floor, and framed newspaper clippings chronicling the life and death of gangster Bugsy Siegel.

"Classy," Jane said when she saw that someone had inked a mustache on Siegel's obituary photo. Using her foot, she sorted through the assembled garbage. It would help if she knew what she was searching for, but nothing appeared out of the ordinary, which she found sad, considering the mess. What if the invention looked like a crushed beer can or a bottle of aftershave, and she walked right over it? Slowly she made her way through the room, then turned and made another pass. Remembering Felix's run-in with the sofa, she unfolded it and stuck the handle of her feather duster in the cracks, finding several dollars in change and a piece of Bazooka Joe bubble gum. "Poor Felix," Jane said, putting the change in her pocket and tossing the gum into the clutter on the floor. "First he was trapped in here, and now he's trapped at Liberace." If they were going to be in-laws, and it seemed they might, Cedric was going to have to tell Felix the truth: Bazooka Joe was the worst bubble gum ever made, and its cartoons simply weren't funny.

Having begun in the sitting room, sorting through the accumulated clutter of men far from home, she thought she had seen everything—until she entered Dougie's room and found Emma Peel in his bed. The blighter had stolen Jane's crush, and it was clear he intended to sleep with her, even going so far as to cover her with a red nightie with cutout nipples. Jane shuddered again. It was enough to make her forget the tight hairnet and sensible shoes she had to don to get in here. Bridget allowed Jane to love one other girl besides her, and that was Emma Peel. "I'm going to kill you, Dougie Smathers," she swore, ripping off the hideous nightie and carefully removing a dialogue bubble taped to Emma Peel's cheek that said, "Oh, Dougie! More, more, more!"

Fueled with a new vengeance, Jane carefully propped her cardboard girlfriend against the wall, then ripped through Dougie's things, a bland assortment of toiletries (all travel size except for the hemorrhoid cream, she noticed with a smirk), loud summer outfits, airplane liquor bottles, and dog-eared spy novels. There was a photograph stuck in one, perhaps used as a bookmark, a black-and-white off-kilter snapshot of two frightened-looking teenagers in outdated clothes. A skinny teenager wearing a borrowed tuxedo and a plaid bow tie, grinned like a jack-o'-lantern as he stood beside a very pregnant girl in a black maternity smock and matching hair ribbon, holding a wild sweet-pea bouquet as tender and young as her pale, sweet face. Had someone not drawn fangs and horns on the girl, Jane would have thought it an image of young misguided love. After she read the inscription—"Dougie and Daisy, Kansas City, 1941"—she stuck the picture in her apron pocket, feeling protective toward the pregnant girl. In the margin of the book she wrote, in code, FUCK YOU DOUGIE SMATHERS. Feeling like a juvenile delinquent, she tossed the book on the mess *she* had made, grabbed Mrs. Peel, and went to investigate the remaining rooms.

After her search turned up nothing (it was not time wasted; she had saved Emma Peel from a fate worse than death—imaginary sex with Dougie Smathers), she left empty-handed, with no invention and no pride. In a way she was glad the room was such a disaster—no one would be able to tell that she'd been there. As she changed back into her clothes in the staff bathroom, she overheard a couple of maids complaining about the agents' behavior. By the end of the first day of their stay, the hotel had received numerous complaints, from staff and guests alike, that the men in the Bugsy Siegel Suite were great big asses. Unable to kick them out—they were, after all, "with the government"—the management had stopped all amenities. The men in the Bugsy Siegel Suite were to receive no more fresh towels, soap, toilet paper, and room or maid service, until they apologized to every one of the 112 females they had offended.

After parting with ten dollars for a bottle of scotch at a nearby liquor store, stocked with overpriced booze and cheap women, Jane left it at the front desk for Dougie, along with a note dripping with flattery. Jealousy had made James Bond attack him, jealousy of all things American—its bountiful food, excellent dental care, and superior nuclear arsenal. Jane hoped that the gift of the little black book, this bottle of scotch, and a trip to a strip show, which she suggested in the note, cringing at the idea of spending time alone with Dougie Smathers, would win back James's "dearest" American friend and win her entry into the spy convention. She spit in the envelope before sealing it, handed it and the bottle to the man at the front desk, and hit the Strip, heading for the Sands and, she hoped, Bridget's arms.

By the time she walked into the Sands, Jane had had time to think it over and had changed her mind. It was too soon in the game to admit defeat. She would not go running to her girlfriend to rescue her from Dougie Smathers. If the booze, boot-licking, and naked women wouldn't do it, she'd simply track him down, shoot him (this time intentionally) with a tranquilizing dart, and leave him in the desert with a six-pack of beer. Then she'd push her way back into the convention and put truth-serum drops into everyone's drink. Pleased that she had figured out a reasonable solution to her problem, Jane walked back out the door into the shimmery heat and neon glare of the Strip, and while she was waiting to cross the street, a car screeched to a stop and she was pulled into the front passenger seat, the driver roaring away from the curb as if being chased by Satan himself. A Dorothy Duncan Defrost-Off contestant also waiting patiently to cross at the light had witnessed the abduction, but by the time she flagged down a police car, she had forgotten the license-plate number. All she could remember was that an aqua Cadillac had taken the man away.

"Hey, Jimmy," Sandy said as she climbed into the backseat, still a little out of breath from pulling Jane into the car at forty miles per hour. Jane was dazed but aware enough to be relieved that she wasn't sitting in a car loaded with drunken secret agents. She still had her spy wits about her, and she was proud of that.

"Sandy, you're pretty strong for someone of your—"

"Beauty?" Sandy said brightly.

"Exactly."

Betty was roaring along the Strip with the confidence and tire squeals that told Jane she had driven many a getaway car. Sandy lounged in the backseat, hanging her feet out the missing window, and sipped a beer. She was thirsty after all that excitement.

Jane was flung against the door as Betty made a spectacular U-turn across two lanes of traffic, then righted the car, which, under the best of circumstances, had a decided list to the left. "Chickie sent her to one of those driving schools for mob wives," Sandy said as she passed the can to Jane. "In case someone tries to kidnap them or take their parking spot at the grocery store."

"I thought you were going to pass the evening at the Stardust?"

"Well," said Sandy, "the Sands is Betty's old stomping grounds, where Chickie used to take her for supper and a show. He'd take me, too, on my birthday."

"We stop here once a week for matchbooks and drink coasters," Betty added. "For our weekly bridge club. We were just leaving when we saw you standing on the corner all alone, looking heartbroken."

"Thanks for rescuing me," Jane said dryly, rubbing her head where it had hit the doorframe. "That woman in the apron had just offered me a pep pill. I'm safe now. You can let me out anywhere." Her chances of finding Dougie Smathers on the crowded Strip were slim, but it beat spending the night in her teepee.

"No can do," said Sandy, passing up two beers and a cheese platter she had liberated from a Sands room-service cart on its way upstairs. "You dance with the one who snatched you."

"It's girl trouble, isn't it, Jim?" Betty asked, looking at Jane longer than at the road.

"Yeah, why were you at the Sands?" Sandy said. "You were supposed to be at the convention center. Did she stand you up?"

"You can tell us," said Betty. "We've been there."

"We know all about shattered dreams and broken hearts," added Sandy for clarification. "I've been married more times than Elizabeth Taylor. It's not something to be proud of, but it's the one thing we have in common, and that means something in this town. Now, Betty here has had a more conventional love life."

"I was with Chickie for twenty-three years," said Betty. "We would have gotten married, but his wife wouldn't let us."

"You could still marry Trini 'the Toe' Toots," Sandy teased. "You could be Mrs. Toe Toots. How does that grab you?"

"Revolting," said Betty, pretending to gag.

"He moved in on Betty during Chickie's memorial," Sandy explained to Jane.

"While I was putting out the raw vegetable platter, he had the nerve to proposition me!" Betty shook her head in disgust.

"Men start crawling out of the woodwork when they smell fresh widow," said Sandy. "There's lots of flesh on parade in this town, and more young girls willing to put up with a big hairy ape for regular meals and maybe a mink stole, but someone as classy as Betty's a real gem, and the guys know it."

Betty corrected her. "The *old* guys know it. But do I seem like the kind of woman who wants to spend her golden years taking care of some old geezer with *ear hair?*"

"God, no," Jane said. "You're much better off with Sandy here." They did make a cute couple.

"Don't I know it!"

"So, Jim, you haven't answered our question."

"I haven't had a chance," said Jane.

"And?" prompted Betty. "Is it love trouble?"

"What other kind of trouble is there?" Jane sighed.

"There's stomach trouble," said Sandy, remembering a spoiled tuna-noodle casserole she had eaten yesterday for lunch. "But love can be as bad as an old casserole sometimes."

It was, Jane thought, the perfect analogy.

"Hush, Sandy," Betty said. "Let Jim finish."

"I don't know what to say."

"It's the same old story," Sandy said, her knowing proclamation followed by a sudden cry of, "Shit! I just lost a shoe!" She pulled in her feet and took off the remaining battered gold moccasin to show Jane. The leather shoe was so old it had formed to Sandy's feet, and Jane could see the imprint of her toes. The shoe looked a size too small. When Betty refused to turn the car around so Sandy could play dodge-'em cars all for the sake of an old slip-on, Sandy shrugged and threw the remaining shoe out the window.

"So," Sandy prompted, "you came to town, you met a girl, she turned out to be a mobster's moll, and you and the boyfriend went to the convention center to duke it out. It happens all the time."

"We've got to get you out of town." Betty adjusted the rearview mirror so she could examine Jane's face, her wide brown eyes narrowing with concern. "That's the mug who realigned your face. If you think you're unlucky now, just wait until those mugs arrange for you to have an 'accident.'"

"You've got to get out of town. To the airport, Betty!"

"It's nothing like that," insisted Jane. "I came here *with* my girlfriend. There are no mobsters involved. I wouldn't even know what one looked like." Sandy reached for her wallet, for the picture of Betty and Chickie she kept in there, and passed it to Jane. Apparently mobsters were short, balding men in barbecue aprons, Jane thought. "Nice legs," she said to Betty, staring at the attractive fortyish woman standing next to Chickie in a skirted swimsuit and heels. Betty fluttered at the compliment, and before it could become a lovefest, Sandy decided to take charge.

"If you've got a girl, what are you doing with two old bats on a Saturday night? Two old bats with nice gams," she quickly added when Betty turned the mirror on her and stuck out her tongue.

"I can't find her. I don't know where she is." While listening to their stories, Jane had concocted one of her own. It was always preferable to build a fiction based on fact; it made it easier to remember and sounded more authentic than a complete fabrication. Unless, of course, one was a master liar like Mimi Dolittle. For several months after Jane had joined up with G.E.O.R.G.I.E., the other agents were divided on the subject of Jane and Mimi's night of passion. But as Mimi spun out of control, her followers distanced themselves, and by the time Mimi threw the infamous jar of vanishing cream at Jane's head, she had few supporters. When word first got around that Bibi and Mimi were involved, Jane wondered what incredible untruths Mimi had told Bibi in order to seduce her.

"You're at Wanda's place outside of town, aren't you?" asked Betty, remembering Jim's mentioning a teepee. It was the only teepee place left anywhere near Las Vegas.

"You brought a girl to Las Vegas and put her up in a different motel? What are you—married?" said Sandy.

Jane waggled her fingers so they could see that she wasn't wearing a ring. "Her mother showed up. She's a duchess and doesn't approve of me." That last part was not an inch from the truth.

"A duchess!" cried Sandy. "Hey, now I can tell people I know royalty!"

"A real duchess or a fake duchess?" asked Betty warily. She was holding back her enthusiasm until she heard the whole story.

"A real duchess. Lady Emerald Norbert-Nilbert Smythe-Pargeter St. Claire, the Duchess of Malmesbury." Jane worried she might have left out a name or two; Bridget had had, after all, seven stepfathers, some more fatherly than others.

"And what does Lady Nordic-Filbert Smitty-Parquet Éclair, the Duchess of Mallomar, have against you? Does she think her daughter's too hoity-toity for you?" The idea made Sandy mad as a wet cat. Anyone should be happy to have Jim as a son-in-law.

"We're living in sin," Jane said. "She's afraid the newspapers will find out." That much *was* true. Emerald knew the nature of their relationship, hated it, but kept her opinions to herself. Bridget was her only child, an independent, stubborn girl, and had threatened to cut her mother out of her life if she didn't include Jane at Sunday family dinners, which usually consisted of Emerald, her husband of the moment, Bridget, and more servants than diners. While Jane was touched by Bridget's attempt to include her, she could do without their weekly dinners with Emerald, a terrible snob who could recite Debrett's from memory but could not remember Jane's name.

"Good for you," said Betty. "Sin has gotten such a bad reputation lately."

Sandy picked up the story line. "You were going to meet secretly at the convention center? It's not the most romantic place for a rendezvous, but it's the last place a snooty duchess would look."

Jane sat back, amused, and let them have their fun.

"But your girl didn't show," jumped in Betty. "And you've been wandering the Strip, heartbroken, looking for her—"

"But you can't find her, because her mother's had her kidnapped so she can be brainwashed against you. Betty, we'll have to check all the churches, starting with the Baptists."

"She's probably gone back to London," Jane said. Being dragged from church to church sounded worse than an evening with Liberace.

Betty made sympathetic clucking sounds, and Sandy handed Jane the last beer. "You must be devastated. This is no time for you to be alone," Sandy said.

"I guess I *could* use some company," sighed Jane. "To take my mind off my troubles." Staying on the Strip might mean running into Bridget, but as long as they remained apart, communicating only through subtle gestures, they wouldn't be breaking any of Miss Tuppenny's rules.

"We're going to show you Las Vegas, Jimmy. But first we'll need something to drink."

They started out with cheap beer at a dumpy Fremont Street bar, a typical "old timey" Las Vegas place and, according to Sandy, the land of hobos and cowboys. During a raucous toast to Annie Oakley, they were ejected from the bar and decided to move their party to the Strip. Standing in front of the Flamingo, they felt a welcome breeze was coming off the mountains, and now Jane could understand the draw of this place, could feel the pulse of neon and the infectious excitement of the revelers, grown-ups out on the town determined to cram a lifetime's worth of debauchery into a three-day holiday. The tourists were easy to spot: the men in their best Sunday suits, their wives dressed to the nines, smiling anxiously, gripping their purses, not sure which way to look or what to worry about more—the kids back home or the scantily clad cocktail waitresses and coat-check girls sizing up and smiling at their husbands?

"The free buffets won't be open for an hour," said Betty, watching Jane become a typical bug-eyed Las Vegas tourist. "We've got time to hit the slots."

"Blow on this, Jim." Sandy held a penny in her palm. "For luck."

Sandy and Betty wanted to give their new friend a real Las Vegas welcome, and nothing said "Hello sucker!" like a shiny slot machine and complimentary booze.

Jane obliged after warning her she'd had nothing but bad luck since her arrival. Sandy stuck her penny in the slot, and the machine swallowed it with a mechanical gulp and spit out a nickel. "You luck is changing, Jim! That's a *fifty* percent return."

"Five hundred," Betty corrected her from her machine across the aisle.

"Guard this baby, it's a winner," Sandy said, scooping up the nickel. "I'm going to get change." Members of a bowling team—the Milwaukee Mudslingers—were milling about nearby, eyeing Sandy's machine. When the red light atop the machine flashed, signaling a winner, gamblers took note, ready to pounce. Once the portal was open, it was bound to happen again, the law of averages be damned.

Slipping a penny into the slot, wondering what Bridget was up to, Jane pulled the lever and felt a rush of adrenaline overtake her as the lemons, cherries, and oranges flew by the little windows. The first batch of spinning fruit stopped. Cherry. Then the second. "Another cherry!" She didn't realize she was talking out loud until the bowling team started to crowd her. It was unusual for someone to become this excited at the penny slots; big wins were possible, but rare. The clientele typically drawn to them were elderly people who wanted to pass the time, arriving with sandwiches and a thermos of coffee and staying all day. Casino management along the Strip were conflicted about their presence. Anyone with a penny was welcome, and they made a ton of dough—but they didn't want their casinos to become flashy senior-citizen homes.

Seeing the commotion, Betty gave up her machine to a pushy nun and joined Jane just as the third cherry clicked in place. "Oh, Lord, I won!" Jane cried, feeling like an idiot as she jumped around to the applause. The clattering of nickels and the bells and lights brought Sandy running from the change booth, and they helped Jane fill her pockets and then their bowling bags. It seemed it would never stop: the cascade of coins, the flashing lights, the questions about her strategy, the spontaneous off-key burst of song from the bowling team—*"Money makes the world go 'round, the world go 'round, the world go 'round . . ."*

As she danced with Betty and Sandy, Jane suddenly spotted Dougie Smathers a row away, sitting at a nickel machine, a bucket of coins between his fat thighs, wearing a baby blue velveteen swinger suit from the Sammi Martini collection. Someone must have told Dougie that light blue went well with bloodshot eyes, because it was the predominant color in his wardrobe. (Being with Sandy and Betty had almost made Jane forget that, only a short time ago, she had rifled through his suit-case.) He looked like a cheap hood, and he was playing the part to the hilt—pinching cocktail waitresses, balancing cigarettes on his nose, and acting like the King of the Nickels.

Jane stopped dancing, and her hand automatically went to her black eye, still swollen under Wanda's thick application of makeup. She hoped he hadn't noticed her amid the commotion. "Is that the bastard who gave you the black eye?" asked Betty.

Jane nodded. "Dougie Smathers. He's a rival insurance agent."

Sandy peered at him through her cat glasses. "He looks as cheap as his suit," she snorted. "That's one of those shitty J.C. Penney Sammi Martini knockoffs. I swear, Betty, Chickie was the last of the really classy hoods." A flash went off in Jane's face, a tourist taking a snap of the lucky winner, and, startled, she jumped, colliding with a tired looking cocktail waitress dressed like a harem girl.

"Complimentary cocktail, master?" the woman purred, seemingly unbothered at getting kicked around by inebriated customers. Jane was about to accept when she saw Smathers slide off his stool and head for the door to the street. Relieved he hadn't seen her, she relaxed and held out her hand for the drink while reaching into her pocket for a tip. Mis-reading her gesture, Betty grabbed Jane by the elbow.

"Let's get him in the parking lot," she whispered, imagining a gun. "There are too many witnesses here." She pointed toward the ceiling, at the cameras fixed into the acoustic tile every couple of feet. Linking arms, Betty and Sandy walked Jane out of the casino, but not before Betty fished around in her wallet. "I could fix you up with a good con-cealer, dear," she said, dropping her AVON CALLING! business card onto the waitress's tray.

Jane clanked when she walked, every pocket stuffed with coins. They had lost track of Dougie in the crowd and didn't spot him in the parking lot, so they decided to duck into a nearby cocktail lounge to count their money.

"It's all yours," Jane said over Sandy's protests as she emptied the bowling bags onto the table. "That was your machine."

"Whoever pulls the lever takes home the cash. It's the law of the land. But I *will* help you count it," Sandy said, and began slinging coins like a pro, stacking them twenty high until a city of little skyscrapers emerged on the tabletop. "Fifty-seven dollars and fifteen cents."

Jane slid a stack to the edge of the table when the waitress brought three beers.

"Fifty-six dollars and fifteen cents," calculated Sandy.

"I can't carry all these nickels," protested Jane. "It will ruin my girl-ish figure."

Sandy hooted. "Betty says you have an awfully nice caboose for a fella."

"Sandy! I never said that!"

"Well, I'm too much of a lady to repeat what you *really* said."

As a flush crept up her neck, Betty cast about for a new topic. "I think Jim should use his winnings and catch a show. You haven't really seen Las Vegas until you've seen a show."

Jane's ass all but forgotten, the women listed all the most popular at-tractions the Strip had to offer. "Wayne Newton's at the Sahara," Sandy said. "He's a real up-and-comer; I predict someday this place will be called Las Newton."

"Liberace's at the Riviera," said Betty. "They say it's the gayest show in town, but tonight's the last night and it's probably sold out. It's too bad Sammi Martini isn't playing tonight. I would have suggested that straightaway."

"Glug, glug." Sandy pretended to drink her beer in one gulp, and then began to gargle.

"Very funny. That's her Sammi Martini imitation."

"Phyllis Diller's taken over his show, according to the attendant at my service station. Apparently," Sandy added with a glimmer in her eyes, "Mr. Martini swam out of town on a whiskey river."

"Who hasn't?" sighed Betty. "There's no one else I'd pay to see, but there's always the water show at the Sands. It's glorious, Jim. You sit in a dark room, eating lobster and drinking champagne, and one whole wall is an aquarium full of beautiful mermaids."

"Do you like seafood, Jimmy? We got crabs once in Atlantic City," Sandy said without waiting for an answer. "That was nice."

"We *ate* crabs in Atlantic City," Betty corrected.

Jane smiled. "Let's see if we can get crabs in Las Vegas."

"You shouldn't spend your money on us, Jim," Betty said through a mouthful of buttery lobster. They were seated at a small round table set with a linen cloth and silver cutlery and elegant flutes of champagne.

"She's right," said Sandy, buttering a roll. "You should buy your girl a present. Casino-chip earrings are always nice. Betty, those bibs would certainly come in handy when you bleach my hair," she added, eyeing a stack on a waiter's tray. "Would it be pushing things to have another shrimp cocktail?" she asked shyly. Jane ordered shrimp cocktails all around, and another magnum of champagne. She had a feeling their waiter wouldn't be so polite once he realized they were paying in nickels.

"Chickie used to take me to places like this," said Betty wistfully, sizing up the women in glittery cocktail dresses. Their own casual attire had been judged unacceptable, but their money perfectly satisfactory, so the manager had seated them in a dark corner next to the kitchen. Each time the door flew open, their view of the wall-size aquarium was blocked and the candle in the center of the table flickered and went out.

Lost in memories of better days, Betty said little, and Sandy knew to let her meander through the past uninterrupted.

"Sorry for the view," said Jane, misreading Betty's silent reverie for disappointment.

Betty smiled and patted her hand. "It smells better back here than it ever did up there," she said, wiping her fingers on a damp warm towel before picking up her champagne glass. "The chlorine makes everything taste a little antiseptic. Who wants to be seen in public in a bib anyway?"

"Everyone here is afraid of germs." Sandy licked butter from her fingers and signaled the waiter for more crab legs. Sipping champagne, Jane watched, amused, as Sandy did her best to comply with the menu's promise of "all-you-can-eat-crab legs."

"Sandy's got a theory about germs and Las Vegas. Sandy's got a theory about everything. That one"—Betty stabbed a finger at her friend—"she's always thinking."

"And your theory is . . . ?" Jane asked Sandy.

"It's a way of making sinners feel clean. Ever notice how the glasses are covered in soap spots? It's no accident. You come here to do things that, back home, would get you kicked out of your church, or the rotis-series—"

"Rotarians," Betty translated.

"—or your nice neighborhood or your marriage. When you go to the airport, what's in the vending machines?"

"Chewing gum?" Jane guessed. "Cigarettes?"

Sandy shook her head. "Moist towelettes made with holy water."

Jane's laugh extinguished the candle. The lights dimmed, signaling the beginning of the show. They were pitched into darkness, and then streams of colored water—aqua and pink and a color Betty called mauve—shot out of plaster dolphins set to each side of an enormous fish tank in front of a mural of the Bermuda Triangle. Four unhappy-looking mermaids fluttered in the water, their arms beckoning like hula dancers'.

"How do they breathe?" asked Jane, who had never learned to swim and found it incomprehensible that someone would willingly put her head underwater.

"There are air hoses hidden in the seaweed," Sandy said. "And King Neptune keeps on eye on them." She pointed out a beefy, short-necked merman sitting on the edge of the tank, with a sinister-looking trident in his hand. "He also keeps an eye on their tips, to make sure they don't stuff any coins down their bra when he's not looking. He gets half, and they divvy up the rest."

"What a miserable way to make a living," said Jane, ashamed that she had barely been able to stand her brief stint as a land maid.

"Most jobs in this town *are* miserable," Sandy said. She should know; she was seventy-two and still looking for the right career. "After paying for your costume and weekly cleanings, your tips are all you have to live on." She put her hand down her shirt looked for the quarter she had stashed there, for emergencies.

"Take this," said Jane, jingling the bowling bag with over fifty dollars in change. "I've got plenty of money."

"Jim, you're being awfully generous," said Betty. "We'd like to do something for *you*."

"You've been charming tour guides."

"Perhaps you'd like to come over for lunch tomorrow?"

"We're having crab salad." Sandy said, signaling for one more platter, then excusing herself. Bowling bag in hand, she sidled up to the tank, climbed three rungs up the ladder, and emptied the nickels into the water, blinking back tears as the chlorine pricked her eyes and nose. When she returned to the table, the fresh crab legs had arrived, along with a telegram for a Mr. James Bland.

"So that's your last name. Bland. Jimmy Bland. Classy." Sandy set the empty bowling bag on her lap and put down a layer of shaved ice from her shrimp cocktail so the crab would be fresh when she got home. "I like it." Her last name, she explained, was difficult to pronounce and even harder to spell, so everyone just called her Sandy. "I've been Miss Sandy, Mrs. Sandy, and Damn you Sandy!"

"It's Beach," said Betty. "Nothing hard about that. Sandy Beach. Now, Jim, what's in the telegram?"

"It's probably from the mermaids saying they don't accept nickels," joked Jane.

Emerald ill. Stop. Leaving on 10 o'clock flight. Stop. Bibi detained by authorities. Stop. Sorry, darling. Stop. You're on your own. Stop. I love you. Stop. Bridget.

"It's from your girl, isn't it?" Betty said softly, reading the distress in Jane's eyes.

Jane nodded and downed a glass of champagne.

"What does it say?" Sandy said as she refilled Jane's glass. Her third husband had sent her a telegram announcing he was on his honeymoon, and would she please get a divorce and send him the papers? "Is it a Dear John-o-gram?"

Jane shook her head and tucked the telegram in her pocket. "She went back to London. Her mother's ill." In order for Bridget to drop out of a mission, Emerald must be dying—or pretending she was. As much as the Duchess of Malomar infuriated Jane, she did hope it was another false alarm. Poor Bridget. Once, while bending over to scold her King Charles spaniel for using an Italian marble floor as a toilet, Emerald got a strand of hair caught in her ruby bracelet. Bridget received a frantic call from Emerald's social secretary, informing her that the duchess had been taken to the hospital with a devastating head wound.

"Her mother probably tripped over her own name," Sandy said. "Let's hope she hit her head, not too hard, but just enough so she suffers from amnesia; that way she won't remember that she doesn't like you."

Betty laughed, but Jane wasn't paying attention. As determined as she was to find the invention on her own, it had been nice knowing that experienced agents were a call away. Then again, remembering her lost wallet and the hotel operator's insistence that there was no Eleanor or Mamie registered at the Sands, Jane realized that finding Bridget and Bibi would have taken more skills than she possessed. She was really on her own now.

Although stuffed with seafood, the ladies still had to think about tomorrow's meals, and so Jane found herself at the Dunes watching thin slices of honey-cured ham disappear into Sandy's bag, along with a loaf of

warm and crusty French bread and a jar of mustard. Jane was in charge
of holding the Tupperware containers as the gals filled them to the brim,
leaving only enough room for the air bubble and that all-important burp.
They had started with chilled vegetable salads, moved on to macaroni
and potato dishes, and were now deciding on entrées.

"The Sahara has the best ham in town," Sandy burbled happily,
pleased by tonight's haul. There would ham and eggs for breakfast, ham
salad for lunch, and ham croquettes for supper.

"Yeah, Wayne Newton sings here."

"After this, pie and pudding. Then we'll give other people a chance,"
said Betty, putting a dish of cool and creamy butter pats in her purse.

"You see, Jimmy, working the buffet table takes the concentration of
a blackjack dealer and the moves of a magician," explained Sandy. "See
the stout gal in the orange muumuu eyeing the roast they just wheeled
out? She's our biggest competitor. She weights ninety-eight pounds with
her shoes *on*. Those are bags of food under there. She's already hit the
Swiss steak, judging by that gravy stain under her arm."

"Does everyone do this?"

"Just the more mature set. It's our city's version of Social Security."

Betty put a plate of pepper steaks and stuffed peppers in her purse.
"We'll move on as soon as the potatoes au gratin pan is refilled," she said,
tapping the top of an empty Tupperware container. A scantily-clad showgirl slowed as she passed their table, flashing Jane a thousand-watt smile
and a come hither look over her plate of corned beef and cabbage. Jane
smiled—how could she not?—but shook her head when the girl slowed.
Realizing that Betty was gauging her reaction, Jane gave her a wink.
Betty blushed and slapped Jane's hand. "You're so much like Chickie."

"Parading the goods," snorted Sandy. "In the old days we knew how
to be almost-nude *and* ladylike."

"Sandy's had lots of high-class jobs. That's why she can be so hoity-
toity."

Slipping a salt shaker into her bag, which was beginning to smell like
a delicatessen, Sandy laughed and began to recite a laundry list of jobs,
beginning with a stint as a chicken plucker in Oklahoma. "I worked in a
paper-hat factory making dunce caps for the Omaha School District,
then I sewed the days of the week on panties. My third husband, Freddy,

moved us here, and I stayed home like a good wife until he lost all our savings in the nickel slots. It took him months, but he managed to spend every penny we had, even the change in the bottom of my purse."

"He was a real stinker," cut in Betty. "Oh, Sandy, the crab's not going to make it. Your bag smells like a smelt factory." Folding her paper napkin into a little boat, Jane inked *"The S.S. Betty"* on the side and placed it on Betty's bouffant. Reluctantly, Sandy took a plastic bag from her pocket and unloaded the crab.

"So you divorced him?" asked Jane.

"I shot him. He's not dead, but he's not happy."

Jane laughed until she realized Sandy wasn't kidding. Betty adjusted her paper-boat hat to sit at a rakish angle on her puff of hair, keeping an eye out for the waiter in charge of au gratin dishes. "It's a great story. I told her she should write it up and send it to *Reader's Digest.*"

"I was cleaning a .22 I kept in my purse. Back then, this town was the wild, wild, West, and every girl carried protection. Freddy decided it was the perfect time to inform me we had to sell the trailer and move in with his sister in Tempe. The jury found me not guilty, on account of the gun having a touchy trigger."

"On account of the jury was all women, is more like it," corrected Betty, her eyebrows knitting together as a warming tray was wheeled to the buffet, steaming like a geyser, then relaxing when she saw that it was only green beans amandine.

"On account of the men in this town think they're too important to bother with shit like jury duty."

Betty held out her hand, and Sandy dropped a quarter in it. "Every time she swears, I get another chance at winning the jackpot," said Betty, warming the coin in her hand before dropping it down her blouse. "A guy won five thousand dollars last year at a quarter slot. It hasn't paid out since, and I've been playing it like clockwork every Saturday."

"That's not a lot to a fella like you, but we retired gals have got to be careful." Sandy peered at the buffet table, to see if any fresh fruit carved in festive shapes had been put out.

"Betty's property taxes are due soon, and her rabbit shortie jacket and diamondaire bracelet aren't going to pay those. I own my trailer outright, but the city keeps threatening to tow it to the junkyard if I don't get new siding. Freddy said I should put aside my paycheck and buy a nice little two-bedroom ranch like Betty's, and come to find out, he was going to the damn bank each week and taking out what I put in. Nothing personal, Jimmy, but I'm glad I shot that man. My kids hate me, but I'm glad I did it. Seventy-two years old and still needing free eats." Sandy sighed, her face aging ten years.

"More husbands should be shot," said Jane, putting an arm around her shoulder. Sandy's back was bony and sharp, the muscles tight and knotted. Behind each ear was a deep cut where her face had been pulled into submission. Afraid she would cry, too, Jane looked to Betty for help.

"Look! It's Zsa Zsa Gabor!" Betty said, pointing at a beautiful blonde in a sleek, white, beaded, cocktail dress and matching eye patch. "She looks like a pirate's girlfriend, doesn't she? I hear she got an infection from her false-eyelash glue."

"Wrong," Sandy said. "I overheard two waitresses last week discussing what happened. Mr. Poo-poo, Zsa Zsa's Maltese, did his business on the carpet in the Lido Lounge, and when she bent down to pick him up, she hit her eye on a cocktail waitress's headlights. You can never be too careful in this town, Jim."

. . . .

twelve

While Jane was luxuriating in all the Strip had to offer, Bridget and Bibi, accused casino robbers, were lying low, trying to forget their plunge into drabness by throwing themselves into a game of poker. Bibi had stolen just a fraction of the deck, and they quickly abandoned the game in favor of a walk, to see the sights. A half mile of parched desert scrub and tumbleweeds later, they returned to the Teepee Village Motor Court, hungry and dusty, and wandered over to the coffee shop. The sandy strip in front of the restaurant had been swept since they arrived a few hours ago, revealing the words "Stop N' Eat" spelled out with green beer bottles turned upside down and embedded in the sand like ostrich heads. Christmas-tree lights drooped from a ripped green awning over the door, the electrical cord taped to the side of the tin house with duct tape. They were officially closed, but Wanda saw the girls outside and waved them in.

"Saturdays out here can be pretty quiet," she said, showing them to a clean booth smelling of ammonia and leatherette polish. "So I usually get a lot of my cooking done." She had baked three meat loaves earlier that evening, she told them, one of which her husband was devouring in the kitchen in front of Saturday Night at the Movies. "There's plenty to go around, and I'd be plenty glad for the company. My husband's glued to the TV." Five minutes later they were facing slabs of grayish brown meat, a mountain of mashed potatoes, canned green beans, small wooden bowls of a tomato-wedge and iceberg-lettuce salad smothered in a pinkish orange dressing, and squares of quivering lime Jell-O. "Eat up, girls. There's nothing worse than cold meat loaf."

"It looks delicious," said Bibi, squeezing half a bottle of ketchup onto hers while Bridget picked up her fork and moved the green beans around her plate.

"So what brings you pretty gals to Vegas all the way from ... *Florida?*" Wanda asked.

"Florida," Bibi nodded, liking the sound of it.

"We're on our way to Los Angeles," Bridget said. "We want to be in pictures."

"Did you know that, according to *Motion Picture* magazine, seventy-nine percent of young women polled chose motion pictures as the most desirable occupation, beating out glove salesgirl, hosiery model, and cafeteria lady?" said Wanda.

"We read that," said Bibi, swiping Bridget's green beans, which looked fresher than hers.

"Most of the girls who come here want to be in pictures. Sometimes they end up in the wrong kind, if you get my drift," warned Wanda.

"I do," said Bibi, remembering the time she had posed as a milkmaid for a butter ad.

Wanda leaned forward, examining their faces, which had been wiped clean of makeup. "You're pretty girls. I'd get out of town before this place ruins your complexion."

"It's the chlorine," Bridget said. She could feel the top layer of her skin peeling as they spoke. One day here and already she felt—and probably looked—months older.

"Hell, kid, chlorine's a preservative, everyone knows that. It's the bomb dust—one dose is worse than a year's worth of pool water. That's why I do all my tanning indoors, under my Elke Sommer Sun Lamp. Sure, they *say* they stopped testing out here five years ago, but I don't believe them. There's days when my fillings hurt. I just know the army's behind it. Of course, some say they're out here looking for flying saucers. They prefer New Mexico, but occasionally one sees the lights of Las Vegas and lands here by mistake. One landed here many years ago, in a sorrel patch behind Teepee Six. That was one reason the chief bought the place."

"Did you actually *see* this UFO?" asked Bridget, thinking that Jane, who collected kooks the way some people collected small dogs or postage stamps, would just love to meet Wanda.

Wanda took a pencil from her beehive and tapped it on the table, choosing her words with care. "It's easy to make fun of this kind of thing. I did when I first came here. Too much sand in the brain, I thought. But then I heard the story, and the more I heard, the more sense it made."

Bibi put down her forkful of mashed potato. "You're having us on!"

"No siree! The guy who used to own this place had a metal plate in his head, from the war. He said the magnetic field of the saucer lifted him through the air. That's all he remembers until waking up on his cot in the kitchen, smelling of muscatel and wearing a strange silver outfit. It was written up in a leading national magazine."

Bibi laughed and scooped up the potatoes. "I thought you were going to say you saw little green men."

"I did." Sinking back into her seat, crossing her arms across her stained uniform, Wanda watched the information sink in. Things happened to her that didn't happen to other people. She had been crowned Most Beautiful Baby in 1919, and twenty years later *to the day*, she had met a creature from outer space.

"Little green men," repeated Bibi.

Wanda nodded. "But I need another beer before I continue. Ladies? Another round?" As soon as Wanda left, Bridget slid her meat loaf into the napkin on her lap and put it on the seat next to her.

"How much of this do you have to drink to see little green men?" she wondered, spinning her empty bottle on the table, spraying Bibi with the last few drops.

"May I remind you," Bibi said, dipping a napkin in her water glass and scrubbing at the droplets of strong beer on the front of her expensive Dior creation, "that this is one of your favorite summer dresses?"

"Don't you have *any* clothes of your own?" Grease had begun to seep through the napkin onto the polished leatherette. "I know why you slept with Mimi. It's because you're the same dress size."

Sucking in a righteous gasp, and a mouthful of potatoes, Bibi said, "I had real feelings for her."

"Yes," Bridget said distractedly, soaking up the puddle with her paper place mat. "You felt her wardrobe would look better on you."

Examining her plastic daisy-petal watch, a sunny yellow face ringed by white petals—a farewell gift from Mimi—Bibi experienced a pang of unidentifiable emotion. It wasn't hunger, she thought, pushing aside her plate. Could it be heartburn? "Our relationship was the most miserable week and a half of my life. And the breakup . . . well, you were there for that humiliation."

"I've been there for all of them," Bridget said, patting her friend's desert-roughened hand, noting that Bibi needed a good moisturizing cream, and fast.

"When I saw Mimi hurl that jar of vanishing cream at Jane, I knew she could never be mine."

It was easy to forget that Bibi bruised as easily as anyone else. "You'll find another girl," Bridget assured her. "One without homicidal tendencies or chronic lying syndrome."

"Of course I will," Bibi said. "But will I ever find another size six with such a nice wardrobe?"

"Don't forget your vegetables, girls," Wanda said when returning from the kitchen, hugging three cans of icy-cold Fresca to her chest. "Sorry, girls, the Chief refused to part with more beer." Smiling when she saw that Bridget's meat loaf had disappeared, she urged her to try the vitamin-rich salad. Bridget put a forkful of pale green iceberg lettuce in her mouth and chewed. It was refrigerator cold, tasteless and watery. Turning her head, trying to be as dainty as possible given the nature of the deed, she spit the lettuce into a napkin. Bibi just gave in and shoveled the whole mess into her mouth.

"Why the looks of doom and gloom? It's the little green men, isn't it? Don't worry; if you see one, send 'em to me. I know how to talk to those creatures."

"It has nothing to do with little green men," said Bridget, wiping her mouth.

"Or green men," said Bibi.

"Or little men."

"I see where you're going with this," Wanda said, taking a long swig of soda. "You're really runaway housewives, aren't you? And you're going to the Dorothy Duncan Defrost-Off hoping to win first prize."

Bibi wiped Thousand Island dressing from her upper lip and observed Wanda. What, exactly, was under that hive of hair and varnish?

"I've heard this story a hundred times," Wanda explained. "You couldn't get jobs at home; what would you have told your husbands? So you spend months perfecting your best recipes, and came here with your suitcase packed, planning on heading to Reno. Oh, you didn't bring too many clothes; you wouldn't want to raise any suspicion. But you did bring your most precious items: a ring you inherited from your grandmother, say, or your high school yearbook. Perhaps the potholders you knit yourself, the ones *he* left on the stove and singed.

"Every year a hundred and fifty-eight women come for the cooking contest, and only one hundred and fifty-five go home. You can always tell the ones who are planning their escape. The minute they get here, they go a little crazy. They think they can smell freedom in the air, but that's only the casino-chip factory in Boulder City. Have you two considered becoming stewardesses if you don't win? You can lie about being married, and if your husbands catch up with you, you can hop a plane and fly away. I only ask because a stewardess checked in this evening. I gave her the unit next to yours, number five. She says a lot of movie directors fly these days, and on just about every flight, one offers to make her a star. She looks like Elizabeth Taylor right before her third marriage. Looks nice in her uniform, too; not everyone can wear such bright orange. I told her that, and you know what she said? 'I know.' Cool as a cucumber."

"Was her uniform a size too small?" said Bridget. "And her eyes

beady and close together?" Their new neighbor sounded like the same
air hostess who had climbed into Jane's lap, offering her shapely body as
a flotation cushion should they crash over the Atlantic. She had worn far
too much makeup.

"Oh, no, she was a perfectly beautiful girl—even the chief said so. But
he thought she looked more like Sophia Loren. He doesn't go to the
movies," she added. "Not enough bathroom breaks."

Through the plastic shower curtain dividing the kitchen and the dining room, they could hear the Late Late Night Movie come on, and
Wanda rolled her eyes in a gesture of mock exasperation. "Thank god
that damn things isn't on twenty-four-hours a day, or I'd never see my
husband." She yawned, getting to her feet, waving away Bridget's offer
to do the dishes. "Hon, I've got a dishwasher back there."

"Don't interfere," said Bibi. Bridget was always volunteering to perform nail-breaking tasks, with no thought to Bibi, whose nails were soft
and chipped easily. People who had grown up with maids always found
domestic work a lot more fun than it actually was. "We lost most of our
luggage in a train derailment in Terre Haute. Our casserole dishes, too."

Wanda looked at their simple shifts with an appraising eye. "I
thought maybe someone gave you those clothes. They won't do for the
Dorothy Duncan folks. They're real picky about who they let in. And you
might want to do something with your hair. It's real pretty, but anyone
can see it's a dye job."

"We're switching to Lady Clairol Ash Brown #31," Bridget said. "So
we'd better go and get started."

Wanda had to look away lest the girls see her tears. Ash Brown #31
had been her late mother's color. Meat loaf and Lady Clairol—it was almost as if Mom were right there with them. Misreading her reaction,
Bridget patted her hand. "I just don't like salad," she said.

Wanda patted her own impressive tower of hair, a good six inches
taller than theirs. "The Chief *hates* mine," she confided, lowering her
voice even though her husband was in the kitchen with the national an-
them blaring. "He says it makes him look short. I say, hon, you *are* short.
I wear a hairnet when I cook and a hat when we go to church, but I'll
never restyle it. The secret to a happy marriage is to have separate in-
terests. It keeps the conversation going. Everyone says it's sex, and

they're wrong. The only way a marriage can last is if a husband and wife spend time apart, having fun. My husband has his shows, and I have my hair. The minister even mentioned it in a sermon last week. He said God wouldn't approve of such a heathen display. I stood right up and quoted my friend Sandy: 'The higher the hair, the closer to heaven.' I bought a crumb cake at the baked-goods sale in the lobby, and then I left. Sometimes I don't think of something to say until I'm in bed. Lutherans," she snorted. "The hell with 'em."

It was after three, and despite their tales of all-night excursions, this had been too much for them. Their heads hung like wilted daisies, Betty's mascara had flaked off, and the chop suey in Sandy's purse was beginning to stink. It was time to go home. But first they had to stop at a grocery store for Clamato and Little Debbie Oatmeal Cakes, their antidote to a night of rich food. Jane offered to run in for them, anxious to get back to the teepee and find out what had happened on Cedric's date.

"The woman in front of me was buying diapers and beer with a casino chip," Jane said, returning to the car with the requested items plus two six-packs of Old Milwaukee and a bag of ice. After loading the cooler, she helped Sandy tighten the rope holding the trunk shut while Betty sat in the car, pouring juice into shot glasses. "Anyone want ice with their Clamato?"

Suddenly a car shrieked into the lot, spraying gravel in the air. A door opened, and Jane was overpowered by a cloud of Hai Karate.

"Mr. Bond. We meet again." She sneezed. Dougie Smathers had found her. She sneezed again and reached for her gun, remembering that she'd left it under the backseat, where she'd tossed it before bending over the fill the cooler. After sampling every item at the Riviera buffet, her trousers were simply too tight to accommodate a firearm. "Jane, someday you're going to need this, and it's not going to be there," Miss Tuppenny had said the day Jane left her gun atop the watercooler. That day had just arrived.

She heard a click. Jane knew it was a gun being cocked.

"Let's talk this over," she said calmly, afraid to turn her head.

"There's nothing left to say but sayonara, Mr. Bond."

"Wait. I might have something you want."

Smathers laughed, wheezing on the intake. "Those old broads? Your taste has certainly matured, but I prefer my women . . ."

He wasn't able to finish before Betty screamed "Duck!" and Jane hit the gravel, scraping her palms and her pride. The passenger door was flung open, hitting Dougie Smathers in the gut and sending him reeling. He bellowed, and as a group of agents jumped out of their rented Volkswagen, Sandy and Betty whooped at their matching baby blue suits. "If it ain't the Dougie Smathers Quartet," drawled Sandy. "Sing us a song, boys."

Confused, perhaps flattered at having been mistaken for recording artists, they began to hum. Dougie staggered to his feet and lunged for Jane, who knocked the gun out of his hand with a karate chop to the arm, punched him in the eye, then threw him into the vocal group, sending them tumbling and ending the painful rendition of "Mr. Sandman." Jane sauntered over to the fallen agents, figuring she deserved a good gloat. Wanting to get home before her Clamato got too warm, Sandy, once again exhibiting remarkable upper-body strength for a woman her age, pulled Jane into the car through the window. Betty roared off with that old getaway-car confidence, performing her best maneuver to date: She enveloped Dougie's crew in a dust cloud that was so thick it clogged the naps of their velveteen jackets. She almost sideswiped the station wagon parked around the other side of the grocery, in which Cedric sat behind the wheel with Felix at his side, both too engrossed in close conversation to notice the commotion the old aqua Cadillac was creating— or Jane's lower half hanging out the window.

Armed with old towels from Wanda, Bridget and Bibi turned on the shower and held their heads under the cold spray, layers of lacquer from their performance hairdos disappearing down the drain. After working the dark brown liquid through their still-stiff strands, they wrapped towels around their heads and set Wanda's egg timer to forty minutes. Bibi lay on the bed, fanning herself with a *Hair Do* magazine Wanda had loaned them, while Bridget opened the bathroom window in an attempt to air out the room, heavy with the chemical tang of hair preparations.

Dye running down her neck, her head boiling under her turban, Bridget used her palm to wipe a circle in the steamy bathroom mirror. Wanda was a doll, but she was awfully awake for a woman who got up at five in the morning to sling hash. They had stood in the coffeeshop's doorway, dying to leave, the heat of the desert blasting at their backs as they watched her reenact her wedding-day march up the aisle, using a napkin dispenser as a bouquet. When the Chief came into the dining room to collect the empty beer bottles (worth a penny apiece), Wanda had just stopped in front of the jukebox altar. "It was here I paused to rethink my decision. My mother kicked me in the butt, and I knocked over the minister."

"Justice of the peace," her husband corrected her. Slouching against the counter in a filthy T-shirt, he chewed lazily on a toothpick, the picture of indolence and filth. When he looked at Wanda, though, his small brown eyes took on a dopey expression. They argued good-naturedly about the dress his sister wore that day. It was blue, Wanda insisted, and she had dyed her shoes to match. It was beer-bottle green, he said, and reached for a shoe box of yellowing color-tinted snapshots from under the counter to support his position. Bridget looked at Bibi, and both knew they'd be stuck there until the end of the wedding reception, so they sat down and opened another Fresca.

"Happy couples are so depressing," said Bibi, stretching out on the twin bed. How they'd both be able to sleep on the narrow mattress was a mystery. "Maybe one of us should sleep on that delightfully soft yak rug. The floor is cooler, and concrete is so good for the back."

"You've sure slept in worse places." Padding around in bare feet, Bridget unpacked her beautiful cocktail dresses and fun new swimwear, not because she would need them but to give herself something to do. If she sat now, she'd be asleep before her eyelids closed, and they still had to finish their hair. Mopping up the bathroom would mean more than scrubbing dark dye from the sink; when Bibi saw her hair, Bridget knew there would be tears.

"Are we depressing?" she asked, holding up a gorgeous white beaded Dior cocktail dress, one she planned to wear their last night here, a night on the town to celebrate their success. "Jane and I?"

"Bloody damn depressing. I've never seen two happier people. If I didn't know you better, I'd say you and Jane and Wanda all take the same brand of vitamins. Say, do you see the woman on the cover of this hair-dye box? She's wearing an apron and holding a casserole dish." Inside was a half-off coupon for a new and exciting type of frozen-food product, Dorothy Duncan Liver Spots. *All the goodness of liver in bite-size pieces!* "We've just dyed our hair with the official hair color of the Dorothy Duncan Defrost-Off."

"We'll blend in *beautifully*." There was no reason now to take the paper stuffing out of her purses; evening wear would be limited, for the rest of the trip, to shortie pajamas, cold cream, and curlers.

"Listen." Bibi put aside her magazine, the page folded down to mark an interesting article about the trend toward ironed hair. "Someone's singing." A girl's clear, sweet voice was coming from the next teepee. Bibi prided herself on her almost encyclopedic knowledge of pop songs and telly commercial jingles, but she couldn't place the upbeat tune.

Bridget shut the window; she could name that tune, and she was livid. "*Fly me to the moon and let me play among the stars*" indeed! An out-of-tune stew on the flight from New York had used an official aviation intercom to sing it to Jane. "It's the same damn stew who took *Coffee, Tea or Me?* a little too seriously!"

"I want to meet her and show her the ins and out of teepee living," said Bibi, hopping out of bed.

"Go ahead, play the vicar's wife. I'll shout when the buzzer goes off."

"My hair!" Bibi's hands flew to her towel turban, and all thoughts of entertaining died along with her natural blond beauty. "I can feel the ugliness through the terry cloth. This is going to be just dreadful."

"We've been through tough times before, Bibi. Remember that cave in France? We were there for three weeks and ran out of chocolate after two days. And we survived."

"I was having my *period*."

"I know, honey. I'm not blaming you. I'm just trying to make you understand that this time we've run out of options."

Unwrapping her towel, Bibi tried not to look in the mirror as she bent over the sink and began rinsing her hair. "It hasn't fallen out," she said cheerfully. "At least I'm not bald. And there's nothing here that can't be undone, right?" When she looked in the mirror, she bit her lip so she wouldn't cry. "I look twenty-five!" wailed the twenty-four-year-old. And where's the brown part? It's practically gray! It makes me look positively dowdy."

"We are *going* for dowdy," Bridget pointed out. "But I see what you mean—it washes all the color out of our skin. I hope we don't run into Jane before we have a chance to dye it back." Bridget's transition from strawberry blond to black had been a difficult one for Jane, whose attachment to Bridget's silken mane bordered on obsession.

"Jane has a single black eyebrow," pointed out Bibi. "She's hardly in a position to criticize. And I don't think we look *that* bad. How could we? In fact, this terrible hair color makes the rest of us us look even *more* attractive by comparison. Tomorrow everyone will be asking, 'Who are those pretty girls? That horrible hair does not do them justice!'"

"We look like extras in a floor-wax commercial." In an unusual display of temper, Bridget threw her boar-bristle hairbrush out the window. Tomorrow morning they would present themselves at the Dorothy Duncan Defrost-Off, being held at the Las Vegas Convention Center, as Mrs. Myrtle Metz and Mrs. Bertha Brightman, sisters from Indiana detained by a train derailment. Once inside, possessing legitimate conference passes, they could be available at a moment's notice should Jane require their services. Although it might involve the thawing of food, it would be worth it. No one could possibly think two ordinary housewives carrying casserole dishes were Mata Haris.

"Sit," said Bridget, motioning toward the closed toilet. She took shears from her cosmetics case and opened Wanda's hairstyle magazine to a feature on America's best-loved television housewives, propping it on the back of the toilet. Combing Bibi's shoulder-length hair until it lay in flat streaks around her face, she raised the shears. "Just close your eyes and think of Mary Quant," she said as long, medium-brown locks fell to the floor. After she had scissored off a good six inches, she began separating the wet locks into small sections, then winding them on narrow foam rollers.

"I hope that when Jane finds this invention, it turns out to be a reversible hair dye," Bibi said, closing her eyes so she wouldn't have to see Bridget's expression. "God knows, we already have enough weapons in the world. Why can't they invent something we really need?"

When they finally got to bed, well after midnight, the stew next door was watching the Late Late Night Movie, *Dracula Goes to Harvard*, with the volume turned way up, and laughing like a loon. The sounds carried through the still desert air.

"I'm afraid of vampires." Bibi shivered in Bridget's arms.

"I'm afraid of stewardesses," replied Bridget. The only way they both fit in the narrow twin bed was to spoon so tightly that, had the fabric of their nighties been any thicker, one of them would be hanging off the side of the bed. The idea of sleeping one on top of the other had been explored, but each girl wanted to be on top. The Teepee Village slot-machine chip had been tossed, and twice it had landed on its edge. They went to bed, their newly shorn brown locks in tight curlers and encased in ugly hairnets, and Bibi cried for almost an hour about her tarnished hair, squandered youth, and martyred glamour. When sleep finally came, it was brutish and short, like life in medieval England. Shortly after drifting off, Bridget had a bad dream involving a stewardess, Jane, and a jar of vanishing cream, and Bibi woke them both by screaming, having dreamed she was the woman on the Lady Clairol box.

• •

thirteen

They had slept badly. Bibi, unhappy about how her new hair color muddied her peachy complexion, had spent more time in the bathroom sighing at the mirror than she had in bed. Bridget woke up each time Bibi bounced back into bed, and right before dawn she gave up trying to relax into sleep on her foam-curler helmet and got up. Grabbing her robe and Bibi's paperback novel, she went outside to sit on the stoop. The air was cool and welcoming, the traffic along the highway sparse and quiet. By the light of the gold torch hanging from her charm bracelet, she flipped through *Valley of The Dolls*, a trail of drugs, sex, and broken dreams, fascinated by the passages Bibi had underlined with a strawberry-scented pink-ink pen. "Complete and utter trash," she murmured to herself, flipping back to Chapter One to start at the beginning. There had to be more to this book than lurid descriptions of drug-addled sex maniacs. It was,

Bibi insisted when she packed it in her cosmetics case, an important resource when trying to understand the psyche of the modern American woman.

An hour passed. The traffic thickened as trucks headed into town, carrying liquor and vegetables and new decks of cards. Then the armored cars rolled by, thirteen of them, one for each casino. By the rosy light of dawn, she could see into the convertibles and sedans fleeing the city, the drivers hunched over the steering wheels and their passengers slumped against the doors, the new sun sweeping their exhaustion under the dusty carpet of desert, an exchange of night for day. "Come back later when you're all bright and shiny," Bridget thought, waving away a sand flea before getting back to her book. She was deeply engaged in the riveting bestselling study of American single womanhood, and barely noticed the aqua Cadillac barreling down the highway, dragging its muffler, until it squealed to a stop, backed up, and turned into the motor court's gravel drive, heading in her direction, shuddering and coughing like a pack-a-day smoker. Pulling her robe closed, Bridget went inside.

"Almighty God, what's that racket?" Bibi cried, sitting straight up. Rolling out of bed and into her slippers, a move she had perfected after spotting the scorpion warning posted on the inside of the door, she put her eye to the dirty triangular window, her mouth agape. "It's a spaceship! I see lights. White lights. Do you hear that horrible noise? Bridget, I really think this *must* be a UFO! Where's my camera?" Gripping her Instamatic, her finger on the shutter release, Bibi flung open the door and started shooting and didn't stop until the oil and exhaust got to her nostrils. The woman standing by the open passenger door had a platter of luncheon meats in one hand, a bread basket nestled in the crook of her arm, and was spreading mustard onto a piece of white bread. Bibi heard a mournful moan from the car's backseat, so she slammed the door.

"Aliens?" Bridget asked brightly.

"We'll have to develop the pictures and see," she sniffed, climbing back into bed and pulling the covers over her head.

Jane unlocked the door to her teepee, wondering about the scream from the unit on her left. Daylight was still a ways away, and already a

Las Vegas drama had begun. Had someone gambled away her ranch house and just realized what she'd done, or had she merely been up all night, now hysterical at the sight of a comfortable bed? Stumbling through the darkened teepee, Jane peeled off her jacket, kicked off her boots, and fell into bed—right on top of Agent Felix Bivens of the FBI.

"Communists!" he screamed, diving under the covers.

Cedric rolled over and stared at her through bloodshot eyes.

"What the hell are you doing in my bed?" yelled Jane, jumping up.

"There was something moving around in my teepee," he explained. "Felix was certain it was a *family* of spiders. When you weren't home at two, I assumed you weren't coming home at all." He looked at Jane, silently beseeching her to understand, to give up her room just awhile longer. "We're in our *pajamas*."

Felix peeked out from under the sheet. "I'm sorry I called you a communist."

"Hello, Bivens." There was no bloody way the chap in Cedric's blue-striped nightshirt was a genius scientist. Sighing, she put her boots back on and picked up her jacket. Felix was pretending he had fallen back to sleep, giving a hammy imitation of a snorer. "Just change the sheets," said Jane, backing out of the teepee and crossing paths with Wanda, in a chenille robe. She was smoking a cigarette, holding two dresses and a paper bag with old shoes sticking out of it. "The girls in Unit Three were in a train wreck," she said. "Two runaway housewives, but that's all I can tell you 'cause they're on the lam. Hey, you got a girl in there? I heard giggling earlier. It sounded like *two* girls giggling." Wanda tried to look around Jane, who blocked the door. Gambling, prostitution, and the mob—all were legal or tolerated, but she had a feeling two secret agents in one bed might set off some alarm. Wanda raised one painted-on brow, and Jane couldn't tell if she was shocked, amused, or simply concerned about the one-person maximum-occupancy rule.

"Airline hostesses. I met them on the plane."

Wanda nodded. "I read *Coffee, Tea or Me?*," she assured Jane with a smirk. "I'm no square."

"We'll be needing more towels—of course we'll pay for them. Would you mind leaving them on the stoop? The girls are a bit . . . shy."

Wanda let out laugh. "What a week! I've got a British swinger, airline hostesses, and runaway wives." After extracting a promise from Jane to keep her nocturnal activities a secret from the Chief, who was a Baptist and might get ideas of his own, Wanda went back to work.

The smell of Old Spice was overpowering when Jane opened the door to Cedric's stuffy teepee. After escorting the perfectly harmless spider out the bathroom window, she stripped down, ripped the blanket off the bed, and fell onto the cool sheets. The giggling next door started up, and Jane laughed. She was both pleased Cedric had finally met someone and thought it ironic that after all his complaining she was sorry she had to listen to it. When the giggling stopped, Jane swore she could hear the same pushy stew from the plane who had sung to her over the intercom, after the safety demonstration. *"Fly me to the moon . . . "* a girl sang, and Jane, certain she was hallucinating, passed into dreamless sleep.

"There is not *one* redeeming scene in this entire novel," Bridget threw the book at the figure huddled under the sheet.

"Sod off. I'm tired."

"You kept me up all bloody night," Bridget said, jumping on Bibi. "'Does this color make my skin look green? Who's prettier, me or Princess Margaret? What if all my hair falls out? Would it be the end of my dating career?'" she mocked.

"I'm sick," said Bibi, pushing Bridget aside and struggling to sit up. She did look pale and a bit green, but it could just be the new hair color against her skin. "Is it possible to get a hangover from meat loaf?" she asked. Leaning against the headboard, she began to undo her rollers, dropping them on the cement floor. She didn't need a mirror to tell her the ugly truth. While she slept, her hair had been brutally curled, surrendering to the iron fist of Dippity-do, and was now tight, controlled, no-nonsense hair. Hair the queen would wear.

"We'll get Vidal Sassoon himself to fix it," promised Bridget. "This is only for a few days—besides, I've always thought you'd look good in something short and sassy." At these words Bibi perked up and ran her fingers through her ruined hair, fluffing the tight curls while Bridget removed the curlers from her own ash-brown disaster.

"At least the dye covers your gray hair," Bibi said brightly. Bridget had exactly one, in the middle of her head, and until now it had resisted all color.

"Sod off." A tentative knock at the door interrupted what could have become a pillow fight, had the room come with more than one pillow.

"It's the aliens," said Bridget, pushing Bibi off the bed with a giggle.

"Girls? It's Wanda."

Bibi put the pillowcase over her head, and Bridget checked the floor for hairy creepy-crawlies before padding to the door. Wanda had an apron over her worn chenille robe and ketchup on one of her bunny slippers.

"I heard you moving around in here, and thought I'd deliver these while I had the chance." Holding out two dresses on wire hangers, Wanda flicked an ash from her cigarette, pushed her way inside, and dropped her bag onto the chair.

"You're up awfully early," said Bridget, all hopes of going back to bed dashed.

"The first breakfast rush is already over. Served eggs and bacon to a whole busload of nuns headed for the Hoover Dam and everyone heading out of Vegas after a crazy night on the Strip."

"On three hours' sleep?" Bridget handed her an ashtray made of a gold-painted clamshell.

"It's these pills my doctor gave me for my nerves," Wanda explained. "I only need a few hours' sleep. Since I had the time, I thought up a winning recipe for you girls. Tabsicles. They're quick and easy and have zero calories. That's where all the food of the future is headed. Zero calories. And I have your outfits." She held up the dresses she had dug up after hearing of their tragic train wreck and lost luggage. Two ugly, wrinkled, dotted-swiss dresses with saggy hems, left behind by Wanda's sister on her last visit, had been transformed into two ugly, pressed, dotted-swiss dresses with razor-sharp hems. "Well, what do you think?" Hanging their costumes on the shower rod, Wanda picked up the stained, neatly folded towels on the edge of the tub. "The fellow next door, his teepee looks like a twister roared through it. Girls sure are neater. I went in there last night to turn down the bed and tripped over his suitcase, right there on the floor! And I'm not even accident-prone.

Did I tell you we're having a centipede invasion? Just flush the little buggers."

Bibi pulled the pillowcase off her head and slid out of bed, taking a tentative few steps toward the bathroom mirror and the cruel light of morning.

"I would have never recognized you," said Wanda. "You look just like the model on the box!"

"We know we're hideous," said Bibi. "This hair is going to be the death of me!"

"I've had plenty of hair disasters," Wanda confided. "A couple of years ago, I chopped off the top of my beehive in the meat slicer, but didn't realize it until my husband pointed it out. Some trucker got a hair-and-baloney sandwich that day! I just pinned on a new cap and went about my business. Everyone asked if the Chief had run over me with a lawn mower. The sheriff even stopped by as a joke to make sure he hadn't. Boy, did I get sick of that one!" She patted her perfect tower of hair with pride of ownership. "It grew back, and in time yours will, too." But Bibi wasn't listening—she was staring at the hundreds of tiny raised dots on the dress, wondering if the bad taste she was forced to suffer through in Las Vegas would follow her back to London. Bridget, who had attended four years of boarding school in a middy blouse and baggy blue serge skirt, was less inclined to collapse under the weight of an unattractive outfit, said, "You pick first. The yellow will be pretty with your 'blue' eyes."

Examining the bust darts and narrow waist, Bibi sucked in her breath and wondered how much weight she could lose in the next ten minutes. "The waistband's so tiny it'll never fit. And the flared skirt is just going to make my hips look bigger." Wanda pointed to a bag on the chair, containing white girdles, satiny peach half-slips, and boned bras, stained yellow under the arms but clean. The shoe selection was ghastly: a pair of tan lace-up rubber-soled oxfords that shouted "I've got a bunion!" and a pair of blindingly white pumps with a low, scuffed heel.

"They were mother's. She had unusually large feet," said Wanda as Bibi held one narrow canoe in her hand and looked ill. Sighing, Bibi grabbed an armload of undergarments and shut herself in the bathroom. Wanda dropped a nickel into the radio and tuned it to the news report: *"Vivian Vance seeks a divorce from her husband of nine months, Wayne Newton's publicist revealed today that the popular singer has received two threatening letters on Sands stationery this past week. The police have asked the public to be on the lookout for a disgruntled fan, most likely female, who dots her i's with a smiley face."* A moment later a shriek echoed through the teepee, which was punctuated by sobs from the bathroom, then the sound of running water.

"Think she's going to drown herself?" asked Wanda.

"If she was going to kill herself, she would have done it last year when she wore mismatched shoes to a Dusty Springfield concert," Bridget said as Bibi emerged from the bathroom in the navy blue dress, a twin to the tragic lemon-curd-yellow number Bridget would have to wear. With her hair combed into a modest bouffant, and a short strand of fake pearls circling her neck, she looked every bit the homey housewife they were trying to emulate, the type of woman who, when not separating her darks from her lights, made fried chicken for her church's picnic suppers and sewed name tags into her children's camp clothes. Her face, scrubbed clean with only a touch of powder and a hint of coral lipstick, looked youthful but blank, as if time hadn't written a story on her yet.

It took considerable effort to get Bibi out of the teepee. After a half hour of soothing assurances that her true beauty still shone through, Bridget finally promised to buy her anything she wanted from the Mary Quant collection. Now, at the Teepee Village Coffee Shop, with a cup of tea in front of her and a western omelet on its way, she seemed restored to her usual good humor.

"If I get one of the new Mary Quant all-weather anoraks, I'd have to get the matching cap."

"Only if you put that salt shaker back," said Bridget. Bibi stuck out her tongue and returned the small ceramic horse to its cowboy mate.

"Now I just have to decide which of the new colors goes best with my creamy complexion," Bibi continued. "Do you think the trend toward bright colors will hold? I'd like to be able to wear it until November, at least."

Bridget leaned across the counter for a piece of the morning paper. Relegated to two corner stools in front of the revolving doughnut case, they seemed to be the only customers who had not committed the menu to memory.

"Are you listening? No. Always reading." Bibi snatched the paper to see what it was that held her friend's interest. "'Will Vivian Vance survive tawdry divorce proceedings or will she lose her status as American's best-loved comedic second banana?'" she read aloud. "Who the hell is Vivian Vance?"

Bridget shrugged and pointed at the bottom of the first page of the Women's Section, and Bibi picked it up and started to read.

"'The annual Dorothy Duncan Defrost-Off competition, in which America's most creative housewives vie for thousands of dollars in cash and prizes, got off to a chilly start yesterday when two disgruntled showgirls dressed as potatoes hurled themselves off the stage during Act 3 of *Frost Side Story*, an original adaptation of a Broadway hit and this year's entertainment. According to witnesses, audience members were just finishing box lunches when the girls, unhappy at having to wear unflattering costumes, caused a near riot by setting their cardboard suits on fire, then putting out the flames by rolling in contestant Marge Milligan's delicious carrot sheet cake, meant for the cast party. When asked if she would bake again, Mrs. Milligan replied, "Yes, I'll bake again."

"'The top prize this year of ten thousand dollars will go to the frozen-food aficionado with the most tantalizing TV dinner.'"

Bibi put down the paper. "I'm not sure exactly what a TV-dinner *is*, but I'm certain we can win!"

"Dope. I meant this." Bridget pointed to the headline: HAVE YOU SEEN THESE GIRLS? Below it were sketches based on witness descriptions that must have been done by one of the caricaturists working the Strip. Two wide-eyed, busty cartoon dames carrying enormous suitcases and tiny guns were posed in front of a slot machine spewing nickels. Both girls were wearing skimpy showgirls outfits with sequins over "the naughty bits." "We have nothing to worry about—my own mother wouldn't recognize me from this drawing," laughed Bridget, reading the caption. "Listen to this: 'A witness has tentatively identified one of the robbers as a Miss Mary Quaint.'"

"Quant!" Bibi cried. "Mary Quant!"

* * *

"Rise and shine!" Felix sang in Jane's ear.

She had fallen asleep in the back of the station wagon after Cedric dragged her out of bed at the god-awful hour of nine o'clock and informed her they were going to tour the J. Edgar Hoover Dam before attempting to rejoin the convention for the one o'clock soup-and-sandwich lunch. "I'm sure that by now the events of yesterday are water under the bridge," he said with the kind of annoying cheerfulness that came from having had a good snog (and perhaps a shag) the night before.

"I doubt it," she murmured, debating whether to tell him about her tussle with Dougie Smathers outside the all-night grocery. Why hadn't she laced that fifth of scotch she had left for him with knockout drops? None too anxious to face Dougie Smathers, and the eye she had blackened, and remembering to be grateful that she had dodged the Liberace bullet, she agreed to go, but first went into the Teepee diner for coffee to go (three cups, with a wink from Wanda), bypassing the last of the stale doughnuts. They would eat at the dam. Once in the car, she stretched out in the back, her head on Cedric's fuzzy-dice pillow, and listened to them debate the merits of indoor flight. It seems Liberace had made his entrance by flying across the stage in an ermine cape, supported by a thin wire. Worried he would crash, it had taken Cedric three songs to calm down.

"That's why we ordered champagne," Felix explained, as if anyone needed a reason to order champagne in Las Vegas.

"I got a little tipsy," Cedric admitted. "So Felix drove me back to the Motor Court. He came in to see my stamp collection—"

"—and by the time I finished admiring his 1961 East Indies Jacqueline Kennedy two-cent stamp—"

"—I was too sleepy to drive him home."

"Safety first," said Jane, giving their act points for timing. Felix must, understandably so, have assumed that James Bond, A Stud, would be uncomfortable with his seduction of Cedric. *The Seduction of Cedric*—now, *that* was a book title, Jane thought. It was her last until she woke forty-five minutes later in a crowded parking lot, with dot impressions on her face. It seemed everyone was here today: the Sacramento California Shriners, Miss Firth's James K. Polk Elementary School fourth-grade class, and the

Gay Divorcée Club of Reno, Nevada. "I'm too tired," she groaned, wishing she hadn't let Sandy and Betty talk her into one last trip to the buffet table for fried cheese in mustard sauce. It hadn't mixed well with the Clamato–and–Little Debbie Oatmeal Cake chaser. "You chaps run along."

Cedric opened the door and stood with his hands on his hips like a stern headmistress. "We didn't come this far to have you miss America's greatest monolithic engineering marvel," he said. "When are you going to have this opportunity again?"

She slithered out of the car, wishing there weren't so many people around so she could pistol-whip him. In the past year, Jane had limited her alcohol consumption to one drink in the evening, and she'd become accustomed to waking up clearheaded. Her companions last night had drunk cheap beer as if it were water, and Jane had done her best to keep up, not wanting to be a party pooper. "Don't let me fall over the edge," she said now, unsteady from fatigue and a queasy stomach.

"Somebody really tied one on last night," Felix teased.

"I don't want to hear any more about your evening," said Jane.

"You promised to be nice to Felix," Cedric hissed in her ear. "If he wants to talk about Liberace, you're to listen and respond in kind. He's on the verge of revealing his invention to me. One false move on your part and . . . well, Her Majesty will be very disappointed."

"Sorry. I had a hard night."

He looked at the dark circles under her bloodshot eyes. "You thought you could find the solution to your problems with Agent Smathers in a bottle, didn't you?"

"In a way, yes." She hoped Dougie was a scotch man and responded to insincere flattery.

"Did you do anything that threatened national security or the success of this mission?"

She wondered how to answer that—would anyone, besides Mrs. Smathers, care that she had blackened Dougie's eye?

The Mormon Tabernacle Choir pulled up in a sleek, noisy tour bus, cutting off Jane's attempt to assure Cedric that she had done nothing scandalous, indiscreet, or illegal. She wouldn't have told him otherwise, not at this sacred site.

"I fixed everything," he assured her. "After the third show, we dropped by the Desert Inn and left a bottle of domestic champagne for Agent Smathers to enjoy."

Cedric passed out the sombreros he had purchased from the Teepee Village gift shop. "It will keep the sun off our faces," he said when Jane blanched at the straw hat with red bobbles hanging from the brim. "I thought you'd like the sleeping señorita," Cedric added with a wink.

Before their tour of the dam, they were led to a small auditorium to watch scratchy, thirty-year-old footage of the dam being built. "Fascinating," murmured Cedric as muscled workers, stripped to their waists and their legs revealed in short shorts, moved boulders and mixed concrete. Safety instructions followed: They were not to stick their gum on the wall of the dam, spit into Lake Mead, or impress their friends by standing on the railing. Before they were taken down into the turbine-engine room to watch electricity being generated—as it turned out, a pretty dull experience—they were asked to stand up, give their name and home state, and tell why they were there.

"It's pretty obvious," Jane murmured, earning a sharp "shhh" from the Girl Scout seated right behind her, who had been kicking her seat since the filmstrip began.

"Medrick Slumberknuckle, London, England. I'm in town with the International Association of Accident-Prone People." This drew a laugh. "I'm here to see a great monument to a great American, an American whose contribution to America is unparalleled." He sat down to warm applause, then popped up and added, "And, may I add, a personal friend of mine. Well, not a close personal friend, more a pen pal."

"Ok-aaaay," said the tour guide, as Jane hid behind her sombrero. Cedric's name-dropping had put an end to the question-and-answer period, so the group headed to a small lift that would take them underground, to the engine room.

After viewing turbines in action for a mind-numbing ten minutes, their group advanced to the entrance of a damp, slippery tunnel that would take them through the body of the dam. Cedric wanted to stay close to the tour guide so as not to miss a thing. Jane noticed that the rest of the group hung back a good distance, whispering among themselves. Afraid they would lose their hats, Cedric and Felix had simply placed the mandatory hard hat over the straw crown of their sombreros. Jane slowed until she lost them, then stopped and let the rest of the group pass her.

"We're supposed to stay together," the Girl Scout nagged as Jane quietly backed out of the narrow tunnel.

"You've earned your bossy badge," hissed Jane. "Now go away."

A Diet-Rite Cola in hand and a generous application of Jean Naté eau de toilette behind her ears, the woman at the card table that served as the sign-in desk for the Dorothy Duncan Defrost-Off Competition guarded the entrance to Ballroom B with the fervor of a religious convert. Upon hearing that the two tardy contestants had lost their paperwork, Mrs. Verda Taylor, 1965 Honorable Mention, E-Z Breezy Marshmallow Dots, shook her head, her tight, gray-streaked auburn bun bouncing on the Peter Pan collar of her crisp white blouse. A larger-than-life cardboard cutout of Dorothy Duncan, America's Best-Loved Homemaker, stabbing the frost off a package of frozen French-cut green beans with a carving knife, loomed large over the table, and Verda Taylor gazed at it like an adoring cocker spaniel waiting for a signal. "What would Dorothy do?" she wondered aloud.

"Let us in?" Bibi said hopefully. Since the woman at the front reception desk refused to let them into the building unless their names were on the roster, they had to sneak in the back way, through the entertainers' entrance, and tiptoe past a golf-cart jockey napping at the wheel.

"You're a day late," Verda scolded. "Without your letter of acceptance, I can't admit you." A tragic tale tumbled out of Bibi, a story involving a cow, a train, a smashed collection of Avon decanters, and a little town called Terre Haute, Indiana. "Our letters of acceptance were destroyed in the fire, but, happily, in a vivid testament to American manufacturing, our casserole dishes weren't even chipped."

The story left Verda Taylor as stiff as one of her husband's starched shirts. She gave them a dry dismissive smile and went back to alphabetizing the plastic-covered name badges in the shoe box on her lap. Bridget, who was welcome at Buckingham Palace and all the right parties, was stunned by the rejection. "Look here—"

"Am I going to have to call a midget?" Verda Taylor said, pointing at a small man in a green jumpsuit whooshing by on a golf cart.

"If you don't let us in, the world will be forever deprived of Tabsicles," said Bibi, trying to appeal to the woman's culinary side. "Do you want that hanging over your head?"

For a moment Mrs. Taylor's face softened. "I'm sorry." She did look a little remorseful. "I simply must uphold the integrity of the contest. No papers, no admittance." Their fate decided, she dropped her eyes and refused to look at them, her short, neat fingernails tapping out the Oscar Mayer Wiener song on her clipboard.

"We'll go," said Bridget. "But I'm going to report your attitude to Dorothy Duncan herself." She dropped her straw handbag, another mother-in-law fashion statement, onto the card table and rummaged for a pen. The bag smelled of peppermint and menthol cigarettes, and she found a cheap giveaway pen from a local bank under a layer of loose tobacco. Verda grabbed a stack of blank contest-entry forms (*win a stainless-steel Deepfreeze big enough to hold a cow!*) and sat on them, forcing Bridget to write on the inside flap of her paperback copy of Betty Friedan's *The Feminine Mystique*, which she had tossed in her purse at the last minute. When Verda saw the title, she reared back as if she had seen a vampire.

"We don't allow agitators to enter our contest," she said, twisting the gold Scotty pin on her blouse. "Go burn your bras somewhere else. Every woman here is perfectly happy being a woman."

"As are we," Bridget assured her, shoving the book back in her purse.

"*As are we,*" Verda mocked her. "You're not even housewives—you're spies."

"Spies for whom?" asked Bridget with a growing concern that their cover had truly been blown. She looked at Bibi, who hadn't heard a word because she was busy making eyes at a pretty young woman in a plain gray shirtwaist dress with a gold wedding band on her finger. The woman was standing off to the side, pretending to polish her name tag while making eyes back at Bibi.

"Just go back to corporate headquarters and tell Betty Crocker to suck an egg!" Verda slammed her hand on the table, splashing her wash-

and-wear rayon blouse with Diet-Rite. She gasped and, close to tears, put her hand up to cover her mouth. Bridget and Bibi stood back, stunned. Spotting the commotion, a woman in a neat tan suit and an ash-brown bob with perfectly scissored bangs, carrying a stack of complimentary *Redbook* magazines, trotted over.

"Now, Verda," Louise Wuebel, 1959 Grand Prize Winner, Scrumptious Scrod Sticks, said in the smooth, modulated tone one used for a quarrelsome child, while lightly touching the woman's shoulder. Verda shook off her touch, and, with her purse tucked under one arm, she rushed off to the ladies' room before the stain could set. The shoe box of name tags that had been on her lap fell to the floor, and Bibi knelt to pick them up.

"I found our name tags," she said triumphantly, holding up two plastic badges.

Louise Wuebel gave them a warm smile as she took her place on the folding chair behind the table. "I must apologize for Mrs. Taylor. Someone showed up with the same prune-whip-on-a-stick recipe she spent months developing, and she's mad as an old hen."

"Poor woman," said Bridget. "With that on her mind, it's little wonder our predicament—we were in a train wreck and lost our letters of acceptance and treasured collection of Avon collectibles—failed to move her. Give her our best, will you, and our apologies for causing her any distress." With that, and a ten-dollar donation to the Not-So-Happy Homemakers of America Fund, they clipped on their new badges and became contestants number 157 and 158, Miss Sandy Beach and Mrs. Betty Skeets.

"You didn't designate a food category when you sent in your application." Louise pointed out the blank line beneath each name and handed them a mimeographed list from which to choose. Bibi picked Quick-'n'-Easy Freezer Desserts, and Bridget selected Hurry Up! I'm a Busy Lady! Breakfast Ideas.

"Have fun, girls," said Louise, handing them their booth number, a package of three complimentary Dorothy Duncan disposable aprons in three new kicky colors—Alluring Avocado, Gorgeous Gold, and Snow-Brite White—and their official convention pen-and-pencil sets. "Just stay out of Verda's way."

Entering a room partitioned into dozens of open cubicles, each a fully equipped miniature kitchen, Bridget wished they had simply apologized to the cast of *Frost Side Story* and begged to be let back onstage. "At least we're at the convention center and closer to Jane," she told Bibi as they arrived at their kitchenette, a turquoise-walled cubicle with bubbling white-speckled mint green linoleum and shabby appliances.

"If the show had gone well, we'd be here anyway, signing autographs and demonstrating new ways to cook vegetables," Bibi pointed out.

"Yes, but now, if we don't want to seem suspicious, we actually have to cook. In ten minutes everyone's going to know we can't even toast crumpets, and Verda will really believe that we're Betty Crocker spies." The two girls had lived together for five years, in which time Bibi had flirted with the notion of a home-cooked meal only once, an experience cut short by a tragic incident involving a pickle fork and a prawn. Bridget could take biscuits out of a tin, make a decent martini, and open a take-away container without breaking a nail. None of these talents would help them now.

"The Toast-A-Thon's not for an hour," said Bibi, checking the schedule. "We've time to practice."

Bridget viewed her reflection in the pressure cooker on the countertop in their kitchen. She thought she looked like one of those pour souls in sensible clothes who went door-to-door collecting for overseas missionaries. "For many reasons, my vanity included, I hope Jane's mission is a smashing success. Although, she could have rung me."

"I told Miss Tuppenny that sending you both was a mistake. My number-one rule of dating: Don't work at the same place as your lover."

"And the number-two rule is . . . ?"

"Always date someone your size. That way, when it's over, at least you have some new pieces in your wardrobe to soothe your shattered heart." Bibi looked down at her feet, admiring her white open-toed sandals with large black daisy clips, another nice "gift" from Mimi, and frowning over the dark brown toe and heel patches of her pantyhose. She would be banned from the Mary Quant boutique if word of this got around.

"I can't believe you wore those," said Bridget. It took only one false note in an operative's appearance to blow her undercover status. Wanda had warned them the Dorothy Duncanites were as strict as nuns—no smoking, gum chewing, or bare toes were allowed.

"I know . . . the hose ruin the effect. I'll just have to take them off."

Bibi hiked up her skirt, intending to peel off her pantyhose and stuff them into the cutlery drawer. A little tingle at the back of her neck alerted her to the fact that she was being watched, and, smoothing her dress over her thighs, she turned to find a girl staring at her from a beautifully decorated buttercup yellow kitchen directly across the aisle. The girl, awfully pretty to begin with, was even more so when bathed by the light of her bun warmer. Bibi gave her a little wave. A pot on the white enamel stove started to boil over, and the girl's face pinked prettily as she drained the steaming beets over the sink. A neatly stacked pyramid of strawberry Jell-O boxes on her Formica table hinted at the gelatinous goodness in store for the lucky judges.

Bridget turned to look. "Don't tell me," she said. "You've suddenly discovered a passion for Jell-O."

Jane, having never been the type to appreciate great monoliths, spent the remainder of the tour standing by the protective railing outside the gift shop and smoking, waiting for Cedric and Felix to emerge from the tunnels. She wondered what it was people found so fascinating about a concrete wall, considering that perhaps Americans had a keener interest in the turbine engine than did the above-average Brit. The next part of the tour would be a walk across the dam, on the road clogged with late-morning traffic. On the other side of the two-lane highway was Lake Mead, the country's largest man-made lake and the setting of *Ladies in the Lake*, a water show playing on the hour.

A charter bus pulled into the lot, the men inside hanging out the windows, hooting and spraying cars with beer. A sheet had been affixed to the back of the bus—HOOVER DAM OR BUST! The *B* was a vulgar silhouette of a woman's breasts. The world's greatest secret agents had arrived. Reassured by the touch of the gun tucked under her jacket, Jane backed into the shadow cast by a life-size bronze statue of President Herbert Hoover and waited for the men to disembark and disappear into the theater. Stumbling, Dougie Smathers, in white Perma-Prest pants and Hawaiian shirt, led the way. On the eye Jane had blackened was a black patch; she could tell, even from this distance, that he was proud of it. He looked like a pirate on holiday. With a swagger, he led his pack to the ticket booth, arguing with the old lady behind the glass wall when she wouldn't take casino chips.

Slipping behind a revolving rack of postcards in front of the gift shop, Jane wondered when the happy couple would emerge and whether Cedric would trust her with the keys to the car. If she let the air out of the tour bus's tires, she would have more time to race back to the convention center, charm her way into the building, and tear the room apart until she found that damn invention. She would have achieved her goal without assistance, and, better than that, she'd never have to see Dougie Smathers again. It was Plan C, her best to date.

Tripping over their own feet, loud and vulgar, the agents headed for the auditorium just as Cedric and Felix emerged from the small lift that had taken them from below ground. Smathers dismissed Cedric's friendly greeting with a rude noise resembling a sow's mating call, and his loyal followers followed his lead. Cedric was mortified.

"Over here," said Jane. "Dougie Smathers is a giant ass," she added as they walked into the small concrete building, its shelves crammed with snow globes and ashtrays, pendants and can openers. "If we had any doubts, that last performance sealed it."

"His eye's been blackened, and he's walking with a limp," Felix said, picking up a giant pencil covered with views of the dam and examining the pink eraser. "Inferior rubber," he said, putting it back on the shelf and wandering off to inspect the official Hoover Dam ballpoint pens. Cedric looked down at his damp socks and sandals and sighed. "I'm running out of socks," he reported.

"I have an idea," said Jane. "Why don't you and Felix continue on the tour and I'll go back to the teepee and have a nap?" It made sense to her. Cedric could combine two pleasurable activities—sightseeing at stupid places and being with Felix—and Jane would be free of them to do what she came here to do.

"There's no need to be intimidated by those thugs any longer," he said. He winked, pointed at Felix, flapped his arms, and did everything but turn a cartwheel. Jane shoved him behind the bath-mat display before the clerk called an ambulance.

"What is wrong with you?"

"Felix is *the* one."

Jane suspected as much. "Don't get your heart broken," she warned. "Holiday romances can be sweet, but they're always short."

"Agent Bond," he said, his face flaming. "Agent Bivens is the *inventor*."

"Well, Bob's your uncle!" laughed Jane. "What is it? What does it do?"

"I can't tell you."

Jane raised her eyebrow, which took considerable effort. "It's . . . a . . . *secret!*"

"He says he had something he wants to give me, and only me, but he's shy and needs time."

Jane closed her eyes and prayed that she wouldn't lose control and pummel Cedric with a souvenir snow globe. She watched in disbelief as Felix took apart a pen and examined the pieces with a jeweler's loupe. There was blue ink on his fingers, his yellow shorts, his brown-and-white checked short-sleeved shirt, and the picture postcard he just purchased of John Glenn orbiting over the dam. Jane knew that there was no way Felix could be the genius inventor—not with this display and not even with Cedric's most recent revelation. It made her even more tired than her hangover, and she could not help being snappish with him.

"I really need that nap, Cedric," Jane said.

"But first I'd like the three of us to grab a bite at the Snacketeria. I feel a bit peckish, and it would nice if you and Felix got to know one another."

"Anything you want, Cedric." She put her arm around his shoulder, and they watched as Felix purchased three snow globes, one, she knew, for each of them. "He's an awfully generous chap."

"And he thinks the world of you. He going to have that cocktail coaster you signed laminated so he can carry it in his wallet forever."

"I'm just an internationally known secret agent," said Jane, hearing a touch of envy in his voice. "You're the one who's bending over backward to accommodate him."

Verda Taylor climbed atop the raffle prize—a stainless-steel Deepfreeze with an easy-clean Teflon interior—and banged a wooden spoon on an aluminum frying pan until even the teakettles grew silent. Oven temperatures were turned down, and fresh aprons were tied around girdled waists as the contestants gathered in a circle around her.

"Your attention, ladies!" Verda cried, casting an eye around the room for stragglers. Bridget and Bibi joined the outer ring of younger contestants, with soft bouffants and figure-hiding A-line dresses that eliminated the need for a girdle. And they weren't *all* married. Bridget didn't need to look at her ring finger to know that the home-economics teacher standing next to her was only a "miss."

Reading into a microphone from a prepared statement, pausing between sentences to graciously acknowledge applause, Verda said, "Welcome to day two of America's most prestigious cooking competition, the Dorothy Duncan Defrost-Off. We at Dorothy Duncan pride ourselves on having our finger on the pulse of today's homemaker."

"I wish," Bibi sighed, looking over her shoulder at their attractive neighbor from the buttercup yellow kitchen, who was standing shyly at the edge of the group. When Bibi waved, Verda glared in her direction. Placing her hand on the back of Bibi's neck, Bridget swiveled her forward. "Smile and pretend you're listening," she whispered. The crowd's energy had started to wane.

That morning's event, the world's biggest coffee-klatch, turned into a fiasco when a friendly discussion about how many Folgers flavor crystals were needed to make the perfect cup of coffee got out of hand. Tempers flared, cups were cracked, and a five-gallon container of a powdery cream substitute was knocked to the freshly waxed floor, creating a sticky situation.

"Dorothy Duncan honors the housewife's commitment to her family by making nutritious, attractive foods anyone would be proud to defrost. Remember, ladies, the kitchen is your laboratory, your job as satisfying and meaningful as any scientist's. Today you face your greatest challenge—to invent a TV dinner so innovative, Dorothy Duncan herself would be proud to serve to her family. You, ladies, are the tastemakers of the future, for who has more influence in today's world than the average housewife?"

"Jackie Kennedy?" someone shouted.

Flummoxed, Verda stopped. She stood atop the freezer, wishing she hadn't worn her new girdle for the opening remarks, then removed her glasses, rubbing the deepening cleft between her eyes. She hadn't expected an answer.

"Ladies!" Verda tucked her script under her arm. "Do you want the world to be a better place?" The only response was the buzzing of whispered conversations as this idea was debated.

"Well, *do* you?" cried Verda. The home-economics teacher raised her hand, then, seeing she was the only one, snatched it back. "If you want the world to be a better place"—Verda paused, wiping her glasses on her blouse before putting them back on—"then feed it *better food!*"

A whoosh of relief passed through the room, and someone began to clap.

Verda went back to her script, taking a minute to find her place. "Nutrition-rich foods such as Dorothy Duncan Frozen Cottage Cheese Cutie. Or Dorothy Duncan Thick-Sliced Frozen Buttered Toast." She paced atop the freezer, denting it with the heels of her sensible tan pumps. "Change begins in the kitchen," she said, pointing to a young contestant with a MAKE POPOVERS, NOT WAR button pinned to the front of her paisley A-line dress. "Not on the psychotherapist's couch or in the legislative branches of government. Ladies"—This was directed at the inner circle, the hard-core devotees, the gals in girdles who wore the torturous device as willingly as their ancestors had worn whalebone corsets—"*you* change your drawer-liner paper each week, don't you?"

"Yes!" came the unanimous chorus.

"What's liner paper?" Bibi whispered.

"Well, it's more often than today's so-called liberated woman changes her dress shields!"

"Dear God, Verda's been in the cooking sherry again," a woman behind them murmured.

A trim brunette in a pristine housedress used a crockpot to climb onto the freezer and, after a short discussion, gently took the statement and microphone from Verda, who was enticed away by a log of thawing chocolate chip cookie dough. Her face flaming, the woman—whom they would later learn was their neighbor, Marge Milligan, 1960 Second Runner-up, Appealing Appetizers, daintily cleared her throat and said, "Verda's just remembered she has a pork roast to thaw, and she's been generous enough to let me read what has always been the highlight of day two opening remarks—the annual poem penned by Dorothy Duncan herself, a dedicated housewife just like you, to celebrate the 1966

Dorothy Duncan Defrost-Off Competition and available at the registration desk as a commemorative booklet." Her voice trembling, Marge Milligan, who had never spoken to a group larger than the PTA, gave a reading that would be remembered each year as the most inspiring oration the contestants had ever heard, next to Richard Nixon's checkers speech.

> I think that I shall never see,
> Anything so lovely as frozen broccoli,
> Vitamin rich, so better than fresh,
> A surefire hit at any bash!
> And up above the sky so blue,
> Airlines serve frozen foods, too!

"I have chills," a woman said, buttoning her pink Orlon cardigan to her neck.

"So do I," a girl whispered in Bibi's ear. "I wish I had something warm to wrap around me." She was so close that Bibi could smell the unmistakable tang of artificially flavored strawberry powder mixed with bovine jelly. And something else.

"You smell like lemons," Bibi whispered, then turned crimson when she heard the girl giggle. She had meant to say something subtle yet seductive, but there was something about this place that made her feel as if her brain was wrapped in sterilized cotton. Had she muffed her opportunity? She turned and faced the girl, whose buttercup yellow apron perfectly matched her buttercup yellow kitchen.

"Lemon Scrub," the girl replied sweetly. "It removes dirt and germs and leaves your hands smelling like a warm summer evening under a lemon tree." She held out one lemony fresh hand. "Mrs. Myrtle Minx, Second Runner-Up, 1963 Pleasin' Pretzel Pie." With her long blond hair, worn in a cascade down her back, and big brown eyes, the movie star she resembled most was Brigette Bardot, if she had warm brown eyes and knew her way around a kitchen.

"And I'm Sandy Beach, Honorable Mention, 1961 Cherry Berry Pie."

"You love pie, too?" Babette cried. "I'll bet you make a heavenly pie."

"The best you've ever eaten," Bibi promised, marveling at her luck.

In her ugly outfit and tragic hairdo, the movie star *she* most resembled was Lassie. "Maybe I'll make you one."

"I'd hate to leave without tasting it," Myrtle said, a rosy dust of color rising from the V of her spotless yellow shirtwaist dress. "But I've fallen into the convention trap and signed up for too many nonrefundable events. Are you going to the apron factory? We're supposed to partner up, in case one of us wanders away. Verda's already asked, but I put her off. I don't want to be tied to *her* apron strings."

"I know exactly what you mean," said Bibi, checking her Mary Quant daisy watch. She was about to say that she was free, gloriously free, but then she remembered why they were here. Poor Myrtle! For once Bibi found herself cursing her life as a spy, and all the lies. Looking around, she saw so many lonely housewives, aching for a kind touch and some stimulating conversation after a day bent over a hot stove. Women everywhere deserved better, and tears flooded her eyes when she thought of the shared sisterhood of put-upon women.

"We're already signed up for the Teflon talk," Bridget jumped in, seeing that familiar lustful look on Bibi's face. She snapped the strap of Bibi's pocketbook, recapturing her attention.

"Perhaps we'll run into each other at the Hostess Hoedown." Myrtle smiled, backing away when Bridget looped her arm through Bibi's.

"I'm making you a pie," Bibi promised as Bridget put more distance between them.

"And I'll wear my prettiest apron when I eat it," Myrtle promised.

• •

fourteen

℈'m having the tuna," was all Jane could say, beleaguered by the Hoover Dam Snacketeria's spread of bright foods in odd shapes laid before her—jiggly gelatin cubes in every color of the rainbow, slices of soft white bread covered in a pinkish spread with olive slices forming a grinning face topped with parsley hair. She hadn't waited in line for food since she was a student at the London High Street Academy and wasn't thrilled about the Snacketeria's offering of cafeteria-style service of sandwiches, salads, and an assortment of beverages. "Tang," Jane sneered, wrinkling her nose as she reached for a Coca-Cola, bypassing glasses of the orange beverage and small cartons of warmish chocolate milk. "Didn't they discover anything else in space?"

"Actually, Jim," Felix said, selecting a scoop of cottage cheese on a bed of lettuce with a cherry on top and placing it on his orange plastic tray, "Tang wasn't discovered *in* outer space, but it is a by-product of the space program, like Teflon and silver lamé." He wiggled a plate of Jell-O, trying to determine the blue gelatinous brick's flavor. "Blueberry," he decided, and put it next to his cottage cheese salad.

"Lucky we came in when we did," said Cedric as they took their seats at a Formica table with attached aqua plastic chairs near a window overlooking the dam. People had started to queue for lunch, and soon there was a line out the door. Women in pink uniforms and hair nets rushed to keep up, slapping turkey on rye and peanut butter on jelly.

"We'd better be out of here before Dougie and his pals get through being bored to death in the turbine-engine room," Jane said, hesitant to start eating her Great American Tuna Melt. "God, I can't wait to get home and have beans on toast."

Felix jumped up. He had dropped cottage cheese on the shorts he'd borrowed from Cedric—shorts held up with a too-big belt, safety pins, and a shoelace. "Pardon me," he said. "I'll just go rinse this with cool water before the milk protein congeals." With that he raced off to the lav. Cedric put down his carton of chocolate milk and looked up at Jane. All morning he'd been remarkably alert for someone with so little sleep, but now he looked like a tired and overwhelmed traveler, with a sunburned nose and a list of sightseeing recommendations he was determined to get through.

"I didn't mean to upset him," said Jane, feeling like an ass for bringing up the subject of home. The way holiday affairs worked, as she remembered, was that all talk of real life was strictly forbidden.

"A dose of reality is what we needed after last night," he assured her, but he didn't sound like he meant it.

"Did I miss anything?" Felix asked when he returned to the table, his shorts damp and his eyes shiny. Jane patted the chair next to her.

"Sit down, Felix. We've been discussing your visit to London. We've already decided, you're coming for the entire month of October. The queen is having a tea for Britain's most important subjects, and Cedric's been invited."

Cedric's mouth dropped.

"Isn't he?" prompted Jane. "Invited to come to London?"

"I'll have to dust," was all Cedric could think to say.

"I do have five years' worth of vacation accrued," Felix said. "But I might lose my job if I take too much of it all at once."

"You will soon be coming into a great fortune," Cedric said, with all the wisdom of a fortune-cookie prophecy.

Felix laughed. "I was thinking that when I get home, I should spend an evening rolling pennies."

"It's an American parlor game, I believe," Cedric explained to Jane when Felix got up to get a Hostess Fruit Pie. Although Jane was eager to leave America's largest man-made concrete monstrosity, Felix wanted a snack pie, and so a snack pie it was.

He had just finished tearing open the wrapper and was eyeing the pastry when a new group of hungry tourists walked into the lunchroom, with Dougie Smathers and his friends bringing up the rear, impatient, vulgar, and loud. Jane winced, sensing a scuffle in her future. The others—the Mormon Tabernacle Choir and the Girl Scout troop, the Shriners and the strippers—all waited patiently in line, but Smathers pushed through to the front, knocking over a bowling team from Kalamazoo, and then held everyone up while he decided between the ham-and-Velveeta sandwich with macaroni salad or a Sloppy Joe with carrot and celery sticks. Jane offered to race them out of there.

"No. I'm sick to death of that bounder," Cedric said, feeling confident because the inventor everyone was after was sitting at *his* table. "He's not ruining my one chance to see a great monument to a great American."

Grateful for the sombrero, she pulled it low over her face, and, having scarfed down her surprisingly tasty tuna melt, she began picking the icing off Cedric's slice of white cake. She wondered what exactly Felix had done to Cedric the night before to give him his newfound courage, and worried that it was misplaced.

"He's an embarrassment to the American espionage community," Felix said as Dougie Smathers spilled pea soup on a nun in an attempt to steal her table.

"And *here,* of all places," Cedric added.

"That kind of behavior would be unwelcome at *any* of America's national monuments," Felix assured him. Dougie seemed to settle, slurping his soup and dripping hot Velveeta on his shirt.

"Certainly Mr. Hoover would like to know of Smathers's behavior," said Cedric, looking dolefully at his piece of naked cake. Jane popped the remaining cake in her mouth, finished her Coke, and wiped her face on a paper napkin.

"Please, let's go before he sees us," she begged quietly from beneath her sombrero.

"He's scratching something into the tabletop with a penknife," Cedric reported, ignoring her.

"Now he's stealing a little girl's Little Debbie Lemon Snack Cake," said Felix, clutching his gift-shop bag to his chest. "Is there nothing that man won't do?" As Dougie Smathers struck terror into the hearts of innocent sightseers, Felix narrated like a radio announcer at a prizefight. "Uh-oh. Dougie's done it this time. He stole the last Ho Ho from an elementary-school teacher! She just hit him with her ham salad sandwich! A lady in a hair net is trying to break up the fight! An open can of peas just hit the floor!"

"That's our exit," said Jane.

"We can't just walk away," said Felix. "Would Joe Friday?"

"We shouldn't interfere with American customs," murmured Cedric, shutting his eyes to the shocking sight of two public servants fighting over a mini cylinder of chocolate cake with a layer of creamy white filling inside. "And what if you get hurt? You're far too valuable to lose in a common cafeteria fight."

Felix continued his narration. "He just pulled off the cafeteria lady's name tag! Now he's shoving her face into the marshmallow salad! I take personal offense at that—my mother was a cafeteria lady!"

"I hate to have to resort to violence," Cedric sighed. "Mother was opposed to any display of brutality, but if no one else will step forward, I fear I must do my duty." Carefully handling each item as if were fine crystal, he emptied his pockets of breakable items: his Instamatic, his

Hoover Dam snow globe, his Liberace commemorative ashtray, and a framed photograph of his mother.

Worried about Smathers breaking more than just Cedric's photograph of Mrs. Pumpernickel, Jane whispered sternly, "Are you sure you want to get involved with that? The man has no shame, and we're already in hot water with him and the rest of the American spies." But it was too late—Dougie Smathers had noticed the trio out of the corner of his eye.

"Look at the sissy!" cried Smathers, pointing at Cedric. He grabbed the lunch lady's hair net and draped it on his own greasy head. "He carries around his mommy's picture."

"Oh, bugger!" Jane's hatred of Dougie commingled with her protective nature, and she threw off her sombrero, jumped over an orange chair, and ruined a perfectly good piece of lemon meringue pie by introducing it to Dougie's face. The fourth-graders gave her a standing ovation, and everyone joined in. The applause died down when Dougie knelt to wipe meringue from his shoe and silently pulled a gun from his ankle holster.

"I told you something bad was going to happen." The Girl Scout stuck out her tongue at Jane, who was now convinced that she was part of Dougie's spy troop.

"Don't you get it? You're not welcome here, Bond," said Dougie, licking lemon curd from his chin. His entourage of trained monkeys stood in a semicircle around their leader, smirking through the Hostess Fruit Pies they stuffed in their mouths.

"Actually, if I may interject, everyone is welcome at national parks," said their tour guide, lunching on tomato soup and a cheese sandwich, seated with his back to the window. "Men, women, old, young, citizen and foreign born. But leave your pets at home."

"Killing me will solve nothing," said Jane. "The people I work for will demand your head." Even with that greasy rug on top, she added to herself. She giggled; it couldn't be helped.

"Yes, sir! Murdering James Bond is a hangable offense," said Cedric, making infinitesimally small slides across the brown linoleum, trying to get closer to Jane without alerting the gunman. "Although, now that I think about it, it's not anymore, not since 1956. But it will earn you life at Wormwood Scrubs. Don't let the name fool you—it's not a nice place."

"Pumpernutters, you've always got something to say, don't you?" Dougie waved his gun around, and Jane felt a few drops of water fall on her head. Glancing above to the air-conditioning unit, she waited, but nothing happened. If the water wasn't dripping from above, it had to come from some other source.

Dougie smiled, revealing large white front teeth dotted with parsley.

"You've got something in your teeth," said Jane, pointing to the toothpick dispenser next to the register. "Let me get you one. Shall I remove the sanitary wrapper, or would you like to do it?"

"Funny, Bond." Dougie affirmed the grip on his gun, and Jane watched water drip onto the toe of his loafer.

"You really do have something in your teeth," Cedric assured him. "It's green."

"Bottom and top," said the lunch lady who had lost her hair net to him.

"It's gross," said the Girl Scout.

"I agree," said Jane, putting her hands in the air and slowly approaching Smathers. "In fact, everything about you is gross. Your hair, your ugly face, your fat stomach, your stinky shoes, the way you talk about women, the way you treat your wife. I can't believe I offered to take you to a strip club as a peace offering, you pig."

"Don't do it, Smathers," begged Cedric. "Bond, *Shut up!*"

"Tell your wife to pipe down," Dougie snarled, shooting a brief glance Cedric's way. It was what Jane had been hoping for. "Go jump in the lake!" she said, stomping on his insole. She grabbed the gun, aiming it at the spot where Dougie's heart was rumored to be, and pulled the trigger. Cedric screamed and covered his eyes.

"Bang, bang, you're dead," Jane said as water soaked the front of Dougie Smathers's baby blue Dacron shirt.

"Whoever the real Sandy Beach and Betty Skeets are, their kitchen has all the charm of estate housing," said Bibi, chipping off a strip of dingy aqua-blue paint from the wall. They were back at their cubicle, getting themselves acquainted with their appliances, finding that the conditions in which they were to prepare Wanda's fail-safe Tabsicles were less than

Dorothy Duncan perfect. "I'm surprised they allow this kitchenette in here," Bibi added. On the fiberboard underneath the old paint was a lipstick heart with the words "Betty loves Chickie" written in a girlish script. The linoleum counter, white with blue starbursts, was littered with cigarette burns. Second-rate appliances crowded the counter: a sea foam green Mixmaster minus the beater, an electric iron with a frazzled cord, a waffle maker encrusted with ancient batter, and an orange fondue pot covered with burned cheese drips. "You'd think they'd treat the survivors of a train wreck a little better," Bibi groused as she opened the door of the turquoise refrigerator, the handle of which was wrapped with sticky black electrical tape. Inside she found a bad smell, two six-packs of warmish Diet-Rite Cola, a stick of unsalted butter, a container of moldy cottage cheese, gherkins swimming in a cloudy vinegary liquid, a half bottle of Tabasco sauce with a crusty neck, and a bottle of Yoo-hoo so old the "Yoo" had separated from the "hoo."

The cabinets presented a similarly depressing collection of dented cans, instant soup packets, musty bouillon cubes, and something called Hamburger Helper that listed salt as its main ingredient. "What's this?" Bibi asked, pulling a six-pack of corn from behind a dusty box of Little Debbie Oatmeal Snack Cakes. The label on one of the cans was peeling, and she finished the job, pulling off a label picturing a bowl of plump yellow corn to reveal the can of Old Milwaukee beer underneath.

Using a fondue fork from the messy cutlery drawer, Bibi chipped away at the freezer frost, hoping to have enough to cool a Crock-Pot of beer as Bridget pounded the bottom of a metal ice-cube tray with a meat-tenderizing mallet, unaware of the easy-release handle on top.

"Let's order in," suggested Bibi, realizing that everyone around them was really cooking. "We don't want to call attention to ourselves by being the only ones here without food."

Bridget poured a can of Tab into the dented ice-cube tray. "We have to add the tongue depressors in twenty minutes," she said, as serious as a scientist in a laboratory, and she set the grease-encrusted stove timer while Bibi poked around the freezer for something to eat, unearthing a soggy box of Dorothy Duncan Liver Spots.

"'Guaranteed to be a party pleaser,'" she read, wrinkling her nose.

"It expired last month." Afraid the old liver juice would contaminate their Tabsicles, Bibi tossed the box in the sink. Marge Milligan, who, it turned out, was their neighbor, looked at them through the window above her sink with the shocked expression of one coming across two girls making curtains from the Shroud of Turin.

"No, no, no, no, no!" she said as she made a mad dash for their kitchenette, hobbling in the new narrow-toe, brown suede pumps she was breaking in for tomorrow night's closing ceremony. She would get to announce the name of the lucky winner of the Deepfreeze, since she had been the winner last year, and she wanted to look her best. Seizing control of the Liver Spots, she threw them back in the freezer, slammed the door, and leaned against it, panting, her fingers crossed, hoping that the delicious and nutritious liver treat wouldn't suffer freezer burn. "Dorothy Duncan's fine line of quality foods is good months after the expiration date," she wheezed. Afraid the woman was going to collapse, Bridget picked a blob of dried jelly off the cleanest cracked-vinyl-covered chair and invited her to sit down. Someone had placed a wooden bowl of plastic grapes in the middle of the small round table, trying to hide a casserole-size scorch mark.

"May I have a refreshing Diet-Rite cola?" the woman gasped, resting her head in her hands. Along with stiff shoes and a tight girdle, she was also suffering bruises and trauma from the *Frost Side Story* fiasco the day before.

"Refreshing," she said after gulping the not-quite-cold contents of the can. "You girls are lucky I was listening," she said, patting her face with the red-checkered tea towel in her hand. "Those Liver Spots are not just the newest star in the lineup of Dorothy Duncan Freezer Goodies, they're your main ingredient for today's homemade-TV-dinner competition. You see that?" In one corner of the hall, on a raised stage, was a three-sided set made with fake oak paneling and a brown linoleum floor. Five Barcaloungers faced a Mediterranean-style console holding a sixteen-inch color television set, and a TV table depicting rustic duck-hunting scenes been placed in front of each lounger. "At six o'clock the television will be tuned to *Bonanza*, and five judges will sit in those chairs and taste one hundred and fifty-eight TV dinners. The winning recipe will join the Dorothy Duncan line of fine freezer foods."

"How much do you win?" asked Bibi, suddenly understanding the allure of the kitchen.

"Ten thousand dollars and the satisfaction of knowing you've made TV viewing that much more pleasant. *And* you get your picture on the box."

"Bibi Gallini's Luscious Liver Spots? No thanks."

Marge looked confused, and Bridget saw her glance at Bibi's name tag. "Sandy," Bridget said, glaring at her friend, "you'd have to use your *real* name if you won. You see"—she tried to distract Marge with another soft drink—"Bibi Gallini is her stage name."

"You're an *actress*," said Marge, her eyebrows raised, popping the top and putting the pull tab in her apron pocket for her friend who made pot holders. "How fascinating. Me, I'm just a housewife from Detroit. Although it's not a glamorous occupation, I was a secretary for General Motors when I met Marv, and I was good at it, too, but I had to retire when I got married—company policy. Sometimes I miss having money of my own." Marge frowned and looked down at the table top, absent-mindedly playing with the pull-tab on her can.

Bibi had stopped listening, too caught up in the intriguing notion that she could be a secret agent by day, and an actress by night. "I've only done community theater," she said, "I use an alias, I mean, a stage name. Many actresses do. My director thinks I could go big time, but then who would be home to put hot meals on the table?"

"With Dorothy's new line of TV dinners, you could do both. If you could teach your hubby how to turn on the oven, that is." Marge laughed. "You'd think with mine being an automotive engineer, he'd be able to operate something as simple as a dial. Whenever I go away, I spend a week preparing freezer casseroles, but they're always there when I get back. I don't know where he takes his meals, but I have my suspicion it involves something fast and cheap."

Or someone, Bridget thought.

"That's not a Tab, is it?" Marge had noticed the empty can on the counter, next to the wooden block of Peel King knives. "Diet-Rite has thoughtfully provided a six-pack of soda for each of our contestants; all other beverages, except Folgers coffee crystals, are banned. You haven't been properly oriented, have you?" She looked disappointed and disapproving, the same expression Bridget's mother had on her face when she barged into her flat and found Jane lying on her daughter's bed, on top of her daughter. Marge, a member of the welcoming committee, started to sag at this assault on her careful preparation. It was as if they had slammed the oven door on her soufflé.

"Our train derailed," said Bibi, knocking the can into the garbage. "We just got here."

"We've got a lot of ground to cover," said Marge with a martyr's sigh. "First of all, you're supposed to build your TV dinner around the frozen entree provided, that being the Liver Spots, and round it out with a vegetable and a dessert. The trays are in the drawer next to the sink. Just write your number on the lid.

"Since you just arrived, you missed the welcoming festivities, including the sunrise Tupperware party, led by Mrs. Tupperware herself, and the first performance of *Frost Side Story*, this year's musical. The show was a disaster! Two dumpy showgirls ruined weeks of preparation by showing up drunk and falling off the stage onto the cast-party carrot cake with white icing I had spent all morning baking. The director himself told me he was looking forward to tasting it. I'm trying to keep my chin up, but I've had other bad luck. Verda Taylor," she said, after looking over her shoulder to make sure Verda wasn't standing there, "borrowed my brand-new Teflon loaf pan and returned it scratched, I overheard a lady say my white icing was colorless, and my new lunch-meat containers still refuse to burp."

Bibi, who had stopped listening after the words "dumpy showgirls," said, "We heard those girls were *pushed* by the carrot because she was jealous of their beauty and talent."

"That's not what Verda Taylor reported. She said they were so homely the director had no choice but to put them in costumes that covered their faces."

At this mention of off-kilter American beauty standards, a speechless Bibi backed toward the counter and the Peel King fine selection of knives (one for paring, one for chopping, and a meat cleaver perfect for a sharp blow to the skull). To move the conversation along, Bridget smiled at Marge and said, "You *must* give me your recipe for white icing. It sounds *so* versatile." Bibi snorted and opened her compact to redo her luscious lips in a muddy orange color that made them look like dried tangerine slices.

"The secret ingredient is Marshmallow Fluff," Marge confided as she wrote the ingredients on a MADE BY MARGE recipe card from the stack in her pocket. Her girdle was feeling a little less tight now that she had gotten some of her unfortunate experiences off her chest. She told them everything she knew about Marshmallow Fluff—how it had started life as filler for bathtub cracks until the inventor accidentally dropped a five-pound bag of sugar into a vat of the compound, with delicious results.

"I guess yesterday wasn't a total loss," she said as a women walked by wearing a FOR THIS I WENT TO COLLEGE? apron. "We've received confirmation that our World's Largest Pound Cake will be in next year's *Guinness Book of World Records*. That's something. And the sharp Wisconsin cheddar arrived." Marge nodded at the enormous wheel of cheese propped next to what was surely the world's largest fondue pot, an enamel avocado monstrosity with two broom-sized wood-handled fondue forks standing guard at either side.

When the stove timer buzzed, Bridget jumped up to put sticks in the Tabsicles, which reminded Marge of the time a Popsicle melted in her purse. Marge popped opened another Diet-Rite, kicked off her shoes, wiggled her toes, and launched into an unraveling monologue that revealed the bitter behind-the-scenes grudges and catfights that only the Dorothy Duncan Defrost-Off could engender. "Did y'all know that Dorothy Duncan started out as a taste tester for a rival frozen-foods company and quit to found her own company when they stole her idea for a giant green spokesman? Verda Taylor is a bitter, jealous, two-time grand-prize loser. She thinks everyone is a spy and isn't afraid to say so. They only let her boss us around because she's Dorothy's third cousin twice removed by marriage. Betty Crocker is actually a very nice lady—don't believe what you hear. I met her at the Piggly Wiggly when she was handing out angel food cake samples. After the outcry last year when Battered Zucchini-on-a-Stick was disqualified because wood, though rich in fiber, is not a food group, Dorothy Duncan stepped in and declared food-on-a-stick a legitimate category. You girls are sure to win at least an honorable mention in tomorrow's Hurry Up! I'm a Busy

Lady! Frozen-Confection-on-a-Stick category. Oh, and be sure to sample Louise Wuebel's Cheesy Liverwurst. Spray food is the 'in' thing this year, very popular with the judges, and her addition of paprika to her recipe adds a foreign flair that just might send the panel over the edge. Personally, I think America isn't ready for paprika. May I suggest you switch to Diet-Rite?"

"Diet-Rite-sicles? It doesn't sound right." Bibi shook her head at all the information Marge had just spit at them.

"What about Icy Cola Rocket Pops? These days it's all in the name. Last year Theodora Smafield won the Grand Prize in the Cunning Canapés category—a Teflon bathtub and a year's supply of Mr. Clean—for her This Little Piggy Cheesy Ring-a-Lings, even though I entered a similar dish called Cheese and Bacon Rounds and mine was actually preferred taste-wise by nine out of ten contestants.

"My girdle is killing me," she confessed, undoing the top snaps through the nubby fabric of her navy skirt. "Honestly, it's good to finally take a load off. I spent the morning gutting fish for my friend Marilyn's Sardine Chop Suey. It's out of this world! If Dorothy Duncan doesn't pick it up, I'm certain Chun King will."

"We're not interested in winning," said Bridget, getting into character. "We're just here to learn from the best and collect some exciting new recipes. Now that I have your white icing, we might as well go home!"

Marge beamed. "If you like white icing, you'll *love* my white sauce! The secret is *Marshmallow Fluff!*"

"Is there any recipe that couldn't benefit from Marshmallow Fluff?" Bridget cried, a little hysterically, wondering if she had packed a sedative and why she was getting excited about all this. Bibi stuck her head in the grimy oven—anything to get away from the white-cream banter that was making her ill.

"That's an electric range, dear," Marge said helpfully, burping daintily behind her tea towel.

The trio regrouped outside the Snacketeria after a park ranger ticketed Dougie Smathers and James Bond for engaging in excessive horseplay and carrying a concealed squirt gun on state-park property. Everyone was in good humor except Felix, who had scraped both knees. "When you reached for his gun, pictures of newspaper headlines about your death swarmed in my poor head. That was a move worthy of the 007 name. I knew you were ready for this mission. How did you know the gun was a fake?" Cedric beamed, taking credit for Jane's skills.

"I saw water dripping from the barrel."

"But he could have been perspiring," Cedric said.

"Dougie is a drippy guy," agreed Felix, wincing as he daubed his knees with hydrogen peroxide.

"I also saw the warning label on the bottom of the barrel: 'Do not fill above line.' I knew the gun couldn't possibly be real."

Cedric made a case for leaving promptly, before Dougie Smathers emerged from the first-aid hut, all the while looking wistfully at the massive concrete structure just achingly out of reach.

"Our friend's no longer a problem," said Jane, pointing to Dougie as he hobbled onto the "Hoover Dam or Bust" bus, looking dispirited and defeated.

"So we can finish the tour?"

"*You* can." She held out her hand. "I'd like the keys to the car, please, and a few hours to myself. I can be back around two. That way you and Felix can see the water show *and* have time to revisit the turbine engines."

"You're leaving us?" asked Felix, clumsily repositioning the bandages on his knees. "What if one of his men tries something?"

"I've got to lie down before I fall down," she said truthfully.

"That's awfully far to go for a nap. Why not just crawl into the back of the station wagon? It's not locked."

"I have to drop by the convention center, too," she said through gritted teeth, hoping that her excuse for going to the convention center alone would help her get out of there sooner. "I have to get something for a friend. And I don't want him to see what it is."

"I can't believe you remembered!" said Cedric. "My birthday is not until December, but still! It must be an awfully big something if you need the station wagon." He was thinking of one of any of the interesting items from the Bachelor Pad of Tomorrow display.

"So you'll give me the keys?" Jane asked with hope in her eyes.

"I wouldn't mind riding along. I'd like to get another pair of bulletproof swim trunks," piped up Felix. "Just in case." Knowing that Cedric would insist on coming along if Felix "the inventor" wanted to, Jane realized she was stuck.

"Why don't we finish the tour and then head to the convention center?" Cedric suggested.

Jane's hopes fell. There was no getting away now.

The dam spanned two states, Nevada and Arizona, and two time zones. Crossing the state line, the tour guide assured them, would be the highlight of their trip. "Today," he said, "you will experience a type of time travel. As you cross into Arizona, you will lose an hour—an hour you will find again by retracing your steps."

"Where does it go?" asked a pregnant woman with four children. "Because I could sure use an extra hour or two." Everyone laughed and headed for the dam, to find out firsthand.

"Aren't you glad you stayed for the final portion of the tour?" Cedric said to Jane, who glared at him through her Ray-Bans. She was never going to lose him.

"And you thought the yo-yo was the only marvel of Yankee ingenuity," he added as they peered over the safety rail of the streamlined dam, 4.36 million cubic yards of concrete fashioned into a simple yet elegant partition that fractured a bleak canyon in two. A crowded roadway allowed cars and delivery trucks to drive across the top of the dam, on one side the concrete wall, on the other Lake Mead, the largest freshwater manmade lake in the Western Hemisphere.

"Imagine, some of the concrete is still drying, yet people have been walking on this for thirty years," the tour guide said.

"There was all kinds of talk about the safety of this place when I was a boy," said Felix, his pale skin taking on a ruddy glow as the wind whipped up the side of the wall, hitting the group with a wallop. "People worried that something this big would throw the earth off its axis. Of course, that was well before space exploration began. I barely remember—I must have been four or five—but my family drove here from Kansas City in 1939 for the grand opening." Cedric counted silently on his fingers, and Jane knew he was adding up their age difference. Gripping the safety rail, Felix leaned over and looked down. "I remember throwing up when my father held me over this railing by my belt so I could get a good look."

"I threw up when Mother lifted me over her head so I could see King Edward VII leave the palace for the last time," Cedric admitted. "I didn't actually see him—I witnessed a large black trunk being placed into a lorry. As it turns out, he and his pug dog were inside." Jane did the math. She was twenty-nine, Cedric was twenty-three years her senior, and in 1936 he had been—"But you were in your twenties!"

"Mother was unnaturally strong," Cedric answered matter-of-factly. "Women in those days had to be."

The agents who arrived in Dougie's crew filed past, shamed by the Snacketeria debacle and the fact that James Bond had once again made fools of them. Smathers was still on the bus, no doubt nursing his bruised ego, but Agent Bob Snurd, who normally clung to Dougie like a bad cold, was not. Trailing behind his buddies, he paused to snarl at Jane. "We're going to get you next year, Bond. When we get through with you, your name will be mud. Do you understand? M-U-D." He paused. "D."

"Go brush your teeth," said Jane. His breath smelled of liverwurst and lime Jell-O and Tang.

"I'm chewing Dentyne!" he shot back smugly.

"No gum chewing on the dam," scolded the bossy Girl Scout, reading from the Hoover Dam safety handbook.

"Yes, ma'am." Bob blushed, running to catch up with his friends.

"And no running!" she added.

They crossed the state line into Arizona and a new time zone, one hour ahead of Nevada, and everyone made the obligatory joke about their watches' suddenly being an hour off. The guide reminded them that gambling was illegal in Arizona. "So if you're planning on placing a bet, please step back over the state line."

As the group paused to look at the view, Cedric amused himself by jumping back and forth between the two states until, he declared, he had forgotten where he was. Felix was swept up in a clump of bowlers arranging themselves like a ninepin layout so their team captain could take their picture. And Jane was standing on the walkway, her back pressed to a commemorative brass plaque that read DEDICATED TO HER-

BERT CLARK HOOVER, OUR 31ST PRESIDENT, THE MAN WHOSE VISION AND TENACITY MADE THIS PROJECT POSSIBLE. Before they'd left for the States, Cedric had talked incessantly about visiting the greatest monument ever erected to the director of a law-enforcement agency. He thought he was standing on a 6-million-ton tribute to FBI director J. Edgar Hoover, and Jane wanted to keep it that way. Afraid that the truth the plaque revealed would send him over the edge, Jane refused to give up her spot, even staring down a nun determined to read the plaque. "It's the Ten Commandments, Sister. I should think you'd know them by now."

"Ninety-six men fell to their death building this dam," their guide said solemnly, asking for a moment of silence, "so we could power places like Las Vegas and perform aquatic feats in clear blue water." He pointed out several bathing beauties in one-piece swimsuits on Lake Mead, riding behind speedboats, rehearsing trick moves for *Ladies in the Lake* that defied gravity. Jane lit a cigarette, attempting to have a quiet moment while still protecting Cedric's happiness.

Suddenly a scream went through the air. A woman on the Lake Mead side was leaning over the rail, flailing her arms. In her hand was a shiny white object. Afraid the woman would fall over and into the lake and certain death, Jane dodged cars across the two-lane highway to come to her aid. The woman stumbled into Jane's arms, making fluttery noises in the base of her throat as she tried to speak. The James K. Polk Elementary School nurse rushed forward with a first-aid kit, and Jane helped her lay the woman on the sidewalk and elevate her feet while Cedric fanned her with his sombrero. The woman handed Jane the shiny white object, a man's slip-on shoe, with a three-inch lift and an odor pad that had outlived its usefulness, and pointed to the lake.

Several tour groups swarmed upon the spot where Nevada met Arizona, jostling for a view of the fainted woman. The tour guide looked over the rail, then shook his head. "Two more months and I would have retired with a spotless record," he sighed, using the walkie-talkie attached to his belt to call for help. A pyramid of showgirls broke apart when a girl screamed and fell off her skis. She had spotted the body in the water, a man in white trousers and a Hawaiian shirt. Jane closed her eyes, feeling sick. She didn't need another whiff of the shoe to know who was down there.

"When I told Dougie Smathers to go jump in the lake, I didn't mean it," she whispered to Cedric as she stepped on her cigarette.

· ·

fifteen

Y ou don't want to miss Louise Wuebel's lunchtime reading, followed by my demonstration of how to make cookie cutters of your entire family," said Marge, standing in their doorway holding several sheets of copper and a blowtorch. "And then we're going to take turns guessing the weight of the World's Biggest Cheese Wheel for tomorrow's Fondue-A-Thon."

"I'm going to take a break from all this excitement," Bibi said, sliding under the table with a can of Diet-Rite Cola and *Valley of the Dolls*. The kitchen clocks chimed the noon hour, and women turned off their ovens, unplugged their percolators, put on fresh aprons, and grabbed complimentary egg-salad sandwiches from the lunch table. Smiling at Marge and hating Bibi, Bridget offered to hold her oven mitts while Marge ran off to get sandwiches "before they all turn bad like they did last year."

After leaving Bibi with the job of answering her compact should Jane ring, tired of hanging around the kitchen watching Bibi try to concoct a romantic new Jell-O flavor using the few pathetic ingredients in their larder, Bridget decided she would join the audience gathering around the makeshift stage, and took a seat next to Marge. After an initial rustle of wax paper, the room grew quiet—just the tick of kitchen clocks and mechanical whirl as the raffle prize defrosted itself.

Louise Wuebel's reading went off without a hitch. Tall, with elegant gestures, the soft-spoken brunette proved to have a stage-worthy voice, deep and rich, with crisp diction. She had performed Shakespeare in community theater for years, and her interpretation of Donna Reed as a scheming Lady Macbeth was a big hit. It was a hard act to follow, Marge learned. Looking dejected, Marge sounded increasingly desperate as she tried to get a rise out of the dozen or so spectators who hadn't wandered back to their kitchen, eager to start assembling their TV dinners. "There are many ways you can use cookies shaped like your family. Mother's Day, for example." Marge consulted her index card. "For what mother wouldn't enjoy eating her children? Or a husband his wife?"

She pulled down the shield on her safety mask and picked up a piece of copper. "I'LL START WITH MY HUSBAND," she shouted with a nervous smile, unaware that they could hear her perfectly behind the plastic shield. "FIRST I'LL MAKE A CUTOUT OF HIS BODY." A minute passed while she cut a crude Mr. Milligan. "OOPS! THIS IS A MISTAKE YOU WANT TO AVOID! I JUST CUT OFF HIS HEAD!"

Women chatted behind her, and Bridget strained to listen. A light touch on her shoulder startled her. "We could use a blowtorch," Bibi whispered in her ear as she slid into the next chair. "Donna Reed woke me. I had no idea she was such an unhappy woman. It's just as well. It was filthy under there—cigarette butts all over, empty Avon samples, and a petrified tuna sandwich. And I found this." She held up a dollar casino chip from the Riviera. "I'll bet it's safe to go back to the strip dressed like this."

"It's too risky. The best place for us is right here, close to Jane, just two ordinary housewives. Let's make cookie cutters. It'll be fun. We'll make a cookie of Mrs. Martini and bite her gun off."

The next event, an informative lecture, "Teflon, Your Second-Best Friend" (the new control-top pantyhose having been voted number one), had ended with a demonstration pitting a Teflon-coated frying pan against one made of cheap aluminum with no magic coating. As a result, the room smelled of burned cheese and singed plastic. Verda Taylor, the creator of the hourlong look at this marvelous example of space-age technology, had forgotten to remove the plastic wrap from her American cheese slices before tossing them in the hot skillets.

"This is worse than the apron-tying contest of 1962," Marge said, fanning herself with her apron, pleased that her cookie-cutter fiasco had been forgotten. "Remember? The contestants got so carried away we had to call the fire department to cut them loose."

"Who could forget it?" said Bibi.

"She made up that ridiculous story as a test!" whispered Bridget as Marge walked away to talk with some other members of the Dorothy Duncan family. "Think about it. My shoes don't fit, you keep calling me by the wrong name, and we obviously have no talent for thawing. When you held up that turkey baster earlier and asked for a demonstration, I was certain she was going to go get Verda. She suspects we're imposters."

Bibi stopped licking melted cheese from her fingers long enough to make a face at her friend. "You're paranoid. Marge doesn't suspect a thing. She's just like your mother—the evidence could be right in front of her face, and she'd still deny it. To Marge we're inexperienced house-wives in need of guidance. If she thought we were Betty Crocker spies, she would have turned us in right away. Of *course* your shoes don't fit. We were in a train wreck. It's why I can't remember my name is"— she looked down at her name tag—"Sandy Beach."

"You can't remember your name because of that Jell-O queen. You made a date with her, didn't you?"

"If we're going to fit in here, we've got to be chummy. 'Notwithstand-ing their nuclear arsenal and enormous military power, Americans are amongst the friendliest people in the world, second only to the French.' Remember that dull filmstrip you made me watch? Are you going to tell me those twenty minutes meant nothing?"

"You know that dating intra-mission is prohibited," Bridget whis-pered. "Otherwise it would have been Jane hanging onto the side of our bed last night." A pained look crossed Bibi's face. The strap on her left sandal had rubbed a spot raw, and Bridget had bumped it. "Not that sleeping with you is a hardship," Bridget assured her.

Bibi slipped off her shoe and looked at her baby toe. "You see this ugly bump? My grandmother had them. It's a *corn*. And I'm only twenty-*four*." She touched the painful spot and grimaced. "It wasn't there this morning when I put these on." Blinking back tears, she ran her hands through her bouffant, forgetting she had smothered her hair with a can of Aqua Net. While trying to disentangle herself, she grew more entrapped.

"I always knew I'd suffer a disfiguring accident while on a mission," Bibi said as Bridget helped her pry her hands from her sticky helmet. Tears rolled down her cheeks as she thought of the cute new narrow-toe black vinyl half boots in her closet back home. Refusing in principle to wipe her eyes with the fuzzy, crumpled, obviously used Kleenex that Bridget dug out of her apron, she hobbled to a bale of hay, part of a display saluting farm wives, and sat down. She knew that fallen arches and foot odor were right around the corner. "I just hope Myrtle doesn't notice."

"It's a very small corn," Bridget assured her. "A *baby* corn."

Bibi groaned. Vegetable humor. She was right to have worried about Bridget's enjoying this part of their assignment too much. Pretty soon she'd be retiring from the spy game to stay home and starch Jane's shorts.

"I have a plaster," Bridget added, digging through her purse and coming up with a bandage in sterile packaging. "It's old, but clean."

"Just be gentle," Bibi sighed. Nodding, Bridget knelt down, her giant gunboat shoes sticking out from under the skirt of her dotted-swiss dress. Bibi held out her foot as if preparing to receive a glass slipper, and Bridget peeled the paper off the bandage. Bending over to position it just so, she saw that the spot on Bibi's toe wasn't a corn. It was a dried onion flake.

"Do you think I'll be scarred for life?" whined Bibi.

"You will if you keep wearing those flimsy sandals," Bridget said, sticking the plaster on Bibi's toe and rubbing hard.

"I haven't anything else to wear. I left the ones Wanda gave me back at the teepee. Unless . . ." She eyed Bridget's shoes and winced. Which was worse? Temporary ugliness or a permanent, disfiguring injury? "For the sake of the mission, would you . . . ?"

"For the sake of the mission," Bridget sighed, slipping off her canoes.

sixteen

Jane was certain that Dougie Smathers had not killed himself. Touring a national monument, pummeling a lunch lady, eating a ham-and-Velveeta sandwich—none of these were the actions of a man bent on taking his life. He was simply too egotistical to deprive the world of Dougie Smathers. The opportunity to brag about having scared the hell out of James Bond would have been enough reason to live.

When she realized that the body in the lake was Smathers, a suspicion confirmed when she saw his name inked under the loafer flap, her first feeling had been that of relief, then shame. There was a Mrs. Smathers who would not be receiving a glow-in-the-dark toilet seat, but instead a visit from the police, with shocking news.

A second shiny white shoe and a half-eaten box of Bugles, the crunchy little horn that tastes like corn, had been found, and the consensus of the crowd gathered at the Nevada-Arizona state line was that it was suicide, plain and simple. The odds were three to one that the man had jumped, and a Rotarian with a keen sense of civic duty and a ten-dollar bill riding on the outcome had lent his hat to the young man setting up the pool. Nobody had actually *seen* the man jump from that spot, but it was agreed that he must have. How else to explain the popular snack item and the man's shoes left on a sidewalk tidied not ten minutes before by a troop of Brownies working on their Community Cleanup badge.

Spectators watched as two police cruisers, one from Nevada and the other from Arizona, met up in the middle of the span. After agreeing that it must indeed be another monumental suicide, the officers argued over points of procedure, as there was typical confusion over which state had the authority to investigate the death. True, the shoes had been found on the Arizona side, but the Bugles had always belonged to Nevada.

While shore patrol retrieved the body, Dougie's crew huddled together, their Hoover Dam pendants drooping by their sides, their sadness contagious to the group and even to Jane and the Girl Scout, who had lost her dessert to Dougie only a short time before. When the body was turned on its back, it was impossible to miss the black eye patch covering his injured eye. As he was hauled into the boat and rowed to shore, Agent Bob Snurd, dressed in a junior-miss version of Dougie's loud attire, looked around the crowd, eyes soggy with unshed tears as he recalled their last conversation. Bob had described his outfit as being perfect for the weather and the occasion as he and Smathers selected liverwurst and ham-and-Velveeta sandwiches and bowls of fruit compote in the Snacketeria, and Smathers had dismissed him with a grunt and then took his chocolate milk.

The death of a secret agent, even a real stinker like Dougie Smathers, was a chilling event. Jane felt a tug in her chest as the body of her fellow agent was brought back to land, minus shoes and half a box of a salty snack food he could have done without. She looked up at Cedric, who had doffed his sombrero and was wiping tears from his cheeks. Felix looked frankly relieved and cast his eyes down, embarrassed by his cold response to his colleague's death, when he caught Jane looking at him.

"Dougie was a bloody idiot," Jane said to Cedric, squeezing his shoulder. "You don't need to cry for him."

"I'm just a sentimental fool," sniffed Cedric, putting his sombrero back on in fear of sunburn. Life must go on. The back of his neck was as red as a beet, and poor pale Felix had acquired another layer of freckles on his spotty arms.

"Once they realize it wasn't suicide, they're going to be looking for someone to pin it on," Jane whispered. "We've got to get out of here. Let's try not to attract any attention."

Cedric drew in a sharp, worried breath. He knew that evidence against Jane would be easy to stack up: busloads of nuns, schoolchildren, and secret agents could testify that she had told the dead man to go jump in the lake. Cedric and Felix stepped in front of Jane and linked their arms, her bodyguards. Cedric was meek, folding quickly under the steely gaze of authority, and Felix was hardly required to defend someone he'd just met, so their gesture, while nice, didn't make her feel any safer.

The rescue mission was documented from every angle by tourists and police alike, and Jane wondered if these images would find their way into vacation slide shows. She imagined the narration upon a family's return: "Here's Martha in front of a body they found floating in Lake Mead, America's water playground." While two tourists argued over the trajectory the body must have taken on the way down, a child seated himself in the middle of the road and began assembling his snap-together model of Hoover Dam (water not included), a souvenir Cedric coveted but had decided against when he found out the price. Jane couldn't wait to get out of there, concerned that someone would take a photo of her at the scene of the crime. "All visitors will be required to give statements to the police," the tour guide announced, dashing Jane's hopes of a quick getaway. "You will not be free to go until the last statement has been taken. This is, after all, a police investigation. Children and women will be allowed hourly bathroom breaks, and if the interviews go on past the supper hour, the Red Cross will bring in sandwiches, coffee, and blankets."

Two additional patrol cars rolled up, one carrying a plainclothes detective who shooed the tourists back so he could examine the scene. Running a finger over the iron rail, oxidized to a rusty red color, the detective frowned, lifted his sunglasses, and examined the substance on his index finger.

"Looks like—" He put his finger to his nose and sniffed. "Yep, it's glitter, all right." He squinted at the silver particles dancing in the bright afternoon sun. Then a puddle of water on the sidewalk caught his attention.

"Showgirl?" suggested a patrolman.

"Christmas-card snow?" shouted out the pregnant woman.

Jane thought it interesting that not one of Dougie's friends stepped forward to offer assistance or identify their fallen comrade. Like husbands forced to wait while their wives tried on dresses, the agents shifted from foot to foot, gift-shop bags dangling from their wrists, looking annoyed, sweaty, and bored. Several were smoking cigarettes and chatting while sneaking looks at their Superman watches (the official giveaway of the 1965 convention). Only Agent Bob Snurd appeared upset, standing facing away from the lake, blowing his nose on a limp black sock. Agent Pierre Camembert took a girlie magazine from his pocket and pretended to read. Bob took a snow globe from his bag and, using it like a baseball, nervously tossed it in the air and caught it until Agent Camembert barked at him to stop, but the distracted agent continued.

"I want a hot dog, and I want it now!" a boy wailed, and a grateful sigh rippled through the crowd.

"Trust a child to understand that life must go on," a woman said. "The little angels . . ." A cheer from the crowd interrupted her. A sodden body on a canvas stretcher with a dead man's open-eyed stare—one bloodshot eye staring blankly at the cloudless blue sky, the other covered with a black patch—was placed onto the Arizona side of the roadway.

The detective snagged his shoe on one of the stretcher's wood handles and pulled it toward him so the corpse's feet, minus the shoes, belonged to Nevada. With a smooth motion born of practice and necessity, he slid his hand into the pocket of the soaking white pants and pulled out a Flamingo swizzle stick in perfect condition. "He's an out-of-towner!" someone shouted, as if the white shoes and Hawaiian shirt hadn't been clue enough. Like paparazzi at a Hollywood premiere, the crowd surged forward, cameras raised and flashcubes popping, the body of someone *just like them* suddenly more fascinating.

"This fellow took a beating recently," the Arizona cop said as he peeled back the eye patch. "By the looks of it, it was within the last twenty-four hours."

A sheet was pulled over the corpse, which was clumsily loaded into a frozen-foods delivery truck flagged down for the job; the Las Vegas County coroner's hearse would be tied up for days at a desert excavation. Jane looked around, not sure whom to be worried about more, and spotted Agent Bob Snurd. Like a kid picking at a scab, he couldn't stop playing with his globe, rolling it from hand to hand. With a personality defined by proximity to power, Bob would need a new bully to hide behind now that he no longer had Dougie to anchor himself to. Jane saw him glance around at the group shyly, like a fellow looking for a pickup, straining to hear the agents surrounding him talking among themselves, and she knew that he would try to make good on his threat to get her, especially since he now had something to prove.

"They must be talking about me," whispered Jane. Cedric nodded, took off his sombrero, and used the car keys to poke eyeholes in it, then traded it for Jane's, clamping it over her head so her entire face was covered. She felt like a lampshade, the red bobbles tickling her chin. The tourists had become quiet, too hot and now too bored to continue speculating about the drowned man. The pregnant woman used the time to balance her checkbook on the top of her tallest child's head.

Bob's snow globe fell from his hand, and the sound of plastic breaking seemed to awaken everyone's interest. The detective picked up the globe, cracked and leaking but intact, tracing the break from the black plastic base to the pimple on top with his finger. "The substance on the rail is snow-globe glitter," he said, comparing the two. "The question is—whose snow globe?" He took Dougie's wallet from the evidence bag and examined the wet but still legible Diners Club receipt inside.

"A shot glass, bar coasters, and a bag of rock candy. But there's no snow globe on this receipt." He held it in the air. "This glitter is not from victim's snow globe because"—he paused for theatrical effect upon the audience he never had—"the victim *had no snow globe!*"

"I saw this on *Perry Mason,*" a man whispered, and people around him nodded. The detective was hailed as a clever fellow, and everyone's interest was revived by this break in the case. The pregnant woman toddled off to the ladies, her third trip since the police had arrived, leaving her children in the care of a Shriner.

Jane felt in her jacket pocket. When she left the Snacketeria, she'd had a snow globe, a gift from Felix. Now it was gone. "Did either of you take my snow globe?" she whispered from beneath the sombrero.

Felix and Cedric shook their heads.

"Someone stole mine and planted it as evidence. Just as I thought: Somebody's *killed* Dougie Smathers, and I'm going to take the fall," she said as the detective put Bob's globe and glitter in an evidence bag. "Who hated him enough to pitch him over the rail?"

"It's usually a family member. That would be Mrs. Smathers. But she's home in Kansas City with their dog, Dougie Smathers Jr."

"Could Snurd have done it?" Jane asked. "Did you see the expression on his face when Dougie ate his pudding?"

"Reason enough for murder, some chaps would say," muttered Cedric, who dearly loved a good rice pudding.

Felix shook his head. "Bob admired Dougie too much to ever harm him. He did everything he could to be like him. When Dougie bought a green Dodge, Bob bought a green Dodge. Bob even got married so he could go on *The Newlywed Game* with Dougie."

"This speculation is pointless," Cedric said. "You didn't kill Agent Smathers. We'll simply tell the truth: We were with you from the time you left the Snacketeria until the body was discovered. We all saw him get on the bus, and that was the last time we saw him until now. You didn't kill anyone."

"It's possible all three of us will be implicated, in which case your alibis won't count," said Jane. "And we can't go to the police." Jane knew she'd never pass the strip search.

"But you're not capable of murder!" said Felix.

Jane cleared her throat.

"Oh." He lowered his voice. "I keep forgetting you're an assassin."

"*Former* assassin," Cedric said helpfully. "It's a kinder, gentler secret service."

"I've got too much class to kill someone with a snow globe," Jane said, and Cedric nodded emphatically. The pregnant woman had returned from the ladies' room with a can of Tab, and Jane realized how thirsty and hot she was. She looked back at Bob, who was now on his tiptoes examining the faces of the people around him, a pained look in his eyes. Just then Felix bent down to pull up his socks (Cedric's last clean pair, actually), and, afraid if she stepped behind Cedric she'd look as if she was trying to hide, Jane froze. At first Bob passed right over her. Unaccustomed to thinking for himself, it took a few minutes for him to realize that the person with Cedric and Felix, the one with a hat pulled suspiciously low, might be James Bond. Like a hammy actor in a silent movie, he did a dramatic double take. His jaw flew open, and he stabbed his finger in the air in her direction. Jane feared that her time was up.

"The charade ends now," she said, putting her hand down her shirt to unpin the bandage around her breasts. It would be the fastest sex change in history, and the only way to get out of there.

Cedric grabbed her arm. "Absolutely not," he hissed into her ear. "If you do this, your brother's name will be worth nothing. There are already enough rumors flying around, questioning his mental health, his taste in clothing, and his rampant abuse of penicillin. *I beg of you.*"

"I cannot be strip-searched!" Jane whispered back. "I'm a woman in men's clothing. If I'm not wearing at least two pieces of women's clothing, I'll be charged with a crime. That will give them plenty of time to build a case against me. Either way it's an international incident."

Cedric shut his eyes and rubbed his forehead, thinking back to his mother's theatrical career. She was a woman who had dressed like a man, on occasion. "If you can't be a woman dressed as a man, you can always be a man dressed as a woman."

Felix had tactfully put his fingers in his ears when he heard the angry whispers. He did, however, understand the gist of the matter: James Bond was in a pinch and needed their help. *He could not believe that the one and only James Bond needed Felix Bivens's help!*—and he offered it when Cedric filled him in. "I made my own costume when I played Peter Pan in a school play," Felix said. "Cover me." Switching places with Cedric, Felix removed his sombrero. By breaking off the prongs of his black plastic comb, he was left with a cutting tool. With a sure hand, he ripped the string of bobbles from the border of his sombrero, crushed the peak until it was flat as a pancake, and tore a hole into the center of the hat. He then repeated his action with Cedric's. With a needle and thread from his pocket sewing kit, he made long stitches binding the two circles together to form a crude skirt. Jane knew not to interrupt a queen when he was creating a new look, so she held her tongue as he took a few extra dear moments to bend the upturned rim so it angled down and then whipstitched the bobble back onto the hem. Entrusting her Beatle boots and socks to Cedric's care, she rolled up her trouser legs and slipped into the "skirt," glad she had shaved her legs for yesterday's performance as a maid. She was amazed at Felix's eye for design and quick work. Even Wanda would have been impressed.

Jane did a quick scan of the group and noticed that Bob had the ear of the detective and was reenacting the Snacketeria scuffle while his friends ate rock candy and examined their souvenirs. Was Bob the only one who would mourn Dougie Smathers? "We don't have much time," she whispered as she tied the front tails of her shirt in a knot at her waist, trying to make her man's shirt look like a lady's blouse. It was a misguided attempt to imitate an outfit she had seen in a Doris Day film, and it didn't work. "I look like a shipwreck survivor," she complained to Felix, seeking his help.

"Wear your shirt out. It will lengthen your silhouette and hide the unfinished top edge of your skirt. And it's a more flattering look for a tall fellow. It will take attention away from your hair," Felix assured her, untying her blouse and pulling the wrinkles out of the fabric. "But it's not enough." They looked at Cedric for help. Sighing, he handed over the colorful silk scarf showing dam piston engines in action, a gift for Miss Tuppenny. Tying the scarf around her hair, pulling a few strands forward to suggest bangs, Jane looked, Cedric thought, frumpy but passably female. There was nothing they could do with the eyebrow. Knowing how she hated it, Cedric had made her attach it with an extra-strength glue used to attach logos to the outside of airplanes. He now regretted such stringent action.

"When she leaves to go to the ladies"—Jane indicated the pregnant woman shifting her weight from one slipper to the other—"we go with her. Cedric, give me your snow globe." She cracked it against the rail, breaking off the plastic base, holding her thumb over the hole so water wouldn't dribble out.

An expression of alarm splashed across the pregnant woman's face; she looked as if her baby-pressured bladder would burst. Dropping the can of Tab, she turned to tread a familiar path. The officer guarding the exit didn't even look up from his racing form. "Just follow my lead," said Jane, shoving her jacket up her skirt. They fell in line behind her, Jane walking swayback to exaggerate her belly. She got past without a blink, but the officer held up his hand and ordered Cedric and Felix to halt. "I'm the father," Cedric stammered in an inspired bit of improvisation Jane knew he would brag about for days.

"Congratulations. I've got three myself. But I can't let you through."

"I'm having *twins,*" Jane said, throwing in a moan. "I'm sure they're coming any minute." She looked over her shoulder. Bob had finished talking to the detective and was pointing to a tall metal waste receptacle wearing Felix's windbreaker and the surviving sombrero. "Holy Mother of God!" she cried, pouring the snow globe's water on the ground between her legs. The officer whitened under his tan, leathery skin as Jane clutched her belly and begged for morphine.

"We've got to get to the nearest maternity ward!" cried Felix. The officer nodded, putting his hand on Jane's elbow, boosting her up the short flight of narrow steps leading to the parking lot. "Hurry," Jane gasped, pointing out their station wagon. Cedric fumbled for his keys, turning out every pocket in the perfect imitation of the expectant father. The three men eased Jane into the back of the station wagon, strewn with fuzzy-dice pillows and candy-bar wrappers. Shoving Cedric into the passenger side, Felix popped behind the wheel and gunned the motor. Leaning out the window, he inquired as to the officer's name.

"Milton," he said. "Milton Steimgh. Badge number seven-three-six-five."

"Milton, we're naming the first one after you," Felix called out as they roared off.

The road back to Las Vegas was a blur as Felix leaned on the gas, glancing into the rearview mirror every few seconds. Jane realized that it was the first time they had actually driven on the right side of the road.

"Dougie could have slipped. He *was* drinking an awful lot. And he had pudding on his shoe." Felix had been trying, unsuccessfully, to talk Jane into believing that Dougie's death had been an accident and that the police investigation would prove it.

Neither Jane nor Cedric was buying this line of reasoning. "Pudding doesn't make people slip over a four-foot-high rail," said Jane. "No matter how drunk they are. Someone tossed him. My money is on Agent Snurd. Did you see how nervous he was? He couldn't stop playing with that damn snow globe."

"I thought he seemed genuinely upset. The rest of Dougie's friends acted as though they were at a company picnic," said Cedric. "It was shock, I imagine."

"Relief is more like it. I don't think anyone liked Dougie. But I'm the only one who told him to go jump in the lake," Jane said again, still in disbelief that her words had become prophecy.

"An unfortunate choice of words," murmured Cedric.

"People say things like that all the time, but they don't mean it," said Felix. "Everyone knows that. When I try to change the channel in the middle of her soaps, my mother says, 'I'll kill you if you touch that knob,' and of course she never has. And when I purchased my swim trunks yesterday, the guy in line behind me threatened to kick my ass if I didn't make up my mind. He didn't, of course. They're merely expressions," he said. "It's not as if we run around killing each other and beating each other up in America."

"A roomful of tourists saw us go at it," Jane said, realizing they were having the same conversation over and over, a result of stress, she was certain. It was a sure bet that none of them had been accused of murder before, and they didn't have a clue how to act. "They saw me shoot him; you think they're going to remember it was *his* squirt gun? Not bloody likely." She hung her head out the window and was sick. "Sorry," she said, wiping her mouth on her head scarf while Cedric sat in the back and sighed over this desecration of his one remaining Hoover Dam souvenir. "Morning sickness," she said, patting the "twins."

At least Felix laughed. Then, growing somber, he said, "I'll tell the truth. I'll say you were with me the entire time, except for that visit to the ladies' rest room when we were in the Snacketeria. But we don't need to mention that."

"Or even talk about it among ourselves," added Cedric, taking his eyes off Felix to shoot Jane a reproachful look. She had promised to use the correct lav!

"I propose we go to the police right now so I can give my statement," said Felix.

"We can't go to the police!" Cedric's voice was shrill. The shock was wearing off.

"But he's not capable of murder—they've got to know that," said Felix.

Jane cleared her throat.

"Oh. Right."

It was the one aspect of being her brother that Jane despised. N. had never considered a situation like this, but G.E.O.R.G.I.E. had. In case of danger, Jane would resume her true female identity and fly out of the country. Trouble was, Bridget had her real passport. She had thought, and rightly so, that Jane might lose it. "Take the turnoff to the convention center," she ordered, "I've got to go back in."

This was her last chance to find that invention. It *had* to be in that room, hidden among the limited-edition Hummel secret agent figurines and the J. Edgar Hoover aftershave gift sets.

"While I appreciate the gesture, now is not the time to shop for my birthday gift!" cried Cedric, thinking of the bag of souvenirs he had dropped on his sprint to the car. Souvenirs with his fingerprints all over them, fingerprints that by now were surely on their way to Interpol.

"I left something behind," explained Jane. "When we get there, drop me at the front door and stay close by—and keep the engine running." While talking she had shed her sombrero skirt and was unrolling her trousers.

"Something that you absolutely *must* have?" asked Cedric. "May I remind you I left a few things of my own at Hoover Dam."

"My *Welcome to Las Vegas!* informational packet," Jane said. It was the first thing that came to mind.

"You can have mine," offered Felix. "I was going to paste it in my scrapbook, but I have other ways to remember my trip here."

"I wrote something on the envelope."

"Something in code? Something that the public must never be privy to?" asked Cedric.

"A shopping list?" wondered Felix.

"'I hate Dougie Smathers.' Let me have a cig."

"No one really liked him," Cedric assured her, handing her his pack of cigarettes.

"No, I wrote 'I hate Dougie Smathers' one hundred times on the back of my *Welcome to Las Vegas!* informational packet. And I left it in the Bachelor Pad of Tomorrow, where anyone could find it. And I signed it."

Cedric unrolled his window, leaned out, and made a choking sound, and Jane switched on the radio and tuned in the Liberace station, hoping the music would soothe his shattered nerves.

. . . .

seventeen

You're just going because your new crush is going." They were in line with a group of women dressed in slickers and rain bonnets, waiting for the signal that the bus taking them to Hoover Dam was ready to board, and Bridget still wasn't sure it was a good idea.

"We're going because our directive is to be available to Jane should she need us," Bibi said tartly. "And since she hasn't rung us, or answered any of your calls, the only way we'll know what's going on is if we spy on her."

Irked that Jane was being stubbornly independent, and a little worried, too, that she had run into complications and was too embarrassed to ask for help, and knowing that Jane's convention was touring the national monument, Bridget had agreed to go to Hoover Dam, but only if Bibi promised to sit with her on the bus, and not with her new girlfriend. "But we've got to be careful. If Jane sees us, she'll know we're following her."

"Nonsense. She won't recognize us in these hideous garments." They had cut holes in rubberized tablecloths and were wearing them like ponchos, and had pinned two of Marge's plastic doilies to their heads—all in hopes of blending in with a group of women dressed in full protective rain gear. It was, without a doubt, the ugliest mission they'd ever been on. "And if she does, we'll just say that, due to creative differences, we had to leave the show and adopt new covers, and are touring the dam along with the rest of the gals.

"Gals—that's what they call themselves," Bibi added, proud that she had picked up housewife vernacular so quickly.

"Aren't you excited that you're going to see America's greatest monolithic engineering marvel?" said Bridget, suddenly burying her face in a *Hoover Dam Fact Sheet* as Verda walked past.

"Don't worry. We could be as naked as Venus and Verda wouldn't notice. A few minutes ago, she was handed a message from Dorothy Duncan, asking her to take over security. Her first job is to check the bus for a lost box of peanut brittle, and remove it before the candy gets crushed into the upholstered seats. She'll be so preoccupied, getting by her will be a breeze."

"I love Breeze. The bubbles tickle my nose," a woman in a clear slicker said, and a round-robin discussion of the product followed.

Pleased that they were finally fitting in, Bridget ventured an opinion. "I have a glass a day," she said, figuring it was a fruit-flavored beverage, like Tang.

"Is that a doily on her head?" someone said, and Bridget slid behind Bibi, her face flaming.

"Did you see their kitchenette?" someone else said in a stage whisper.

"It's like something from *The Beverly Hillbillies*. Like they pulled up in their trailer and drove right in."

Bibi put an arm around her friend. "Remember, I've got a can of itching powder in my purse," she said cheerfully as the line began to move.

Bridget stood on tiptoe, peering over a sea of badly styled hair, looking for their only friend there. "Where's Marge? She was so excited about seeing Hoover Dam."

"I bumped into her in the ladies' room, and she said she was going, but she wasn't in rain gear, and there was a wicker purse in the crook of her elbow. It's obvious she was lying."

"Because?"

"Think of it—wicker? Water? She's just asking for trouble. And you know how Marge likes to blend in with the other gals. She so friendly and helpful; it's clear she's too insecure to commit the social gaffe of carrying the wrong purse, even if it is only to tour a slab of concrete."

Since they'd only known Marge since nine o' clock, it seemed a little soon to analyze her, but what else did they have to do? "I do think there's trouble at home," Bridget said. "When she cut off her husband's head earlier, I got the feeling it was a subconscious act." She rolled her eyes. "We're so bored we're looking for intrigue at a *defrost-off*."

The line started to move, headed by the gals who, apparently, knew all there was to know about the product named after a puff of air. Bridget held back, considering sending Bibi to Hoover Dam so she could stay behind and put itching powder in their spare girdles, which, thanks to Bibi, she knew that all contestants kept hanging in their broom closets, next to their auxiliary aprons. A turn to the left would take them to the front door and onto the luxury bus, where Verda was checking underneath each seat for crumbs. To the right, down a long corridor, was the meeting place of the International Association for Accident-Prone People.

Bridget paused at the intersection, and Bibi took advantage of her hesitation. She crouched on the carpeted floor while exclaiming, "I've lost one of my secretarial school faux pearl graduation earrings!" Bridget, surprised by the turn of events, tripped over her and landed on her hands and knees, her plastic doily flapping over her face like a displaced toupee. Perhaps leaving a coded telegram for Jane at the front reception desk would have been better than enrolling in this contest, Bridget thought, listening to the giggling. Bibi grabbed her ankle.

"I'm not going to endure a bus full of women wearing vanilla extract behind their ears just so I can see Jane," she whispered.

"I'm glad to see you've come to your senses." No matter what Bridget wore, or how she tortured her hair, surely Jane, who knew her better than anyone, would see through the disguise.

"It's settled," Bibi said. "We're going to break into the convention and have a look around." Peeved at having never been invited, simply because her top-secret organization was *so* top-secret that the British Secret Service didn't know it existed, Bibi was determined to find out what went on behind that door.

Unwilling to admit that she had had that very same thought, Bridget said, "And what if we're caught?"

"We stopped by to get information about their organization to take back to the clumsy citizens of Terre Haute. The door was open, so we went inside to dust. While in there, we fell asleep. They're not going to kill two innocent housewives. Could it be any worse than facing Mrs. Sammi Martini?"

"But what if we find the invention before Jane does?"

"We'll put it right back," Bibi promised.

The two halls were divided by a long corridor containing public restrooms and a bank of telephones, and when they rounded the corner, intending to dump their ponchos and doilies into a trash can in the ladies' room, they were surprised to find Marge making a call. Bridget started to say hello, then stopped when she heard the catch in Marge's voice. They snuck into the lav to listen, leaving the door open a few inches. Marge's conversation had nothing to do with their mission, but neither did Liver Spots.

Marge was clearly annoyed. "Yes, dear, I know Monday is your poker night, but I have to stay on here a few more days. Why? Because Dorothy Duncan has selected me to appear on her show, to share my secrets for getting lipstick stains out of my husband's shirt collars. No, I'm not still angry, Marv, but I won't cut my trip short to come home and make sandwiches for you and your buddies. It's called mustard,

Marv—*that's* my secret ingredient! I have to go now; we're going to Hoover Dam. Yes, Marv, I'll bring you a paperweight." She dropped the receiver into its holder and put her head in her hands. They couldn't tell whether she was laughing or crying, and she quickly regained her composure, blowing her nose on the edge of her apron before picking up the receiver again. "Operator," she said. "Get me Reno, Nevada."

"Someone's getting a divorce!" Bibi sang in a whisper.

While Marge dug through her purse, muttering something about never having a pen when she needed one, they took the opportunity to slip out of the bathroom and head for their original destination. Marge must win, Bridget thought. A divorce, whether one was a duchess or a Detroit housewife, didn't come cheap.

There was no one guarding the spy convention door, no Verda Taylor noisily alphabetizing name badges while keeping an eye out for interlopers. Bridget tiptoed to the door and put an empty condensed-mushroom-soup can against it, listening just in case any agents had stayed behind. The floral wreath had wilted, its white carnations edged in brown, the sash sagging much as Marge had when she discovered that the girls were allergic to cheese and couldn't be on her Fondue-A-Thon team. "Good Luck, Unfortunates," Bibi read, draping the floral ribbon over her chest, looking like the winner of a sad and disturbing beauty pageant.

Bridget knocked, the sound muffled somewhat by the white cotton gloves she had snatched from the White Glove Inspection Team. Using an old trick she had picked up from Miss Tuppenny, Bridget knelt down, opened her compact, removed the razor-thin mirror, and slid it under the door, confirming her initial suspicion. No one was home. The lock was so flimsy, all it took was a twist of a butter knife and they were inside.

They bolted the door behind them, booby-trapping the handle with the mushroom-soup can so they would have ample warning of intruders, wishing they had accepted Wanda's offer of casual-knit cardigans. The heat from 158 hot-dog-bun warmers made the temperature in their convention hall pleasant, but in this spy sanctuary, the air conditioner was churning out frigid air even though the room was uninhabited.

"Maybe the invention needs to stay cold," Bridget said as she waited for her eyes to adjust to the dimness, the thin beam from her miniature charm bracelet flashlight ineffectual in a space this size. She could barely make out the row of booths and tables running the length of the room, and the tall glowing tower at the far end. Moving cautiously forward, they saw the dark object rising from the center of the room, circular in shape and humming ominously. "Don't touch it until I disarm it," warned Bibi.

Bridget gave a long, low whistle as they crept toward the object. "If that's it, we're going to have a hell of a time stealing it."

"We can steal it," Bibi assured her. "But can we get it home?" Glass crunched under her shoes, and she slipped on an olive pit and slid into a booth. Terry-cloth beach wear rained down on her head. Struggling from under a mound of surprisingly heavy swim trunks, she instinctively checked the damage to her hair, pleased that the Aqua Net had held so well. Wanda was right: It was the strongest hairspray ever made.

"NASA coats their space capsules with it, to protect them from the sun. That's why it's so cheap. Tons of it is made in a secret government factory, and what doesn't get used right away becomes consumer grade," she had told them. Until now Bibi hadn't believed her. "If we don't get our hands on the invention, perhaps we could bring home a can of Aqua Net?" Bibi suggested as she pulled up her bra straps and retrieved the huge shoes that had popped off her slender, size-six feet.

"Bibi, are you changing your clothes?" They always carried paper dresses and panties in their purses in case of emergency, and it sounded like Bibi was making use of them.

"Yes, Bridget, I've suddenly decided my outfit isn't quite to my liking. Would you hold my purse so I can give myself a manicure?" Bibi's snippy response was fueled by the knowledge that Bridget's concerns were not without merit. Once, while chasing Lord Sillitoe down Chelsea Street, she had ducked into Mary Quant to pick up a pair of red vinyl ankle boots with shiny silver buckles, on sale and the last pair in her size. She learned a valuable lesson that day: When tracking down a miscreant member of Parliament, do it in comfortable shoes. For weeks she walked on blisters, the boots kicked under her bed, their presence a sad reminder of her folly.

"Miss Tuppenny expects more than hairspray," said Bridget. "Come on, let's keep looking."

Bibi was thrilled to discover the revolving spring-loaded bed's abilities, and she squealed in delight. She hopped on, and it wasn't until she developed a nasty case of shag-carpet burn on her legs that Bibi heeded Bridget's warning to stop playing with it. "A concussion's the last thing you need," Bridget pointed out, to which Bibi rolled her eyes and insisted she had taken adequate precautions by fashioning a helmet from a bulletproof terry-cloth robe, which she planned to steal for dangerous missions at the beach.

Bridget was getting more frustrated by each humming minute. There was no evidence of this elusive, unnamed gadget, this breakthrough available only in America that promised to revolutionize the spy world, and their only reason for being there. She picked up a tube of Dehydrated Space Pizza and unscrewed the cap, releasing an overpowering bouquet of oily pepperoni and musty cheese into the room. "Maybe this is the secret weapon we've been looking for," she said, holding her nose. Bibi judged the Space Ice Cream inedible, except for the fudge sundae, which tasted chalky but had a pleasant fizz and a fruity aftertaste.

"Do you think Marge will notice we're not on the bus?" asked Bridget, examining a table of party favors. She was hard-pressed to tell the squirt gun pistols from the real one in the secret compartment of her cosmetics case.

"We'll say that at the last minute our Crock-Pot cracked, and we had to hold the parts together while the glue set. She'll think we're crafty, in the good way."

"I heard she and Verda are running against each other for the Most Personable trophy. Marge has got my vote."

"Why would anyone want a trophy?" Bibi sniffed. "They're so hard to decorate around, and a catastrophe waiting to happen if you have inflatable furniture."

"Verda definitely wants that trophy and will stop at nothing to get it—including finding the Betty Crocker spies," Bridget said.

"I miss being a casino robber," Bibi sighed.

"And it's only a matter of time before Verda finds us. When you were off testing the wiggle factor in our neighbor's Jell-O cubes, Marge told me that the contestant who turns in a spy will be rewarded with a lifetime supply of floor wax, and you know how shiny Verda's floor is."

"What if we invent ginsicles?" Bibi said, eyeing the bottles stacked in a pyramid on the bar. "And left them on Verda's table with a note from Dorothy Duncan asking for her opinion? Being drunk will get her kicked out of the contest. Then we can stop hiding behind major appliances every time we spot that miserable cow."

"Not a bad idea," Bridget admitted. "It *would* be a scandal." In deference to the large number of Mormon housewives in attendance, no alcohol was allowed in the room. Because the complimentary beverages, Diet Rite and Folgers coffee crystals, contained caffeine, the Utah contingent had drawn their wagons around Aisle 7, Booths A to P, marking the area with gaffer's tape and designating it the "no-stimulants demarcation zone." A sign saying as much had been posted.

"I have a feeling the gadget we're searching for is locked in some hotel safe. Unless it's a glow-in-the-dark toilet seat or super-strength Hai Karate cologne. *Or* the jet-propelled riding-lawn-mower."

"I hope not," Bibi sighed, shoveling tubes of fried chicken, ham salad, and potatoes au gratin into her purse. "We'd look pretty stupid sitting on one of those. Can you imagine riding through London on a *lawn mower?* Talk about obvious. I never did understand secret agents who like to show off their weapons. We might as well strap rocket launchers to our scooters. Still, it would be funny to show up at work on one, claiming *it* as the top-secret invention. Imagine Miss Tuppenny's expression when I ride into her office—"

Clapping her hand over Bibi's mouth and turning off her flashlight, Bridget whispered, "Did you hear the can rattle? Someone's at the door." Bridget clutched her purse, which contained a supply of smoke bombs. If they used them, Jane would know they had been sneaking around her convention.

"Should we scale the walls and go out through the windows, or stay here and bluff our way out?" Bridget whispered, rubbing the face of her Lady Timex, which contained a climbing wire and two small, but strong, grappling hooks.

"The walls," said Bibi. While she knew they could bluff their way out of the situation—i.e., they could be housewives drunk on cooking sherry, looking for a place to hide—she also knew they would not be allowed to take the bed with them. So why bother with a face-to-face encounter when it would be so easy to climb the walls?

They crept toward the door, intending to jam the lock with a dollop of Dehydrated Space Pizza to give them some getaway time. Bibi peeked under the door, spotting the tip of a black shoe.

"There's only one agent out there," she whispered in Bridget's ear. Bridget screwed the cap back on the pizza tube, and stuck her butter knife in the lock as the man on the other side jiggled the handle. Bridget pressed on the knife. This went on for some time, until the agent landed a hard kick in the middle of the door and ran away.

"Did you get it?" Cedric switched off the radio when Jane got back into the car, which was hidden behind a frozen foods truck, the engine idling. Felix, thank God, was still at the wheel. He wasn't as talented as Betty, but he was willing to ignore the posted speed limit.

"Get what?" Her shirt was soaked by her race through the building, a man in a golf cart on her heels. She had knocked over a Defrost-Off contestant, then wasted more time retrieving the dozens of meatballs that had fallen to the floor. When security arrived, Jane had fled.

"The incriminating evidence!" Cedric's shirt was soaked under the arms, and his face was as red as a beet. The cellophane tape holding him together was threatening to give way.

"Of course I did."

"We must burn the envelope immediately," said Felix, tossing a book of matches over the seat. He hit the gas, sending Jane flying as he maneuvered his way through the parking lot and out into the street, almost sideswiping a television news truck. "If you watch enough *Perry Mason*, you'll know that if you don't get rid of the evidence, the police will eventually find it." Once on the Strip, he slowed down, blending in with the afternoon traffic.

"I ate it," said Jane.

Calmer now, Cedric turned around to offer her an antacid tablet, and Felix said, "I wondered what was taking so long. According to my waterproof Timex, you were in there almost five minutes. That's more than four minutes too long for my comfort. I'm not used to espionage in action. I'm afraid I may be a bit of a liability."

"It shouldn't have taken that long," scolded Cedric, Mr. Espionage. Jane put the chalky tablet in her mouth, wondering if it had been the inspiration for Space Ice Cream. She was going to need a cigarette after this, to clean out her mouth.

"I was afraid the pressure of my pencil had left marks on the pages inside the envelope. So I ate the entire packet."

Felix whistled, long and low. "You fellows are the real thing."

"I've never been so glad to see a teepee in my life!" Cedric cried when he pulled the station wagon into the designated parking spot behind the coffee shop. He got out and stretched, then patted his stomach. Fast getaways, in real life or on the telly, always made him hungry. "Do we have time for a bite before we go on the lam?" he asked Jane, who had anointed herself Queen of Sheba, and was barking orders like a drill sergeant.

"Absolutely not. You're to get your things and be back here in five minutes. And don't let Wanda see you." Throwing her jacket over her head, she ran to her unit, key in hand. The rocks ringing the teepees had been watered; the plaster flamingos, stenciled with each unit's number, had been lovingly wiped clean of dirt and spiderwebs and polished to a pink luster. There was other evidence of Wanda's homemaking skills: The stoops had been swept, and the plastic begonias in the window boxes had been dusted and their wire-stemmed leaves bent in fresh poses. Wanda had also raked and seeded a patch of topsoil under the window, making a homey garden, and topped it off with an empty turnip-seed packet taped to a pencil stabbed in the earth.

One tidy row had been trod on, and Jane knelt to pat damp earth over it, knowing that turnips would never blossom in the motor court. Because the little garden lay in the shadow of the window box, it wasn't until she got down on one knee that she saw the daisy imprints. Mary Quant was a household name in her house, thanks to Bibi's passion for all things daisy, and she knew that *the* summer shoe was a white patent-leather sandal with a big black daisy at the heel, with a special rubber sole that left an imprint of daisies on soft surfaces. Bibi had come to work one morning in tears, having scuffled with Princess Margaret over the last pair at a Chelsea boutique and lost. But when she showed up the next day wearing the shoes and a smug smile, no one dared ask how she'd acquired them. Thus Jane knew that where there were daisy prints, Bibi could not be far behind, and she flung open the door to her teepee, half expecting to find Bibi stuffing the wagon-wheel lamp into her suitcase.

"I am so bloody glad you're here," Jane said, and stopped in her tracks, finding Wanda sitting on the floor grooming the buffalo-hide scatter rug next to the bed, a can of beer on the floor next to her.

"Howdy, stranger," she said. "It's nice to see you, too. I wish my husband would be that happy."

"Did a girl come by for me?" Jane asked, hovering in the doorway, ready to run at the first sound of a police siren.

Shaking her head, Wanda reached for the cigarette she'd left burning on the bedside table, already spotted with black burn marks, evidence of her carelessness. "It's been quiet as a graveyard around here since the second breakfast rush ended. It's always like this on Sundays. That's when I do the weekly scorpion sweep-out. I saved your unit for last. Didn't think you'd be getting home anytime soon, because I knew you were going out to the dam. Most people spend the whole day there. When I heard the news on the radio, I rushed right over here to get this place in shape, figuring you'd be back sooner than I thought. The radio said they were turning people away."

"It was terribly upsetting," said Jane, shoving the bag containing her sombrero skirt behind the twig chair. "I'd rather not talk about it. In fact, I'd like to be alone. Do you mind?"

"Not at all. I'm just about done here." Wanda nodded vigoriously, releasing into the air a cloud of peroxide to compete with the smell of lemony furniture polish and mothballs. Her lacquered beehive crackled, and when she brought the cigarette to her mouth, the glowing ember teased the dry wisps of her bangs, and Jane got ready to jump for the bucket of sand in the closet, Wanda's homemade fire extinguisher. "The Chief's in a bad mood. They preempted *The Secret Storm.*"

"Sorry about that, Wanda," Jane said as she went to the bathroom to splash cold water on her dusty face. Nothing she said or did was going to hurry Wanda; her best course of action was to act natural. "That dam is damn dusty," she said, making Wanda chuckle. Grit had taken up residence under Jane's nails, and she unwrapped the bar of perfumed soap and scrubbed her hands and face, drying them on a stiff towel with another motor court's name on it. "Next time you pinch towels, you should get them from a fancy hotel," she added as she draped it over the shower rod.

"Oh, I'd get caught. The Chief's the one who likes to flirt with the law. I'm too . . ."

"Lutheran?"

Wanda guffawed, spilling beer on the buffalo rug. "*Chicken.* He sets everything up, and I just keep my mouth shut. A wife can't testify against her husband."

Their crimes seemed fairly tame, Jane thought. Twice she had seen a patrol car in the lot, its occupants enjoying, or at least consuming, a meal at the picnic table under the wires of the jury-rigged electrical system that began at the utility pole along the highway and stretched to each structure in the motor court. It wasn't the only evidence of their parsimony. The words "Nevada State Women's Correctional Institution" were stamped on Jane's blanket, and when Cedric had paid for breakfast yesterday, the money had gone not into the cash register but into a battered toaster on a shelf above the griddle, the Chief's hidey-hole from the tax man.

"Give me one, hon," said Wanda as Jane lit up a cigarette from the pack in her nightstand drawer. Retrieving two cans of beer from the Styrofoam cooler at her elbow, Wanda tossed one to Jane and popped the tab on hers, sucking the cold foam as it ran down the side. Suddenly exhausted, Jane closed her eyes and held the can to her temple. Five minutes, and then she'd tell Wanda she was going out for some fresh air, leaving her suitcase and dice pillows behind, and not come back. A life spent in cool, drizzly weather had left her poorly equipped for these long, sunny days and chokingly hot air, and the novelty of sleeping in a teepee had worn off five minutes after she'd unpacked her bags. And she was probably wanted for murder. She was ready to go home.

"Are you sure no one came by or called?" she said. "Could the Chief have taken a message and forgotten to tell you?"

"Today's his day of rest. He doesn't speak from sunrise to sunset. He got the idea from a sword swallower who stayed here last year." Wanda paused to pick a short, stiff hair out of her new brush. "Did that fellow go over the wall or into the lake?"

"The lake."

"I'm not proud of it, but I have a cousin who tried to push her husband over the railing on the other side, hoping his face would be flattened so they wouldn't be able to identify him. She was never too bright. Anyone who's ever watched *Dragnet* knows about fingerprints. Plus, a cheerleading squad from Nevada U. caught her in the act."

"Did she go to jail?"

Wanda's eyes narrowed, two dark slits set under frosty blue eye shadow. "Damn fool took her back. Told the cops he slipped on some kid's Creamsicle and that Lois wasn't dangling him, she was grabbing onto him for dear life. The squad leader said otherwise, but after Stanley bought them new uniforms and pom-poms, she changed her tune." She squashed her empty can and tossed it into the wastebasket. "They say love is blind, but it's stupid, too. They moved to Boulder City for a fresh start. We go there once a month to play cards, and I bring my own beer and dip. You can never trust a woman who's got murder on the brain."

She struggled to her feet and took a look around. "Twenty minutes from stem to stern," she said proudly, checking the man's watch face pinned to her blouse. Her housekeeper's outfit consisted of baggy blue shorts covered in spotty bleach marks, a sleeveless white blouse with old sweat stains under the arms, and bare feet. "Room looks nice," she said surveying her work with a mother's pride. The windowpanes sparkled, a clean scratchy blanket was draped on the bed, and the plastic lariat stitching on the wagon-wheel lampshade had been tightened. "I've just enough time to have a quick look in your friend's room. He said he heard scurrying under his bed and was certain it was a family of spiders."

"I've already checked," said Jane, not wanting Wanda to find Felix among Cedric's possessions.

"If we've got an infestation, I gotta tell the Chief so we can bug bomb the teepees. It's the law."

"It was just his . . . shoes."

"Walking around?"

"The odor pads were breathing."

"Poor fellow. The Chief has to wear those things twenty-four hours a day, even to bed. I buy them by the gross." Lingering in the doorway, she swept the room again with her eyes, which landed on Jane, who fumbled in her pocket for a tip. Wanda shook her head and looked Jane right in the eye. "Look, Jim, I've got to tell you something, but if the Chief catches me, there'll be no end to the yelling tomorrow." Dropping the cooler and bucket on the bed, she took the beer can from Jane and finished it in one long swallow, wiping her mouth with the back of her hand.

"What is it, Wanda?"

"It was murder." She kicked the door shut behind her.

What was murder, Jane wondered? Being married to a man who never spoke? Serving hot dishes in hundred-degree heat? Carrying a head of hair the size of a small missile?

"The fella at the dam. He was murdered."

Jane dropped into the twig chair, immediately getting a painful splinter in her ass. So it had been decided. Dougie Smathers had been murdered. "I was there. He fell and drowned. I saw the body. There was no evidence of murder."

"Several witnesses saw a man bash him over the head with a snow globe, then hurl him over the edge. The cops came by with a description of the suspect. A dashing, dark-haired man with a distinctive sneer, and his harmless sidekick, a chubby fellow in shorts. There's a third man, but nobody remembers what he looks like. The police came here because criminals like to check into little out-of-the-way places, thinking it's safe. It's not. Especially since they're saying the victim, who was registered at the Desert Inn, had a Teepee Village Motor Court chip in his hand."

"I didn't—"

"I don't need to hear it." Wanda held up a dishpan hand. "You're a good tipper and make your own bed—that's not really what you'd expect from a cold-blooded killer. But I do business in this town, and half my customers are cops. I'll give you a twenty-minute start. Take our car. If the Chief squawks about it, I'll say I forgot it when I went to town for peroxide. Don't head into the Mojave—you'll die there. Go to Los Angeles and get lost. I figure you can hop a tramp steamer and be home in a couple of weeks. Try and change your appearance. Stop dressing like a preacher. Pluck that eyebrow. Wear a big hat. Just get out of town."

"We had nowhere else to go," said Jane when Betty opened the door.

Betty nodded that she understood. During her years with Chickie, people had dropped in out of the blue more times than she could remember, sometimes hiding out in her sewing room for weeks. "You're welcome here anytime, Jim, and your friends, too. Sandy will be thrilled to see you again. I'm sorry I can't be of much help to you until the bridge game ends. I'm expecting the gals any moment." Her demeanor perfectly suited this place. Jane had anticipated a decor more in keeping with a Betty who stole all her meals. Instead of this model of comfortable, middle-class normality, she had imagined the kind of bland landscape paintings and battered wood furniture typical of inexpensive hotel rooms, disassembled and brought home in the trunk of Sandy's car.

The front door led directly into the living room, an icy blue oasis designed around a formal portrait of a serene Betty that was hanging over a white brick fireplace. The soft sky blue color was present throughout the room, in the blue-on-blue narrow-striped wallpaper, formal nubby-silk drapes, and the thick carpet, its even rows of brushed nap evidence of a recent and thorough vacuuming. The white sectional sofa was as fresh as the day it had fallen off the truck, its virginal state preserved by custom-made plastic slipcovers Betty had ordered from a place in New York. The covers had been removed only once, for Chickie's memorial. A traditional funeral had been out of the question; there was no body, and Betty wasn't his actual wife. Officially, Chickie Skeets was still a missing person, but the pinkie ring Betty received in the mail the day after he went for a ride with some associates was all the confirmation she needed. She draped the front door in black crepe and invited their friends over for baked ham and fond remembrances. She and Chickie had had a good run, and after a day spent crying over old police reports and a Super-8 movie of their trip to the Grand Canyon, she had donated his suits to a Fremont Street mission and gotten on with her life.

"Stay on the runner," Betty said, rushing them through a corridor hung with family photos, the blue carpet having given way to a sturdy, low-pile olive. They were welcome to hide in the master suite until her bridge club, three women pulling into the drive in Sandy's aqua Cadillac, broke up. Though gracious, Betty was obviously flustered by their arrival, but her manners were Emily Post–perfect. She was the quintessential lady of the house, trying to maintain her composure in the face of unexpected fugitives from justice.

After instructing them on how to treat her steam-cleaned carpet, she excused herself, explaining that she had to roll her cheese ball in chopped nuts and set out pretty soaps in the guest half-bath. "You'll recognize the cheese, Jim," she said with a wink. "Now, these walls are thin, so keep your voices down. If the ladies find out I've got three wanted men in my bedroom, I'll never hear the end of it. The bathroom's across the hall. Make sure no one sees you. Don't use the fingertip towels— those are for the girls. And keep your shoes off my spread."

A minute later the house was filled with the sounds of women laughing, talking, admiring each other's hairstyles, new shoes, nail polish. The weather was discussed, then discarded for a more important topic: Vivian Vance's divorce from her bullfighter husband.

"Who's Vivian Vance?" asked Jane as she kicked off her boots and sank onto the cushioned bench in front of Betty's dressing table, a blond-wood skirted affair covered with expensive perfume bottles, most of them empty. "Dear Abby" columns clipped from the *Las Vegas Sun* were taped to the perimeter of the round mirror, dispensing advice on everything from Mexican divorces (were they legal, and did the wife have to know?) to advice to new widows (how do I keep the wolves at bay?).

The bedroom was coral, in all its variant tones, from shell pink to a dark reddish orange. The ceiling and carpet were the same gingery shade, radiating a richness and warmth lacking in the formal front room. The home was a remnant of better days, a museum of Betty's life with Chickie, a life that had included money to pay for hand-loomed carpet, imported French bed linens, and the woman who came in twice a week to keep them pristine. The only evidence that Betty had once shared this room was the leather catchall on the bureau, with Chickie's gold initial cuff links, a handful of coins, and the diamond pinkie ring Betty was trying so desperately to hold on to.

Heeding Betty's stern warning, Cedric took off his sandals to prevent dragging dirt all over the room and put them neatly by the door, in case he needed to make a quick escape. The television had been switched on in the next room, and chatter subsided as grains of sand slipped through an hourglass and *Days of Our Lives* quieted all discussion of Hollywood morality.

"Vivian Vance is the greatest second banana in the history of television," said Felix. Fascinated by the feminine candy-box room, he stood in front of a low-slung blond-wood bureau, his hands in his pockets, admiring Betty's Avon collectibles.

"Why did she marry a bullfighter?" said Jane, examining an empty bottle of White Shoulders with a thin skin of a dried, amber-colored liquid at the bottom. "Where on earth did they meet? Did he wear his bullfighter's costume to the wedding?" She realized she was running her mouth on these questions to avoid the real things that were on her mind—mainly this: Were they really going to be arrested and tried for the murder of Dougie Smathers? Would N. leave them to twist in the wind, or would he use his influence with the queen to save them? If her brother's eyebrow transplant was a success, would N. even want her back? And did Betty have any of that berry pie left from last night?

"Well," said Felix confidentially, "I read in *Small Screen Star* magazine that they were introduced by Elizabeth Taylor at a party honoring the tenth anniversary of one of her jewels."

Cedric paced the room, leaving deep prints in the thick pile carpet. He hated to interrupt such convivial conversation—it was the first time Jane and Felix had really connected—but other inquiries were more pressing.

"How do you know this woman?" He was hoping Jane would say she was an American agent. The pin-neat house, the bridge club, the cheese ball covered in nuts—all pointed to a picture of Middle America reflected on the television shows he had made part of his research. This woman had the perfect cover for a spy.

"Betty and her friend Sandy gave me a ride to town last night. They think I'm here for the accident-prone convention."

"So she's not one of us?"

Uncertain which "one of us" he meant, she shook her head, figuring it covered all bases, field, and teams. "She's just a nice woman helping out a friend."

"She can connect us with the dead man. What if she calls the police?"

"She won't."

"That's not enough," he said. "When you're wanted for murder, you need it in writing."

"You trust *him*," she whispered, gesturing toward Felix, who was now standing at the bank of windows across the room, scrutinizing the neat pleats on the floor-length chintz curtains and pretending he was hard of hearing.

"He's a fellow agent."

"*He's a pencil sharpener.* I'll bet Betty's got more experience in these matters than both of you together."

"She's still a civilian! You've put us in grave danger by bringing us here," he hissed.

"Betty knows not to say a word—she's been doing it all her life," Jane argued, still trying to keep "quiet" even though she wanted to scream.

"You *had* to fight him. You couldn't just walk away."

"He started it."

"Nowhere in the annals of spydom has 'He started it' been an excuse for such bad behavior."

"Well, he did pull a *gun*. Anyway, this is not what I signed up for! I didn't want to stay in a hot little teepee, and I especially don't want to listen to this right now. Another word from you and I quit!" Betty poked her head in and put her finger to her lips, the universal sign for "Shut the hell up." Felix quietly backed into the open clothes closet, pretending to admire Betty's selection of slightly outdated but still-elegant dresses.

Cedric glanced down at his feet, covered in Hoover Dam dust, and ran his hand over his sunburned forehead. When he looked at Jane again, he saw *Jane* and not the man who had tormented him for years by planting plastic spiders in his desk and bending his paper clips. "I'm sorry," he murmured. "I lost my head. If you say Betty's trustworthy, then she is. I do trust your judgment." Obviously embarrassed by their outburst, he turned to Felix and said, "I should think most secret agents don't feel comfortable enough to express their feelings to one another in this manner, eh?"

"I really am just a clerk," Felix said from the closet. "Mr. Hoover signs my paychecks, but I've never been part of an investigation or even held a gun." Torn between his loyalty to Cedric and his admiration for James Bond, he decided on a conciliatory smile and then went back to reading the labels in Betty's dresses.

"I should think few secret agents would insist on watching the end of *Batman* before running for their lives," said Jane. While she was chatting with Wanda, Cedric had become engrossed in television.

"Although I now see the folly of that decision, I will say, in my defense, it was an episode I'd never seen. In any case," he said, changing the subject, "I think it would be best to keep certain aspects of our mission out of the final report." Jane picked up a black marble ashtray from the bureau and offered him a cigarette as a truce. Had they stayed for the Betty Crocker coconut-cake commercial, as Cedric had wanted, they could be in jail, but there was no sense belaboring the point. He ventured a smile and shook his head. "Silk is very flammable." He pointed to the spread. Jane went to the window, drew back the curtains only slightly so as not to catch the attention of casino workers' children playing in the street, and raised the casement, leaning her arms on the ledge and blowing the smoke outside.

Cedric's gaze wandered over to Felix, who was peeking into hatboxes stacked on the floor of the long, narrow closet. Through the thin walls, they could hear the ladies talking about the man at the dam.

"We may be writing our final report from a jail cell despite Betty's help," said Jane. "And we won't even finish our mission." Groaning, Cedric pushed himself off the soft bed and lit a Kools, a brand Felix highly recommended for its refreshing taste, and taking up a post beside Jane.

"I'm confident the death will be ruled an accident, no matter what the eyewitnesses say," he said assuredly, exhaling out the cigarette smoke, his lips pursed in an imaginary kiss.

"I must stop threatening people in public. Someone's always watching."

"You weren't the only one. The lunch lady did threaten him with a paring knife."

"Yes, but I told him to go jump in the lake. And I'm the one the agents hate. What would they have against *her?*"

"She was mingy with the cake," said Cedric. "Those were awfully small pieces."

"Then there should be frosting on the rail, not glitter. Wanda told me they found a Teepee Village Motor Court chip in Dougie's hand. I had mine in my pocket, and, like the snow globe, it's gone." Jane wished Wanda had taken her chip for the table leg instead of Cedric's.

"Do you bring your *real* passport?" he whispered, tracing a crack in the sun-bleached wooden windowsill with his thumbnail.

"I'm not listening," Felix reminded them.

She nodded, forgetting for a moment that Bridget had it, and rubbed the hair between her eyes, which would no doubt leave a real scar once she was a girl again.

"And the right costume?"

She shook her head. She had packed a girlish getaway outfit, a simple dress made of plasticized paper, but she had used it to block the sun leaking through the shade on her teepee window. And she had given the sombrero skirt to Wanda, who wanted to wear it for that night's enchilada supper.

Cedric eyed the open closet, and Jane blanched. "Absolutely not," she said when he pointed out a blue silk cocktail dress with flowing sleeves.

"Not even a pantsuit?" suggested Felix, picking out a pair of flared-leg tan slacks made of durable polyester, paired with a simple matching blazer. This was making her unreasonably cross. It wasn't just the clothes. As much as Cedric annoyed her, he was her partner and should know that she was not someone to cut and run.

"I'm not leaving without you," said Jane. "If we can't see our way clear of this mess, we can make our way to the British embassy in Washington and request asylum." Sandy would probably relish the idea of transporting fugitives across the state line.

"There are brass knuckles in here," Felix announced when he opened the last hatbox. His nose was peeling and itchy, and he scratched it with the metal object until Jane took it from him and put it back. "You haven't asked my opinion, and I know there are things you can't discuss in front of me, but why not take a page from *The James Bond Action Book*?" he said. "We at the FBI use it for training exercises, then try our hand at the quiz at end of each chapter. I was going to bring the office copy for you to sign, but it's not allowed out of the building."

"Bloody good idea. From now on, Felix, you're the brains of this operation," said Jane. "Your job is to remember everything I've ever taught you, and come up with a plan."

"I'll get right to work."

"What are we going to do?" asked Cedric as Felix sharpened a pencil with his penknife, transferred the shavings to the wastebasket, moved the perfume bottles and cold cream jars to one side of the dressing table, and began making notes.

"I'm going to take a nap," said Jane, kicking off her boots and pulling back the coverlet, folding it neatly at the foot of the bed.

"Betty said not to disturb her spread." Cedric lay back on the divan, letting his feet dangle over the edge. Felix had several sheets of notepaper spread across the vanity and was drawing some sort of map.

"She just said not to put my shoes on it." The pillowcases gave off hints of lavender and Aqua Net, Wanda's remedy for everything from droopy beehives to ant invasions. "I'm starving," she said. She could smell coffee and cinnamon rolls. "I don't need a helipad on the roof of my building or a decoder ring fluent in thirty-nine languages, but a hot meal would be nice."

"If someone didn't bleed the budget each year so he could have his own private submarine, we could abandon certain cost-saving measures, such as requiring agents to pack a sack lunch for all assignments within England's borders," Cedric replied.

"Perhaps it's time for James Bond to retire. Permanently. He could jump off Hoover Dam, leaving behind a signed confession and an empty martini shaker."

"And why did he kill Mr. Smathers?"

"To get to Mrs. Smathers, of course."

"It would make sense, but N. would hurt us in a manner hitherto unknown in the history of human civilization," Cedric cautioned. "Then he'd make me return the silver-plated stapler I received at my farewell luncheon."

"And it would be exhausting to write the obituary. As his sister, I imagine the task would fall to me. If I included each one of his romantic conquests in the list of survivors, a special edition of the *Times* would have to be published to hold them all. It would be the world's longest obituary."

When her amusing suggestion drew no response, she picked her head up from the pillow and squinted at Cedric. He was asleep, as was Felix, his head on a pile of papers, a cozy scene had they not been wanted for murder. Jane lay on her back and stared at the ceiling, covered with yards of coral silk fanning out from a wildly extravagant baroque-style chandelier of entwined mermaids and crystal drops. The air-conditioning unit set into the window kicked on, a low hum that dulled the voices from beyond the wall. The moist air being pushed around the room settled on her skin like a sleeping potion, and her last thought before drifting off was that she had come to America's Sin City and the most sinful thing she had done was steal a bar of motor-court soap.

eighteen

"Where have you girls been? I was so worried when we got to the dam and you weren't in your seats." Marge breezed into their kitchenette tying on a spotless apron. Her hair was freshly combed, her face powdered, and rouge had been applied to her cheeks; a little too much. There was no sign of the unhappy, soon-to-be divorced Mrs. Milligan as she flitted about their kitchen.

Bridget and Bibi exchanged curious looks. Marge hadn't been on the bus; they had heard it drive off before stumbling upon the domestic dispute. Bridget stuck the bottle of gin they had liberated from the convention next door under the sink, behind the trash can. "The entire time I assumed you were in the bathroom, but come to find out it was Verda, practicing her prune rosettes. Do you have a Diet-Rite handy?" Marge seemed pretty happy for someone whose convention experience—bad Tupperware, a faulty apron tie, a trophy for the Most Boring Craft Demonstration—should have been the low point of her housekeeping career. Instead she looked like a new woman, the serene twin to the friendly but burdened woman who had shadowed them all day. A little too happy, Bibi thought, wondering if Marge had been dipping into the bottle of "Mother's Little Helper" Bibi had uncovered in her spice cabinet.

"We didn't go. The other contestants made fun of our impromptu slickers," Bridget said as she pinched herself, trying to bring up a few tears.

"They're just bitter women married to men with ring around the collar," Marge said sweetly, popping the top on her soda and throwing the tab in her purse. "How about a little pick-me-up before I tell you the news?" She held out her soda can and nodded at the sink. "That's where most of the girls keep their bottles," she said. "And the linen closet. No one goes in there. The dog-food bag's a good place, too."

"What the hell," sighed Bridget, opening two more sodas. Marge seemed overly cheerful, and her voice had a hysterical edge. They gathered round the wobbly kitchen table, the top so damaged by hot dishes and cigarette butts that drink coasters were unnecessary, and Bridget poured gin into each of their cans. Marge pretended not to notice, sipping her drink, ladylike, through a straw.

After two gin-and-Diet Rites, Marge went back to her kitchen to put the finishing touches on her frozen dinner for that night's *Tantalizing TV-Dinner* competition, which came with a ten thousand dollar top prize. Although Bibi desperately wanted to win—her half would go a long way to realizing her dream of owning the entire Mary Quant fall line, the box of Liver Spots in their old Frigidaire, the main ingredient of their dinner, had disappeared.

Deciding that it would seem suspicious if they didn't have an entry, they scoured the cabinets for ingredients that would add up to a meal.

The other contestants already had their dinners in the freezer and were lounging in their kitchens, crocheting pot holders and drinking coffee and gossiping about Betty Crocker.

"Does Metrecal freeze?" Bridget said, blowing dust off a dented can of celery-flavored diet soup.

"I don't see why not." Bibi found some sardines in oil and a jar of Cheez Whiz, and decided to pass on the French dressing, which had something green growing in it. They mixed the ingredients thoroughly and poured the goopy mess into the aluminum tray provided them, added plenty of salt, and popped it in the oven.

"Now we need a vegetable and a dessert," Bridget said, examining the contents of the Frigidaire. She bit her lip, thinking about what she had learned from Marge that day. Salt made everything taste better. Wieners were the basis for many a festive party food. Beets from a can, placed on a lettuce leaf and sprinkled with sugar, made a quick and nutritious side dish. "Are gherkins vegetables?"

"I don't see why not," said Bibi, taking the barrel-shaped jar from the bottom shelf and unscrewing the rusty lid. She took a sniff and put it back. "But I smell why not."

"Let's skip dessert," said Bridget, closing the door on a handful of soy sauce packets and a jar of old mustard. "Of course, we'll never win without a dessert." Bibi groaned and handed Bridget a package of lemon Jell-O mix. Must every one of her souvenirs be sacrificed? Adding hot tap water to the box, Bridget shook it until it sounded mixed, then popped it in the freezer.

"Smells like you're making progress in here," sniffed Marge, sticking her head through their shared window, the sheer white curtains framing her face like a new bride's. If the heavenly aroma coming from her kitchen was any indication, Marge would surely take top prize.

"It stinks," Bibi said frankly.

"A bad smell is just nature's way of telling us it's nutritious," Marge said kindly.

"What are we going to call it?" Bridget peeled back the foil lid, turning her head to avoid inhaling the fishy steam. Most of the Metrecal had boiled away, leaving tiny parched fish coated in burned Cheez Whiz, floating in a shallow pond of low-cal celery soup. "They look like they're decomposing," said Bridget, holding her nose. "And smell like it, too."

"Once we let it air out and add the side dishes, it will be more appealing," Bibi assured her, waving away the fumes before the smell could bond to her hair spray.

"At least our Jell-O turned out," said Bridget, taking the box from the freezer and peeling back the cardboard, proud of her contribution. Bibi helped herself to a ginsicle, her fondest creation yet, and hopped onto the countertop, watching Bridget chop off the corners of the frozen block so it would fit in the dessert section of their aluminum tray, now comprised of select sardines charred almost beyond recognition, a springy vegetable cut into slivers for easy digestibility, and an icy lemon-flavored dessert that was a new twist on an old favorite.

"I could use some help here," Bridget said, her fingers stained yellow.

Without an argument, Bibi slid off the counter and got her a ginsicle, like a born-again hostess. Since deciding she absolutely *had* to win this contest, Bibi had become every inch the lady. She had washed off the tattoo of Mary Quant she'd drawn on her arm while Marge was explaining how to turn on the stove, returned the little Amish people salt-and-pepper shaker set to Louise Wuebel's kitchen, and even put a drop of vanilla extract behind each ear. Her purse had found a permanent home in the crook of her arm, and a demure pink cardigan with real fake-pearl buttons was draped over her shoulders, again, courtesy of Marge. Bibi had even borrowed a plastic red bell pepper from someone's kitchen centerpiece and boiled it until it tasted just like the peppers her mother used to make.

Bridget couldn't believe her eyes. "I miss the old Bibi. When is she going to return?"

"After we win the ten thousand dollars."

Marge, who had come by to give them some last words of wisdom, took one look at their meal and exclaimed, "Oh! Sardines! What a surprise!"

Bibi jumped up. "That's what we'll call it! *Sardine Surprise!*"

"Why, that's a great idea, dear." Marge beamed at her student.

The less confident of the two, Bridget confessed that it hadn't turned out the way they intended, and Marge put a motherly arm around her shoulder and said, "There are some things in life we must learn to accept. Surprises are one of them. Who knows why bad things happen? Why does Cheez Whiz become crusty when it's overcooked? Why did my friend Edna's hair fall out after her last perm? Why do people have white carpeting, then are surprised when it gets dirty so quickly?" Marge was being kind. She knew full well, as did Bridget, that they would never win, not up against entries like Scrod-kabobs and Hot Dog Hooray! Bibi still seemed blindly (and unrealistically) convinced they could walk into a cooking contest, throw together some expired food products, and waltz off with the grand prize.

"I hope you girls win," said Marge graciously. Her apron, made of crisp white cotton with dancing vegetables escaping a giant paring knife embroidered along the hem, reminded Bibi of their embarrassing stage debut, and she stared at Marge, wondering if their neighbor had figured out *who* had ruined her carrot cake and was taunting them. "See you at the finish line!" Marge sashayed around to her kitchenette for her entry: Marge's Own Meatloaf à l Orange, Creamed Corn à la King, and Flaming Cherries Jubilee. She had given them a taste earlier, and, except for the small fire that had started when Bibi got her paper napkin too close to the dessert, the experience was heavenly.

"This is woman who *really* wants to win," Bibi said to Bridget when Marge showed them the homemade tray for her homemade dinner.

"Isn't it obvious? She needs the money for a divorce."

"We need the money, too," said Bibi. "Let's go, the line's forming!" Bibi held on tight to their precious dinner, sliding into place behind Louise Wuebel and her Swiss Steak Delight, and counting the number of women in front of them. "We're tenth. Is that good or bad? Will they have forgotten us after they've sampled nine dinners, or will ours be more memorable because it came early on, when their palates were fresh? I'll bet no one's ever tried freezing Jell-O before," she burbled happily, pleased that they had been able to throw together an entire meal in less time than it took to wash her hair. She might even write a book and call it *The I Really Hate to Cook Book.*

"I think our dish is so memorable that it won't matter when they eat it," said Bridget truthfully, wondering if they'd be laughed out of the contest.

Bibi nodded. To give their meal some added zip and without first consulting Bridget, she had tucked a Valium into each of the sardines. She had sacrificed the last of her dolls to culinary science, all except for the one wedged in her molar, to be swallowed in case of emergency. She *did* have, in Wanda's mother's purse, a travel-size bottle of truth serum, and a joint, also to be used in case of emergency. "I'm so excited," she said, bouncing on the heels of her shoes. "I already know how I'm going to spend my half of the prize money. How about you?"

"We're not going to win. But if we do, I'm sending it to Oxfam."

Bibi pouted. "Charity begins at home, Bridget. The British economy is in a slump, you know."

"Perhaps the queen will send you a thank-you note for your selfless devotion to crown, country, and Mary Quant." Bored with standing in line—the contest was supposed to have begun seven minutes ago—a woman behind them had peeled back the foil on her entry and was eating her peas.

"If I promise to wear her clothes on the Dorothy Duncan TV-dinner box, do you think Mary would give me the outfit?" asked Bibi expectantly. Frozen foods would be a wonderful way for the British designer to move into the American market.

"I'll have Mother ask."

"You never take me seriously. I'll bet you your half of the prize money that our Sardine Surprise! wins." Confident of their success, Bibi took out her compact and, staring at herself in the mirror, practiced looking surprised.

"Bibi, how many ginsicles did you eat?" Bridget knew that Bibi was not this overzealous on the other side of the pond.

"Just three. Marge had one when you went to the lav. That's when she told me the secret to good cooking."

"Gin?"

"Mrs. Dash's Spicy Onion Medley. It makes everything a *party*."

Women were lined up, still and silent, carrying their piping-hot dishes in oven-mitted hands, in anticipation of presenting their trays for judging. Four of the five judges—the author of a popular booklet on cocktail-party canapés, a newspaper columnist whose beat was the casino buffets, the chief froster at the most prestigious wedding-cake bakery in town, and a gal from Reno who held "Cooking for One" classes for new divorcées—had each taken a seat in the Barcalounger of their choice and were talking among themselves, their voices hushed, their tone respectful, in keeping with the gravity of the occasion. The TV-Dinner Winner would be announced tonight, over fruit cocktails. The festive atmosphere had gone chilly. Suddenly girls who had thrown baking soda on their new friends' grease fires now found themselves competitors and had to adjust to their changed circumstances.

Bibi stiffened her shoulders and refused to look at the contestant behind them, whose TV dinner smelled suspiciously of sardines. "I think we've found our spy," she whispered to Bridget, wagging her head in the direction of the girl before moving up a step.

"No shoving!" barked Verda from the head of the line, her feet firmly planted on the gaffer's tape marking the first-place position. Her Pruney Tooney was tastiest right from the oven, when the intriguing combination of prune and canned tuna was at its best.

The judges gripped their forks, ready to begin. The opening strains of the theme from *Bonanza* came through the console speakers, signaling the women that if the judging didn't commence in the next few minutes, they were all going to miss the first part of the show. Louise Wuebel, who had volunteered to help out by refilling the napkin dispensers on each TV table, smiled at Verda and said, "We have a surprise mystery judge. She's expected to arrive any minute."

"I'll bet it's Angie Dickinson," said Bibi when they heard the door from the corridor swing open and the oohs! and aahs! coming from contestants at the back of the line. The girls strained to see, but a row of kitchens and a woman's bloated bouffant were in the way. "I wonder if Angie Dickinson loves Cheez Whiz as much as I do," Bibi said.

The contestants waited patiently as the mystery judge made her way through the room, pausing to pose for snapshots and to sign oven mitts.

"Come on," Bibi muttered. Her sardines were losing their sizzle.

The Meat Loaf queen turned around and nodded her agreement. "I don't care how famous our mystery judge is, my sauce is beginning to congeal. It's probably some actress; they're notorious for being late," she sniffed.

"Then it *is* Angie Dickinson!" cried Bibi. The rumor raced up the line, and when a tall, golden blonde in a glamorous bouffant, wearing a mink coat and enormous dark glasses, made her way to the set, Bibi's heart went thump-a-thump. She hadn't believed Bridget when she said Angie was in town. Had she time to place a love note amid the sardines? "Hold this," she said, shoving the tray at Bridget and digging in her purse for pen and paper. There was nothing to write with, so Bibi made a sexy lip print on back of her Toni home-permanent coupon, then reapplied the same color to her lips, knowing that Angie was clever enough to put the two together. She wrote Miss Dickinson's first name on one of the sardines, with Mrs. Dash's Spicy Onion Medley, glad now that she had accepted Marge's gift of a complete set of Mrs. Dash's flavored food enhancers, and then rolled the paper kiss into a tube and stuck it in the sardine's mouth. She'd give up her dream of appearing on a TV-dinner box if only she could have one date with the beautiful movie star.

"It's as if fate has brought us together," she exclaimed earnestly to Bridget.

"I was just thinking the same thing," Bridget said dryly, cupping Bibi's chin in her hand and rotating her head so she was facing the set. The fifth judge had finally removed her mink and dark glasses and was seated comfortably in the last lounger, one napkin on the lap of her baggy capris and another tucked into the collar of a spotless baby blue blouse.

"Our surprise judge is Mrs. Sammi Martini!" cried Verda Taylor. "Let the defoiling begin!"

Sandy woke the three fugitives when she snuck in with three 7-Ups and a tray of salty mixed nuts, Ritz crackers, half a nutty cheese ball, and the news that the bridge party was breaking up. Knowing they were in here had made it hard to keep her mind on her cards, and she quit when her losses reached three dollars, her absolute limit. Slipping off her gold sandals and stretching out on the king-size bed, she let her head hang off the edge to keep her hairdo from being squished. Her long, skinny legs were clad in the same aqua stretch pants she had worn yesterday, but were now paired with a gold boxy top. "Stretch pants," "aqua," "boxy"— all words that had entered Jane's vocabulary only when she arrived in Las Vegas.

"Betty says not to ask you why you're here. The less she knows, the better, has always been her policy. Unless you're dying to talk about it." She ate a cashew and, when no one spoke up, said, "Did you hear about that guy going over the dam?" Banishing the nut bowl to the bedside table—all the good nuts were gone anyway, leaving just bitter walnuts and peanut shards—she took a butterscotch candy from her pocket and popped it into her mouth. Crinkling the wrapper between her fingers, she gave them the latest KMOB update. "The dead guy was from Kansas, in town for the International Association of Accident-Prone People conference. Christ, this place will host a shindig for anyone. Sorry," she added, remembering Jane's affiliation with the group. "Whose idea was it to drag a bunch of trippers to a *dam?* I'll bet you three bucks he fell while trying to snap a picture of one of those bathing beauties on skis. Probably hungover, too. Half the people here are walking around with one. The other half's workin' their way toward one! Man, I could use a drink myself, but when the girls are around, it's strictly soda and coffee. You'd think they were *Lutherans!* Betty spends the whole morning polishing and dusting so she can pretend she has a girl who comes in. She shoves all her real crap—her jigsaw puzzles and Jack LaLanne exercise equipment—into Chickie's office. It stays there for a day, and then she drags it all out and it begins to look like a real person lives here again. Betty won big, so we're sending out for Chinese. I'm supposed to take your order."

Cedric wiped cheese off his fingers and then did something Jane had never seen him do—he reached for his wallet, removed ten dollars of the queen's money, and instructed Sandy to order anything she wanted. "Anything but squid." The "I'll need a receipt" he added was vintage Cedric, proof that he hadn't entirely lost his mind, and Jane went back to eating the soft, nutty cheese, a hodgepodge of Velveeta and cheddar that had found its way to Betty's kitchen via Sandy's refrigerated bowling bag.

* * *

The bridge group gone, Jane, Cedric, and Felix followed Sandy into the kitchen, looking forward to their meal, their first real one of the day.

"Everyone always ends up in the kitchen," said Betty, who had disappeared into her bedroom dressed like Loretta Young, in a neatly tailored blue poplin dress with white cuffs and sensibly heeled shoes, and returned looking like an extra on *I Dream of Jeannie*. Her shocking chartreuse velvety hostess gown had been made by Sandy, a Christmas gift, and the gold leather slippers were part of her uniform from occasional stints as a coin washer at the Aladdin. When the doorbell rang, Betty took a dollar from an orange-juice can in the deep freeze in a nook off the kitchen. The dollar tip bought her goodwill, double the fortune cookies, and a mystery container of leftovers from the night before that had been ordered by someone but never picked up. While she was at the door, Jane discreetly replaced the dollar in the freezer and couldn't help but notice it was big enough to hold a body.

Sandy tucked a tea towel into the waistband of her slacks and did a quick wash-up of the Wedgwood teacups that Betty took from the china cabinet for special occasions, like funerals and bridge club. "Jimmy," she said, wiping the delicate porcelain with a soft cloth and a gentle touch, "I hope you're not spending all of your hard-earned money on us."

"Thanks to my associate's careful handling of our bankroll, we've barely touched our reserve," said Jane.

Cedric coughed softly. "I only now realize I left most of our money behind, in my sock drawer at the teepee," he whispered as he fiddled with the rooster and hen salt-and-pepper-shaker set, leaving a scattering of salt on the yellow Formica tabletop. "That ten was all I had."

"Don't worry, old chap. I've got some money," Jane said, patting her trouser pocket with most of Cedric's Secret Service–issue bankroll. Betty and Sandy's money troubles were over—for now. "I'm the new treasurer of this group."

"Knowing the pressure on you to gamble, I put most of our stipend aside for a rainy day," he said miserably. "And now it's gone."

"Well, it almost never rains here," said Sandy. Carefully, she placed the cups and saucers on the top shelf of a narrow walnut cabinet housing a collection of blown-glass circus figurines and then polished the glass door with the edge of her towel.

"Anyway, it's not a good idea to carry around much cash, especially here," Sandy added, handing Jane five Flamingo Coffee Shop paper place mats while she scavenged through a messy junk drawer for plastic forks. Not everyone could handle chopsticks. "Once you get off the plane, you're in danger of having your pocket picked. People hang out at the airport looking for the ones with the hay between their teeth. I can't see anyone following you, Jimmy, since you're so man-of-the-world, but Fred here looks like an easy mark. Nothing personal. I don't mind a little man."

"It's Felix."

"Like the cat?"

"Yes," he sighed. "Like the cat."

Sandy dealt paper plates as if they were cards, then leaned against the counter and pulled her cracked cigarette case from her bra. "Betty must be talking that guy's ear off," she said, taking short, hard puffs so she could finish her cigarette before their meal. "She's a travel bug. Honestly, if *National Geographic* programs were on twenty-four hours a day, her butt would be stuck in a chair. You should talk to her about carrying cash. She got robbed in Mexico once and had to come home early on the bus. Don't you have Diners Club? I only ask because it seems you can't go anywhere nowadays without one."

"I was turned down," admitted Cedric.

Betty rejoined them with the hot food and a story about the delivery boy's encounter with a famous starlet, who, when she didn't like her fortune, she demanded a screenwriter be called in to write another one. Shaking their heads over the ridiculous behavior of some people, they arranged themselves around the table, a four-seater expanded to accommodate five by a drop leaf and a stepstool from the laundry room as a fifth chair, and passed around dripping paper cartons of shiny, fragrant food.

"It's squid!" said Betty with a little laugh when she opened the mystery carton. "The free dish is *never* squid. You must be some kind of mind reader," she told Cedric as she passed the container over his head to Sandy.

"I had a run-in with a particularly mean squid during a visit to a South Pacific island," he explained. "I've never been able to look another one in the eye since."

"I feel that way about my third ex-husband," Sandy said, squinting at the piece of squid on her chopstick before popping it in her mouth and gnashing it between her teeth. Conversation ceased as they tucked away three orders of moo goo gai pan, egg rolls, fried rice, and the garlicky squid, and washed it down with cold beer. The kitchen was the sunniest place in the house, the butter yellow walls and gay rooster-print curtains more suited for a farm kitchen than a showcase suburban home, the walnut curio cabinet the only formal touch. On the yellow tile countertop was a small portable TV, which bookended a lineup of shiny chrome appliances whose pristine appearance suggested an ornamental rather than functional role.

"This room is nice, isn't it?" said Betty, watching Jane take in the place, lingering over the CLEAN UP THIS MESS! cross-stitch sampler above the sink. "Everyone always sits in here and talks. The rest of the house was Chickie's design. It's pretty, but hard to keep up. His mother stitched that. She never did approve of my housekeeping skills."

"My grandmother tried to teach me to sew," said Jane. "I kept poking myself and bleeding on the cloth."

Felix brightened, as they had hit upon a topic dear to his heart. "Me, too."

Betty took Jane's hand in hers and turned it, palm side up, running her fingernail down the palm. Jane reddened, and Betty gave her a little wink. Chickie Skeets had been a lucky man.

"You have small hands for a man, very fine-boned," Betty said.

"Betty's got a crush on you," Sandy said in a singsong voice.

"I'm giving him a reading," Betty shushed her with mock seriousness. "And I'm old enough to be his mother." They all leaned in as Betty examined Jane's hand, clucking over a scar at the base of her palm, a memento of the day Mimi Doolittle kidnapped her.

"Do you see a good end to this trip?" asked Cedric.

"It's never that specific. And it's hard to read Jim's hand because of the scar. It interferes with the lifeline. Other one, please." Closing her eyes, she held Jane's hand, her skin cool and dry, then gave it a gentle squeeze, letting Jane in on the joke. When Jane squeezed back, a little smile played at Betty's lips and she said, "I see trouble ahead. Girl trouble. Beware of the blonde. She means to do you harm."

"That's me!" snorted Sandy. "If by harm you mean I'm gonna make him do the dishes, you're damn right. There's nothing I like better than seeing a man in an apron." Betty laughed and gave Jane back her hand.

Jane did the wash-up under Sandy's supervision, while Betty put away the leftovers, letting Cedric burp the Tupperware, as yet unavailable in the UK. Betty played with the TV rabbit ears, and eventually a *Road Runner* cartoon came into sharp focus. She switched the channels around until the five o'clock news came on.

"How can anyone think that rug is real?" Her hands on her hips, Sandy lit a cigarette, picking a piece of tobacco off her tongue. "Honestly," she said, pointing at the Ken-doll newscaster, "would you go out in public like that?" Patting her beehive, which looked even shinier than it had yesterday, and a tad taller, she said, "Thank God women don't go bald."

"At the top of the news: The Vivian Vance divorce took an ugly turn today as she described, in open court, how her bullfighter husband forced her to wear red at his fights."

"I don't know why she married that man," said Felix, wiping the tabletop with a sponge and straightening the chairs.

"The threats against Wayne Newton continue. According to the FBI, a string of menacing letters has been sent to the popular singer, suggesting he should 'diet.' They're looking for an individual with a broken typewriter and poor spelling."

"The kook behind that is going to be sorry," said Betty, glaring at Sandy as she plunked five earthenware coffee mugs and a bottle of saccharine zero-calorie sweetener on the table. "Nevada is the strictest state in the nation when it comes to punishing people who bother famous personalities. I was at the grocery store yesterday, and the lady behind me is a matron at the women's correctional institution up in Last Gasp. She told me that not only does the prison have a dress code, but there's a hair code as well. Hair spray and bobby pins are not allowed, 'cause they make good weapons. It's permanent waves all around."

"No wonder prisoners riot," said Sandy, checking her reflection in the glass door of the curio cabinet.

"Police are looking for three suspects in the murder earlier today of Dougie Smathers, a Kansas City man, whose body was found floating in Lake Mead. According to witnesses, a fight that started in the Hoover Dam Snacketeria over the last Ho-Ho quickly turned ugly as one of the suspects flashed a knife and suggested he and Mr. Smathers settle their differences out-of-doors. It was the last anyone saw of Mr. Smathers, until his body was spotted by sharp-eyed sightseers. When asked if he was very upset by the day's events, the man's best friend, Bob Snurd, also of Kansas City, said, 'Yes, I'm very upset.'

"Although two of the suspects have been identified, their whereabouts remain a mystery. Their last known location was the Teepee Village Motor Court on State Road 1. According to the owner and his wife, the men were tidy, polite, and made their own beds.

"Again, police are looking for three men, considered armed and dangerous. Two are British nationals, James Bland, approximately thirty and described as devilishly handsome, and Cedric Slumberknuckle, approximately fifty years of age, with average looks and a stout build. Witnesses were unable to come up with a description of the third man, believed to be a short American. In lighter news, the Dorothy Duncan Defrost-Off continues, and gourmands everywhere await the outcome of the homemade TV-dinner competition. We'll be there live tomorrow to meet the winners."

"And so will we," Sandy sang back at the television. The seriousness of Jim's situation hadn't hit her yet, because her mind was fixed on one thing and one thing only—the debut tomorrow, at the Dorothy Duncan Defrost-Off, of her latest, and greatest, invention.

Betty got up and switched off the television, then plugged in the percolator. There would be none of that lousy instant coffee in her house. When the coffee had percolated long enough, she filled six cups, one for each of them and the last for Chickie. She could use his help right now, and the extra cup was her way of letting him know he was needed. Cedric blew his nose on a paper napkin, the truth finally sinking in. Jane's fear that they would be accused of murder wasn't just a case of female hysteria—they were fugitives from justice. A conga line of the important people in his life passed through his imagination—the queen, N., his mother were she alive, his neighbor Mrs. Figgis, Lady St. Claire—and all were disappointed in him.

"It's all conjecture," said Jane. "Dougie Smathers and I had a bit of a row in the Snacketeria—over *pie*. There was no woman involved." This was accompanied with a subtle lift of her eyebrow and a shake of her head. Betty and Sandy thought the deceased had been sent by Emerald, the "Duchess of Mallomar," and Jane was trying to head off any questions about Bridget, certain that Cedric would crack like an overboiled egg if he knew she had told civilians details of her private life. With a wink and a smile, Betty and Sandy assured her that the message had been received.

"He pulled a gun on Jim!" cried Felix. "And Jim took it away and shot him with it!"

"You're a big help, Felix," said Jane. "Betty, it was a water pistol." She felt that a deceased mobster's mistress might understand the complexities of the case better than anyone there. "The next thing I know, he's floating in the lake. The three of us were together the entire time, but, unfortunately, during our fight I told him to go jump in the lake, in front of witnesses."

"Witnesses can be bought," Sandy snorted. "The dead man's friends no doubt paid them off."

"And I bet the dead man was a real jerk, and up to no good. The big lummox deserved what he got," Betty said passionately.

"It's as if you knew him," Felix murmured, smiling a little to hear Dougie Smathers described in those words.

"Well, I don't believe it. I haven't known you long, but men who have burped my Tupperware and washed my dishes without chipping a one are no more killers than I am. Hell, the contents of my refrigerator are more likely to kill than one of you guys." Betty got up to get the coffeepot. They would need some more mental stimulation to figure this one out.

They all put on their thinking caps, and a fair amount of time passed as they sat quietly around the table, sipping the bitterly sweet coffee, contemplating their situation. Cedric broke the ice.

"I may have put on some weight since retiring, but I'd hardly call myself stout," he sniffed.

*   *   *

They waited out the results of the TV-dinner competition with the other contestants, milling around the family room set, sipping strong coffee and chomping nervously on sugar cookies so sweet Bibi could feel new cavities forming. While Bibi ruined her teeth, Bridget kept an eye on the plate of cookies she'd saved for Marge, who had returned to her kitchenette to scrub her linoleum with a toothbrush. "I'm just so darn nervous, girls," she said, offering to scrub their floor while she was at it. Marge was their only friend at the competition. Bibi and Bridget were shunned because their appliances had frayed cords, their oven mitts were dirty, and when their contribution to the round-robin discussion "Keeping Up with Dust" had been to suggest that the women simply not bother, or make their husbands do it, only Marge had clapped. It was further proof of her unhappy home.

"I should relax," said Bibi, craning her neck to see if the judges had returned a verdict. After each meal had been tasted, they secluded themselves inside the giant enamel fondue pot. That was twenty minutes ago, and Bibi was getting antsy. She had seen Mrs. Sammi Martini's look of surprise as she peeled back the foil on their dinner. It wasn't clear whether the laugh that followed was one of delight or derision. "She knows it's us. We'll never win now."

"She didn't recognize us," Bridget assured her. "*I* don't recognize us. And we'll never win because our meal is disgusting. Honestly, Emerald feeds her dogs better meals."

The cookbook author climbed out of the pot and asked to speak to Verda, who brushed cookie crumbs off her blouse, retied the floppy bow at her neck, and raced over, hoping she had been called because it was *she* who had won and they wanted to congratulate her personally before the public announcement. Dreams of being included in the author's next book, perhaps one entirely devoted to prune dishes, were dashed when the judge admitted they had reached a stalemate. They all wanted another taste of two dinners. The author whispered the numbers in Verda's ear, and Verda lit up like the stove light on a new Hotpoint oven.

"We've lost," sighed Bibi. "Lost to *Prunella.*"

* * *

The last crumb of the last sugar cookie had been eaten, but the judges were having trouble picking a winner, for the first time in Defrost-Off history. There were, it seemed, two TV dinners that merited the award, but only one could win, and the judges had asked for additional time to discuss the pros and cons of two very different meals. The air crackled with tension, all eyes on the fondue pot. A light supper of hot dogs and baked beans had been provided, but few, besides Bibi, could eat.

"We've already lost." Bibi shrugged, spraying cheese, then relish, on her sympathy hot dog, her third. It didn't matter. Bridget had already ruined her dream of appearing on the box of a frozen dinner by pointing out an obvious fact: If they won, the check would be made out to total strangers.

"Unless we can find someone who will agree to have the check made out to her, for a cut of the money," Bibi said, unwilling to let go of this, her latest "biggest dream."

"Marge would do it," said Bridget. "And she'd refuse to take a penny of it. But she's not going to win, either. Verda's got it locked up. Did you see the TV-tray covers she knit for each of the judges? I should think that persuasion of any type would be against the rules."

Bibi decided it was not the time to admit she'd stuffed the sardines with Valium. If only she had known that greedy Mrs. Sammi Martini was going to be a judge, they would have this whole thing as wrapped up as some of Marge's leftover meat loaf.

. . . .

nineteen

How an agent should proceed when wanted on suspicion of murder hadn't been covered in the G.E.O.R.G.I.E. manual, and Jane's one chance of escape, leaving the country using her real passport, had left with Bridget. It was dumb to have given Bridget the passport for safe-keeping; Bibi's idea, that Jane should have it sewn into the lining of her underwear, would have made far greater sense had Jane not had a propensity for losing things. Her wallet (not her doing), a snow globe (she now remembered putting the gift shop bag on the sidewalk so she could remove a pebble from her boot, and then walking away), the Teepee Village Motor Court chip (she had a hole in her pocket), and her plastic comb (last seen in their car at Hoover Dam and now existing somewhere in thin air).

While she silently berated herself for her stupidity—underesti mating these men could prove fatal to her and the mission—she half-listened to the conversation around her. Cedric's insecurity had flared up like a bad rash, and the conversation had turned to weight-loss tips.

"Well, it's time for Andy," said Betty, cutting Sandy off in the middle of a product pitch for Metrecal, a liquid diet guaranteed to drop a pound a day.

"Betty never misses the *Andy Williams Show*," Sandy explained, putting out her cigarette. Smoking was not allowed anywhere but the kitchen and garage. "Not even on the day of Chickie's wake."

On orders from Betty, her guests picked up their kitchen chairs and moved them to the pristine living room, and set them in a neat row in front of the blond-wood television console. The rabbit ears hidden behind a potted plant came out, and while Betty warmed up the set, Sandy brought in the evening cocktails, five cold cans of Old Milwaukee.

"If you spill on the rug, Betty will kill you," warned Sandy as she played waitress, remembering their accident-prone problem. She had three high-class spillers on her hands. Felix, fearing the wrath of the gun he had earlier unearthed in the hatbox, declined the drink. Jane took two and put a dollar on Sandy's tray. Sandy laughed merrily and stuffed it in her bra. Although it was warm in the house, Cedric also passed on the beer, not wanting Felix to think him a lush and thereby unworthy of his invention. He was sure that once the shock of being a stout suspected murderer passed— by morning, he hoped—the sale could be arranged. Felix would *have* to take the check now. He'd need it for a good attorney, for although he hadn't been named as a suspect, and no one from the convention or the dam remembered his name or what he looked like, anything could happen.

"Was Chickie your husband?" asked Cedric, keeping his feet planted the plastic runner.

"The late Chickie Skeets was Betty's married boyfriend," Sandy answered. "Only Betty doesn't really like to talk about him."

"Forgive me for introducing a painful subject."

"The show's about to start," Betty shushed, turning up the volume.

"Chickie bought her this house," Sandy continued in a whisper. "His wife knew all about it. She didn't care as long as he paid the bills. When Chickie Jr. went away to college, Chickie moved in for good. Six months later he was dead. Some business associates took him for a ride."

Cedric nodded sympathetically. "With the way people drive these days, it's a wonder there aren't more fatalities."

"I couldn't agree with you more. So then Betty was a widow, only she wasn't really, but since the house was in her name, she got to keep it. The real Mrs. Skeets came over and threatened to tell the IRS Chickie had bought the house with ill-gotten gains—those were her exact words, even though you just know her own living-room suite fell off the back of a truck. She has some nerve! Betty was too much of a lady to kick her can out the door, but she did let the air out of that woman's tires while I was putting her through the rinse cycle, if ya know what I mean."

"And that," whispered Jane, "is the abridged version."

"What a fantastic invention," said Cedric, marveling at the full-spectrum color screen, widely touted as "better than real life" and something he had never seen before in Great Britain. He wiped beer foam from his upper lip, taking care to put the can on the coaster provided. Good sense had given in to the spirit of the moment, and when Sandy served the second round, he took one, if just to make himself seem less like a fuddy-duddy in front of Felix. Although Betty's attention was riveted to the TV while Andy Williams was on the air, during commercials she became a bubbly hostess, getting up to turn down the volume, sipping her beer and chatting with her guests. It was like visiting old friends, thought Cedric, glad now that Jane had brought them here.

"I've never seen anything like it," Cedric continued.

"I think so, too," said Sandy, thinking he was talking about her newest creation, highly absorbent cocktail coasters cut from simple kitchen sponges. "I keep telling Betty it's going to be the latest thing."

"You can't get anything like it in England." When Cedric said this, Sandy lit up. She hadn't thought about overseas sales.

"You should take one home with you," she said. "Show it around. You could work on commission, sending me orders and then delivering them when they get to your side of the ocean. Someone with your classy accent could probably sell a million."

"Let me mull that." He hadn't thought of becoming an authorized television dealer, but his memoirs were almost finished, and soon he'd be searching for some new way to occupy his time. Television might very well be the ticket. "I will sleep on it and let you know, dear lady."

"Did you hear that, Betty?" Sandy said. Suddenly she didn't mind that her other latest invention, liquor-on-a-stick, had been turned down by every casino in town. "I could be real big in England. Maybe not as big as the Beatles, but in everyone's home just the same."

"Shhh," said Betty, turning the volume up.

"Maybe the queen would like to try one," said Sandy.

Jane knew that Cedric's feelings had been hurt when the newscaster had called him stout, and she hoped her mention of his association with royalty would shore up his ego. "Cedric, why don't you ask her next time you see her?" she said.

This information caught Betty's attention, but Andy was back with his special guests, the Osmond Brothers, and so she held her questions for later.

"Bo-o-o-ring!" Sandy hollered at the screen, slouching in her chair with her bare feet dangerously close to the glass-topped coffee table. Betty agreed that the youthful barbershop-harmony group was not her cup of tea. "I just want to watch until the end, to see what color sweater Andy wears for the last song." Andy appeared in an emerald green V-neck, and again Cedric marveled at the full-spectrum picture. "He looks better in blue." Betty shrugged as she switched off the television, closed the console doors, and put the rabbit ears back behind the potted plant. "Now," she said, standing in front of the row of chairs, like a schoolteacher about to begin a lesson, "tell us all about the queen."

"It's nothing, really." Cedric blushed before launching into his version of how he came to be one of Britain's most celebrated subjects. "It was a cold and rainy afternoon, not fit for man nor beast. Still, I ventured forth to attend a prestigious, invitation-only charity auction for the Daughters of the Dispossessed Aristocracy, one of the queen's pet organizations. Her Majesty was in attendance at Grunby Hall that evening, as were members of a nefarious gang of malcontents who went by the indecorous moniker of the Sons of Britain."

"Hold on," said Sandy, running to the kitchen. "I need another beer." When she returned with drinks all around, he continued.

"Little did I realize," he said, politely sipping his beer, "that as I stepped across the threshold and onto the Italian marble floor of the Great Hall, its red damask walls the dramatic backdrop for Lord Wooley-Booley's extensive taxidermy collection, that by evening's end I would foil a kidnapping plot, assuring my place in history. The evening was a brilliant social success, except . . ." He took another sip of beer, and they all leaned forward, even Jane. His story got better and better each time he told it, and she thought for the first time that his memoir could possibly be a success.

"Except?" cried Sandy.

"Except I had the sneaking suspicion that something was not as it should be. Whilst dining on a most delicious kidney canapé, I had a sudden urge to visit the library."

"That's the polite way to say bathroom over there," Sandy whispered to Betty.

"The door was shut but unlatched, and when I peeked inside, I was witness to a shocking scene. Lady Lettie Finhatten, the wife of a very important member of the House of Lords, was standing in her undergarments, trying to talk Her Majesty into trading frocks."

"She wanted the queen's dress?" said Betty, sounding as if she didn't believe him.

He nodded. "It's almost unthinkable. Unwittingly, I had uncovered a kidnapping plot, arriving just as the queen was overtaken by chloroform. Rather than go for help, I leapt into action, taking on the gang of villains single-handedly. A few karate chops to all the right places"—he demonstrated his moves, careful of the crystal lamps—"and the would-be queen-nappers were begging for mercy. They are now behind bars, except for Lord Wooley-Booley, who met an unfortunate death at the hands of some spoilt cheese straws."

"You're pulling our legs!" hooted Sandy. "Serves us right for asking. No more beer for you, buddy!"

"No, it really happened," Felix piped up. "There was an article about it in our company newsletter. I wish now that I'd saved it."

"It's true," said Jano, who had been there. Parts of it, at least. Cedric had walked into the library and seen Lady Finhatten try to change costumes with the queen. And then he had passed out, which is when Bridget and Bibi waltzed in and, with a few karate chops to all the right places, saved the monarchy. Because G.E.O.R.G.I.E was a top-secret organization that never went public with its triumphs, they threw all the credit to Cedric. The knot on his head—he had hit an elephant-leg wastebasket midfaint—explained his case of amnesia, which prevented him from remembering his heroic deeds. His account of those missing fifteen minutes had come from Bridget, who dressed it up like a Christmas goose, a gift to a stuffy old gent who had come into their lives and absolutely refused to leave, and to whom they had grown attached.

"Her Majesty knighted me for my efforts," he continued, "and I have been contracted to write my memoirs. An American TV company has expressed interest in turning the story into a weekly variety show—a tasteful one, naturally. And next month I'll be taking tea at Buckingham Palace with Her Majesty and ten thousand other very special subjects."

"I'll be the very first person in Las Vegas to buy your book," said Betty, taking a bridge pad and a pencil from her end-table drawer. "What's the title?"

"Tentatively, *Your Humble Servant: The Cedric Pumpernickel Story,* but my publisher is pushing for *I Saw England, I Saw France, I Saw the Queen in Her Underpants: The Cedric Pumpernickel Story.*"

The girls limped up the dusty drive, their feet too swollen to fit into their shoes, their dresses wrinkled and grubby, not at all like the perky housewives that had left that morning, Wanda could recognize them only by their perfectly coifed hair, twin testaments to the superiority of Aqua Net over all other brands. Wanda had taken up her evening post at the picnic table out front, with a cooler of Fresca, her smokes, and a paperback copy of *Valley of the Dolls* from the Las Vegas Library, under a dying palm tree stuck in a kiddie sandbox, its trunk held up by a rope tied to a wooden Indian chief holding a fork in one hand and a cup of coffee in the other. It provided the only shade for miles, and Wanda swore that when it finally fell and had to be dumped in the desert like some poor sap, she was going to put a fake wooden tree with enormous plastic palm fronds in its place.

Wanda set down her book, marking her place with her squashed cigarette pack. With enough Bug-Off, nights in the desert could be delightful, and sitting out here, listening to the traffic, made her feel like she was going somewhere.

"Did you hear about the murder?" she greeted them. Wanda had promised Jim she'd keep her lip zipped for twenty-four hours, and she was a woman who kept her promises, but it didn't mean other people couldn't talk about it.

"You want to talk murder?" Bibi groaned. "We stayed until nine o' clock to hear the results of the TV-dinner competition, and the judges were still debating it!"

"There's got to be something criminal involved," Wanda said, hoping they'd pick up the hint.

"Of course there is," Bibi said with disgust. "Some people have no concept of fair play—or how their actions affect others." Verda's obvious courting of the judges would surely tip the vote in her direction.

"It's true. You'll never believe how many people think they can pretend to die and then live here. There are guys who, for ten bucks, will swear in court they saw you disappear into the desert." After taking a long drink of her Fresca, Wanda wiped the back of her neck with her dish towel and pushed back in place the few locks of brittle hair rebellious enough to escape the hive.

Bridget suspected that Wanda had inhaled too much Bug-Off.

"I've never been so exhausted," said Bibi. She had new respect for cooking-contest competitors. As Marge had tried to impress upon them, it wasn't all cream and cheese. "First we labored to prepare a nutritious and delicious meal and then stood in line to deliver it, all without a single 'Thank you' or 'It looks yummy!' And someone trying to get in good with Mrs. Martini, the celebrity judge, kept playing the same Sammi Martini song over and over. Honestly, I wanted to lock her in a broom closet!"

"Art irritates life," Wanda said, wiping cigarette ash off the picnic table and crushing her empty cans with the heel of her shoe. "People disappear here all the time. Every couple of years some big winner decides to ditch Bertha and the kids. He buys himself a used Caddy and a sharp suit and thinks he's Sammi Martini. A few lucky throws at the craps table, and he's sure he's got the magic touch. Then he meets a showgirl, and before he can jump the noose, he settles right back down. A couple years later, he's in the same boat: He's got another bunch of kids, and now he's really stuck. You can only die once."

"Don't the wives come looking for them?" said Bridget, sitting at the picnic table and kicking off her shoes. She thought she might be getting a corn. A real one.

"Some do. I heard a story about a guy whose bereaved wife came to Vegas for a widows' convention and took a tour of the candy factory over in Boulder City and found him making nougat, trying to support his new family on fifty bucks a week and all the peanut clusters he could fit in his pockets."

"Did she shoot him?" Bibi would sure as hell shoot someone who got a job in a chocolate factory and didn't tell her.

"She already had his pension," Wanda said, her words slurring into a yawn. "Why give that up?" Raising her arm so she could flick her ash into her seashell ashtray can took effort. She must have cut three hundred Jell-O cubes for the diet lunch rush. She had prepared thirty lunch boxes for a tour group of nuns headed into the desert to check out reports of a Virgin Mary sighting in a sorrel patch, made Jell-O from scratch, cleaned the units, and done her hair. It was a typical day for a small operation with no hired hand to fall back on, days that went well into the night.

Wanda continued, aware that she was saying too much, peppering them with anecdotes whose veracity even she questioned. But she couldn't help herself. Except for the fellow who was wanted for murder and the nuns, who were fussier than they had a right to be—twelve wanted their crusts cut off, and no one wanted mustard—she hadn't had a real conversation all day.

"It's a real puzzler sometimes, the things people will do. Like the guy who died in the middle of a poker game. His wife wouldn't let them take him away until she played out his hand. By then he was so stiff they could have just rolled him out."

"I know exactly how he feels," said Bibi. "My head hurts, I have dish-pan hands, and every time I take a step, the corn on my toe throbs. I am not going to the awards ceremony tomorrow smelling like a cheap little fish." She abandoned Bridget to the rambling of Wanda, knowing she'd have time for a nice long soak in the tub before their overworked but re-markably lively hostess ran out of stories.

"Your friend is delicate, isn't she? It's why I didn't tell her about the time a murderer stayed in Teepee Number Four. This was a long time ago. A long, long time. Not recently."

Worried that the "long, long time" was an unconscious warning about the length of this story, Bridget got to her feet. "I'd love to hear all about it," she said, "but we've got a full day ahead of us."

Slipping on Bibi's flimsy sandals, the back strap threatening to come off, Bridget pushed herself up from the old picnic table, which left a splinter in her palm. It was the least of the day's indignities. Having been in such close proximity all evening to Mrs. Martini had left Bridget with a bitter taste in her mouth. In truth, part of the taste had come from the piece of broccoli chewing gum she had sampled, but not all.

After a bit more conversation about what the other contestants had worn, Bridget dragged her feet back to the teepee. When she entered the room and saw Wanda's handiwork, she felt ashamed that she had rushed away. There were fresh linens from the Nevada Correctional Fa-cility for Women on the bed, their suitcases were stacked neatly in the closet, the baby-doll nighties last seen on the floor had been hung up, and the bathroom sparkled. Wanda had even left the evening newspaper and two now-melted Hershey Kisses on the nightstand.

Bibi was submerged in bubbles, her tanned legs draped over the side of the tub, a tame light pink polish drying on her toenails. Her hair clung to her neck like seaweed, the Aqua Net having released its hold after a good soaking in hot water and a bout of vigorous brushing that broke the handle of her cheap plastic hairbrush.

"Don't try to get a comb through it," said Bibi as her friend stood, looking into the mirror, tugging at her helmet of hair. "Soak it in hot water until you feel it melt. Then soap it three times with Prell, and you'll have hair as stunning as mine." Picking up a limp strand, she made a spit curl in the center of her forehead, then sank into the water, cloudy from cheap motor-court soap. Sighing, Bridget wrapped a towel turban-style over her hair and opened a jar of cold cream. Perched on the lid of the toilet, she covered a day's worth of common household dirt clinging to her fair skin and removed it with scratchy toilet paper, someone having used the last of her cosmetic puffs to keep her toenail polish from smudging.

"Wanda says we can take the dresses home with us, but she needs the purses back," said Bridget, resting her feet on the edge of the tub. "She's a little odd, but awfully generous. And lonely, I think. All those stories . . ."

"My purse is ruined. The Space Ice Cream melted and made a kind of smelly glue. I can't unstick my Kotex pads."

"I'll run right out and buy another frumpy purse. Anything else?"

Bibi pulled the chain with her toe and watched the dirty water run down the drain. "You always become a crabby cow when Jane doesn't ring," she said, peeling the bandage off her corn and examining it. "Just ring her."

"I promised her I wouldn't interfere," said Bridget. "But if you think—"

"Hey, my corn fell off!" Bibi cried. "My days of ugly shoes are over! This makes up for having to listen while Mrs. Sammi Martini took credit for a hairstyle I designed—with a *little* help from you, of course."

Ignoring her, Bridget rubbed moisturizer into her clean skin and decided she would not ring Jane.

"Stop worrying," said Bibi. "It causes wrinkles." She checked her polish to see if it was dry and got out of her bath, leaving wet lumps of cotton on the floor and an Aqua Net ring around the tub. Slipping on a shortie nightgown, she sat on the bed and toweled her hair, eyeing the chocolate kisses. Bridget turned on the faucet to give the tub a good rinse. The trickle that came out was cold and rusty, and she decided to put off her own bath.

After slipping into a shortie nightie much like Bibi's, only not so "shortie," Bridget lay on the bed and thought about the odd twists this mission had taken. They had been dancing potatoes, then casino robbers, and now Defrost-Off contestants. "Do you think Marge is going to get a divorce?" she said, rolling over on her stomach and watching as Bibi cleaned out her purse. Her travel-size bottle of truth serum was sticky, but the cap was still screwed on tight.

"I do. That's why she lied to us about going to Hoover Dam." Looking back, Marge had seemed awfully quiet on the afternoon's attraction. "When we overheard her talking on the telephone, I think she was going to book a room at a Reno divorce ranch, and was afraid she'd be kicked out of the contest if anyone knew."

"Poor Marge, I hope she wins. She'll need a bankroll for her new life. How much could she possibly have saved as a housewife?"

"She's pretty thrifty," said Bibi, afraid that Bridget was going to jinx their chance of winning by suggesting that Marge needed the ten thousand dollars more than they did. "She told me she saves five dollars each month by cutting her own hair. And she erases her paper plates so she can use them a second time."

"Another couple hundred years of that, and she'll be free of old Marv," Bridget said dryly. "I don't care *who* wins, as long as it's *not* Verda Taylor."

Except for a girlfriend who stole her panties and tried to collect ransom money, which Bridget had paid, she had never encountered such a mean and crazy women. Back home there was sneaky Mimi to worry about, but she was more likely to steal Bridget's favorite lipstick and grind down the tip than rob someone at gunpoint or hold up a cooking contest because she'd chipped a nail and had to wait for a manicurist to be brought in to fix it. That last one was merely a rumor, but, having spent time with Mrs. Sammi Martini, Bridget could well believe it. The singer's wife had softened her on Mimi. Except for the vanishing-cream incident, the secret agent was little more than an aging juvenile delinquent compared to Mrs. Sammi Martini, who, Bridget suspected, played the same sad song over and over. "Perhaps Mrs. Martini will choke on one of Verda's prunes, and fall into the fondue pot, where her body won't be discovered until tomorrow afternoon, when the Fondue-A-Thon begins. By then, she'll be smothered in cheddar."

"You *are* tired," said Bibi.

"Then, Verda will die of embarrassment. 'Like potted cheese that has been left out too long, Mrs. Verda "Prunella" Taylor quietly expired today at the Las Vegas Dorothy Duncan Defrost-Off, the victim of prune pudding poisoning. In other news, police are searching for the saboteur who kidnapped an expired box of Liver Spots.'"

Bibi applauded, her mouth too full of gooey chocolate to congratulate Bridget on having just relinquished her Goody Two-Shoes style.

The dripping faucet woke Bibi, and after it became obvious Bridget was not going to wake up and fix it, she rolled out of bed and walked into the bathroom, catching a glimpse of herself in the mirror. She looked almost as ugly as the passport photo Mimi had retouched with a pen, adding curlers and a light mustache to what had been a sexy head-and-shoulders shot. Bridget had been subjected to a similar indignity, with a hairy mole attached to the tip of her pert nose and a pirate patch drawn over one eye. Going through customs in New York had been an exercise in humility. Held up in line for over an hour as the customs official poked about in Agent Pumpernickel's Marmite, looking for drugs, they had drawn stares and whispers, and not the good sort. They should have never taken the same flight as Jane and Cedric, or let Mimi get her hands on their passports.

Bored and awake, she padded around the teepee, looking for something to do. Bridget had fallen sound asleep shortly after plotting Verda's demise. Usually a pleasant bedtime story like that ensured Bibi a good night's rest as well. But tonight she was restless. The muscles in her legs were twitchy, and she knew it would be hours before she would get back to sleep. Why had she snuck off to the lav today to finish her novel? She could read it again, but she had a feeling that *Valley of the Dolls* wasn't as exciting the second time around. There was a Bible, the racing form, and a late edition of the *Las Vegas Sun,* another of Wanda's motor court touches. Bibi snapped on the lamp next to the splintery chair and settled in to read all about Vivian Vance's day in court. Starting with the back section of the paper, the women's pages, she began with "Strip Search," a gossip column about celebrity comings and goings. The famously reclusive Mrs. Sammi Martini, sporting a new and flattering hairstyle, had offered to judge the Dorothy Duncan TV-dinner contest, and the Chamber of Commerce had declared tomorrow Mrs. Sammi Martini Day, in honor of her charitable work. "All she did was sit in a fondue pot and eat!" Bibi muttered, wishing she had someone to complain to. "It wasn't as if she designed an exciting new clothing line that has defined an entire generation of women." Mary Quant had received the Order of the British Empire for her contribution, and all Mrs. Martini would get, and deserve, was an ugly brass plaque, yet it nagged at Bibi that anyone would think so highly of such an obvious sociopath. If Bibi had known then what she knew now, she would have left Mrs. Martini's peroxide in longer. Dry, brittle hair with noticeable split ends would have served her right.

· ·

twenty

A desert breeze licked at the hem of their cocktail dresses, twin Dior creations with beaded bodices and satin skirts, one champagne, the other black. The heat had loosened its grip on the city; the brightness of day under a cloudless sky was replaced by cool neon. Next to the simplicity of the Teepee Village Motor Court, and Wanda's unreserved friendliness, the Strip seemed louder and gaudier than it had last night, too crowded and impersonal, the hip swingster veneer rubbed away to reveal a sucker's game. When Wanda had called a taxi for them, she put in an order for casino soap, twelve bars if they could fit them in their tiny clutch purses. Bibi had laughed at the modest request and promised to come home in a taxi filled to the brim.

Bibi forgot all about her planned soap heist when they walked into the Sands and two women in stiff brocade dresses and pillbox hats made of owl feathers rushed over, autograph books in hand, and asked if they were on television.

"Why, yes," Bibi purred as flashcubes went off in her face. "I've been on *Bonanza* and"—she strained to think of another program—"*The Andy Williams Show*! And this"—she put her arm around Bridget—"is my older sister. She does commercials for Lady Clairol. Have you seen the one where the housewife cleans her oven and banishes the gray from her hair at the same time? That's my dear older sis."

"Isn't that Zsa Zsa Gabor?" said Bridget, pointing to a sexy blonde in a snug gold gown feeding quarters into a slot machine. When the women craned their necks to see, she gave them a helpful shove, then grabbed Bibi's hand and pulled her into the cocktail lounge.

"I'm sorry I didn't put you in a television show, too," said Bibi. "I can't think when I'm being admired."

"We have bigger problems than *Bonanza*," said Bridget, ordering two zombies at the recommendation of the cocktail waitress, who told them the drink was the top seller on the Strip.

When Bibi had awakened her with the news that Jane was a suspect in the Hoover Dam death of conventioneer Dougie Smathers, of Kansas City, Bridget had accused Bibi of inhaling too much Aqua Net. After Bibi shoved the paper in her face and she read the front page of the *Las Vegas Sun*—CONVENTIONEER MURDERS SNACKETERIA HERO, POPULAR SNACK CAKE IMPLICATED IN DEATH—she shot out of bed, knowing they had to find Jane.

According to the newspaper account, dozens of eyewitnesses, including a tour bus–load of Catholic nuns, claimed that a Mr. James Bland showed up at the dam drunk and disheveled, cursing at an innocent Girl Scout and making unreasonable demands on the Snacketeria cafeteria ladies. When Mr. Smathers attempted to intercede during a quarrel over a Ho-Ho snack cake, it was claimed that the man, a foreigner, threatened to beat him about the face and neck with a souvenir snow globe and toss him over the rail.

"This doesn't sound like Jane at all," Bridget cried, frantically ringing Jane on her compact transmitter. There was no response. When she read farther down the page, below the fold, she shrieked when she saw a sidebar story in which the suspect's wife, interviewed by phone from their London home, admitted that her husband had both a bad temper and an addiction to Ho-Ho snack cakes. "Listen to this: While reminiscing about her husband's bad temper, *Mrs. James Bland,* who now finds herself the wife of a suspected murderer, unwittingly confessed to this reporter that Snacketerias have a way of bringing out the worst in her husband, adding that her woman's intuition told her the snow globe in question was one her husband had purchased for their collection. 'We keep them on the mantel,' she added before bursting into tears. Authorities are investigating Mr. Bland's behavior at a number of international monuments, including the Great Wall of China, Big Ben, and Disneyland. This stinks of a setup" said Bridget. "Two people fight in public, and ten minutes later one falls off a dam. The suspect's *wife* lets it be known that her husband has a temper. Remember when Wanda told us about the man in the candy factory who faked his own death?"

"You think this Dougie Smathers did the same?"

"Forget the fact that James Bond does *not* have a wife. The evidence lines up too easily. After a public fight, conveniently staged in front of impeachable witnesses, a man falls, or is pushed, off a dam. The suspect's wife lets it be known that her husband has a temper, a fondness for the type of snack cake that started the argument, and most likely purchased the murder weapon just a short time before, from the gift shop."

"Are you sure we're not still sleeping?" said Bibi.

They had selected the Sands for two reasons: because Jane thought they were staying there, and might very well be waiting for them, and because of its seafood restaurant with a giant aquarium filled with "real" mermaids, something that might appeal, in a macabre way, to a drowned man. Dougie Smathers had checked in to the hotel late that day, under his own name; more proof that he was alive. "What an amateur," sniffed Bibi. "We've already had so many names, I can't remember who we are right now. What kind of secret agent is he?"

"A dead one," said Bridget, "when we get our hands on him. Wanda says you can't die twice in this town. I'm going to prove her wrong."

"You're in a mood," said Bibi, raising her hand to order another drink. Bridget shook her head. "We have to pace ourselves. We could be out all night chasing Dougie Smathers." The photograph she had clipped from the newspaper showed a thickset middle-aged man in an apron and chef's hat, barbecuing hot dogs at a suburban backyard party. Although the picture was out of focus and Bibi had spilled foundation on it, Bridget had studied his face until she was certain she could pick him out of a crowd. He had the large, hairy ears of a criminal.

They moved from the bar to a black leather banquette against one wall of the cocktail lounge and watched the casino crowd. The next twenty minutes were spent flashing their chewing-gum-foil wedding rings at potential suitors and trying to talk over the patter of ventriloquist Trixi Stix and her puppet, Pixie. The only evening bags Bridget had packed were satin clutches made from the same fabric as their dresses, one champagne and one black beaded brocade number, and they had traded purses to give some contrast to their outfits. No bigger than a paperback, the bags were meant to carry a compact, a lipstick, and a key. By cutting the lining and removing the batting that gave them shape, they were able to pack tranquilizing dart guns, a roll of strong tape, and handcuffs.

Bibi had just finished her zombie and was looking longingly at Bridget's half-full glass when a manicured hand reached for her empty one. Bibi looked up to tell the waitress she wasn't ready, but when she saw who the hand belonged to, she knew she was going to need that second drink. The woman laughed, flinging off her white mink coat and sliding in next to Bibi, who grudgingly scooted over.

"This round's on me," Mrs. Sammi Martini insisted, playfully slapping Bibi's hand when she went for her purse. Bridget managed to get to her dart gun and bury it in the folds of her skirt.

"You do remember me?" She smiled at them, looking confident that they would. "I'm one of the judges of the TV-dinner competition." She had undergone a personality transplant and was now charming and attentive, admiring their couture dresses, shimmery lipstick, Lucite pumps, and tall, glamorous bouffants. She exclaimed over the charm bracelet on Bridget's slender wrist. "How unusual," she said, examining the gold charms. "A tiny gun, a little knife, binoculars, a flash light . . . How did you come by something this unique?"

"It's a family heirloom," said Bibi.

"And very delicate." Bridget pulled away. The last thing they needed was another accidental weapons discharge.

"Fascinating. I have a bracelet at home like yours. Tiny records of my husband's hits. I keep begging him to quit the business before I sprain my wrist."

Escape, it seemed, was impossible. Afraid to rile Mrs. Martini lest she remember where they had first met, they agreed to have one drink with her. "But you can't tell anyone," Mrs. Martini said. "Although the winner's already been selected—don't ask who it is! Verda said if I let it slip before tomorrow morning's live telecast, she'll throw *me* off Hoover Dam! I can't be fraternizing with the contestants. Where is that waitress? Excuse me, girls." Leaving behind her mink, Mrs. Martini walked up to the bartender and snapped her fingers, barking out her order. It was the Mrs. Sammi Martini they knew and loathed.

Excuse me," Mrs. Martini hiccupped twenty minutes later. "I have to go to the little wife's room." Too plastered to stay atop three-inch heels, she kicked off her gold satin pumps and walked out of the lounge in her stocking feet. As soon as she disappeared into the busy casino, they had a hurried conversation; in her condition Mrs. Martini might forget where she was going, and come right back.

Bridget and Bibi had each independently come to the conclusion that Mrs. Martini was toying with them. "Did you see her brush up against me when she reached under the table to take off her shoes?" said Bibi. "She's been giving me signals all night."

"She's signaling that she's onto us," said Bridget.

"Impossible!" Although they did look stunning, it was a different kind of look than their usual youthful, carefree beauty. "First off, our hair is a different color and much shorter. We look like the Betty Skeets and Sandy Beach she met today, only much better. She doesn't suspect us of anything more than being prettier than she is. Can't you see she's *flirting* with me?"

"You thought Wanda was flirting with you when all she was doing was trying to get sand out of her eye."

"I had jet lag, and it put me off my game. In nine out of ten cases, I'm right."

"You *have* done a remarkable amount of research in the field," admitted Bridget.

Bibi suddenly smiled and waved, and Bridget turned around to see Mrs. Martini slowly making her way back to the table, leaning on strangers for support.

"I say we grab the fur and get out of here," Bibi said.

"Good idea. Let's *all* go to prison." Bridget picked up the loathsome coat and put it on the seat next to her, out of Bibi's reach. A piece of paper fell out of one of the pockets. The familiar orange lip imprint on the back of a Toni home-permanent coupon glittered in the light, the lipstick not even faded, and Bridget glared at Bibi, sliding the coupon across the table. "How are you going to get out of this one, Miss Popularity?"

The answer to the question—for they had faced this dilemma before—was always the same. Flipping open the top of her enormous freshwater-pearl ring, Bridget spiked Mrs. Martini's drink with a strong kick of sleeping powder, then stirred it with a cherry stem. "You can lead a horse to water," she said, crossing her fingers, hoping a dart in the ass wouldn't be necessary. "Your mission, Agent Gallini, is to use your charms to get Mrs. Martini to finish her drink."

"No sooner said than done," said Bibi, sucking in her cheeks and putting a wad of paper napkins in her bra to create more cleavage.

"You look like you're sucking on a lemon," said Bridget.

"You know I've always wanted cheekbones," Bibi replied.

Bridget sighed, annoyed they were having this conversation at that very moment. "Bibi, you have cheekbones. Everyone has cheekbones. Otherwise your face wouldn't stay up."

"Easy to say when you have the bone structure of Jean Shrimpton's older sister. Prominent cheekbones are sexy. At least this season they are. Face it, your looks are why Jane fell for you."

"True, but my winning personality and impeccable manners are why she stays. Not to mention I shag like a minx."

"I remember," sighed Bibi. "Come to think of it, Jane has good bones, too. Everyone's got them but me."

"Everyone's got what, darlin?" Mrs. Martini was back, and if they hadn't known better—they had each been in every lav on the premises at separate intervals on their soap expedition—they would have thought there was a bar in the "little wife's room." "I hope someone hasn't finished my drinkie-poo!" she squeaked, reaching for her glass while attempting to sit down, and landing on the floor. Bridget grabbed the glass while Bibi grabbed Mrs. Martini, throwing the inebriated matron a charitable peek down her dress. "To the two prettiest girls at the Dorothy Duncan Defrost-Off!" Mrs. Martini cried, as she slipped back into her seat and raised her glass. Bridget held her breath, hoping she wouldn't drop the doctored drink, and Bibi wondered if sleeping with Mrs. Martini would get them the prize money. Before she could further explore the idea, Mrs. Martini threw back the zombie and almost immediately closed her eyes and slumped down in her seat, pulling her coat over her like a blanket.

"We've committed so many crimes already," Bibi sighed, eyeing the coat. "We've used the names of presidential wives without written permission, we've trespassed, destroyed both a sheet cake and a choreographer's reputation, discharged a lethal weapon in a crowded casino, stolen the identities of two housewives, and drugged the wife of a famous singer."

"So what you're telling me is that we've left out grand theft. You *may not* stuff the bloody coat under your dress, Bibi. We're going back to the convention tomorrow." Bridget grabbed her own purse and satin wrap, leaving a nice tip, knowing that some poor waitress was going to have to haul the trash in their booth to the curb. "The owner of this coat will be there. Remember, there's an invention we still have to steal?"

A look of contrition washed over Bibi's attractive and, yes, round face. "I forgot all about it. Somewhere between Lady Clairol and Mrs. Dash, I stopped thinking of myself as a secret agent and became Sandy Beach, housewife."

"Well, just call me Betty," agreed Bridget.

"Betty? Sandy?" A strikingly handsome woman wearing a ruby red cocktail sheath with a white chiffon wrap stopped them as they were leaving the cocktail lounge. "I barely recognized you!" After brushing aside the wispy bangs that framed her dramatic dark eyes, she put her hands on either side of her bubble-top bouffant and seemed to be adjusting it, as if it were a hat she could take off. Bibi thought the shape of her fashionably pale lips looked familiar, but it was Bridget who figured it out—the vanilla extract behind the ears was a dead giveaway.

"Marge?" Bridget stepped back to take in the complete picture, while Bibi openly stared. Was this the same woman who saved five dollars a month by cutting her own hair with a manicure scissors?

"I'm buying you girls a drink," Marge said. "You're my best friends at the Defrost-Off—don't let Louise know I said that—and I want to have a drink with my best friends."

"We'd love to, but we're meeting someone. Besides, Sandy's Mormon," Bridget said, wanting to get out of there should Mrs. Martini wake up with her real personality. "And she's already broken all ten of their commandments."

"Then one little drinkie-poo couldn't hurt," said Bibi, suddenly feeling awfully attached to her new best friend. If she had only realized Marge was this attractive, she would have flirted with her.

"You may have a Coke," Bridget said, her voice stern and a bit too loud. She was a tiny bit tipsy herself. "But when it's time to go, I don't want to hear one word of complaint. You'll see Marge again tomorrow."

"You see the short leash she keeps me on?" Bibi complained as she and Marge linked arms and walked back into the lounge. Someone had tented Mrs. Martini's face with a menu from the bar and tucked the coat around her legs. The piped-in music had been turned up, to mask the snoring.

"Dear, that's what friends are for," Marge said.

A little of Verda's grasshopper spilled on her pale pink blouson top as she slid over to make room for the girls. "You look familiar," she said, licking the corner of her mouth where some of the green liquid had settled.

"If there was a Most Glamorous Defroster trophy, you two would surely win it," said Louise Wuebel shyly. "I've never seen dresses that pretty. We're staying at the motor lodge on Fremont, but I did some window shopping at the Flamingo the other night. There's a really cute little dress shop there, Dotty's Dresses. I saw Zsa Zsa Gabor trying on eye patches. We were only at the Flamingo because Verda promised her twins she'd bring home something with a pink bird on it. Show her, Verda. She's got a whole purseful of matchbooks and cocktail stirrers."

"Of course, Marge here would beat them hands down. Imagine spending your pin money for a whole year on one dress and a fancy hairdo," Verda said bitterly. Her own gingham going-out dress looked like a potato sack next to the glamorous getups in this place. She squinted at them over her glass. "Don't I know you two?"

"Of course you know them," said Marge, after ordering Bibi's Coke. "These ladies are Dorothy Duncan–ites." She tapped Bibi on the hand. "I wanted to call you girls and tell you to be at the convention center by eight o'clock tomorrow, for the announcement of the winner, but I couldn't find your registration card. Where are you staying?"

"In a horrid little place outside of town," said Bibi. "The only phone is guarded by an Indian chief." Bridget glared at her, and Bibi shut up.

"We have met before, haven't we?" said Verda, scooting closer. "I know we have."

"Oh, cheese sticks! No more alcohol for you!" said Marge, taking her drink away.

Louise Wuebel patted Verda's hand and, speaking slowly and clearly, said, "They're your competition, dear. Sardine Surprise!"

Bridget toyed with her pearl ring. Louise was being much too helpful. Verda pursed her lips and pulled in a breath through her pinched nose, her large, rounded bosom puffing out like a pigeon's. "So we're competing against one another," she said icily.

"Verda, that's the point of a contest," Marge chuckled. "You'll have to forgive Verda. When she ruined that Teflon fry pan, the representative took back her complimentary waffle iron."

Before she could get control of herself, Bridget began to giggle. Louise grew pale and inched away from Verda, who was giving Bridget a murderous look. Marge, getting the joke, clapped a hand over her mouth to stifle a laugh.

"I was imagining a complimentary waffle iron," Bridget explained. "'My, Verda, you look lovely this evening.'"

Verda looked confused. "There's nothing amusing about it. My husband, Ernie, says that my waffles are his only reason for living." This made them laugh harder, and even Louise began to chuckle quietly behind her napkin. Verda slung her pocketbook over her shoulder and tried to squeeze past Louise, ending up stuck in her lap.

"We're not laughing at you, dear," Marge giggled.

"We tease you because we love you," Bibi said, putting a hand on the woman's stiff shoulder. Verda pushed her away, and Bridget laughed, reached into her purse for a bar of stolen soap, and slid it across the table so Bibi could wash out her mouth.

"Ernie is crazy about you, Verda," Louise said, trying to find a way back into the prune lover's good graces. She was her best friend and neighbor, but, as every Dorothy Duncan–ite knew, Verda could be a real bitch when she was crossed.

"He's *crazy* about my waffles."

"Because they're so complimentary!" Bibi snorted, spraying Verda with Coke.

Dabbing at her dress with a cocktail napkin, Verda hissed, "I'm going to inform the selection committee that you have engaged in behavior unbecoming to a contestant. None of you will win the Mrs. Dorothy Duncan Defrost-Off crown this year—or ever!" She spoke as if she had the title wrapped up, and Bibi was overcome with a burning desire to be Mrs. Dorothy Duncan Defrost-Off 1966.

"I think our friend is here," Bridget said, tipping her head toward the bar.

A Dougie Smathers type had walked into the cocktail lounge and taken up residence on a stool, and was chuckling over the dirty joke on a cocktail napkin.

Bibi blinked *I see him, too* in Morse code, getting sloppy toward the end, forgetting to put the second *o* on "too." Though they were a little tipsy, Bridget tried to contain herself. It had been easy to find Dougie Smathers, and they couldn't let simple luck make them cocky. They still had a mission to compete, and it might not go so smoothly as this.

"Oops! I've lost my shoes," she said, and disappeared under the table, where she popped a Sober Up! tablet.

"They obviously didn't read the morals clause on their registration form," sniped Verda when the girls walked away, craning her neck to see who this "friend" was. "If *he* doesn't have a wife waiting for him at home, then my Pruny Tooney isn't the most delicious combination of fish and fruit in the history of fish-and-fruit dishes."

"Maybe he's a cousin," Marge said.

"He's a married man, cheating on his wife." To punctuate this view, Verda picked up her glass and slammed it on the table, drenching herself. Slapping away the tissues Louise presented her, she grabbed her straw handbag and stormed out.

"Poor Verda," Louise sighed. "Everyone but her knows Ernie's having an affair with a woman who makes the fluffiest pancakes on the block." Louise couldn't help but feel that her decision never to marry had been the right one. "I could see how he would get sick of her waffles. No matter how tasty they are, it's still Verda serving them up."

"I had no idea there was anything like *that* going on at home," said Marge. "She hasn't behaved any differently than in past Defrost-Offs."

"You can count on Verda to be as regular as . . . well, as regular as Verda." After looking over her shoulder to make sure Verda hadn't snuck up on them, Louise leaned over the table and said, conspiratorially, "Now, Marge, you simply *must* tell me where you got that dress!"

"Those sensible shoes have ruined my feet," complained Bibi, hopping onto a stool at the horseshoe-shaped bar, directly across from their target. She kicked off a high heel and rubbed her sore foot while Bridget stared at Dougie Smathers through the binocular charm on her bracelet. The man's chubby cheeks and large ears looked familiar, but it was the hair—thicker and longer and darker than in the newspaper photograph, with a forelock that fell rakishly over an eye covered by a black patch—that clinched it. The wig, so big it flopped around whenever he turned his head, stuck out like a hat on a pig. When Bridget saw the mark on the back of Dougie's hand a mole the shape of Iowa that had been visible in the newspaper photo—she knew they had their man.

"It's him." Bridget patted the purse resting in her lap, feeling the hard steel of her tranquilizer gun. It had been too easy to find him, and either they were exceptionally gifted secret agents, or he was a dolt. She thought it was a little of both.

"What an idiot. Doesn't he know that a bad disguise is worse than no disguise?" His outfit, a cheap, light blue Sammi Martini velveteen suit, was tight around the chest, and when he raised his arm and snapped his fingers, his rude way of ordering another drink, she could see sweat stains under his arm. He was nervous, wishing, perhaps, that he hadn't ventured forth from his hotel room. He was, after all, dead.

"Why don't I throw the fire alarm, and we'll grab him while he's running out the door?" said Bibi. "These people look like they could use some fresh air."

"I'll bet you he's the first one out the door."

"I'll bet you he steals the wheelchair from the old lady drinking beer, and rides out."

"I'll bet you he puts that suit on his expense account."

"I'll bet you his knickers are made of velveteen."

"I'll bet you he has more hair on his back than he does on his head, wig or not."

"I'll bet—" A tap on Bridget's shoulder cut off a perfectly horrendous mental image of hairy velveteen knickers, and the grateful girl turned to see who had rescued her from such a thought, hoping it was Jane.

"Pardon me, miss." A waitress in a mermaid outfit set two fruity drinks in front of them and said, maintaining her plastic smile while rolling her eyes, "The gentleman cleaning his teeth with a swizzle stick sends his regards." Her eyes swept over the two girls, assessing them from under long, false eyelashes. "I'd get a shot of penicillin before letting him anywhere near *me,*" she whispered. Bridget tipped her a twenty.

Bibi lost the coin toss. She put her shoe back on, threw Bridget a dirty look, and inched around the bar until she was at Dougie's side. Engaged in scratching his underarm with the very same swizzle stick he had used to clean his teeth, and leering at he didn't notice the attractive girl in the chic cocktail dress standing at his side, looking a little ill. When he finally realized he had a nibble, he turned away, took the stick from under his arm, and mopped his face with a napkin, leaving bits of soggy paper sticking to his sweaty cheeks. When Bibi whispered in his ear, he fell off his stool.

"I have a wife, my high-school sweetheart. She trusts me completely."

He had fallen off his stool when Bibi suggested they go somewhere more comfortable, and followed Bibi out the bar and through the casino, strutting like a peacock. He lost his nerve when they got to the parking lot.

"She would kill me if she knew what I was doing." The swizzle stick was now down his back, the sound of his scratching making Bibi nauseous, and she noticed blue marks on his wrists and neck, the dye of the suit bleeding onto his skin.

"Are you worried I might fall in love with you?" purred Bibi, who was glad she had popped an antacid tablet before approaching him.

"Women are always falling for me," he bragged, suddenly the swaggering lothario once again.

Bibi had to stifle a gag. This was the most grotesque kidnapping she had ever participated in, and she was relieved and impressed when Bridget, who had run ahead to find an inconspicuous automobile, drove up in a very un-Bridget choice of cars—Sammi Martini's gold-plated Cadillac.

"She's out for the night," said Bridget when Bibi frowned at the sight of the gaudy, easily identifiable, car. "Come morning, she won't even remember where she left it."

Dougie was beginning to make some noise, whining about his happy home, lovely wife, and someone named Dougie Smathers Jr.

He was annoying her, so Bibi decided to get right to the point. She blinked back tears as the dart gun went off too soon, and ripped a hole in her purse—sure the pain was worse for her than for Dougie, she averted her eyes as the dart tore through the cheap velveteen suit and embedded itself in his fleshy thigh. The two G.E.O.R.G.I.E. girls dragged him to the back of the car by his shiny white loafers, impressed by the staying power of the wig adhesive as his head scraped the asphalt.

"Are you going to kill me?" he whimpered, only now realizing this probably wasn't a date.

"Dougie Smathers, your biggest fantasy is coming true," Bibi said, taking hold of his feet as they hoisted him into the trunk. "You get to spend the night with two beautiful women. Now, you'll shut your yap if you want to wake up tomorrow."

Those were the last words Dougie Smathers heard before the trunk door closed over his head and he slipped into a drug-induced sleep.

Dougie Smathers lay on the gravel and snored like a seal while Bridget crept inside the teepee and opened the bathroom window. They pulled him inside feet first, bumping his head on the windowsill.

"Poor Mrs. Smathers," said Bibi as they chained him to the toilet. "I'm sure she would have made a lovely widow." She was thinking of Dougie's confession tomorrow morning, on live television, that his death was an elaborate practical joke. She imaged very few people would be amused by the announcement, not the FBI, or Mrs. Smathers, or the manufacturer of her beautiful beaded bag. And certainly *not* Jane.

Dougie stirred, burped, and rolled on his side, exposing a strip of pink flesh through a small rip in the seat of his trousers. His snoring resumed, and although the room was stifling, they closed the window lest Wanda overhear.

Sitting in the dark in a cloud of Bug-Off, enjoying the cool breeze, Wanda had observed the girls hoist a body out of the trunk of a car and push him through their bathroom window. She assumed it was one of their husbands, who had caught up with them and somehow fallen into the trunk. She could tell they wanted privacy—they were whispering and keeping their heads low—so Wanda shrank into the shadow of the palm tree, taking her bug spray with her. A lot had happened at the Teepee Village Motor Court that day: Wanda had witnessed the stewardess, a bad tipper and a bit of a cold fish, climb out her bathroom window earlier that evening, her black hair now blonde and styled in a glamorous upsweep hairdo, dragging a full-length white mink coat behind her. The police arrived a few minutes later; they turned Jim's teepee inside out, left white powder everywhere, and used the toilet and forgot to flush. Then she and the Chief had quarreled after a clumsy cop backed his patrol car over the main power line, shutting off their electricity for most of prime time.

Weary from having entertained the Chief until the power was restored, Wanda felt her feet still throbbing from her too-tight tap shoes. If Jesus Christ himself appeared and walked on the water dripping down the side of their house from a malfunctioning air-conditioning unit in their bedroom, she wouldn't have lifted a finger to call anyone to come see. Her husband had made her promise she'd keep out of people's business. He said this after she confessed to turning their station wagon into a getaway car. "If you want to give advice, get a column, Wanda," he told her, and he was right. She *should* have a column. These girls' marriages, though, could not be saved.

The sedative was wearing off, and when Dougie awoke and realized they weren't swingers, and this wasn't some kinky game, he yelled for help. Bibi grabbed a gauzy Dior scarf from Bridget's suitcase and shoved it in his mouth. He gasped for air, snorting through his nose. Bridget had to sit on the edge of the tub and compose herself while Bibi tied a second scarf around his head, to keep the first one in place, and shot him again with a tranquilizer dart. "Dior would just die if he could see how we were treating key accessories from his fall line," Bridget said as she went to lie down. Wanda had been in again, this time leaving a box of chocolate-covered cherries on the nightstand, with a note wishing them good luck.

Bibi joined Bridget in bed, but their sleep was interrupted a few hours later when, well before dawn, Smathers again regained consciousness and began pounding his head against the sink pipes. Bridget checked his airflow, at gunpoint. The diaphanous material of the couture scarves allowed for plenty of oxygen, but the head banging worried her. They could continue to tranquilize him, but he needed to be coherent for his confession.

Their first hour of guard duty passed companionably. While their prisoner lay on the floor trying to scream through his fashionable gag, the girls did their nails, taking turns holding the gun, and discussed current affairs. Bridget expressed concern about the military buildup in Southeast Asia, and Bibi shared her fears about the devaluation of the Swiss chocolate standard. In hour two they decided to act out the plots of their favorite movies. During Bibi's modern-dance interpretation of *It's a Mad, Mad, Mad, Mad World,* Smathers flung his body around on the hard tile floor and pretended he was dying.

"No time off for good behavior for you," said Bibi. His rude behavior earned him a punishment so cruel they agreed they'd keep it out of their final report. Sitting just outside the bathroom door, so he wouldn't have to strain to hear, and sharing the box of chocolates, Bridget used her years of finishing-school elocution lessons to transport them all to the world of Neely O'Hara and her Dolls. After twenty minutes he started to whimper, and then he grew still. When he rolled on his side so they wouldn't see him weep, they knew they had won.

They laughed and Bridget continued reading aloud through her yawns, wanting to finish the chapter. Neely had just overdosed on pills, caught her husband cavorting with a naked starlet, and discovered her first gray hair when Bridget's eyelids slid shut.

twenty-one

By seven o'clock it was a hundred degrees, and Wanda's resolve of the night before, to stay out of her tenants' business, had given way, along with her deodorant, to natural curiosity. She had seen the girls drag the man into their teepee and, right before dawn, seen the stewardess drag him right back out the same window. "Please don't let him be dead," she prayed that morning, kneeling by the cash register while the Chief read a biblical passage about smiting and smoting. "And if he is dead, don't let anyone know they stayed here." Five killers were one too many for a small motor court. "Amen."

By the time she sat down, Wanda had served seventeen cheese omelets, burned a loaf of toast, forgotten three orders of prune juice, and run out of pancake syrup. When the diner cleared out, the only customer left was a regular who knew how to help himself to coffee and doughnuts, so Wanda went to the kitchen for a Clamato and a smoke.

"Watch the ashes," the Chief grumped when she leaned in to take a peek at his latest creation, a sheet cake for the First Avenue Mormon Church, in honor of their one-millionth conversion.

"Doesn't seem right they can convert you without your permission," she said, poking a finger into the chapel, then licking tabernacle blue off her finger.

"Bah!" he said. "It would do you good to watch church once in a while." Now that they had been banished from public worship, he watched a televised Methodist service every Sunday, rising early to candle the eggs and praise the Lord. "I told them that you're a heathen. You're being saved at the eight o'clock service."

"I'll go put on my fancy underpants," she said. "Hon, your sky is too gray. It looks like it's going to rain."

"The sky is fine. It's my Jesus I'm worried about." He picked up a pastry bag of snow-white icing and and filled in the face of Our Lord. Two blue eyes followed.

"Jesus needs to sit under my sun lamp," Wanda said.

"Go poke your nose in someone's business," he laughed, dripping the icing and inadvertently giving Jesus a third blue eye.

As if God had read his mind, a taxi pulled up, and Wanda's interest in the Chief's religious-cake-making business instantly waned. A handsome woman in a beautifully pressed blue housedress and low-heeled suede pumps got out of the cab, indicating to the driver that she wanted him to wait, and walked toward the diner with an unsteady gait.

That woman has never walked on gravel in heels, Wanda thought as she dipped her pinkie in redemption-red icing, licked it, and hustled to her post at the counter. This woman looked like she had a story, and Wanda was all ears.

"I'm looking for two girls," the woman said, taking care not to slam the screen door. Wanda liked her already.

"Aren't we all!" the Chief yelled, and Wanda closed the curtain to the kitchen.

"There *may* be two girls staying here," Wanda said, refusing to commit until she knew what this was about. "Who wants to know? Coffee?"

The woman nodded. "I was out until eleven. I haven't done that since I was in high school."

"Why were you up so late? It's gambling, isn't it? I'll bet you lost everything but the clothes on your back. Don't worry, the coffee's on the house."

The woman laughed at the idea. "Bingo's my game."

"Do these girls owe you money?"

"Heavens, no! I'm a contestant at the Dorothy Duncan Defrost-Off and I have good news for them. They've got to get to the convention center right away."

"Why? Are they making breakfast?" asked Wanda, wondering if she had any Poppin' Fresh biscuits in the freezer. The girls were awfully nice, but couldn't cook worth a darn. They just didn't seem like the housewife type.

"They've won first place in the TV-dinner competition! And they're going to be on *The Dorothy Duncan Show!*"

Bridget put her hand on the knob of the bathroom door, uncertain of how to proceed. Sure, they were an underground spy organization, but they still stuck to the terms of the Geneva Conventions. It was a violation to withhold a prisoner's basic privileges, something she had forgotten about last night. They should have at least given him a candy bar—a Hershey Bar, since he was an American—a towel and a bar of soap, and allowed him to write a letter home.

"He's not in there," Bibi yawned. She must have sleepwalked her way to the bed, and then fallen asleep on her beaded clutch, and it stuck to her face when she raised her head. "I put him in the closet around four so I could hit the loo myself. I took off the chain and cuffed his hands to his feet. I figured even if he gets through that dinky closet door, he wouldn't be able to get very far. I don't particularly like having a hostage," she added, pulling the purse off her face. "This must be what it's like having a baby. You can't go away and leave it alone, they stink up the loo, and they keep you up all night. Do you realize we've had only five hours of sleep since we came to America? The bags under my eyes have bags of their own."

"Did you know that during the war agents crossing the Atlantic in submarines weren't allowed to speak above a whisper for fear the German wolf packs would find them? That they spent months crawling along the ocean floor without one glimmer of day? And female agents sneaking into France had to swim the Channel with a one-hand stroke so they could hold their purses above water?"

"Bridget, I really don't see where you're going with this, besides showing off your expensive public-school education. I'm sorry people had to live underwater and carry their own purses, but please don't interrupt me when I'm complaining. My feet hurt, and it feels like I'm about to get another corn. My face is puffy, my skin is dry, and I think I just started my period."

"Not in my favorite pajamas!" said Bridget. She pulled Bibi out of bed and pushed her into the bathroom. "Get dressed, and hurry. It's time we let the prisoner out."

"Leave him there until we're ready to go."

"Aren't you worried he's not getting enough air?"

"There *is* a keyhole." Bibi wrapped a towel around her hair and began to rub cold cream on her face. "I'd be happy to leave him in the closet all day, so his wife can have at least one full day of happy widowhood."

"Bibi, that's a terrible thing to say! Mrs. Smathers is probably heartbroken," Bridget said, running the tap water so she could brush her teeth. She was tired. Her legs felt heavy and thick. And her head ached.

"I'm sure she'll recover from his death quickly," said Bibi. "And for your information, even though I washed the dresses, I'm not wearing that horrid frock again today." After she'd moved Smathers to the closet, she had had just enough energy left to rinse their drip-dry dresses and hang them over the tub. "If Marge can have a makeover, so can we."

"Good idea," Bridget said, as she began her morning beauty regimen. "Fashion *is* more important than freedom. Once Mrs. Martini finds out who we really are, she can apologize for trying to rob us. And when the Sands calls to ask why we fired a weapon in their casino, we'll just tell them we're secret agents and that it's none of their business."

"After he confesses, can we go home?" said Bibi, wiping the cold cream from her face and examining her skin in the mirror, alarmed at a splotch of new freckles on her cheeks. "We'll bring back a can of Aqua Net and tell everyone it's the secret invention. Marge says it takes crayon off wallpaper."

"We're not leaving without that invention," said Bridget, although in all honesty it was the last thing she cared about.

After they dressed and finished their makeup and hair, relying on Aqua Net to fight the force of gravity after forgetting to put in curlers the night before, they opened the closet door to find that Dougie Smathers, in a feat worthy of Harry Houdini, had escaped. The only evidence he'd even been in their closet was the greasy stain his hair had made on one of Bridget's light summer dresses.

"Unbelievable!" Bridget cried when she picked up the handcuffs and examined them. There was no sign that the lock had been tampered with, no scratches or marks. "These were opened by a professional." They had taken away his shoes, wristwatch, and swizzle stick—anything that could become a tool or a weapon.

"Maybe Wanda snuck in to leave us additional unattractive outfits, and found him in our closet. Thinking he was one of our husbands, she drove him out to the desert and left him there," suggested Bibi. "He's not hiding in one of your dresses, is he?" She had once climbed into a coat, still on the hanger, to escape a store security guard.

"Wanda would have left a note," said Bridget, swatting at the dresses hanging in the closet and feeling like an agent in training. She had never fallen asleep on an assignment before. "I wonder if she saw anything peculiar last night?"

"Why don't we ask her?" said Bibi, tossing the handcuffs under the bed when she saw the scene through their window. "She's outside our teepee, jumping up and down and waving her arms. And she's got Marge Milligan with her."

. . . .

twenty-two

Betty had bunked in Chickie's office on his old army cot, turning the master suite over to her guests, two of whom snored soprano all night. Just before dawn the sawing stopped, and Jane was able to eke out a few hours of shut-eye on the stiff divan, her long legs hanging over the edge, the newlyweds having claimed the bed. As a man wanted for murder, she rather thought she'd have first pick, considering her future sleeping arrangements might involve a concrete cot. If Cedric had gotten his way, she would have slept in the bathtub, on Betty's nice rose-colored guest towels.

As Jane flipped like a fish in a frying pan, trying to get comfortable, her thoughts were not of her home and her lover and their cushy bed but of the large sectional sofa next door in the living room. In the middle of the night, she had gotten up for a glass of water and some cold wonton, leaning over the sink and eating it right from the carton with her fingers so she wouldn't have to do any more dishes. On the way back to the bedroom, she lingered in the doorway of the living room, admiring Betty's sectional: the deep seat, the plump cushions, the cool-looking plastic slipcovers. Afraid to even sit down, fearing her body heat would melt the plastic and leave an indelible mark of her transgression, she'd crept back to bed.

The morning started out stormy. Cedric got off to a bad start by accusing Jane of keeping him up all night with her snoring. "You stick with that story," she said, sipping from her mug of steaming Nescafé. The miniature reel-to-reel tape recorder in the handle of her suitcase had clicked on when she tripped over it on the way to the bathroom, recording a night of symphonic snoring. She couldn't wait to see his face when she played the recording of his nearly inhuman guttural sounds. Being wanted for murder would almost be worth it.

"For a suspected murder, you're in a chipper mood," said Sandy, setting a platter of toaster strudel on the lazy Susan in the middle of the table and rolling an icing tube between her palms to soften it. Not much of a sleeper, Sandy had let herself into the house just after seven, then woke them by banging around the kitchen, preparing a hot and hearty breakfast. Using a steak knife to cut the tip, she dripped the icing on the strudel in narrow, even ribbons, just like on the package.

Betty stomped into the kitchen, every hair in place, wearing the velveteen hostess gown and gold slippers from the night before. She made a growling noise deep in her throat and plugged in the percolator. "Don't talk to her until she's had her coffee," warned Sandy, and Betty nodded, sat down, and hid behind the sports section of the Las Vegas *Sun*. As much fun as it was to have fugitives in her home, she was more accustomed to breakfasting alone, reading the paper at a leisurely pace, then turning on the transistor radio above the sink for "The Martini Hour" on KMOB, each morning at eight. Chickie had hated the guy, but Betty had never lost her schoolgirl crush on him. Blocking out the image of Chickie frowning at her from the grave, she'd close her eyes and pretend Sammi Martini was singing just for her.

Jane rifled through the pile of newspapers, looking for the front page, but Sandy had used it to line Betty's garbage pail. These fellows knew they were wanted for murder; there was no use rubbing it in with the headline JAMES BLAND WILL FRY, SAYS DA. She had thought about saving part of the front page for Jim. The police sketch made him look like a movie star, but the one of his friend was downright unkind. He wasn't really shaped like pear.

When Felix finished reading the funny pages, Sandy took them and went right to *Mary Worth*, who was, no surprise, sticking her nose into other people's business again. For fun, she and Betty would write their own dialogue, giving Mary Worth a gangster boyfriend and a foul mouth.

"What's the weather going to be like today?" whispered Cedric, tempted to go sockless. Where he was going, he wasn't sure, having abdicated power to Jane, who seemed too content to not have a plan.

"The weather's always the same here," said Sandy, keeping her voice down. "It was hot yesterday, it will be hot today, and it's gonna be hot to-morrow. The temperature will drop after sunset, and you can expect a light breeze coming off the mountains."

"Sandy has always dreamed of being a weather girl," Betty said, emerging from behind her paper, clear-eyed and awake after her coffee, ready to face the kind of day typical of life with Chickie. Although her back hurt from sleeping on the stiff cot, it had not been an unpleasant experience. The blanket had reeked of Chickie, a blend of Aqua Velva and menthol cigarettes.

"When I was growing up," said Sandy, "good girls didn't appear on television."

"That's because television hadn't been invented yet," Betty pointed out, opening the refrigerator door and moving items around on the bottom shelf. "Here it is," she said, putting the top layer of a frothy wedding cake, the plastic bride and groom still attached, on the table. She poked at the icing. "It's still good," she said when her finger left a dent. "Not too dry. Who wants a piece?" Cedric was the only one among them who did not raise his hand. He had never heard of anyone having cake for breakfast; it made his teeth ache just to think of it.

"I'll just have another toaster strudel, if you don't mind," he said.

Using Betty's electric carving knife, a free gift that had come with her custom plastic slipcovers, Sandy cut the bride and groom apart, then tossed the mister into the trash and put the bride on the lazy Susan, between Mrs. Dash and the A.1. steak sauce bottle. "This marriage could not be saved," she explained as she picked curls of plastic off the table.

Jane, who felt like she was always doing dishes, washed her mug, then held out a soapy hand for the debris, so it didn't end up on the floor. "Everybody hang on to your mug," she instructed, opening the cupboard under the sink with the toe of her boot and throwing away the curls. "I'm not doing any more dishes until tonight, so if you misplace it and want tea, you'll have to steep it in the kettle and pour it down your throat." This was aimed at Cedric, who, though he lived alone, always had a dozen or more teacups to wash at the end of each day.

"Isn't he just like Chickie?" Betty said to Sandy. "Jim's done the dishes once in his life, so now he thinks it gives him license to complain."

"Ha, ha," said Jane, rinsing the sponge under the tap and squeezing the water out of it. They picked up their mugs so she could wipe the table, and Cedric made a mental note that the Campbell's tomato soup mug was his.

Betty twirled the lazy Susan, staring at it as if it were a roulette wheel and she had her money on black. "Sit down, Jim."

Jane wiped her hands on a tea towel and took a seat across from their hostess. She felt guilty. "I didn't sit on the sofa," she said.

"It's not that." Betty smiled. "Now that we've all gotten some rest and can think clearly, it's time we discussed your situation. The dead guy. How did you know him?"

"We're all with the International Association of Accident-Prone People, a group working to meet the needs of the habitually unlucky," Cedric said before Jane could open her mouth.

"If you're so accident-prone, how come we haven't seen any of you trip or hit your head?" said Sandy. "Jimmy, when we were out all night, you didn't stub your toe once."

"I slipped in the shower this morning," offered Felix.

"Everyone does," Betty assured him. "Jim, it's time you tell us the truth, 'cause we're in on it now."

"And we're gonna bust a gut if you don't tell us," added Sandy.

"We've put you in an awful position," said Jane. "We made sure we weren't followed, if that helps. And we ditched the car a half-mile down the road."

"I can shoot the dot off the letter i," said Betty. "Chickie made sure of that. And Sandy once had a job wrestling alligators. We can take care of ourselves just fine, and I suspect you can, too, Jim. But three of you together make an awfully big moving target."

Cedric sucked in his stomach.

"You can tell us. We won't go to the cops," said Sandy.

"Okay," said Jane, lighting a cigarette to give her time to think.

Cedric's palms started to sweat, but the napkin dispenser was empty. Proving what he had come to believe, that they were uncannily in tune with one another, Felix reached over and deposited his napkin on Cedric's lap.

"I'll answer your questions as truthfully as possible, without putting you in any danger or leaving out any juicy details," Jane said after a few puffs. Betty smiled, and her expression softened, and Jane knew she had said the right thing.

"The dead guy, was he blackmailing you?" asked Betty. She had woken early, well before dawn, to listen to the birds and mull over Jim's situation, trying to imagine what Chickie would do. If Jim had offed this guy, it was for a good reason. She had had the urge to kill once, when one of her neighbors, a retired army captain, threatened to tell Chickie's wife about his infidelity unless Betty agreed to attend a Liberace concert with him. Blackmail was an ugly thing.

Jane nodded.

Cedric coughed.

"Why?"

Jane paused, realizing that "I don't know" would probably not suffice.

"He was blackmailing all of us," piped up Felix. "We're all in this together."

"That leaves out one of the most common motivations for blackmail: a romantic triangle," said Sandy.

"Yes, it does," said Jane, glaring at Felix. Sucking slowly on her cigarette, she blew a smoke ring that settled around the condiment jars. Felix obviously did not want to be left out, and she would oblige him. "I shouldn't do this," she finally sighed.

Fearing what Jane was about to say, Cedric picked at the last piece of cold strudel, wanting to keep his hands busy and off Jane's neck.

"You mustn't reveal what I'm about to tell you," she said. "You'll be signing our death certificates."

"The coroner signs those," Sandy said helpfully, and Jane thanked her with a smile.

Betty hopped up and switched on the transistor radio above the sink, just in case the room was still bugged, and plopped herself down next to Sandy. They exchanged excited looks, and Sandy began to hiccup. Betty put her arm on Sandy's and gave it a squeeze. She hadn't seen her friend this nervous since the time they stole their first complete Thanksgiving dinner.

"There was no blackmail. And you're right; we're not accident-prone," Jane said. "We're spies."

Cedric sucked in air so fast the piece of strudel lodged in his throat, and he jumped up, kicking over his chair, and clutched the edge of the table as Sandy whacked him on the back with a wooden breadboard. When he caught his breath, Jane made him sit down. "Let me continue," she said as she pinched his arm.

"Cedric and I work for a British manufacturing concern, and we were sent here to infiltrate the convention. Felix here has invented something everyone wants, and we—and the others—came here to offer him a large sum of money for it."

"What is it?" broke in Sandy. "I can't stand not knowing!"

"She's like this at the movies, too." Betty shook her head. "What's going to happen? Is he going to die? Will romance win out? I tell ya, it'll drive you crazy."

Jane had lost her train of thought.

"My invention," piped up Felix. "You were about to offer me a large sum of money."

"Right. Anyway, the dead man—Dougie Smathers—tried to smother Felix in a hideaway sofa bed so he could steal it."

"I could hardly breathe," said Felix.

Sandy nodded. It had happened to her. While working as a maid at the Stardust, she had reached too far into the back of the sofa while looking for change and was almost swallowed up. "Not all furniture needs to be dangerous furniture," she said. "I have this idea for an invention—"

"So when you fought with Dougie Smathers, the real killer used the opportunity to get rid of two competitors," Betty jumped in, averting a detour into Sandyland.

"Correct, dear lady," said Cedric. "And now we're wanted for murder, and Felix's marvelous invention has fallen into the hands of a nefarious gang of thugs."

"No it hasn't," said Felix. "I carry it with me at all times. When I went back to the hotel on the night of the Liberace concert, and Dougie dangled me over the balcony by my feet, I realized I wasn't welcome there. So I put my valuables in my pocket. I was waiting for the right time to show you."

"No time like the present," said Sandy. She understood now why everyone had been so interested in her coasters last night; they were people who appreciated a good idea. After Felix showed off his invention, perhaps she could show her new one as well.

"What is it?" Sandy poked at Felix's invention with her nail. It was made of paper, two pieces that had been glued together on three sides. The open end had a flap, like on an envelope, that folded outward. It was about the size of a man's dress-shirt pocket.

"I call it the Paper Pocket. This is just the prototype," explained Felix. "I'll use white glue instead of rubber cement on the finished one. It will be neater."

Cedric picked up the contraption and looked inside. "It has a nice, spare design," he said, handing it to Jane. "It's awfully innovative," he added, seeing Jane's frown. "And the white paper makes it look crisp and clean."

"Don't be afraid to take it for a spin," Felix said, handing him a ball-point pen with a leaky barrel. "What's great about paper is you can erase it or simply throw it away. Each day you wear clean clothes to work; why shouldn't your pocket protector be as fresh as your shirt?"

"It's ingenious," said Sandy, crooking her index finger and poking the air, chanting, "Ka-ching! Ka-ching! Ka-ching!"

"Excuse me?"

"You'll sell a million! No, two million! Disposable things are the wave of the future," she said knowingly, having invented paper swimsuits long before they caught on. "It's fun to throw things away. Say, what about paper shirts? And ties. No more laundry."

"And you could write things on your arm and not worry about ink poisoning," put in Cedric. "And if the ink was invisible, you could write things you didn't want anyone to read, but still have a record of it." It was genius in its simplicity. Cedric was proud—he had been right all along, and he continued to prove his knighthood an honor to the queen.

"What if the paper was made of rice, so if you were lost somewhere, you could literally eat your shirt?" joked Jane. Surely they hadn't come all the way from London for *this*. "And the invisible ink can be made of lemon juice, to ward off scurvy."

"That's the smartest thing I've ever heard," said Sandy. "God, Felix, no wonder people are killing each other to get to you."

After Felix's presentation they sat around the table, and debated their next move. Buoyed by his success, Felix was animated and confident, certain they could investigate Dougie's death on their own and find the real killer. "This very same thing happened on the *Fugitive*," he said. Sandy nodded.

"But we don't have a whole season to find the real killer," she pointed out.

"After a night to sleep on it, I've decided that the only way out of our dilemma is to contact our superior in London, and arrange for an exchange of prisoners," Cedric said.

"Absolutely not. While you were snoring and I was *trying* to sleep, I came up with a theory. Betty, is there any more coffee?" Sandy scrambled for the percolator, and after Jane had taken a leisurely sip, Betty yanked the cup out of her hand. "You'll get it back when you talk. Now, talk!"

"I think Bob Snurd did it."

"But he was Dougie's best friend," Felix said. "They did everything together! Bob even named his son Dougie Smathers Jr."

"But sometimes, best friends feel like killing each other." She gave Cedric a sideways glance. "I saw the look on Snurd's face when Dougie took his pudding. He was furious."

"Dougie *was* always teasing Bob," said Felix. "Pulling his chair out from under him, setting his desk on fire, poking his finger in his dessert."

"Exactly. So Snurd, pushed to his limit from years of juvenile behavior, snapped and decided to take advantage of the location. *He* killed Dougie and threw him over the side."

"But he was so upset when they brought up the body," said Cedric. "And the others just stood there, chatting as if at a garden party."

"I've seen this before," said Felix. "On *Dragnet*. With Dougie dead, the other men felt free to express their true feelings. No one really cared about the dead man but Bob, and when his body was dragged ashore, Bob regretted his action. He cried from a mixture of guilt and sorrow. Guilt because he's the real murderer, and sorrow because a special relationship died that day along with his friend. Died in the cool, clear water of Lake Mead," America's playland.

"So now that the murderer has been identified, all we have to do is find him and force a confession out of him. Betty, do you still have Chickie's brass knuckles?" asked Sandy.

Betty nodded and took a sip of Jane's coffee. "And the pearl-handled pistol he gave me for our anniversary." She hadn't felt this alive since Freddy the Finger had spent a month hiding in her sewing room.

"We'll find that bastard," said Sandy. "And then we'll make him sing like Caruso. We have something to do later this morning, and Betty might be doing hair, but other than that we're free. Right, Betty?

She nodded. "I have a wig restyling later, and that's it. He's gonna leave it in the carport, so I don't have to be home."

Sandy borrowed Felix's leaky pen and started a list. "We'll put on disguises and break into the killer's hotel room and look for evidence."

"What kind of evidence?" asked Cedric.

"Letters from the killer's wife. It's possible she and the dead man were having a torrid affair and he found out about it. That's why he snapped. And since they were already at Hoover Dam . . . It happens all the time on *Perry Mason*. We'll make sure to watch it tonight. Maybe we'll get ideas. His clients are always being accused of something they didn't do."

"Maybe Raymond Burr will agree to defend them," Betty said dryly.

"Do you mind if I turn on the news?" Jane asked no one in particular. Mrs. Snurd had not been sleeping with Dougie Smathers. Jane doubted Dougie's own wife was sleeping with him. "I want to see what new evidence they have against me." She snapped on the black-and-white television.

An alarming thought raced through Cedric's mind. "Do you think the queen has heard about this?" he said, touching the gold medal on his dressing gown.

"Yes, Cedric, I believe Her Majesty *does* watch local Las Vegas programming," Jane said, adjusting the antenna until the squiggly horizontal lines went away.

"Meow!" said Sandy.

"Sorry, old chap. I'm on edge this morning."

"I'm *allergic* to cats," said Felix, looking around fearfully.

"At the top of the news, Vivian Vance has dropped her divorce action and has reconciled with her husband of nine months. They were seen leaving the courthouse yesterday, arm in arm, Miss Vance dressed in a stunning red suit. America's best-loved second banana released a statement today expressing her gratitude for America's prayers. And now, a word from our sponsors." Three cigarette commercials later, the news resumed.

"Since yesterday afternoon the dragnet thrown up around the city has snared one hundred and sixty-two drunk drivers, a shipment of counterfeit casino chips, and a truckload of cheap knockoffs of the Sammi Martini line of men's formal- and casual-wear suits, but no fugitives from justice."

"Not a bad likeness," said Jane as a flattering police-artist's sketch of her appeared on screen.

"You look like a movie actor," said Cedric glumly. "Look at that head of hair."

"They've captured you nicely, Jim," agreed Sandy. "You should ask them for a copy."

"The thickness of your hair is a bit exaggerated, don't you think?" Cedric added.

"Shhh." Betty pointed at the TV screen, where two more drawings had appeared.

"Authorities are also looking for these men, believed to be traveling companions of the raffishly handsome accused killer, an Englishman by the name of James Bland."

"Why is that potato wearing sandals?" said Sandy.

"That would be me," Cedric sighed. Soon they would be calling him Cedric Plumpernickel. The third illustration was an outline of a male figure, with a question mark where his face should be. *"The third man, believed to be a shadowy underworld figure, has not been identified."*

"You're much better looking than you are in that picture," Sandy assured Felix.

"It's high school all over again," he sighed. "My yearbook portrait was an empty box with the words 'Fred Bivens, We Hardly Knew Ye' underneath."

"A memorial buffet, catered by the Dorothy Duncan Defrost-Off contestants, will be held today at the convention center for the survivors of the Hoover Dam massacre."

"We're entered as contestants," Sandy told them. "But we're only going today, the last day, because that's when the Dorothy Duncan show is filmed. I haven't figured out how, but I'm going to demonstrate my latest invention on national TV!"

"And now, live from the Dorothy Duncan Defrost-Off . . ."

A blonde with a deep tan and big white teeth smiled into the camera and licked her lips. *"Good news, gourmands! A winning dish has been selected in the TV-dinner competition! Las Vegans Mrs. Betty Skeets and Miss Sandy Beach will receive a check for ten thousand dollars for their inventive entrée, Sardine Surprise! According to judge Mrs. Sammi Martini, the fish dish left the judges smiling and begging for more."*

"We've won ten thousand dollars!" Sandy jumped up and danced around the table with Felix.

"They've won ten thousand dollars," Betty said. "I told you we should have gone the first day. Now someone's got our name tags." On the screen two girls in dotted dresses stood next to a big blonde in a white mink coat holding a giant check. Invited to say a few words, one of the girls stepped forward and grabbed the microphone out of the reporter's hand.

"I'd like to thank my friend Marge for teaching me how to turn on the stove. And Mary Quant, for making such nice shoes. Lastly, I would like to send a message to another contestant by the name of Verda Taylor. Go suck an egg. And thank you, Dorothy Duncan, for the check."

Jane, who had no interest in cook-offs and had been examining her boots for signs of wear, looked up. *Mary Quant?*

"Why is the other girl tapping on her shoulder bag like that?" said

Betty, getting a closer look. Those young girls would look good in the new short haircuts, and she'd tell them so after taking back her name.

"It's a tic," Sandy said knowingly. "I read in *Reader's Digest* that one out of one hundred and twenty Americans suffers from the embarrassment of uncontrollable muscle spasms. According to nine out of ten doctors, appearing on live television may make it worse."

"It's *not* a tic," said Jane, staring at the fast-moving fingers. "It's Morse code!" Using the leaky pen, she filled Felix's Paper Pocket with dots and dashes, then translated them into words, trying not to show her excitement.

"What did she say?" asked Sandy. "It's a cry for help, isn't it? They've been kidnapped by a brainwashing cult of happy housewives and forced to wear dotted Swiss."

Jane worked out the final words of Bridget's message:

Honey, good news! Dougie Smathers is alive! We kidnapped him last night, but he managed to escape. We'll get him today at his memorial buffet and turn him over to the police. We'll look for you at the airport tonight. Forget about the invention. I love you. P.S. Do you hate my hair?

"It's exactly as Sandy said." Jane laughed from relief. She crumpled the paper and put it in her pocket so she could save it for her scrapbook of cute notes from Bridget. "It's just a tic."

"You've got to take me with you when you go to the Defrost-Off," Jane said, following Betty to the garage as she took out a bag of trash and the remains of the wedding cake. Betty checked the cardboard box under the mail slot. Two circulars, a past-due bill from the water department, and a note from her neighbors wondering if she knew anything about a damaged tricycle. Sighing, she tossed the circulars into the garbage and put the bill and the note in her pocket.

"This garage is such a mess," Betty sighed.

"Is that a yes?"

Betty ignored her and pushed aside a large carton, marked SANDY'S CRAP, resting against a wall. Behind it was a safe, and in that safe was a pearl-handled pistol. After she put the box back in place, Betty let it rest in her palm, remembering the day Chickie had surprised her with it, then ran a finger over the engraved message. *Happy Anniversary, Doll!*

"It has a message engraved on it—see?"

Jane squinted in the dim light, finally making out the faint words. "What a thoughtful gift."

"In case he had to go on a trip, Chickie wanted me to be able to protect myself. In all his years as a businessman, he took only one extended vacation on the taxpayers' dime. Chickie was very civic-minded. He tried to save the state money, so each time he was arrested, he convinced the cops to let him go. What he didn't pay in taxes he made up for by staying out of jail."

"Are you going to take me or not?" Jane folded her arms over the soft fabric of her silk pajama top, waiting for Betty's battery to run out. It had better happen soon; when Jane reached for Felix's pen, her bandage, thrown on while she was still sleepy, had shifted, and her left breast was threatening to make a surprise appearance. "There's a hundred dollars in it for you."

"I don't charge my friends for helping them," Betty sniffed. "Nor do I lie to them. You're not the only one around here who knows Morse code."

"Yes I am."

"Okay, you are. But I know some things. The pretty girl signaling you is your girlfriend. The duchess had her associates follow you to Las Vegas, where you planned to marry. They grabbed her, and then sent you a telegram saying she had left. She's on the lam, hiding out at the Dorothy Duncan Defrost-Off, and her mother's thugs are framing your for the murder at Hoover Dam."

"Well put," said Jane.

"I'll take you." Betty was never one to stand in the way of true love. "And I even know how to get you in there."

twenty-three

$\mathcal{I}$t was only when she and Bibi were standing on a makeshift platform in front of the television camera, trying to wrest their check away from Mrs. Sammi Martini, that Bridget came up with the idea of signaling Jane. The chances that she was watching the TV-dinner award presentation at eight o'clock in the morning were slim, but that was no reason not to try. Mrs. Martini didn't seem to notice the tap-tap-tapping as she drummed out a message on the side of her patent-leather pocketbook. Bridget prayed it would do some good.

A reception for the girls had been set up in front of the mock family room, and while sleepy contestants nibbled on Pop-Tarts and sipped coffee, the judges lolled in their loungers, exhausted from last night. Sardine Surprise! had risen immediately to the top of their lists, but one judge had held out until after midnight, finally confessing that Verda Taylor had offered her a Teflon blender to vote her into first place. After she left in tears, with Verda's bribe hidden under her skirt, the scrumptious sardines were declared the winners and the remaining undisgraced judges took a taxi to the top of the Strip and ate their way to their hotel.

Bibi had just bitten into a chocolate Pop-Tart when Verda climbed on top of the first-prize deep freeze with a microphone in her hand.

"Uh-oh," said Louise Wuebel, who had been having a pleasant conversation with Bridget about an idea for a cheese-based snack to be called Cheese Louise. "She did this last year, when she lost the Fritter Fry." As the second runner-up, Verda would receive an envelope of Dorothy Duncan coupons and nothing more, and Marge, who had placed third, would go home with a new apron.

"Good morning, losers!" Verda shouted into the microphone, and women put down their coffee cups and Pop-Tarts and clapped their hands over their ears.

"I just want to say . . ." said Louise wearily.

"I just want to say," shouted Verda, her feet planted on the freezer as if she were staking out a claim.

"That I was robbed . . ." Louise continued.

"That I was robbed!" But before Verda could tell them about her missing blender, someone pulled the plug on her.

Bibi, a little drunk on power and her newfound wealth, kicked off her shoes and climbed atop the breakfast bar. "Good morning, winners *and* losers!" she cried. The women around her giggled, and Bibi basked in their approval.

"Get down from there," Bridget said, tugging at her skirt. "Don't antagonize Verda," she whispered. "The last thing we need is for her to harass us again."

"If she says anything, everyone will think she's just bitter," said Bibi, waving to Myrtle, whose all-Jell-O dinner had received extra commendation from the judges for its bright colors and wiggle-ability, before climbing down. While Bibi signed autographs, Bridget waited for her to come to her senses. When it seemed like that wasn't going to happen anytime soon, she pulled her away from her adoring fans and into the wedge of space behind the world's largest cheddar-cheese wheel, waiting to be rolled up a steep ramp and into the world's largest fondue pot.

"Will you quit acting like the queen at a corgi race?" Bridget scolded, taking the rhinestone tiara from Bibi. "And stop flaunting this. You're only making Verda angrier. She's already petitioning to have the decision reversed. And after you told her to suck an egg, she started telling everyone that we've stolen the recipe for her prize-winning *Prune-a-doons*."

"That's ridiculous. We don't even know what they are."

"She's already planted evidence. Marge found a bottle of prune concentrate in the cupboard under our sink, behind the bottle of gin. She said she was looking for a scouring pad, but I think what she really needed was a drink."

"It's never too early for cocktails in this town," Bibi said, adjusting her yellow ribbon winner's sash. How lucky that she had picked the blue dotted Swiss dress to wear today. "At least Marge had the pleasure of competing."

"Marge should have won, Bibi. Did you add anything to our dish when I wasn't looking? I know you have a bottle of truth serum in that purse of yours. What else do you have?" Bridget had a feeling Verda wasn't the only one with her hand in the pot.

"The secret ingredient is *marshmallow fluff!*" Bibi cried as she grabbed the tiara and ran.

The tragic death of their fellow conventioneer had led the women of the Dorothy Duncan Defrost-Off to open their hearts, and freezers, to those fortunate enough to have survived the Hoover Dam massacre. For the first time in the history of the event, these angels in aprons put down their individually wrapped pot pies and worked as one to create a smorgasbord that said, "We're glad *you're* not dead."

Recipes based on the government-approved food pyramid had been selected, and Marge Milligan, known for her light touch and flair for the arts, had been asked to make a liverwurst portrait of the deceased.

Marge was poking pockmarks into Dougie's chubby cheeks with a toothpick, using a grainy newspaper photograph of him barbecuing, when she saw her young friends standing in her doorway, looking concerned. Wiping her brow of the sleeve of her pink rayon blouse—there was no trace of the siren from last night—Marge waved them in. "I'll make a pot of coffee," she said, looking down at her handiwork in disgust. It had taken an hour to sculpt just the bulbous nose. "Why don't you two celebrities take a load off and I'll make a batch of fluffy biscuits."

"We'll have Pop-Tarts," Bibi said, taking a box from her purse and tossing it at Bridget with a cheerful "Catch!" Her aim was purposefully off, and while Bridget bent to pick up the box, Bibi quickly slid the newspaper Marge was working from onto a chair, where she could sit on the headline: JAMES BLAND WILL FRY, SAYS DA.

"Would you ladies like a taste?" Marge put a plate of crackers and a discarded liverwurst ear on the table, and Bridget scooped a piece of lobe onto a cracker, just to be polite, and then slipped it into Bibi's purse when Marge turned her head. Bibi was engaged in trying to get to the Pop-Tart inside the airtight foil package.

Marge was gracious even in defeat, Bridget thought, watching their friend as she leaned over the sink, up to her elbows in liverwurst. If it weren't for them, and Verda's bribery, Marge would be headed to Reno and a new life. If they did get anything out of that check, Bridget vowed she'd split it with Marge, who, after all, had shown them how to turn on the oven.

"Oh, kittens!" Marge cried, surprising them with the depth of emotion in her voice. "I've gotten liverwurst on my blouse!" Tears formed in the corner of her brown eyes. "Marv is going to kill me! His mother gave me this!"

"What did I tell you?" Bridget mouthed to Bibi as she jumped up to help. Bibi grabbed the dishtowel hanging on the refrigerator door and handed it to Bridget, covering her sash with her arm so it wouldn't become meat-soiled. After scrubbing her hands, Marge used a damp cloth to wipe the spot, leaving a faint pink splotch just above her left breast. Unsatisfied, she decided to soak the blouse.

Bridget couldn't bear to stay. "Marge is the unhappiest housewife here. There must be some way to get that check cashed so we can help her," she whispered to Bibi as walked into their kitchenette, leaving Marge to her Borax soak.

"I'd be willing to pay for a bus ticket to Reno," said Bibi, feeling slightly guilty for their Valium edge.

"She'll need to start over. That means clothes and shoes and kitchen gadgets. Did you see how happy she was last night, and how nice she looked? She was trying out the new Marge."

"Haven't we enough to do?" said Bibi. "We've got to find Dougie Smathers and get him to confess, then find Jane, and, if she doesn't already have it, find that bloody invention. I hope it's a miracle remedy for corns, because I'm getting another one."

Bridget looked down at Bibi's feet, resplendent in scuffed white shoes the size of loaf pans. "I'm surprised you didn't wear your Mary Quants for your television debut." Bridget had considered trading her tie-up tan canoes for the feminine sandals, but hadn't, knowing Bibi would want them.

"If *someone* hadn't hidden them—what the—?" Bibi searched her memory for an expression suitable to the scene before her. "Oh, bloody kittens!" she cried.

There were sardine cans everywhere—piled on the stovetop, sitting

in the sink, crammed in the cupboard, and stacked on the chairs. Someone had brushed to the floor the pile of congratulatory telegrams that
had greeted them that morning, best wishes from Lady Bird Johnson,
Vivian Vance, Truman Capote, and Betty Crocker, among others, and
stacked the table high with cans of Metrecal diet celery soup.

"I'm done cooking," Bibi declared. "If they want to taste *Sardine Surprise!* they'll have to wait until Dorothy Duncan comes out with the TV-
dinner." Besides, except for the emergency Valium in her molar and a
few put aside for the flight home, she was all out of the secret ingredient.

"No more marshmallow fluff?"

Bibi shook her head.

"We'll use *my* secret ingredient," said Bridget as she reached into
her purse for her bottle of truth serum. "A drop in each little fishy should
guarantee us everything we need to know."

"Can't we just make Dougie Smathers a special Pop-Tart?" asked
Bibi. She'd been about to eat the last one in the box but put it aside after
one lick of the frosting. Bridget was convinced that Dougie Smathers
would attend the buffet. It was, after all, his funeral luncheon. Their
question was, how to trap him a second time?

"It's too risky. What if someone else gets it? And if we target him,
he'll get suspicious. We don't want to risk jogging his memory about last
night." A delicious smell came from Marge's kitchen, and Bibi's stomach
rumbled. Despite what the manufacturer said, one Pop-Tart did not
make a hearty breakfast.

"He's probably next door right now, bragging to his friends about
what he's done to Jane. You have her passport?"

Bridget nodded. She had Jane's passport in her purse, along with a
paper dress for her to wear on the plane. Jane wouldn't like it, but she'd
like a jail cell even less. "We're going to have to get Cedric onto that
plane somehow. If we leave him here, he'll fall apart."

"I don't have my special inks, but if Jane nicks his passport, I guess I
could give him glasses and a hat using my Dorothy Duncan pen-and-
pencil set.

"While you're at it, make a passport for Dougie. We'll send him to
Iceland, care of Mimi Dolittle."

"Knock, knock!" Bridget turned her head as Mrs. Sammi Martini entered the kitchen, holding the giant check she had refused to hand over while they were on the air. Grateful for the scuffle, as it took attention away from her rapid signaling, Bridget was now so angry with the greedy woman that she refused to look at her. "We're busy," she said, shoving the truth serum in her apron pocket. "And that check belongs to us."

Mrs. Martini looked hurt. "Of course it does, dear. That's why I brought it." She put it on the table and pulled out a chair, perching on the edge. "Got a match?"

"No." Bridget leaned against the stove and folded her arms.

Mrs. Martini searched her purse and came up with a gold lighter. "Oh, look, I have one." She lit a Kools and eyed Bridget through a smoke ring. "You're angry, and I don't blame you. It wasn't very nice, what I did to you girls. I want to make it up to you."

"You want to go back on television and hand us the check?" said Bibi.

"Don't let's pretend." Mrs. Martini put her cigarette out on the table-top. "I have a proposal. You can't cash this check anywhere in town. The minute you step into a bank, I'll inform the police that I've caught the girls behind the casino robbery. It takes more than an ugly outfit and a bad hairstyle to fool an expert," she said when Bibi's hand went to her hair.

"Get to the point," said Bridget. "How much do you want?" She had to get this woman out of here before she slapped her.

"Half. If you sign the check over to me, the manager of the Sands will cash it. We'll split it on the spot."

Bridget broke the check in two and threw the pieces at her. "Get out."

Mrs. Martini shrugged and pushed herself up, stepping on her coat in the process. "If the check doesn't get cashed, no one wins. Think about it, Eleanor. And, Mamie, tell your friend to control her temper. There's a local ordinance protecting celebrities and their families from the riffraff that floats through this town. If I get so much as a paper cut, the police will take you away."

"Give us a minute," said Bibi, gesturing for her to step outside their kitchenette.

"If I'm left alone with her, I'm sure to break at least one ordinance," Bridget warned. Bibi nodded and agreed she'd be the one to go. She understood Bridget's impulse but she wanted the money more than she wanted Mrs. Martini to pay for her crimes. Besides, she relished another round with their biggest nemesis.

Bibi waved her back in. "When do you want to do this?"

"Now." Mrs. Martini taped the pieces together and held out a pen. "You both have to sign." Rattled, Bridget started to scribble her real name, then caught herself. "There," she said, pushing the check across the table. "Now get out."

"Four thousand, nine hundred and ninety-one dollars and fifty cents—our half of the take." Bibi bent over the kitchen table and emptied her bra, and Bridget scurried to pick up the hundred-dollar bills floating to the floor. Bibi gave one last shake, and two quarters rolled out. "She made me pay for gas," she said, explaining the missing nine dollars and fifty-cents. It had been hard not to laugh when she saw that Mrs. Martini was driving the same gold Cadillac they'd stolen the night before and left behind a wedding chapel down the road from Wanda's, but it wasn't as funny when, on the way back to the convention center, Mrs. Martini pulled into a service station and demanded Bibi fill the gas tank, clean the windshield, check the oil, and then buy her a Hershey Bar. After all that, she made Bibi sit in the backseat on an old blanket as the speakers blasted an 8-track tape of Frank Sinatra's "The Lady Is a Tramp" in her ears.

"We've more than paid for this mission," said Bridget, neatly stacking the bills and hiding the bundle in a flour canister. "I'm relieved it went smoothly. No one at the Sands recognized you?"

"When you're with the big Martini's wife, you don't exist." This had been a disturbing, albeit necessary, part of the transaction, and one she did not care to repeat. Bibi knew that her need to be the center of attention was the only thing standing in the way of a meaningful relationship with Dusty Springfield. "I swear the same people are still at the same slot machines."

"Was she was gracious about splitting the money?" It had run through Bridget's mind that Mrs. Martini might want to parade Bibi through the Sands in order to have her identified and arrested.

"Remarkably," Bibi said in all truth. "She handed me the bills without a word and even waited while I counted them. The last time I saw her, she was in the lav." Bibi had gagged and chained Mrs. Martini to a sink in a ladies' room at the other end of the convention center that was now closed for repairs. But why burden Bridget with petty details? All Bridget wanted to know was if Mrs. Martini was out of their lives. Unless the woman happened to have a blowtorch in her purse, the truthful answer was yes. Bibi sat down carefully on a kitchen chair, trying to keep the five thousand dollars stuffed in her panties from crackling.

"There's a five-gallon drum of celery-flavored Metrecal over at Marge's with our names on it," Bridget said, handing Bibi a clean apron and tying on one herself. "We'd better get busy. Lunch starts in an hour."

· ·

twenty-four

Yˉou are the ugliest woman I have ever seen."

Cringing under Sandy's honest assessment, still smarting from the leg waxing, Cedric tore off his wig and stomped up the stairs, tripping on the diaphanous material of the paisley hostess gown, the only thing in Betty's wardrobe that fit over his hips. His Adam's apple had been hidden behind a triple-strand imitation-pearl choker, his pasty skin warmed with a self-tanning lotion, his round face thinned with a careful application of blusher, and his narrow greenish-brown eyes, the color of sludge, opened up with bright green eye shadow, heavy liner, and thick false eyelashes. Refusing to shave his eyebrows, straggly caterpillars shot with gray, Sandy had to blot them out with a heavy foundation, then draw delicate half-moons above, giving him a startled look, as if he had seen himself in the mirror and hadn't recovered.

"I did my best, but he looks like Ethel Merman. He just isn't a very pretty woman," said Sandy, scrubbing lipstick marks from the back of her hand, her palette for the brownish-orange lip color she'd applied a quarter of an inch outside his thin lip line. Snapping the lid on a tub of foundation the consistency of spackle and the color of bubble gum, she freshened her own lipstick and said, "I hope he's not crying up there. The glue on his eyelashes needs to set five more minutes." After plugging in the hot rollers, she lounged in the barber chair, waiting for the red light to flash. The chair, white enamel with a black leather seat, was one of a pair Chickie had brought home, hoping to encourage Betty's interest in the beauty business. A mug by the name of Phil the Peeper had spent a Saturday helping Chickie turn this part of the basement into a beauty salon, with a wash station, two chairs, a professional hair dryer, and a vanity table with a light-up mirror. A homemade folding cardboard screen, decoupaged with movie-magazine pictures of Hollywood stars, had been Betty's contribution, a way to block off the rest of the room, a dark and dusty repository for Chickie's junk. Wives, girlfriends, and occasionally the daughters of Chickie's associates would come to her in the middle of the night, for a get-out-of-town-quick hairdo. They passed on word of Betty's talent and reasonable prices, and during the day she still did prom hair and bang trims, mostly for the grandchildren of old associates.

The bathroom door slammed, and Felix, who was under the dryer reading *Photoplay* and had missed the little drama, raised the hood and looked around. Any woman would envy his silky blond hair, which Betty had back-rolled on slender sponge rollers, intending to attach a shoulder-length fall from her collection of hairpieces.

"Where's Cedric?" asked Felix, folding back a corner of his magazine so he could return to the photo layout of Vivian Vance at home with her husband. Sandy took the opportunity to check his set, unrolling a curler and testing the bounce of the still-damp curl. Spraying his head with a setting lotion that smelled like coconut, she snapped the curler back in place and turned the heat setting to high. "He's getting a glass of Clamato," she said, pushing Felix's head under the hood. With his slender frame, he could fit into any one of Betty's dresses. Jim was too tall, and Cedric was too big, but Felix was just the right size, and Sandy, who had done makeup for the Ice Capades, couldn't wait to get her hands on him. The prettier she made him, the more the other two would fade into the background, ugly stepsisters to Felix's Cinderella.

"You're going to look fine," said Betty, patting Jane's shoulder and wrapping a towel around her neck before applying a mud masque to minimize the pores. Jane's face had been dissected by Betty's experienced eye into three problem skin zones: oily nose, dry forehead, and sun-damaged cheeks. Her bones were good, though, strong but refined. Betty refused to proceed unless Jane agreed to part with the middle section of her eyebrow. Jane nodded, cracking the mud setting up on her face, and Betty took her professional tweezers from their case and ordered her to hold still. "Grip the armrests if you have to, but don't move."

Jane yelped when Betty grabbed hold of a hair and yanked as hard as she could. When nothing happened, Betty pulled harder, as if raising a beetroot. Jane screamed, tears running down her cheeks. The solvent for this problem was in a laboratory in London, at the secret offices of the British Secret Service.

"Men are such babies," Sandy scoffed, walking over to examine the eyebrow in question. "Try giving birth. Then you'll cry." A sincere apology followed when Sandy got a good look at the situation through a magnifying glass. "You're an odd case. You've got practically no beard, but your eyebrows you could knit together and sleep under." She climbed up on Jane's lap, pressed one hand against Jane's forehead to steady herself, and held out her hand for the tweezers.

"Sandy's better at this kind of thing," Betty explained, stepping back to give her room. "I faint at the sight of blood." So, it turned out, did Jane.

When she came to, she could hear Cedric lumbering about upstairs, hear the teakettle whistling and a chair being dragged across the kitchen floor. Sandy climbed the stairs, smoking and wheezing, and a short, muffled conversation followed, ending in laughter.

"I'll bet she's showing him my secretarial-school graduation photo," said Betty. "It's always good for breaking the tension."

"I guess it worked," said Jane. Balancing on stacked heels, his surprisingly small feet the same size as Betty's, Cedric gracefully descended the stairs, tripping only once on the hem of his hostess gown. Behind him, praising his dainty step, was Sandy, with a plain blue suit and a woman's tennis outfit slung over her arm. Two copper chain-link belts, attached with paper clips, circled Cedric's waist, giving shape to his dress and diverting attention from his heavily made-up face and stiff black bouffant wig—a swim cap, actually, and Chickie's last gift to Betty. When Chickie took his final taxi ride, she had told them sadly, the contractors were pouring concrete for a pool Betty now couldn't afford to finish.

"You're just in time, Cedric," Betty said, taking a Lucky Strike from the pocket of her gold lamé smock and standing back to view her work. She had stuck a long, dark wig on Jane's head and was trying different styles. "I'm thinking of giving Jim bangs, to cover his prominent forehead. Something young and fun, like a Marlo Thomas flip."

"Sounds good," Sandy said. "But I'd take it easy on the flip, Betty. This outfit is more Jane Hathaway than Marlo Thomas." Holding the jacket of the blue suit against Jane's back, she checked the fit and decided it would do. "I'll let the hem out a couple of inches," she said. "And you can wear the baby blue Dacron blouse Chickie's sister gave Betty. The shoes are going to be a problem, Jim, but if you let us cut up your boots, we can make a passable pair of low-heel boaters. A little schoolmarmish, but better than the army boots you've got on."

"Cuban-heel Beatle boots," Cedric corrected her, knowing how attached Jane was to her shoes.

"I'd rather do hard time," Jane said. She'd wear a skirt to save herself from going to jail. She'd even wear makeup and carry a purse. But she'd sooner turn herself in than give over her boots to a woman with manicure scissors and a fair knowledge of women's shoe fashions.

"Chickie would have said the same thing," sighed Betty, remembering when her bedroom closet was filled with luscious Italian leather wingtips instead of bundles of magazines for the neighbor kid's paper drive. "And he *did* hard time. Well, you'll just have to go in your boots. If people mention it, tell them your doctor prescribed them."

"I look like the aunt who always gets shut up in the attic," Cedric said when Betty lined them up in front of the hall mirror for a final inspection. "The one everyone hopes *won't* come to Christmas dinner."

"You don't have to go," Jane reminded him.

"We're not sending you there alone to find the real killer," said Felix, gripping the handle of his tennis racket and bouncing his hand on the strings. Although he was slender enough to fit in Betty's clothes, Felix's height ruined the effect, turning average-length dresses into minis. Accustomed to wearing trousers, he refused to go about in public with his thighs showing, but he had been amenable to Betty's tennis dress, which came with a pair of sturdy undershorts. Athletic shoes from Chickie's one foray into athleticism— table tennis—were made to look more feminine by Sandy, who had glued red pom-poms to the ends of the laces. With his fine blond hair pulled back and a matching hairpiece waving down his back, he looked, as Sandy put it, "Like some Harvard guy's tennis-playing fiancée."

"We decided. It's all for one and one for all." Felix tossed back his new hair, admiring the soft, bouncy wave as it brushed his shoulder.

Betty looked them over and gave her honest assessment. "Felix, you are simply adorable. You could walk into the Las Vegas Country Club and look perfectly at home.

"Jim, you make a decent-looking gal, more the librarian type than a television star. I still think the boots are all wrong for the suit, but that hairstyle is real cute on you."

"You look like the kind of gal I'd like to take home and redo," said Sandy, giving Jane another coat of concealor on the hairless, bloody spot between her eyes. "You know the type? Good face, good hair, but no fashion sense. Why be dowdy before your time? I always say."

"He's not going to the prom," said Betty, adjusting Jane's sock breasts so they sat higher on her chest. "It's not like the Dorothy Duncan gals are any better looking."

Earlier, when Betty gave them walking lessons—heel, toe, heel, toe— Jane thought it was odd to be mentally measuring her step, walking with her pelvis tucked in so her buttocks would sway. "You'll pass." That had been Betty's assessment, Sandy's, too. Where, though, was her Adam's apple, they wanted to know? And her beard? And why did the fake breasts look so much more natural on her than on the other two? "I'm actually a woman," said Jane, and after they helped Pumpernickel off the basement floor and gave him an ice pack for his bloody nose, she told them the truth, about a dark period in her country's history and a fluoridation experiment gone horribly wrong.

Sandy had nodded in sympathy. "There was a similar tragedy here in America," she said. "In the fifties. A peroxide tragedy."

"And you," Betty said, aiming her gaze at Cedric, who was biting his fingernails, ruining his very first manicure. Betty reached up and fastened a chain with a giant gold sun pendant around his neck. "Cedric, half of any girl's beauty is her personality. Not every girl has to be a Miss America to be considered attractive. Be charming and gracious, and when people speak of you later, that's what they'll remember."

"Everyone likes a funny gal," chimed in Sandy. "Do you know any jokes?"

"A chap told me ripper the other day about the queen," he said. "There's a knock at the door of her throne room. 'Knock, knock.' 'Who's there?' 'It's the Keeper of the Clocks, mum.' 'I haven't the time today.' 'No, mum. That's my job.'" Jane was the only one who laughed, and only because Cedric's impression of the queen was so very good. "It suffers in translation," he said.

"I get it. She was on the toilet, and this fellow barges in," said Sandy.

"The joke is about a misunderstanding," said Jane. "The fellow who keeps the clocks running is there to fix hers, but the queen thinks he's asking her for the time. My uncle was the assistant to the Keeper of the Clocks before the war, so I know about these things."

"No, the joke is that a servant calls her 'mum,'" said Cedric.

"There are just some things you can't do by the clock," decided Sandy. "Skip the laughs, just pile on the accent real thick. You people have a neat way of making everything sound more interesting than it is."

"I'm wearing a purple paisley tent and gold wedgies and an ornament as big as a dinner plate. I hardly think anything I say will deflect from my appearance. Must I wear this representation of a ball of incandescent gas around my neck?"

"It adds bulk to the top half of your torso," said Betty.

"And it gives people something pretty to look at," Sandy added helpfully.

Cedric pulled himself up to his full height, five feet eleven inches in heels, and adjusted the strap on his shoulder bag, which kept threatening to slide off the shiny synthetic fabric. "I have been awarded the Order of the British Empire, taken tea with the queen, and was named one of England's most unusual personalities for the year 1965. I guess this is what they mean when they say, 'How far the great have fallen.' Face it, I look like Benny Hill. I could have the sparkling personality of the Queen Mum and the wit of Prince Philip, and all people will talk about are my pear-shaped body and enormous head."

"Who's Benny Hill?" asked Betty.

"Our Jerry Lewis," he sighed, tugging at the cap of stiff hair perched on his head like a stuffed raven. While measuring him for a wig, they'd discovered his secret: He had an exceptionally large head, which, Jane thought, explained his devotion to his mother, who had given birth, as did women of her time, at home, without benefit of anesthesia. Jane felt sorry for the old bean, having Felix see him like this. When Cedric first tried on Betty's tent of a dress, Jane hoped that it would discourage him from going, which would make her life that much easier. Finding Bridget and Bibi would be hard enough without him on her trail.

To avoid more conversation about his hideous appearance, Cedric changed the subject. "Why have you not told me before about your uncle?"

"Because he turned out to be a Nazi sympathizer. When war broke out, he went to the Bahamas to wind the Duke of Windsor's clocks. He hasn't been heard from since '51, when he came 'round our flat for a loan and my mother threatened to shoot him."

"My brother Barney kicks puppies," Betty admitted, her cheeks pinking, the flush of embarrassment spreading to her neck as she thought of her brother and his legal troubles. "We're all ashamed. He's not allowed in pet shops or near parks, and he has to inform the police when he wants to leave the state. I've been thinking about getting a lit-tle dog, something small that will keep me company when Sandy's not here and that I can take with us when we go out to eat. If I do, I'm going to tell Barney he's not allowed in my house anymore," she decided.

"We are not responsible for the crimes of others," said Cedric. "Just our own." On that happy note, they filed out to the car, piling into the backseat while Betty tied a yellow chiffon scarf around her hair and rummaged through Sandy's glove box for sunglasses she'd left there. Betty had had her outfit for the closing ceremony, a dressy daytime number and faux alligator pumps, ready for weeks. Her best summer-weight worsted-wool dress was a classy number with clean lines, picked up at a church sale, donated by a lady who apparently did not believe in dress shields, and skillfully repaired by Sandy. Sleeveless, it showed off her slender tanned arms, marred only by a smallpox-inoculation scar just below her shoulder. The white bodice was as crisp as a fresh piece of typing paper, beautifully ironed on the lining side with a touch of rose water. A line of black piping divided the bodice diagonally from waist to shoulder. The cocoa brown skirt finished it off, a warm, rich tone much like her hair when it was freshly rinsed. Her legs were bare, and her shoes were out of fashion but handsome and in almost perfect condition.

Betty smiled at the fellas in the backseat, Jane's face obscured by the heavy, cold box in her lap and her prop casserole dish on top of that. "What's in this?" Jane asked, feeling something drip down her leg.

"Frozen corn dogs," said Betty, checking her lipstick in the rearview mirror. "They're leftovers from last year's Girl Scout Jamboree. Sandy sewed badges onto sashes, and I put hot dogs on sticks."

"And this is your entry?" asked Cedric, trying not to let disappointment creep into his voice.

Betty laughed. "Hell, no. That's just ammunition for Sandy's truly remarkable device."

"Is it something so revolutionary it will change our lives forever?" asked Jane, poking Cedric in the girdle to get him to stop playing with his bangle bracelets and pay attention. "Is it by any chance one of the marvels of the atomic age? The most fantastic thing to come along since invisible ink?"

"You must have read the article in the *Las Vegas Shopper.*" Betty laughed and slapped the car seat. "She put that last bit in as a joke. Boy, will Sandy will get a kick out of this!"

"I don't understand," said Cedric, who wasn't really listening; he was cleaning out the purse Sandy had lent him. It smelled of roast chicken.

"Good," said Jane, patting his knee. "Hey, where's Sandy? My corn dogs are melting."

"I'm right here." The door swung open, and a proper, churchgoing type slid behind the wheel. Gone were the red stretch pants and stained white shell of that morning; in their place was a sedate black dress with a rounded white collar and decorative cuffs. Sandy had lowered her beehive a few inches, and left off the casino-chip earrings in favor of pearl clips.

"Betty, I need your seat." Betty squeezed into the back, and Sandy put a carton on the passenger seat and secured it with the seat belt. Then she slipped back behind the wheel and turned on the motor. While the engine warmed up, she turned around, laughing when she saw Felix perched on Cedric's lap. "Get it over with," she said.

"You look very nice, Sandy," they all said in unison.

"Well, I feel like an ass," she said as she backed out of the driveway. "I'm six inches shorter, my girdle is killing me, and I think my dress shields have shifted."

"Welcome to my world," Cedric muttered.

"We're all in this together." Felix nodded. "It's one for all and all for one. We're the Five Musketeers!"

"More like the Five Mouseketeers," Sandy chirped as they roared, off, leaving a dented garbage can in their wake.

They rode in Sandy's aqua Cadillac, four dames squeezed together in the back so that Sandy's latest invention could be up front—cushioned by round sofa pillows and strapped to the seat with rope—where she could keep an eye on it. "On the last day of the contest," she explained, "the VIPs show up—cooking editors from major Nevada newspapers, the president of the Wisconsin Cheese Council, representatives from the Aluminum Industry, the man who invented Teflon. This year there will be twice as many people, since your accident-prone folks' convention will be joining us for the big lunch, to mourn their fallen comrade. No pun intended."

"The guy was a rat," said Betty, who had known, the minute she saw his photo on TV, that he was scum. "You can always tell. Character shows up in the ears."

"Is it wrong to use a buffet-style luncheon in honor of a dead man as a showcase for an invention?" Sandy wondered.

"I don't see how it could be," said Cedric. "As long as your display is tasteful."

This was exactly what Sandy wanted to hear. "People have been discovered at cook-offs before. The guy who figured out how to make

Minute Rice cook faster, and the lady who gave the colander its name were both at the Ritz Cracker Crumb-Off in 1964."

"The woman who invented the lazy Susan is the second-richest person in Iowa," Betty added. "I have the *Reader's Digest* with her story in it, if you want to see it."

"Pretty soon the name Sandy Beach will be as famous as Nelda Crump, the first person to knit a toilet-paper poodle."

"The suspense is killing me," said Cedric. Not, though, as much as his girdle. "May I ask . . . ?"

"I've been sworn to secrecy," Betty said, sitting on her right hip, her back crushed against the door. "And I'm usually her guinea pig for these breakthrough products." She leaned her head on Jane's shoulder, to steady herself. "Thanks to Sandy, I've had my stomach pumped more than once."

"I thought I was gonna make a fortune with my idea for premade kids' lunches in Rocky and Bullwinkle bags, but pediatricians hated it. Said it would add to the rising juvenile delinquency rate."

"I didn't understand the connection," said Betty. "Most of the delinquents here are married men. Their wives are home spreading peanut butter on bread, and they're here doing things they ought not to. Is it like that in England?"

Cedric shook his head, the gold balls on the end of his dangling earrings swatting his cheeks. "We favor Marmite." They could hear a wistful longing in his voice, and Jane knew he was missing home. "If all goes well, we'll be headed home soon," she told him, patting his large, paisley-covered knee.

Felix stopped plinking the strings of his tennis racket.

Cedric brightened at the thought. "Should any of you decide to visit London, you'd be welcome to stay at my home. I just had central heat installed. My late mother's room overlooks the garden and is quite comfy. Just ring me in advance so I can dust."

And move her body to the attic, thought Jane.

Sandy left them off in front of the convention center with her invention in Jane's care. "Are you willing to take a bullet for this box?" she asked.

Smiling, Jane pulled back her bulky suit jacket to reveal the gun tucked in the elasticized waistband of her skirt. Sandy relaxed enough to light a cigarette. "There's bologna in there," she said. "Go inside before it bakes in this heat. I'll park the car."

"Sandy invented bologna?" said Cedric when she drove out of sight. He gripped the front of his hostess gown, stretching the synthetic material. "Oh, dear, you must not have it over here. She's going to be disappointed when she finds out Lord Bologna holds that patent."

"Sandy knows all about bologna," Betty assured them, holding the door so Jane could walk the box inside, into the cool air. Even on the last day of the convention, the line to enter the building was long and slow-moving. Contestants who had dropped out last night, certain Verda had sewn up first prize, now wanted back in, so they could go home and brag that they had helped comfort the stricken survivors.

A woman ahead of them at the registration table put her casserole dish on the floor so she could dig through her purse. "I know I have a license," she said, panic ringing in her voice. She had discarded her name badge, and needed identification to get in. "I don't drive very often. My husband says there are enough women drivers on the road as it is. But I do have one." The woman behind the registration desk threw up her hands and announced that all were welcome. Technicians for the Dorothy Duncan show, local news crews, and food suppliers and florists had been giving her trouble all morning, and she was tired.

"I'll be back," Jane told Betty. "Tell them I went to the lav, and not to wait for me. I'll meet you inside." The crowd in the lobby spilled into the corridor; no one noticed Jane slip away.

The horseshoe floral arrangement of dying white carnations outside the spy convention door had been taken away and replaced with an arrangement of black carnations shaped like a cross, a gold ribbon with the words, HOPE YOU WERE INSURED! cutting a diagonal across the somber field of black. Propped against the metal stand holding the arrangement was a condolence card from the Sammi Martini Line of Fine Men's Sportswear, Inc., offering to provide a brand-new Nehru suit should the family wish to bury the dear departed in the utmost of style.

Jane put her ear to the door and heard shuffling inside.

The handle on the other side of the door rattled, and Jane felt her muscles tightening for attack. She had been trained in hand-to-hand combat and the use of firearms, and she had just recently lived through the most brutal tweezering in history, but the idea of entering this room made her feel like a child entering a Halloween spook house. She took a deep breath, put her hand on her gun, and knocked on the door.

Jane favored the direct approach. She'd request a moment with Bob Snurd, telling him that Mrs. Snurd was on the telephone. Then, when they were in the corridor together, his head would be introduced to the butt of her gun.

A drop of truth serum, and a confession about how Dougie had faked his own death, and Jane was free. But first she had to get them to open the door.

"Open up, you wankers," she muttered as she knocked again.

"No swearing, dear," a woman admonished her, pushing her aside and banging at the closed door. Assessing Jane's outfit with a dismissive glance, she said, "Those are the ugliest orthopedic shoes I've ever seen." Unaccustomed to being criticized by someone in a starched gingham dress and rooster apron, Jane bristled, trying to remember that she was a lady and was to act the part no matter what. The woman, who Jane now realized was the one who had gotten her thrown out of the convention, banged on the door again, and it opened a few inches. A man looked out, obviously annoyed by the intrusion.

"I've come to comfort you," declared Verda, her grip on the paper in her hand tightening.

"Thanks, but we're in mourning."

"That's why I'm here. Food fixes everything," she insisted, pushing against the door with her hip.

"Lady, we don't want company."

"Who is it?" someone called out.

"Dames with food."

"The Chinese we ordered?"

"Better than that!" She completed her assault on the door and stepped inside, with Jane right behind her. Reading from her script, she announced, in the same tone Christ must have used when delivering the Sermon on the Mount, that "I, Verda Taylor, one of the contestants of the 1966 Dorothy Duncan Defrost-Off Competition, have taken time from my busy day to organize a luncheon in honor of your grief. I hope you'll find comfort in our assorted entrées, creamed vegetables and crisp salads, side dishes and desserts, all made with fine Dorothy Duncan ingredients and love."

In her haste to organize an event that would cast a good light on Dorothy Duncan, and repair her own reputation, Verda had forgotten one crucial detail: to invite the mourners.

"It's at one o'clock. Don't be late," she snapped. "The news cameras have already been set up, and if you don't come, I'll call your wives and tell them what you *really* did in Las Vegas," she said smugly, knowing what husbands were capable of when away from home.

Jane went unnoticed as the agents talked among themselves, clearly unnerved by the woman's threat. Dougie's "death" had thrown a spotlight on their convention, and Jane realized that they all must have been up all night dismantling the secret-agent playground, expecting the police or the press or even the grieving widow to descend on them. The spring-loaded bed had been replaced by a child's crib with a doll's head caught between the slats, the bulletproof-swimwear booth now sold rubber nonskid bath mats, and the Bachelor Pad of Tomorrow was gone, replaced by a bathroom set boasting a hair dryer with a frayed cord, a puddle of water on the slippery tile floor, and a toaster perched perilously close to a full tub. The only thing that looked familiar was the column of glow-in-the-dark toilet seats.

"Hurry up and decide. My liver is drying out," warned Verda, shifting her weight from leg to leg.

Agent Camembert, who was standing on the top rung of a ladder pinning up a fire-retardant sheet for a safety film, stared at the intruders, ran a hand through his Bobby Darin wig and smiled. *"C'est magnifique!* It would be for me impossible to refuse a woman of such beauty."

"No funny stuff," Verda warned. "You show up looking decent. Suits with ties. And try to control your ... *affliction*. Stay away from the chicken—I don't want you choking on the bones. Take small, even steps, and watch out for runny white sauce."

While Verda was being shown the door, Jane backed away, scanning the room for Bob, and bumped into the lunar module, now a Safety First Model Home. She crept inside and locked the door behind her. The space capsule had been redecorated in "shabby early ranch," and as she looked around, she imagined lashing Bob Snurd to the wobbly kitchen chair with the frayed electrical cord. A distinctive whine floated through the module's air vent, and Jane tripped over a hockey stick on her way to the small bubble window facing into the room. Scraping off an old Nixon campaign sticker, she peered out the concave safety glass.

"I'll go to this stupid lunch, and then it's back to Kansas City for me." It was Dougie Smathers, live and in person, sitting on a riding mower, flicking ashes into a barbecue grill, wearing what looked like a dead squirrel on his head.

"My wife is going to kill me when I get home," he chuckled, looking in the direction of the toilet seats. "I'd better bring her a gift." He scratched at the fake sideburns glued to either side of his round face, then tugged on his wig.

"What about Bond?" someone asked. Jane drew her gun.

"What *about* Bond?" Dougie spit.

"Dougie, this joke has gone far enough. Do you know how much trouble you'll be in when they find out you're alive? This is more than a misdemeanor hotfoot, Doug. It's a felony in this state to pretend you're dead and let someone take the blame for it." It was Dougie's best friend, Agent Bob Snurd, talking, and Jane realized she had misjudged him.

"I'm an amnesiac, see?" said Dougie. "But I remember who I am just before they flip the switch."

"That's genius!" cried Bob. "That will teach Jimbo not to interfere when you want a second snack cake." No, she hadn't.

Quietly, Jane counted the bullets in her purse. There weren't nearly enough to take on every agent in the room. And if she emerged shooting, surely someone would shoot back, and the image of a dead Jane wearing a dull navy blue skirt would haunt Bridget forever. She slipped the gun into her purse and then got as comfortable as she could, trapped in a snug skirt in a tiny trailer. Her pantyhose already had a run in them, and she hoped it wasn't a portent of things to come.

A woman's shrill laugh startled her, and Jane realized she had dozed off with a cigarette in her hand. It would have been funny under different circumstances, but Jane wasn't laughing when she put out the smoldering ash on the brown shag carpet. This trailer had no emergency exit, although it did have a fire extinguisher mounted on the wall. She looked closer; it was just a cardboard tube painted red. Another almost-inhuman shriek came through the vent, and Jane peered out the window and saw Dougie Smathers and a tall blonde in a white mink coat standing on the patch of Astroturf out front. The rest of the room seemed empty. Smathers was trying to cozy up to the woman, offering her a cigarette while sliding his arm around her shoulder. She stomped on his insole, and he let her go.

"Oh, my word," Jane whispered, realizing who she was seeing through the concave glass. Her hand went immediately to the bald patch behind her ear, so expertly hidden.

"Stop crying, Dougie!" the woman shrieked, hitting him on the head with a rolled-up magazine. Her coat hung crookedly off one shoulder, and she looked like she had survived a hair-pulling contest. Drawing a gun, she motioned him toward Jane's hideout. "We're going to have a little chat." She was limping. Sweat patches appeared under the arms of Dougie's jacket, the same powder blue Sammi Martini swingster suit he had worn the other night. It looked like it had been slept in.

"Get in there," the woman said. "We've got things to talk over." Up until that moment, Jane had been enjoying the little scene, but she ducked below window level when one of them rattled the knob of the trailer. Jane tried to squeeze into the television console, a long and low Mediterranean-style walnut cabinet with a backboard that she discovered came off easily. Her pull on it activated a reel-to-reel tape with a man's scolding voice: "*To reduce the risk of fire or electrical shock, do not remove this backing. Always have this unit repaired by a certified technician.*"

"Shh," said Jane, covering the speakers with a child's fire-retardant blanket. Fearing electrical shock, she crouched behind the cabinet instead, armed with a ceramic owl statue, the only object in the room that wasn't bolted down. She was a lousy secret agent. Bridget would never have put her gun in her purse, then forgotten it by the door.

"My men will be back any moment to rescue me," Dougie threatened.

"Thanks for the tip," said the woman. Jane heard the door to the room slam shut, then counted to ten and crawled out of the trailer, knowing now why Betty had insisted she wear dress shields under her Dacron blouse, despite its easy wash-and-wear-ability. "You never know when you're going to need extra protection," she had advised Jane as she showed her how to attach the absorbent cotton pads to her slip-straps. "I don't much care for the blouse, but it's unpleasant to have damp underarms." Yes, Jane thought, it certainly was.

. . . .

twenty-five

Glad now that she had packed her best mourning apron, Verda Taylor puttered around her kitchenette, putting the final touches on a special dish that would surely be the most memorable one of the luncheon. She had asked for some time off from her official duties, to finish her gift to the memory of the deceased, three hundred prune Jell-O Dixie cups, now setting up in her Frigidaire.

Her goal was simple: When the same news team that had been there that morning returned from covering Wayne Newton's unveiling of his new swimming pool, they would find a gentle domestic tableau under way—the feeding of the unfortunates in a lavish banquet put together by Verda Taylor, who would have come up with the idea on her own had Louise Wuebel not mentioned it first. The reporters would be there in time to witness a special dish, donated by two generous prize-winners, made with love and expired Liver Spots, begin its assault on the intestinal tracts of the unlucky judges from last night, who had been invited to partake of this meal.

Using a syringe she'd taken from a diabetic contestant's purse, Verda melted the contents of a box of Ex-Lax in a saucepan and filled the syringe, injecting each liver croquette until it was as plump as a milk-fed calf.

Tying her starched black apron around her waist, Verda set her dial to two hundred degrees, and popped her croquettes, which had a pleasant chocolatey smell, into the oven for a slow roast. She was penning a flowery description to go next to them on the buffet table when Louise barged into her kitchenette. Verda crumpled the strawberry-scented paper and shoved it in her apron pocket.

"Verda, we've got a problem." The bow on Louise's wash-and-wear blouse had come undone, and her slip had started to creep down on the right. "The women claiming to be Betty Skeets and Sandy Beach won't leave; they want their badges and complimentary pen-and-pencil sets! And they've brought Ethel Merman and her tennis coach with them! And *they* want complimentary pen-and-pencil sets, too!"

"Let them in." Verda shrugged, turning her head so her friend couldn't see her smile. She had known all along that something was wrong with those silly girls, who had stolen her tiara, and Louise had just confirmed it. Verda had caught her spies, and as she closed her eyes, as ten thousand clean dollar bills danced in front of her. Goodbye, Ernie!

"But everyone knows that Mrs. Sammi Martini and Ethel Merman hate each other," Louise said.

"Then put them on opposite sides of the room," Verda said calmly. "Really, Louise, if you can't handle something as simple as this . . ." She gave an exaggerated sigh and slumped into the rocking chair she had brought from home. "All I wanted was some time alone, to collect my thoughts and jot down a few poetic musings on life and death."

Louise cringed under the rebuke. "It doesn't make any sense that four women have the same two names. I should call headquarters. We don't want any trouble, on this of all days."

"Louise, the answer is as obvious as that ugly mole on your neck that you think you can cover with a scarf. Betty and Sandy are common names. I must have made a mistake when I wrote out the name tags, and the first Sandy and Betty were too polite to ask me to fix it."

"That makes sense," said Louise, and Verda nodded. "Golly, Verda, whatever you have baking in your oven smells out of this world!"

"Your slip is showing," Verda said nastily.

* * *

Jane tailed them, watching as Mimi forced Dougie Smathers into an air-conditioning vent off the main hall, in a corridor rarely traveled these days, as its rooms were closed for the summer. Not wanting to interfere, Jane watched Dougie being sealed in with a blowtorch, then watched his jailer saunter off.

"Ding, dong," Jane sang into the vent. "Avon calling."

"Bob, is that you? Get me out of here," he pleaded. "You know I'm afraid of small, enclosed spaces."

"It's not Bob," said Jane, crouching by the vent and keeping her voice soft. "It's James Bond, your Avon representative. And I should think you'd be more afraid of heights after what you've been through."

"Wide-open spaces," Dougie Smathers whispered to himself. "The Grand Canyon. Outer space. Oklahoma. The automotive department at Sears." Fearing he would go mad before she had a signed confession, Jane tapped her gun on the grate, and he stopped babbling. She shoved Betty's bridge pad and a pencil at him and started to dictate a simple confession that exonerated James Bland, Cedric Slumberknuckle, and Felix Bivens of any blame in any incident related to this terribly un-funny joke. "And sign it. And now a second note," said Jane. "To the Snacketeria ladies, apologizing for the mess you made and offering to replace their hairnets."

"You'll let me out when I'm done?" he whimpered.

"Is there anyone else who deserves an apology?" said Jane. The pages piled up as Dougie Smathers, trapped like a sinner in a confes-sional, wrote poorly worded letters to every woman he'd ever met, starting with the nurse who had attended his birth. Each time he con-fessed to another crime against womankind, Jane let him take a drag off a cigarette.

"Your penmanship is dreadful, Dougie," she said, her legs cramping from sitting on the floor. She had her signed confession, and a good many more, but it wasn't going to be enough. She got to her feet and stretched, and the scribbling stopped.

"Bond, you're leaving me?"

"I'm going to get more paper and something I can use to get you out of here. Jesus, Dougie, you've been a real jerk, haven't you?" Jane ground out her cigarette under her heel. There had to be some cooking implement that had the same prying properties as a crowbar.

His fingernails raked the grate. "What if *she* comes back?"

"Keep your gob shut and stay as far away from the opening as possible." All Jane wanted was a confession on live television. After that, Mimi could have him.

Verda took her place at the head of the banquet table, laden with each contestant's prize dish. The dessert section was a little heavy on the gelatin molds, and Verda made a mental note to discourage the gals in the future from relying on this delicious but simple dish. The man they were mourning had fallen from a great distance, and the least they could do was spend a corresponding amount of time in the kitchen. She smiled as she looked down the dozens of kitchen tables pushed together. She had tried to make everything nice, positioning her prune Jell-O Dixie cups so they spelled out the heartfelt sentiment BETTER LUCK NEXT TIME. She thought herself clever that the message looped around her beautifully dressed silver serving platter of liver croquettes, set atop a chafing dish to keep them warm and enticing.

As the men straggled in, she pushed a piece of limp hair off her forehead. An hour standing over a prune separator had wilted her coiffure and caused her left false eyelash, an experiment in glamour that wasn't going well, to become separated from her lid without her approval. "I'm too busy feeding poor unfortunates to bother with my appearance," she said loudly, hoping the overweight woman lingering nearby wearing a ghastly muumuu would get the hint and wipe off a layer of her own makeup. The press would be here any minute to witness this largesse, and ladies in shorts, pants, or hostess gowns were forbidden to be a part of Dorothy Duncan's happy family.

"I think that's Ethel Merman," said Louise, setting out her Weeney-Beany Casserole, then picking up a sardine in Cheez Whiz sauce and gulping it down in one bite. "Yummy," she said before realizing she had just sampled the winning dish in front of Verda, the sore loser.

"Someone's got a big mouth," said Verda, adding quickly, "I mean Ethel Merman. She's always talking about things that should never be talked about, not even at home."

"Some of the gals here really like her. She was on *The Carol Burnett Show* last week and—"

"It's women like Ethel Merman and Carol Burnett who are ruining it for the rest of us," Verda snapped. "These contestants are getting younger and more opinionated, and we're being squeezed out like so much moldy tomato concentrate in an expired tube. Did I tell you I caught someone trying to sneak in a book by that witch Bertha Friedman? She says we should burn our bras, let our children play with matches, and run our husbands over with our station wagons."

"I had no idea," Louise said, sneaking sardines. She wasn't really listening; she'd had enough of Verda's bitching.

"You've got to keep current, Louise. Join a civics group, subscribe to the *Reader's Digest*, listen to Lady Bird's weekly radio show. We can't sit silently at home anymore. If we don't speak out, they'll never know how much we detest bossy women running around like—"

"Men?" Sandy poked her way into this oddly fascinating conversation, wondering who this Bertha Friedman was. She and Betty had held back, waiting for the cameras to roll, and they were hungry, bored, and worried about Jane, who had disappeared. Worried his charade would be revealed, Felix also had disappeared, into the hall to practice his serve, leaving Cedric to wander around like a lost soul.

Sandy emptied a basket of seeded rolls into her purse, more out of habit than hunger, and sniffed a prune Jell-O cup, curling her lip and putting it back. This did not go unnoticed by Verda, who blamed Louise for letting this odd-looking stranger in.

"I'll let you gals in on a secret," Sandy said, "but you have to swear you'll keep your lips zipped. That *is* Ethel Merman in that paisley frock, leaning against that enormous wheel of cheese. Ethel Merman and Bob Hope are planning to star in a musical about the generation gap, and they got permission from Dorothy Duncan herself to audition real housewives for the supporting roles, mature women with good figures."

Although her thighs chafed against the strong elastic, Verda was glad she had struggled into her girdle that morning. "I can still fit into my high-school Future Homemakers of America apron," she said smugly, eyeing the puff of flesh above Louise's narrow patent-leather belt.

Betty, lingering nearby, grew wide-eyed and bit her lip. "The man who wrote and directed *It's a Mad, Mad, Mad, Mad World* just signed on. Surely you've heard he's up for an Academy Award." *Photoplay* had given her a fair grasp of movie lingo, and a real appreciation for Loretta Young.

"Orson Welles?" cried Verda.

Betty nodded, eyeing a platter of thinly sliced luncheon meats. "Miss Merman doesn't want the girls to know she's here; that's why she's keeping a low profile. She's jetting off to a fat farm tonight, and you know how sensitive famous personalities are about their glandular problems. If you're really interested in a role, make her visit here a pleasant one. Flatter her. Tell her you have all her records. Laugh at her jokes. Admire her jewelry." She winked at Sandy.

"Say no more," said Verda, marching to her stunningly modern gold-and-avocado kitchen to run a comb through her hair and powder her nose. Slapping an expression of admiration and awe on her sour little face, she marched down the aisle to fame and fortune. Much as she'd been on her walk *up* the aisle twenty-seven years ago, she was unsteady and afraid she might faint, but now, unlike that day, she had no sudden urge to flee. Twenty-seven years of cooking meals and scrubbing floors, matching socks and ironing her husband's shorts, scouring her wallpaper every week, whether it needed it or not, were finally going to be recognized. "What do you want—a medal?" her husband would say when she'd mention how tired or lonely or bored she was. Yes, she wanted a medal.

Cedric headed toward the buffet table, hoping to get lost in the crowd lining up for lunch. His resolve to have a simple light meal, some prune gelatin and perhaps a carrot stick, wavered when he spotted the baked chicken dish with pineapple rings. The woman responsible for this delightful combination cut him a large piece of breast, with three slices of fruit, and it was downhill from there. One couldn't have chicken without a starch. Nor a starch without a proper dessert. Each time he put down his plate or emptied his coffee cup, someone was there to replace it, and as a result his muumuu was getting snug. Americans *were* friendly, he decided, watching two women argue over who got to bring him his third slice of mock apple pie. He was prone to nervous eating anyway, and plucked at the centerpiece, swallowing two grapes before realizing they were plastic.

Jane seemed to have abandoned him. Sighing, he sank into a Barcalounger and kicked off his wedgies, telling himself he'd go on a slimming diet as soon as he got home, just Weetabix and weak broth for a week, and brisk morning walks to get his blood moving. Finished with practice, Felix had passed on dessert after being asked to take the "for" side in a discussion of women in athletics, and Cedric was able to relax his stomach muscles for the first time since they'd met.

"You have the tiniest feet for such a big . . . *talent!*" said a woman in a morbid black apron. "Hi, I'm Verda." She was holding an aluminum pan of hot food, the steam fogging her glasses.

"Perhaps later," he said. "I'm feeling rather bilious. I had one too many helpings of mackerel in cream sauce."

"Are you practicing for a role?" Verda asked, sitting in the chair next to him and resting the pan on her lap. Grease began dripping down her pantyhose into her shoe and, when that was full, spilling onto the floor, splattering Cedric's purse. For Verda the 1966 convention would be remembered as the year she burned her Teflon and dripped on Ethel Merman. She tried to keep the happy expression on her face, which was proving to be quite difficult. She couldn't remember now if the liver croquettes in her pan were the laxative-free ones.

"Pardon?"

"You know, pretending to be an English lady."

"That's rather funny, actually because as it happens I'm an Englishma— Oh! I am. Practicing my English. The queen's English, that is. Right-o. Pip, pip! Jolly good."

Verda giggled. "You are so funny! I love your muumuu," she said, her hands fluttering to her hips, broiling under her girdle, hoping that everything she said came across as sincere, especially since she thought someone of Ethel's size shouldn't be eating mackerel in cream sauce. "It looks so cool and comfy! And the pendant really dresses it up. I think muumuus can go anywhere these days, from the PTA to the opera. Lady Bird has one she wears in the privacy of the White House. She says so in this month's *Redbook*. And Liz Taylor wears them all the time with a turban and diamonds.

"I read they're making muumuus for men now, and purses. That would be good thing to put in a comedy sketch, don't you think? A man in a muumuu carrying a purse. What could be funnier?"

"There are women wrestling under the banquet table," said Cedric, trying to divert her attention so he could slip away to the men's room. Each time he tried to use the ladies', a swarm of women followed him inside, offering to hold his handbag and asking if he needed a sanitary napkin, something no man had ever offered him in the gents'. Were women expected to tidy up even while they were in there?

"The girl in the dotted Swiss is one of our TV-dinner contest winners," said Verda, watching as Bibi tried to hog-tie celebrity guest judge Mrs. Martini with the string from a pork roast. She took off her glasses and rubbed her eyes, then looked again, trying to think of something pleasant to say. "They're such *nice* people—I can't imagine what they're doing," she hastened to say when she realized that Ethel Merman was also staring and rubbing her eyes. "Please do not assume this is a common occurrence among the contestants." Before Verda left to report this unusual activity, she took a candid picture of the star holding her liver, wondering if it would be all right to use the picture as that year's Christmas card instead of one of her and Ernie in front of their aluminum tree.

"You wrestled Mrs. Martini to the ground and hog-tied her while I was stuck here slaving over sardines? Bibi!" Bridget wiped her cheesy hands on her apron, plopped into a chair, and put up her feet. "I'm not working if you're out having fun." Bridget had accidentally ingested just a touch of truth serum, and she thought it best to stay out of sight until it wore off, lest she expose Dougie Smathers for what he *really* was—a secret agent.

"Relax, she got away," groused Bibi. "*You* can hog-tie her next time."

Marge hustled into their kitchenette. "There will be *no* more hog-tying," she scolded. "You know better than that. You've been banned from future Defrost-Offs, I'm afraid. But I was able to talk Louise Wuebel, who has inherited Verda's role as convention nag, into letting you stay through lunch *only* if you promised to stay in your kitchen and make more of your delicious sardines. They are being gobbled up! A reporter from *Life* magazine is coming to interview Verda Taylor about her experiences as an average contestant, and you girls have been banished from the main floor until she's left." Marge slipped off one of her tight new pumps and rubbed her heel. "I'm afraid you girls have dropped in popularity. A poll has been taken: fifty-nine percent of the women present thought you two should be stripped of your title, 21 percent would never have women like you over for coffee, and 12 percent liked your outfits."

"I'm sorry, Marge," said Bibi soulfully. "Sorry for everything." She felt bad putting Marge in an uncomfortable position.

"I'm just concerned for you girls. Verda is fuming mad. She witnessed the whole thing and thinks you've destroyed the Dorothy Duncan image."

"Imagine being Verda Taylor," snorted Bridget, in a very unladylike manner. "It must be awfully tough being queen of the world's most embarrassing fruit. Mother calls them 'dried plums,' but prunes, sweetie, are prunes."

"She's been in the cooking sherry," Bibi winked and hustled Marge out of there before Bridget could say something she'd regret. Truth serum—no kitchen should be without it.

"Did you take off your knickers?" cried Bibi, after saying goodbye to Marge. There was a pair of panties on the floor that hadn't been there earlier.

"It's nothing you haven't seen before," said Bridget. "God, it's hot in here! My bra is killing me."

"Don't!" cried Bibi, getting a little taste of what it was like to be around *her.* "We're already in enough trouble. Mrs. Martini wanted me *arrested.* Then what would happen to Jane? She'd go to jail."

"I'd get my gun and rescue her!" cried Bridget. "Bang! Bang!" The corresponding scream from Marge's window shook Bridget back to her senses. "Marge!" she cried, and they tumbled over each other trying to reach their friend, afraid that Dougie Smathers had risen from the dead in Marge's kitchenette. Bridget was relieved and surprised to see Marge hugging a Crock-Pot full of money, and not a sweaty man in a powder blue tuxedo.

Now it was Bibi's turn to scream. Sick of sitting on so much cash, she had hidden Mrs. Martini's half of the prize money—money she had promised to return, on threat of arrest—in the safest place on earth— Marge Milligan's broken Crock-Pot, not realizing it was where Marge kept her iron pills. Tears streaked Marge's face, and she ran to hug them. "You girls are so sweet I could eat you with a spoon!" she sobbed. "I accept your generous gift!"

"Bibi, how uncharacteristic of you to be so generous!" Bridget hugged her friend. When she saw the tears in Bibi's eyes, she said, "You can have my portion to spend as you please, perhaps on the Mary Quant fall line?"

"I've got to go call Marv!" Marge was in a tizzy, digging through her purse for a dime while trying to tie on a clean apron. "Do you have change for a hundred?" she laughed. "Boy, is Marv going to be surprised! I wish I could see his face when I tell him that we're going on a second honeymoon after all!"

Cedric was back at the buffet, about to sample a Weenie-Beany when he saw Jane, looking dusty and disheveled, walk into the room and disappear into a kitchenette, emerging with an electric knife under her arm. The women were clustered around the buffet table, eating and chatting and, by the looks of it, having a grand time, while the men stood back, clustered in a tight group, looking supremely uncomfortable. He noticed that Agent Bob Snurd had his eyes fixed on the entrance. The blob of liverwurst Dougie Smathers on his plate had gone untouched.

"Jane, where have you been?" Cedric slipped on a butter curl and almost broke an ankle catching up to her. "I've had nothing to do but go out of my head with worry."

"Don't get excited," said Jane, wondering what the stains were on the front of his muumuu and if Betty had seen it yet. She whispered, "Dougie Smathers is alive."

His clapped his hands over his mouth and his face turned red as he held back a scream. Jane pushed him behind the giant cheese wheel leaning precariously against one wall. Their plans had changed. If she could bring Dougie Smathers to justice without giving away her identity, she could be freed without Bridget having to see her like this.

"He's been welded into an air-conditioning vent," said Jane. Like a dog waiting for his master to come home, Agent Snurd stared at the door, unwavering in his attention.

"I'm going to get him out and march him in front of the cameras so he can confess. I got a confession in writing, too," she added, showing him the wad of papers.

"I'll get Felix," said Cedric. "It's best we leave Sandy and Betty out of this. But what if—" He swallowed hard, his forehead beginning to resemble a frozen-food package left out on the counter, the beads of perspiration threatening Betty's careful application of foundation. "What if he recognizes me? When it gets back to N. that I wore a muumuu on duty . . ." As he blotted his face with an embroidered tea towel, Jane assured him he was completely unrecognizable.

"Your own mother wouldn't know you."

"My mother was a woman with impeccable taste. She'd die if she saw me out in public in a glorified dressing gown." Flicking a bit of fluff from his shoulder, Jane smiled and tried to put her hands in her pockets, then became annoyed when she realized there weren't any. Looking him in the eyes, seeing close up how Betty's skillful blend of blue and green shadow did indeed bring out the hazel in his otherwise ordinary eyes, she said, not unkindly, "Your mother *is* dead."

All hell was breaking loose at what was meant to be a dignified farewell to a dignified man, and Verda Taylor was steamed. A trespasser had walked in and stolen Verda's culinary thunder simply by opening a silly carton and unveiling the strangest contraption she had ever seen, outside of her husband's battery-operated revolving tie rack. The woman wasn't even wearing an apron, yet the contestants flocked to see her, sitting on each other's laps when the last folding chair was occupied, leaving Verda to guard the plastic cutlery, her liver croquettes untouched. This interloper, seventy if she was a day, introduced the Slice-O Dice-O Matic, "the most important invention of the nuclear age. This product will revolutionize your life, ladies! It will slice, it will dice, it will even butter your bread!"

The woman was shameless, hawking her invention like a carnival barker. Verda had never seen anyone ham it up like this, every gesture exaggerated, each twist of the dial accompanied by a speech reminding the women of how much time they'd save with this gadget in their kitchens.

"A chicken turns into perfectly sliced luncheon meat in seconds," the woman said, stuffing a whole baked chicken into the opening on top. "You don't have to take the meat off the bone first—this remarkable machine does it all for you. Put your bird into the extra-large opening, and hit 'debone.' When the grinding sound stops, hit 'slice,' remembering to dial in the desired thickness. Your meat will shoot out within a minute, in plastic, freezer-ready pouches. Questions?"

Verda couldn't hear the question, but the answer told her all she needed to know about the type of woman who would have this in her home. That woman was lazy.

"No, it can't make your sandwich for you, but it can slice the bread *and* the meat *and* the cheese, all at the same time, while the mixer attachment on top spins up a batch of homemade mayonnaise." Meats, vegetables, bread, condiments, cake, frozen foods, and even the lighter woods, like white ash, could apparently be run through this revolutionary new product.

"Can it slice tomatoes for finger sandwiches?"

"As skinny as you please," the woman assured them, putting a tomato into the contraption and setting the dial to "sliver." Her assistant, the old bag in an ugly dress who had told her about Ethel Merman, walked through the audience showing off a neat row of tomato slices as thin as butterfly wings, on a platter Verda recognized as her best Melmac pot-roast plate. Everyone had to see for herself.

"Honestly," said Verda to no one in particular, "the last time I've seen people this excited was when Playtex added two more hours to the Sixteen-Hour Bra."

"There is nothing this baby can't handle!" the inventor said, rather too loudly. The juggling act that followed, in which her assistant tossed her food donated by audience members, was an embarrassment. Half of a cooked ham became sandwich meat, then ham salad, and then croquettes, all with the push of a button. Verda thought it took all the mystery out of leftovers.

"Can it slice this?" Verda cried, pitching a can of cranberry sauce at the woman's head. When she caught it, people laughed as if it were a comedy routine.

"I didn't know Verda had a sense of humor," someone said.

After a quick consultation with her assistant—too old, really, to be running around with bare arms—the woman popped Verda's cranberry-sauce can into the machine and hit a series of switches. When Verda got married, someone had tied empty bean cans to the back of the borrowed car that would take the new Mr. and Mrs. Vern Taylor to their honeymoon cottage at the La Brea Tar Pits. The clanking that followed them all the way to Los Angeles was a minor annoyance compared with the sounds coming out of this miracle machine. It shook. It whined. It shuddered. It did everything but stand up and salute the flag. It stopped suddenly, with no warning, just beautiful silence. Then it spit out a decorative tin plate stacked with slices of everyone's favorite Thanksgiving side dish, gelatinous cranberry slices, with an origami turkey on top, made from the label on the can.

The women clapped so hard that soufflés fell for miles around.

That's when the reporter from *Life* margazine arrived and made the Slice-O Dice-O Matic the centerpiece of what should have been Verda's story.

Sandy was crowned unofficial queen of the contest—unofficial because she hadn't defrosted anything, or learned the company song, and queen because no one had ever invented a product that could both slice *and* dice. Every woman who witnessed the demonstration, including the reporter from *Life* magazine, promised to go home and write letters to appliance manufactures, demanding a close look at this marvelous new product. "We'd buy a thousand outright," said a shy Mormon girl.

"Jimmy, I could just split my pants!" cried Sandy when she saw Jane and Cedric emerge on the nether side of the as-yet-unfondued cheese wheel. "Betty and me are going to be rich!" She grabbed her friend's hand, and they spun around, whooping, seeded rolls flying out of Betty's purse and hitting Verda in the eye.

"We're going to be on national TV! We've got *five minutes* at the end of Dorothy Duncan show!" cried Betty.

"Want a cold one?" Sandy opened her purse and took out a chilled six-pack of Old Milwaukee. "Just keep it in your purse," she said as she distributed the beer and plastic straws. Everyone felt like celebrating after the good news.

"They're talking about you in the hallway," said Cedric, rocking back on his heels, sipping cold beer from a straw. Things had ended beautifully: Felix was going to give the British Secret Service exclusive rights to his Paper Pocket®. Dougie Smathers was alive, and as soon as he was exposed for what he really was—alive, but not a very nice man—he and Jane would no longer be wanted for murder. And he was seriously considering a second career as a color-television distributor.

"Is it true the Mormon Church has placed an order for ten thousand units?" Cedric asked, wondering if the religious institution needed some televisions to go along with their Slice-O Dice-O Matics.

"I heard twenty thousand! Sandy, we're never gonna to have to steal food again," said Betty.

"We're gonna *buy* food and sneak it *into* the casinos," Sandy laughed.

"Chickie would die if he heard this from me, but from now on we're honest women."

"There's no time like the present." Sandy removed a Bundt pan from under her skirt and gave it to Cedric to hold. "That feels better," she said. "Let's all make lists of what we want." Sandy handed out sheets from a Dorothy Duncan stationery set she had recently picked up and cast around for one of those complimentary pen-and-pencil sets. Jane balled up her paper and said, "I want three things. I want to go home. I want you to promise to visit us. And I want to sit on Betty's couch."

As Sandy and Betty wrote out their "Now that We're Rich" lists, Jane pulled Cedric aside for a chat.

"I'm going to free Dougie Smathers, and I'll need your help. I'll do all the talking. That way he won't have a reason to recognize you. You just hold the gun."

Jane patted her purse, feeling the pistol and extra round of bullets through the thin material, and wished, again, that she had pockets. The gun had proven too heavy for her skirt's waistband, despite the manufacturer's claim that the space-age polymer that bound the elastic fibers together could support the weight of a Volkswagen with an elephant inside. A bit of an exaggeration, Jane thought, marveling at the American way. Breathing through her nose as a plate of orange sardines in a light green sauce was carried past, Jane laughed when Sandy speared one and put it in her pocket.

"Excuse us, ladies," Cedric murmured as he clutched his stomach, pretending that the sight of the sardines sickened him. He hung onto Jane's sleeve and moaned, whispering, "Here's our chance. Let's go get Dougie Smathers." What he thought was an inspiring impromptu performance turned out to be a flop, as Sandy and Betty saw right through him, putting away their lists and demanding to be let in on the action.

"That rat bastard who's trying to frame you is going to be sorry if he tangles with us," Betty said, polishing the brass knuckles that Chickie had left her for situations like these. Betty's pearl-handled revolver, which she had fired only once, was pinned firmly in the thicket of Sandy's beehive, easy to access yet beautifully hidden in case of a weapons search. "Let's go get him," Betty said excitedly. It felt like old times.

Jane could have done without the audience, but they seemed so eager to help that it was impossible to say no.

"The dead man's trapped in a cooling duct."

"P-U!" said Sandy. "And I was thinking it was the liver croquettes that smelled so bad."

"No, he's alive, and we have to free him."

But when they got there, all that was left of Dougie Smathers was a cigarette butt and a tatty toupee.

As she searched for Dougie and Mimi, Jane worried about her safety, her reputation, being spotted by Bridget and causing her to lose all desire for her, and if the cheap pantyhose would give her a rash. When Jane spotted Bridget and Bibi sitting in a shabby kitchenette in the same dotted-Swiss dresses and short brown hair they'd worn on TV, she ran to the ladies' and ripped off her Marlo Thomas wig. "No, honey, I do not hate your hair," Jane practiced to herself as she looked in the mirror. "But I do hate mine." She quickly filled the sink with hot water and harsh soap powder from the dispenser, ready to admit that she might need help. But before she could start scrubbing off her makeup, Betty came through the door and grabbed her arm.

"I guess you found your girl."

Jane nodded, smiling, looking into the washbasin at the disappearing soap bubbles. Betty removed the stopper, and the drain sucked up the scummy water.

"She can't see me like this. I won't let her," said Jane.

"You'll look like a man in girl's clothing if you don't put this wig back on."

"I've got my clothes in the car. In the boot. Will you get them?"

"Is it a blue airline bag with a white strap?"

Jane nodded, then groaned, knowing there was a problem. "What happened to it?"

"Sandy took it out before we left. She needed the space for the quarter cow she's going to chop up on her five-minute segment. It's my fault, really. I insisted she bring it. I told her, 'Sandy, you're going to look like a darn fool without it.' And I was right." Jane remembered seeing a strange-looking carcass in Betty's deep freeze, but hadn't wanted to pry. Betty took her makeup bag from her purse and set it on the mirror ledge.

"Before you put your hair back on, let's freshen your makeup. You don't want your girlfriend seeing you with flaky eye shadow and dry lips."

"I don't want her seeing me at all."

"Nonsense. Plenty of men wear their girlfriend's clothes."

"She has much better taste that this." Jane looked down at her plain suit and black boots. She might feel better if she made a better-looking woman.

"Hey! Chickie loved that suit."

"Sorry. I'm sure you look beautiful in it." Betty had Jane look up toward the ceiling as she applied a fresh coat of mascara to her stubby eyelashes and then had Jane bat them until they dried.

"I said *Chickie* loved that suit."

Jane smiled at the image of the gangster in blue serge, and Betty seized the opportunity to brush on a soft peach lip color. "That's just between us girls," she winked, handing Jane a breath mint.

All eyes were on Sandy as she stood in Verda's kitchenette, rehearsing her segment for the show, using the cardboard cutout as a stand-in for the real Dorothy Duncan, who was en route in the company jet from her cozy kitchen at corporate headquarters in East Lansing, Michigan. Verda Taylor's kitchenette, the set for the show, had been judged most photogenic, due in no small part to Verda's obsessive attention to detail. She was the only contestant who had brought her own major appliances, on the bus all the way from Ohio, and come a day early to lay a new linoleum floor, a brick pattern in dark gold, the perfect platform for her shiny avocado stove and refrigerator. Her Most Stylish Kitchen citation had come with the mixed honor of seeing all her hard work on TV—without her. To accommodate the television cameras, three walls had been knocked down, ruining her black-and-red rooster-themed vinyl wallpaper. She wanted to cry when she saw the camera cables snaking through her lovely room, leaving black marks on the scuff-free flooring. Her rooster pot holders were smudged with cow blood, her barnyard curtains had been taken down and replaced with ugly blue ones—a better backdrop for Sandy's hideously bright hair—and her new Formica table was bowing under the weight of the Slice-O Dice-O Matic.

"Verda?" Sandy interrupted. "Would you be a doll and let us borrow your overhead projector?" A last-minute change in Dorothy Duncan's schedule would push back the taping by a half hour, enough time for the audience members to learn a brand-new company song.

"This is not a communist country, missy," Verda muttered into her handbag. It was time for a valium. "It's not share and share alike. It's a democracy, where people buy their own stuff and keep it to themselves."

"I didn't catch that."

"It's under the sink," said Verda, swallowing her pill dry.

"That girl's staring at me," Bibi whispered, dunking a sardine into a pot of warm cheese. They had run out of truth serum long ago, having no idea if a doctored fish would make it to Dougie Smathers's gullet, and were now cooking out of sheer boredom.

"Now we know what it's like to be a housewife," said Bridget. "I'm glad you confiscated my gun." Each time they tried to escape their prison, sneaking past Marge, who was sitting at her kitchen table with brochures spread before her, planning her honeymoon, someone would walk them back sternly and put a sardine can in their hands. Everyone was crazy about the dish, but terrified of Mrs. Martini, who had undergone a personality change after eating too many of them and was running around the room viciously critiquing contestants' hairstyles and dresses.

"Look. She's pretending to read a magazine now."

Frowning, Bridget looked up. The tall girl in the ugly suit *was* staring at them. And she had a friend, an attractive older woman in a very tasteful dress.

"We don't have any tall brunette agents with bad taste, do we?"

"Just Jane." They laughed at the idea of Jane in a dress.

"She's not being very subtle," said Bibi. "I like a girl with a little more finesse."

"Nobody but you picks up someone at a Defrost-Off, Bibi," giggled Bridget. Bibi waved at her with a sardine, and the girl watching them dropped to the ground, on her face.

"Ouch. Maybe you should go over and talk to her," suggested Bridget.

"If I'm not attracted to her, what's the point? She's not my type."

"But I thought everyone was your type."

* * *

Louise Wuebel was all business as she walked up to their kitchenette and stood in the doorway, looking exasperated. "We're going to allow one of you to leave so you can fix two plates of food. You have fifteen minutes. The show will be taping soon, and Mrs. Martini has been kind enough to agree to stand in for Dorothy Duncan, who's somewhere over the Grand Canyon." Louise hadn't been aware of Mrs. Martini's sudden personality change when she offered her the guest spot, and now she regretted having been blinded by the bright light of celebrity. "There is to be no wrestling, name-calling, hair-pulling, pinching, spitting, or hog-tying. If you agree to these terms, sign here." Meekly, Bibi, who won the coin toss, signed Sandy's name to the typed statement, happy to escape their kitchenette, which had taken on the odor of a fishing boat.

When Jane saw Bibi leaving their kitchen, and Bridget standing in the doorway, she threw herself to the ground again, taking Betty with her this time.

"Gunfire?" Betty whispered, shielding her head with her hands as Chickie had taught her.

"Girlfriend," Jane whispered back. "She looked me right in the eye and looked away. I think she recognized me and couldn't bear it."

"Oh, Jim," said Betty, getting to her feet and putting out her hand to help Jane up. "She's not looking for a *girl.* She didn't recognize you. Why don't you just walk up to her?"

"I just don't feel right." Jane struggled to her feet, testing her right leg, the one she had landed on when she'd been ejected from her own convention. She had come down on it hard again, and she limped behind Betty, taking small steps on the slippery no-wax linoleum, which smelled of bleach and soap powder and Dorothy Duncan's signature fragrance, pine.

"Did you find him?" Cedric asked Jane when she limped up to him. Betty wandered off to find Sandy, leaving them to speak openly. Only there was nothing to say.

Jane shook her head, depressed by the sudden change in their fortunes. The man she was accused of killing had disappeared—again—and her lover was completely repulsed by her.

"I think Dougie is gone for good this time. I do have his confession, but it would be much better to have him here, live and in person."

"I imagine it will take time to verify his signature," Cedric sighed. "The police will have to be involved."

Sagging like a deflated dirigible, Cedric turned to the buffet table for comfort, fixing himself a plate of sardines and salad, just to settle his stomach. Talking Jane into taking a moment off from playing secret agent, to clear her head, he led her to two free Barcaloungers. "It's nice to be able to put your feet up," he commented. "Especially when you've been in heels all day. It makes the blood flow to the brain. Good for thinking."

"I'll add heels to the list of complaints," sighed Jane. "Cedric, this mission is over. I've got Dougie's confession, even if he doesn't pop up again. The game had been played, and I don't even remember why we came here." Her head was throbbing, and she was close to tears. For Jane to get her passport, Bridget would have to see her.

"Why, for Felix's invention, of course," he said brightly as he sucked down a sardine. They were the most delicious sardines he'd ever had, and he wondered if he could talk the prizewinners into giving him the recipe.

Jane looked over at him and felt a tenderness she had thus far found impossible to access on this trip. He was in love. "You don't really believe . . ."

He shook his head, his earring reflecting the television camera lights. "No," he said honestly. "It is a wonderful idea, though. I'm going home with a boxful. My consolation prize, I guess." He dropped his plate on the floor, suddenly in need of an antacid. He felt close to tears. "My first—our first—real mission, and we fail miserably."

The "our" in his statement touched Jane. In all their missions together, he had been top dog, and she N.'s puppet. This was the first time Cedric had spoken of them as a team. It was rather sweet of him, and she tugged on the bell sleeve of his muumuu and flashed him a wry smile. "You know what I think? I think we *have* found the invention. We can bring back Sandy's Slice-O Dice-O Matic. It is the only 'revolutionary' invention I've seen around here. Excluding four-foot platinum hair, that is."

"But the report from my American source said—"

"You can't trust any spy reports," Jane said. "Especially my brother's. It's one thing I've learned."

"I've learned you can't hurry love," sighed Cedric. "I asked Felix to come back with me, so we could further explore our compatibility, and he's gone off to think about it. I hope the thing he's thinking about is a chubby fellow in a purple paisley muumuu, and whether he's willing to cross an ocean for him."

"I thought he was playing tennis," said Jane, closing her eyes and counting the hours until the flight home. She was drifting off when she heard a sigh, and opened her eyes. In the short time she had rested, he had hit the buffet again.

"Sardine?" Cedric elbowed her. "I had to fight a tall, rather forceful, blonde woman for these. She was back for her third helping." Jane raised her eyes at this, trying not to inhale anywhere near the stinky dish. "I'm a nervous eater as you know," Cedric added unnecessarily, picking up his plate again. "I think there's also cherry pie."

"Cherry pie?" Jane sat up. "I *love* cherry pie."

"You're not just being filthy again, are you?" he asked.

"I like pie. Take it any way you like. But let's go get some before it's gone."

There was a line when they got to the table. The secret agents had come back for seconds, and Cedric looked downcast when the man at the head of the line took the last liver croquette.

"He's already eaten several pieces," Cedric complained to Jane, who was standing behind him in line, trying to peek over his shoulder, keeping an eye out for Dougie and assessing the pie situation.

"The man has no consideration for others." His paper plate sagged under a large serving of Weenie-Beanies, and Jane stood on tiptoe and spotted the last piece of cherry pie, about to be swooped up by the chap holding up the line.

"Ladies first!" she shouted, pushing Cedric foward. As a celebrity, he should naturally rate better service. Thinking Jane meant him to have that last piece of pie, Cedric elbowed his way to the front of the line, behaving as he believed Ethel Merman might. Jane jockeyed for first place, knowing she was acting childish, and she and Cedric reached for the last piece of pie together, knocking into the chap who, as first in line, naturally thought the pie was his.

Jane had just grabbed the piece when the man shoved her hard, grabbing the pie as she fell into Cedric, becoming lost in the voluminous folds of his muumuu.

"Dyke," the man murmured, looking dismissively at her shoes. And then he looked up.

They had found their man. In a move that would have made Miss Merman proud, Cedric stepped forward and calmly wiped the smirk off Dougie's face with a plate of hot Weenie-Beanies.

"Ethel Merman just threw food on Dougie Smathers!" Bob Snurd cried. From across the table, Bibi watched in wonder as Miss Merman pulled off Dougie's wig in a scene reminiscent of one in her favorite novel, *Valley of the Dolls.* How many celebrities attended this cook-off?

"You've unmasked me . . . *Ethel Merman?*" Dougie scrunched up his face and stared.

Cedric thrust out his chest. "No, it's Sir Cedric Pumpernickel, and you've put my friend in grave danger. Everyone!" he cried, grabbing Dougie by the scruff of his neck and pulling him off the ground. "This is Mr. Dougie Smathers, who is not, as you can see, dead." Dougie tried to pull away, pretending it was all a joke.

"I've got to get a picture of this!" Dougie cried. "Sir Pumpernickel in his bathrobe. Does anyone have a camera?"

"It's a muumuu," Cedric sniffed, gripping him harder, and Dougie began to sweat.

"Can't you take a joke?" he asked, smoothing his real hair nervously. He peeled off his sideburns and threw them on a side of ham.

"Have another pie, Ethel?" Agent Camembert cried as he snapped his picture, and Jane saw Cedric release his grip on Smathers and fold into himself, no longer Sir Pumpernickel but the man her brother had teased mercilessly for years. He headed right for a potroast.

Jane wished their mission could have ended on a happier note. Although they had proved her innocence, Dougie Smathers was still an asshole who hadn't been taught a lesson.

As Cedric stuffed himself, Dougie joined his chums, filling a plate with liver croquettes smothered in A.1. Sauce. He once again played the jester, juggling condiments and making pineapple-ring earrings for his friends. "Where are the good-looking broads?" he asked, holding up a pair. He crammed a croquette in his mouth and swallowed. And then another, and another. Cedric wasn't the only nervous eater in the room, Jane noted.

"I've never seen Cedric so confident," said Bridget, who had snuck out of her prison while the fight diverted Louise's attention, and was hiding behind the partially eaten bust of Dougie Smathers. "Jane's safe," Bibi said, averting her eyes at the sight of Dougie cramming liver treats in his mouth. "But where is she?" In the scuffle, neither of them had noticed the girl in the blue suit stand by the table, eating the last piece of pie.

As they situated themselves in the front row of the audience (Betty and Sandy had reserved them two seats), Jane looked around, trying to spot Bridget and Bibi. It proved to be too difficult, however, in the sea of Ash Brown #31. Dorothy Duncan contestants and secret agents alike had gathered around the makeshift set to watch Sandy go through her paces. She had set up her machine and positioned her cow so it would be easily accessible. Her spot would run for only five minutes, but it was the most important five minutes of her life as an inventor.

"What a day we're having! First we find the invention—or two inventions, actually, then we exonerate ourselves, and now we get to see behind the scenes of a television show!" Cedric said, regaining his stolen composure.

"It is wonderful, isn't it?" Jane said, still a bit on edge, wondering where Mimi could be and what she had up her sleeve. Had Jane not been so vain, she wouldn't be the only one here with the knowledge of Mimi's presence. But this was forgotten as she watched Sandy become a star.

"Smile, Sandy, so we can position the lights to bounce off your teeth," the director said. She had remembered to put Vaseline on her teeth, and her mouth slid open in a grin.

"Now, Mrs. Martini, stand next to Sandy and admire her machine."

"Bo-r-ing," Mrs. Martini mumbled as she instead climbed atop the buffet table, insisting everyone stop talking and pay attention to her.

"It's impossible not to," Jane said to Cedric, realizing she was the only one who knew Mrs. Martini's true identity.

"I wonder if all the Defrost-Offs are like this?" he whispered back, casting around for the subject of his next book.

"I've got something to say," Mrs. Martini continued, prompting Bridget to snap open her purse for her tranquilizer gun. They were seated in the back row, wanting to watch but afraid to get too close.

"Where are my darts?" Bridget whispered to Bibi, who had palmed a one-shot lipstick pistol.

"I hid them. I was afraid you were going to shoot someone. Like Mrs. Martini. Here," Bibi said, unclipping her earrings. "Two smoke bombs. Everything else is in my purse."

"Where?"

"In the vegetable crisper."

"Would you shut your cake hole?" screamed Mrs. Martini, stomping her feet and sending the Jell-O molds on the buffet table into spasms. "Don't you two ever get sick of gabbing?" She was looking right at them.

"She's one to talk," Bibi murmured, clutching the lipstick. She'd like to sit here and watch Mrs. Martini have a nervous breakdown, but not if she was going to get nasty.

"You thought you were done with me," Mrs. Martini said, making an awkward jump from the table, knocking over Verda's prune cups. She pushed aside Dougie, who was still stuffing himself with Verda's Liver Croquettes, stopping a foot from Jane, who was, like everyone there, too fascinated to move.

"Those high cheekbones. Those lips." Mrs. Martini stroked Jane's face, and when Jane raised a hand to stop her, she put Jane in a headlock and kissed her. When she released her, her hand became tangled on Jane's necklace and the cord broke, scattering Betty's second-best set of faux pearls.

"So *that's* where you were all night!" cried Cedric, jumping out of his chair and placing his hands on his hips in an age-old feminine gesture of disapproval. "You are *just* like your brother!"

"Oh, there's Jane," Bridget said dryly.

"There's another one?" said Sandy. "Oh, goody. One for me and one for you, Betty."

"Shut up and sit down!" Jane hissed at Cedric, yanking him unceremoniously back onto his chair. She was afraid that Bridget might hear and misconstrue it. "She's someone my brother shagged, and she recognized me despite the costume." She was a woman dressed as a man dressed as a woman, and she'd had enough of it.

Bibi stared, wondering how she could have spent hours with Mrs. Martini and missed *this* aspect of her personality.

"What the hell kind of convention is this?" Dougie Smathers shouted.

"You!" Mrs. Martini's arm shot up and pointed at Jane's tormenter. "You can easily be disposed of. So shut your cake hole or I'll shut it for you."

Dougie shut his cake hole and crept off to the safety of a Barcalounger, taking the rest of the liver along.

"Anglophile," Bibi sniffed. "I wonder what other words she's learned."

"So far it's just cake hole, cake hole," said Bridget. "She's not really doing anything, but the anticipation is exhilarating. We are very bad people, Bibi, for wanting to watch this. We should call an ambulance. The woman has clearly gone over the edge."

"I see another cake hole that needs to be shut!" Mrs. Martini screamed, and this time Bridget blushed, feeling like a schoolgirl who had talked out of turn.

"That's the third cake hole," Bibi muttered to Bridget through clenched teeth.

Cedric, who was having a hard time keeping up, did understand two things. Mrs. Martini was having a nervous breakdown, and he really needed to use the ladies' room. He stepped forward. "Dear lady, may I offer my assistance? Perhaps a cup of tea to calm those jangled nerves?" Several women raised their hands, offering their services. "See?" Cedric said soothingly. "A nice cuppa—there's nothing better when you're having a bit of a knock."

Mrs. Martini paced back and forth along the set of the television show, five yards or so of Verda's dear linoleum that grew scuffed under her feet. She stopped to lean on the countertop and catch her breath, and when she slipped on one of the pearls from Jane's necklace and almost fell, a ripple of concern swept the crowd.

She climbed atop the countertop and faced her audience, some seated in folding chairs, some snacking on cold cuts from the buffet. People behaved as if this were another entertainment, another *Frost Side Story,* but without the music. Another Las Vegas act, a little racier than expected, but something to take home and cherish. A good dining-out story.

"Now she has another phrase," whispered Bridget. "I'll bet you a pound she uses it right away, lovey."

"A *bit* of a knock?" cried Mrs. Martini. "A *bit* of a knock?"

Bridget felt a giggle coming on, and ducked behind Bibi. The woman was a bitch, but they were better armed.

"I'll tell you the same story I've been telling everyone." She pointed to Jane. "*We* were in love until *she* came along," she said, gesturing toward Bridget.

"Me?" asked Louise, who had left the front desk to find out the source of the ruckus and was standing near Bridget and Bibi. Her heart sank when she saw that it was Mrs. Martini on Verda's countertop. "I don't know that woman."

"Well, I've never met either of you." Jane had to laugh, trying to keep up the charade, wondering what Mimi would do next. This was getting beyond the pale.

"That's precisely why I left you. You refused to acknowledge our love. Not to her—or her—or her." Mrs. Martini pointed all around—at Bridget, at Bibi, but mainly at Jane.

"Who? What?" said Cedric, certain Mrs. Martini had included him by mistake.

"This is strangely familiar," whispered Bibi.

Mrs. Martini rolled her eyes and threw her hands into the arms. "For a year I held my tongue and kept quiet about what was really going on." A buzz raced through the audience as the women realized they were about to hear juicy gossip about America's best-loved singer. She had their full attention now.

"Oh, Christ. More Sammi Martini stories," Bibi said.

"I can't go to Iceland!" Mrs. Martini shouted. She abruptly stopped moving and pulled her coat close, shivering despite its warmth and the heat from 158 ovens. "I don't know anything about puffins. I just don't care. All I care about is Jane. And not going to Iceland. I hate snow. I hate ice. I don't hate Jane. I love Jane. I hate the snooty bitch who stole her away from me. And Bibi"—she shrugged—"Bibi's fun, but she's no Jane. I can't go to Iceland. It's cold, and Mary Quant has yet to come out with a really good winter line!"

"Oh, God, what's the protocol for this?" asked Bridget, opening her compact and punching in Miss Tuppenny's code. Transatlantic calls were iffy, and the static often made it impossible to hear the voice at the other end.

"A shot to the leg," said Bibi as she offered Bridget, the better marksman, her lipstick pistol. "Before she spills the beans on G.E.O.R.G.I.E.!"

Before Bridget could take aim, Mimi charged into what had become a fearfully quiet audience. She pushed Bridget off her chair and onto the floor and straddled her, and the audience stood up to watch and cheer, thinking they were applauding an avenging wife.

"Look here!" Jane cried. "I'm the only one allowed to do that!"

Mimi grabbed a handful of Bridget's hair and pulled hard, expecting a wig. A little hurt that Mimi didn't want to straddle *her*, Bibi jumped into the fray, grabbed Mimi's hair, and tried to pull her off Bridget.

Jane, meanwhile, was blocked from participating in what amounted to a gentle version of female mud wrestling by Cedric, who believed her when she said she didn't know this woman, but who felt, nonetheless, that she'd had a hand in some part of this mess.

"Forgive me," Jane said, stomping hard on his insole. He shrieked and let her pass, and she pushed Bibi aside, grabbed Mimi around the waist, and pulled hard. Hanging onto Mimi wasn't the problem; she locked her legs around Jane's middle and refused to budge until Sandy spritzed her with some spray cheese from her purse, and Betty pushed a handful of Ritz crackers in her face. Jane let go, and Mimi, dazed, holding a lank of Bridget's hair, walked the drunkard's path toward the buffet table.

"What the hell is going on in here?" Verda Taylor, who had been on the telephone with the Las Vegas Airport, put her hands on her hips and glared at the girls lying on the floor, their hair a mess and their dresses hiked up above their knees, and at the celebrity judge who had turned out to be more work than she was worth.

"I've got to get that cheese wheel over to the pot, and I need a volunteer to help push. Gentlemen?" A bloated Dougie Smathers, a real cheese lover, held up his hand, trying to get in good with some of the lonely, bored housewives. When he got home, his wife was going to kill him.

"We've got to get this place cleaned up!" Verda barked. "Dorothy Duncan's jet will be touching down at any minute!" Several girls offered to help, no longer wishing to be witness to a drama if it wasn't Mrs. Martini's, though they really weren't sure what was going on.

Verda and Dougie had no sooner gotten the wheel rolling when Mimi pulled a gun from the pocket of her stolen white mink and trained it on Jane. "It's *finito* for you, dearie. Time for you to vanish."

"Oh, fuck," Jane said, reaching out her hand for Bridget's. Her gun was in her purse. Her purse was on the buffet table. And she was going to die in girl's clothes.

"Honey, it's not working," Bridget whispered in her ear.

"*Now* we're having relationship problems?" Jane cried.

"The *gun* doesn't work. Bibi disabled it when—" The feel of Jane against her, the warmth of her body through the polyester dress . . .

"Do you hate my hair?" Jane whispered back, and Bridget shook with laughter.

"Pay attention!" Mimi cried. "There is *nothing* funny about this."

"Excuse us!" Verda shouted. "Cheese wheel coming through!"

"Cheese off!" Mimi screamed.

Confused, Verda, who had taken the lead position and was guiding the cheese toward its destination, explained that the afternoon Fondue-A-Thon was another attempt to earn a spot in the *Guinness Book of World Records*. She was facing Dougie Smathers, and as she swung her arms out to indicate a wide turn, she accidentally smacked Mimi in the back. Verda was a strong woman, who mowed her own lawn and wasn't afraid of automobile maintenance, and her hands were broad and flat. Verda had been voted Most Difficult in a secret poll, for her nastiness and destructive gossiping.

But she hadn't meant to hit the girl.

And Bibi had meant to take Mimi to the airport herself, instead of relegating the task to a new agent.

When Verda hit Mimi, Mimi stumbled, slipping on some spray cheese that had fallen off Sandy's Ritz. Verda dropped her end of the cheese wheel—she was, in essence, the brakeman—and tried to grab Mimi, too, certain she had something in her kitchen that would remove spray cheese from mink, but succeeded only in making Mimi's tumble worse by pulled the bottom of her coat out from under her. Dougie, hoping to get a peek at her panties, let go of his end, and the cheese stood alone, untethered, swaying on the uneven floor.

An oven timer chirped, Dougie Smathers burped, and Bibi shut her eyes and screamed as the world's biggest cheese wheel, a sharp Wisconsin cheddar, crashed down on Mimi Dolittle, ending a lackluster espionage career and guaranteeing her an entry in the *Guinness Book of World Records* in the Most Embarrassing Death category. Women rushed forward, cheese slicers in hand, but there was nothing anyone could do.

$\mathcal{C}$edric and Felix were working Jane's nerves, giggling and singing along with *The Sound of Music*, the in-flight movie. They were newly in love, and Jane tried to be patient with their idiocy, but when they started feeding one another airline peanuts, she had enough of the happy honeymooners and moved to a row of empty seats near the rear of the plane. The return flight to London was only half full, and she sat as far back as possible, glad for the island of space between her and the other passengers. She had her first report to write, and, along with detailing the events of their mission, she had to explain the death of a G.E.O.R.G.I.E. agent. Cedric and Felix had selected the cheese-croquette dinner, proof that love was blind; had they not seen the giant cheese wheel crush Mimi Dolittle, or the housewives frantically slicing their way to the girl pinned under five hundred pounds of extra-sharp cheddar?

Jane didn't think she'd ever be able to eat another piece of cheese, not even a nice aged Swiss. Balancing her scotch and soda on the pull-down meal tray, Jane took a Dorothy Duncan pen-and-pencil set (compliments of Sandy, who had helped herself to a dozen and handed them out at the airport as parting gifts) and began composing her report on the back of an airsickness bag. The tragic news would not be a surprise for Miss Tuppenny. As Mimi was being peeled from the cheese wheel, Bridget had run out of the room in tears and placed a transatlantic call to G.E.O.R.G.I.E. headquarters. Bibi, shaken by the death of a girl she had once loved (for about ten minutes), stood mute, staring at the macabre scene, and then, wanting something to remember her by, stepped forward and removed the pair of Mary Quant sandals on Mimi's trim size-six feet.

BRITISH AIRWAYS FLIGHT #313
LAS VEGAS TO LONDON
AISLE 14/SEAT E

18 September 1966
MEMO: To Agent Louise Tuppenny, Chief of Operations,
    G.E.O.R.G.I.E.
FROM: Agent Jane Bond, 007-and-a-half
TOPIC: Death by Cheese Wheel: The Mimi Dolittle Story

The following is a spotty reconstruction of the final days of Agent
Mimi Dolittle, whose exile to Iceland (after an attempt on my life)
began with a detour through Las Vegas, Nevada, and ended in
her death. Her objective, I believe, was to undermine our mission
by any means necessary.
    The evidence against the deceased is stacked like a Vegas
showgirl's figure.

Jane put that bit in knowing that Bibi would make a copy of the report and show it to Bridget.

After checking into the Sands hotel under the name of her idol,
Marie Antoinette, Agent Dolittle proceeded to interfere with every
aspect of the mission. The following is a list of what we know of
Agent Dolittle's actions:
    • She impersonated a sexually aggressive and very attractive
air hostess on the flight over, trying to start a fight between
myself and Agent St. Claire, who was accompanying me mainly in
spirit.
    • Then, at gunpoint, Dolittle forced a desk clerk at the Sands
hotel (where Agents Gallini and St. Claire were staying under the
names Mamie Eisenhower and Eleanor Roosevelt) to erase their
American names from the register, making it impossible for me to
find them after my wallet was lost in the line of duty.
    • After overhearing Agent Gallini brag about having the key to

Sammi Martini's penthouse, Agent Dolittle kidnapped Mrs. Sammi Martini and tied her to a vibrating bed in a Motel 6 in downtown Las Vegas, and fed the box nickels until Mrs. Martini agreed to hand over the key to her husband's penthouse.

- Pretending to be Mrs. Martini, Agent Dolittle let Agents St. Claire and Gallini color, set, and style her hair before attempting to rob them at gunpoint.

- Having failed to relieve Agents St. Claire and Gallini of their money, Agent Dolittle turned her attention to me. Disguised as a nun, she followed me to Hoover Dam and, after witnessing my Snacketeria scuffle with Agent Dougie Smathers, suggested he "play dead" while she framed me for murder, planting snow-globe glitter and Bugles, an American crunchy corn snack, as evidence.

- While I was on the lam, she turned her attention back to Agents St. Claire and Gallini, increasing their jet lag by checking into the teepee next door to theirs and watching the Late, Late, Late, Late Night Movie at a high volume. Then, after Agents Gallini and St. Claire located and kidnapped Dougie Smathers, intending to expose the "prank," Agent Dolittle snuck into their teepee in the dead of night and freed Agent Smathers, whom she later welded into an air-conditioning vent at the Las Vegas Convention Center.

There was more, but Jane was running out of airsickness bags. Everywhere Mimi went, she had left a trail of deceit, fear, and candy-bar wrappers. The details were still pouring in, accounts by all types of people—secret agents, hotel maids, tourists, and the pool boy—that painted a picture of a deeply disturbed and really rude girl. The woman in the mink bikini walking the leopard? It was Mimi, hoping to scare Bridget and Bibi off. And where had the choreographer gotten the idea for the potato costumes? Someone had left a five-pound bag of Idahos at the dressing-room door. Her animus hadn't been confined to her fellow agents. Mimi had put sugar in salt shakers all over town, added dirt to the jar of Folgers set aside for the judges, and eaten the bangs off the Dorothy Duncan butter sculpture.

Jane looked ahead at the emergency exit row, where Bibi lay sleeping on half of her new inflatable paisley sectional sofa, Mimi Dolittle's sandals clutched to her chest. After inflating the furniture to show to Jane, Bibi couldn't get the air valve unstuck, so she had carried it onto the plane, explaining that she worked for the airline and was testing a new style of furniture that doubled as a life raft.

Regarding our original mission, it is unclear whether there ever was a miracle spy gadget. Although I was exonerated in the first death of Dougie Smathers, due to the recent events, my fellow spies who were attending the conference still refuse to speak to me, leading me to conclude that G.E.O.R.G.I.E. girls are not the only ones who consider my brother a jerk, information to keep in mind on future missions. Two inventions were uncovered in Las Vegas:

• The "Pocket Pal." Invented by FBI Agent Felix Bivens (Agent Pumpernickel's new boyfriend—more on that later!); this is a disposable paper pocket, designed to fit a man's shirt pocket and hold biros.

• The "Slice-O Dice-O Matic." Invented by Las Vegan Sandy Beach, this contraption performs a variety of food-related maneuvers, including apple coring, chopping, slicing, dicing, and deboning. It also sharpens pencils. I see absolutely no spy application here, but it would be nice to have one for the lunchroom. They will be available by Christmas, from an American company called Ronco.

The cheap ballpoint was leaking, and, lacking a Pocket Pal to protect her Marks & Spencer shirt, Jane dropped the pen into the last airsickness bag and shoved it into the seat pocket in front of her. Jane was positive Mimi had been on the verge of revealing her identity as a double agent; G.E.O.R.G.I.E. would have lost four agents that day, instead of one. It was the best possible way to look at it, Jane decided, aware, too, that she would mentally replay Mimi's final moments and wonder what she could have done to save the girl. She picked up her drink and leaned back in her seat, knowing now what Bridget had meant when she'd tried to describe the melancholy that followed the end of a mission. Jane turned on her side, her back to the aisle, and closed her eyes. She didn't see the girl in the white Chanel suit, wearing a short Sassoon haircut that emphasized her pretty, heart-shaped face and wide green eyes, walk down the aisle toward her, but she smelled her perfume and opened her eyes in time to see Contessa Fagiolo Ravioli brush past her. Keeping to their agreement to have no contact on the plane, Jane could only stare as Bridget sashayed down the aisle and disappeared into an unoccupied lav. An air hostess walked by, holding a tray with a miniature bottle of champagne on it, and Jane knew that it was headed for Aisle 7, seats B and C, to the other two agents in love on this flight. She'd had enough. She picked up her drink and dumped it in her lap.

"Crikey!" she cried as she jumped up, her pants soaked. "I'd better get out of these wet pants!"

Death By Liver Dabs

By a staff reporter

The widow of a man who ate himself to death by consuming more liver croquettes than is generally recommended said today that her husband, Mr. Douglas Smathers of Kansas City, Kansas, had been told by his doctor to avoid organ meats. As to why her husband consumed large quantities of the forbidden food, Mrs. Daisy Smathers replied that he was a man who feared nothing, "not even liver." Mrs. Smathers has vowed never to remarry, in honor of her husband and their life together. "Once you've had someone like Dougie . . ." Overcome by grief, the new widow was unable to finish her thought.

Douglas Smathers is survived by his wife, Daisy, their poodle, Dougie Smathers Jr., and many, many admirers, too numerous to list here.